The House of Wolf
Enemy Planet Book I

Paul Lentz

(This is Book II in "The Stuff of Life" tetrology.)

Ty Ty Press, Peachtree City, Georgia
Earth Analogue III

The cover and the illustration of *Bo-taoshi* on Page 19 were created by Mike Dillard (www.mikedanimationstudio.com).

Illustrations on Pages 1, 5, 14, 17, 23, 72, 88, 120, and 167 were created by J.R.C. Dyer (www.jrcdyer.com).

The image of the sarcopterygian (*Tiktaalik*) was created by the National Science Foundation and is in the public domain.

The image of a homotherium is by Sergiodlarosa, at http://serchio25.deviantart.com/art/homotherium-serum-149618044, and used under terms of a Creative Commons Attribution license.

Other line drawings, charts, maps, and diagrams were created by the author.

ISBN-13: 978-0-692-19022-7 (Ty Ty Press)

10 9 8 7 6 5 4 3 2 1

iv

Other books by the author:

"On Ty Ty Creek: Sweet Potato Pie, Moonshine, and other Southern Traditions"

"The Stuff of Life: Book I"

"Holy Fire"

"The Cry of the Innocents"

Upcoming books:

"Enemy Planet: Son of Wolf"
("The Stuff of Life, Book III)
Early 2019

"Three Planets" (Working Title)
("The Stuff of Life, Book IV)
2019

Books are available on Amazon.com.
https://www.amazon.com/author/paullentz

For information about
upcoming books check
www.PaulLentzAuthor.com

Dedication
To Rebecca Watts, friend, mentor,
and leader of
Peachtree City Library's
Writers Circle
Peachtree City, Georgia

TABLE OF CONTENTS

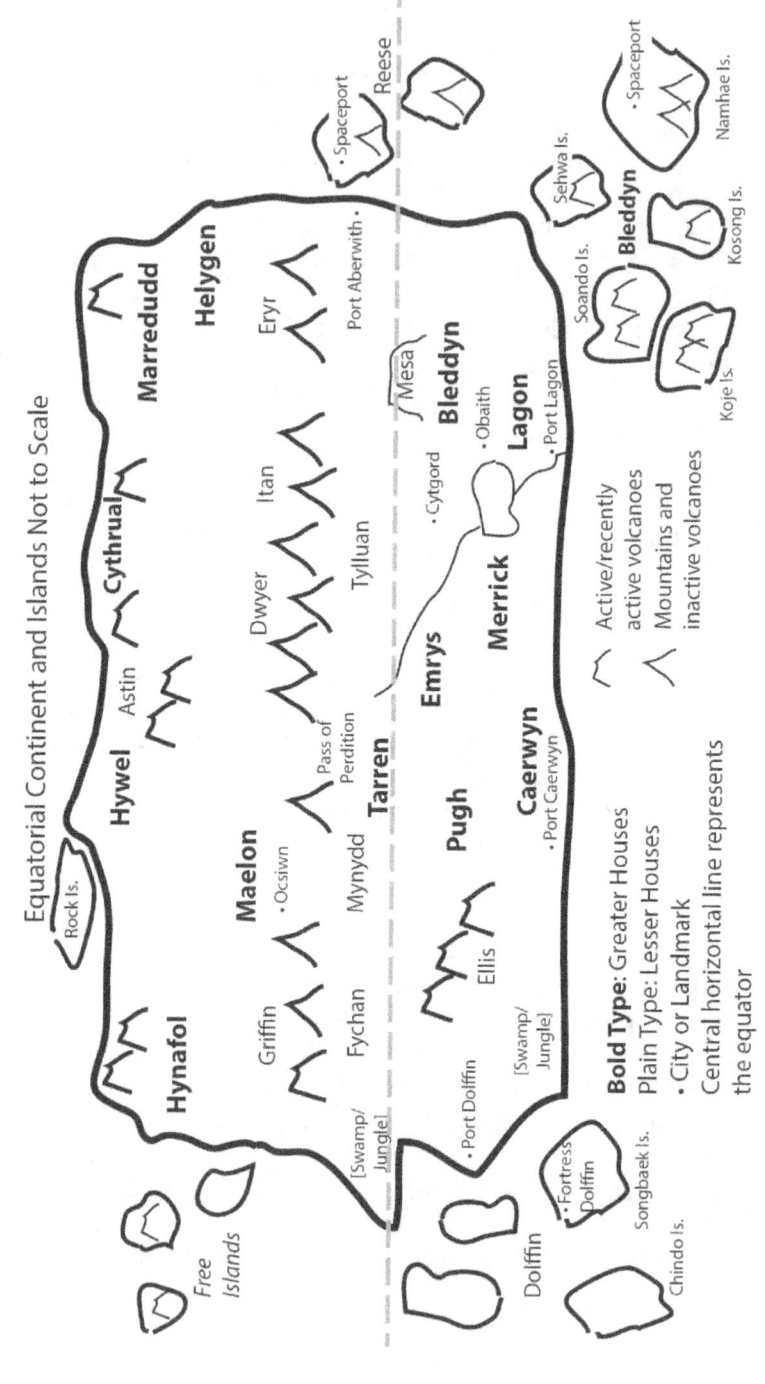

Equatorial Continent and Islands Not to Scale

Free Islands

Rock Is.

Hynafol

Griffin

Maelon
• Ocsiwn

Fychan

[Swamp/Jungle]

Hywel

Astin

Pass of Perdition

Mynydd

Tarren

Dwyer

Itan

Cythrual

Tylluan

Marredudd

Helygen

Eryr

Port Aberwith •

Mesa

Bleddyn

• Obaith

Cytgord •

Emrys

Merrick

Lagon

• Port Lagon

Pugh

Caerwyn
• Port Caerwyn

Port Dolffin •

Ellis

[Swamp/Jungle]

Dolffin

Fortress Dolffin •

Songbaek Is.

Chindo Is.

Reese

Spaceport •

Spaceport •

Sehwa Is.

Bleddyn

Soando Is.

Namhae Is.

Kosong Is.

Koje Is.

⋀ Active/recently active volcanoes

⋀ Mountains and inactive volcanoes

Bold Type: Greater Houses
Plain Type: Lesser Houses
• City or Landmark
Central horizontal line represents
the equator

viii

This narrative is based largely on Telor Bleddyn's journal and those of his father and younger siblings. Some scenes are based on the records of the Council of the Res Publica and of House Bleddyn's Privy Council, and the reports of spies recorded in the house archives.

— Itol Lagon, Archivist and Recorder

Chapter 1: Elevation

Thirteen members of the Council of Greater Houses sit on the High Dais. I am Gens Bleddyn's eldest son and a lieutenant in his Home Guard. I sit in my father's seat to the right of the First

Speaker. Llywelyn, my Brother-minus-two years, is heir apparent and should be here, but he and his companions are playing war games in the mountains. The matriarchs and patriarchs of Lesser Houses plus family and friends sit on benches along the sides of the chamber. Council Guards from neutral houses watch from the rear.

My siblings and their surrogates stand with Father. The infant's surrogate stands at Father's right. She is a daughter of House Caerwyn. Her womb nurtured the child after his mother's egg and Father's seed were combined in a laboratory. The infant's mother is a starship captain who will not return to World for centuries.

Gens Bleddyn elevates my Brother-minus-twenty-years. "I present to the Council of the Res Publica my tenth child-of-the-blood, Garreth." At the moment Father speaks, three people in the benches stand and lift weapons. "Gens Bleddyn dies today," one cries.

I am first to react. Before the second word reaches the mouth of the enemy, I stand, raise my energy pistol, and fire. The assassin who spoke, falls, but his dying hand squeezes the trigger. The burst of energy misses Father and strikes the First Speaker. Garreth's surrogate sees my movements. Without hesitation she turns, lifts her own weapon, and fires on a second enemy. He dies, but not before the energy from his pistol rakes the wall behind the High Dais.

Other surrogates drop to the floor, protecting their children with their own bodies while looking for targets. Father remains standing, seemingly untroubled. He clasps Garreth to his breast and wraps him in the ceremonial robe he wears over his uniform. He faces Council, confident his family will protect him and their new brother.

In the benches, a third man falls to a scuffle of raised fists and flashing daggers.

"He is dead," a voice calls from the melee.

He is dead. So are two other would-be assassins and so is the First Speaker. He is the ancient Gens Hywel. He holds the Speakership of the Council for one solar year in a millennia-old rotation among the Greater Houses. He is an innocent, struck down in one of the vendettas that are the true rule of the people – the Res Publica.

The assassination attempt is a foolish thing. Even if the attackers had killed Gens Bleddyn – my father – and all the family present at the ceremony, House Bleddyn – the House of Wolf – would not die. Father has many children, brothers and sisters, aunts, uncles, and cousins. The attack was not against the house, but against its patriarch, the Gens.

2

~~~~~

After the Council adjourns, Gens Tarren, historic enemy of House Bleddyn, approaches Father. "Gens Bleddyn, this was most unfortunate. Most unfortunate. It is lucky you are so well protected. I assume you will cancel the celebration of your son's elevation."

Father sees the man's deceit. "No. We will celebrate the birth and elevation of my son Garreth and we will honor Gens Hywel."

~~~~~

In the hours before the banquet, while his large family greets their guests, Gens Bleddyn sits alone in his den. He thanks and then dismisses Garreth's surrogate. A wood fire crackles in the winter hearth. A glass of *dŵr y bywyd* sits at his side. Called the "water of life," it is five-times distilled ethanol, aged in oak casks for a thousand years. It is rare, and it is special. He sips it now in a private celebration of his son. Garreth bears the name of an ancient leader of House Bleddyn who is known for both bravery and modesty. *Modest and brave*, Father thinks. *We, House Bleddyn and the Res Publica, need both.*

I enter the room through a hidden panel by the hearth and kneel on the stone floor.

Father gestures me to rise. "The attack was ordered by Gens Tarren," I say.

"There were no survivors to question," Father responds.

"None among the Council, Gens, but there was a move at Academy. Your daughter Bethan was targeted but is safe. The—"

"Telor, you once called me *Father*, not *Gens*," Gens Bleddyn interrupts me. "You called my other children your brothers and sisters."

My face pales as colorless blood rushes to bronze cheeks.

"I am sorry, Father."

"Come, sit beside me. You saved my life and your newest brother's. You were the first to react, to fire, and to destroy an enemy. Now, share this glass in honor of Garreth. Then you may tell me what you have to say."

I sit in the second chair before the fire. Father raises his glass and says, "To your brother Garreth, to whom you will be Mentor, his teacher – and protector." He sips, the potent liquor barely touching his lips. He hands me the glass.

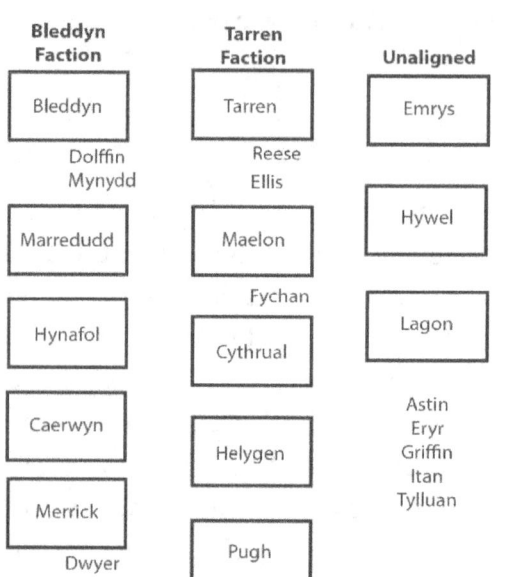

House Alignments c. 200,365 C.E.

Bleddyn Faction	Tarren Faction	Unaligned
Bleddyn	Tarren	Emrys
Dolffin Mynydd	Reese Ellis	
Marredudd	Maelon	Hywel
	Fychan	Lagon
Hynafol	Cythrual	
Caerwyn	Helygen	Astin Eryr Griffin Itan Tylluan
Merrick	Pugh	
Dwyer		

"To Garreth, my beloved brother," I say, then, "And to my father." I touch the glass to my lips. The ethanol burns my tongue and fumes rise through my head.

Father takes the glass from my hand, sips again, and says, "To you, Telor, Son-of-the-blood and son of my heart." He vows silently to repeat those words at the banquet, to make his pledge public and binding. But now, he asks, "What happened at Academy?"

"Sister Bethan and her element were on the sports field when two opponents tackled her. It was a legitimate move until one of Bethan's classmates saw a force-blade in a boy's hand. The glow of energy that turns a dagger into an unsanctioned weapon is unmistakable. At considerable risk, the girl seized the hand of the boy with the blade and foiled the attack. Your agents on the faculty arrested the two boys who tackled Bethan. The boys were given to me.

"One is a scion of Lesser House Astin. Astin is unaligned. I confirmed the boy was not part of the attack. His tackle was part of the game. The boy with the force-blade is a scion of Lesser House Fychan, aligned with House Maelon."

Father frowns. "And Maelon is aligned with Tarren. Fychan wishes to curry favor with him."

"That is what I see, Father. The boy's instructions were to wait until he received word of your death, leaving an empty seat on Council and causing confusion at Academy. He did not follow orders. Perhaps rather than wait he struck when he saw opportunity."

"How did he expect to escape?" Father asks.

"He cited an ancient custom that killing in vendetta cannot be punished except by Council. The boy claimed vendetta based on his house's alignment with Maelon and Maelon's alignment with Tarren. It is not certain the Academy faculty would be bound by this custom. I was not bound."

Father understands that I executed the boy. It was my right and duty.

Father steps to the fireplace and puts another log on the fire wolves before turning to me. "What you found is uncomfortable and dangerous. The attackers in the Council Chamber held forged passes. They were mercenaries, but there is no record of their hiring. I will offer condolences to Gens Fychan on the death of his house's scion at Academy. I will link the attacks in Council and at Academy so he knows I am aware of his treachery."

"What about Maelon, Father?"

"We have no proof of complicity, nor are we likely to find any. For the moment, we will focus on Fychan, where we have proof. We declared vendetta against Tarren two hundred millennia ago, sixty millennia before my grandfather's father was a child. Vendetta has taken on a new face. Never has Tarren tried to assassinate one of my children. We will respond publically and strongly."

I think of the trust my father has given me. I speak with confidence that exceeds my twenty years. "A public response may not be necessary, Father. And, it may not be prudent given the current balance of power between you and Gens Tarren. A secret, surgical strike at House Tarren will reverberate through his allies, including Maelon."

"What might we do?"

I watch my father's face and see understanding and agreement. What I propose will take several years to accomplish. That is but a moment in a lifespan of ten centuries, much less the extended lifespan of millennia given to starship crews and those of the High Blood, but House Bleddyn plans for millennia.

≈≈≈≈

After Telor leaves, Gens Bleddyn stands and faces the fire, for several minutes. He unclips a communicator from his belt and summons his second eldest son, Llywelyn, who has returned from his play in the mountains.

Llywelyn enters and bows, but does not kneel. It is his privilege as heir apparent. He does, however, wait for his father to speak.

"Llywelyn, you know what happened at Council. A member of Lesser House Fychan attacked your sister at Academy. There is reason to believe Fychan was also behind the attack at Council House. I will instruct Field Marshall Lloyd to increase the alert state of the Home Guard at all locations. You will inform your companions."

"Do you have a role for us, Father?"

"Continue to train them as you have been, but be wary." Bleddyn steps from the fire, signaling dismissal.

Llywelyn closes the door and walks to his quarters. *Father put his bastard, Telor, on the Council dais because I was late returning from the exercise. He should have put Delwyn. She's next-eldest legitimate child at home. He favors the bastard Telor too much. Now, Father will declare vendetta against a Lesser House, but has no role for me. At least I will not be part of his debasement of our house. Vendetta against a Lesser House? I could wipe Fychan off World in a day if I commanded the Home Guard.*

~~~~~

Fortress Bleddyn is open for the celebration of Garreth's elevation. Guards are especially vigilant after the assassination attempt. I watch Father greet friends, those who want to become friends, those who seek advantage, those aligned with our enemies, and those known to be enemies. *It is easy to place everyone into these categories. But is it useful? More important, is it correct?*

Nearly three thousand people attend the banquet. Father sits at the center of a long table on the raised dais. Llywelyn's surrogate, who is senior, sits at his right. Garreth's surrogate will be honored at this gathering and sits at Father's left. Llywelyn, Garreth's Brother-plus-eighteen years, moves to his seat beside his surrogate.

I enter, but before I find my seat near the end of the table, Father takes my elbow and seats me at the left hand of Garreth's surrogate. This honor does not go unnoticed by Llywelyn nor by others attuned to house politics. Delwyn and Daffyd, my Sister-and-Brother-minus-eight, sit at my left. They are twelve years old and their surrogates no longer accompany them.

After Gens Bleddyn uses the ancient words to salute the elevation of his newest son, he keeps his glass raised. He acknowledges the First Speaker who died today. This is expected. Then, he turns to his left and speaks the words he shared with me earlier. He keeps his glass raised and names me Mentor to the infant Garreth. This is unexpected. Normally such an appointment is not made until a child's third year. *This means I will have to change his diapers.* I see in Father's face his understanding of my thought.

The guests lift their glasses, but some exchange quizzical looks at the deviation from protocol. Father sees and makes note of them. I think he is pleased to feel the loyalty with which I respond to his words and salute my newest brother and my younger brother, Llywelyn, the heir apparent.

Scions of Bleddyn 200,365 C.E	
Telor	20
Llywelyn	18
Bethan	15
Delwyn	12
Daffyd	12
Aelwen	6
Rodric	3
Garreth	Infant

~~~~~

Grandfather elevated me when I was born, although I was Father's natural son by a concubine. Had he not done so, I would have been declared bastard. When Father became Gens, I became heir presumptive of House Bleddyn. It was only for two years. I was a toddler when Llywelyn, son of both Father and his wife, was born. Llywelyn became heir apparent, and I moved down the line of succession. Since then, six more children-of-the-blood have been born and I am eighth in line. I am firstborn, but eighth. Dynastic wars have begun with less provocation.

—Telor Bleddyn, Journal

~~~~~

Llywelyn invited many companions, young men and women he met at Academy, to join him upon graduation. They live at Fortress. They continue their training in Llywelyn's dojo and firing range. They take meals together and exercise in the mountains, jungles, and sand dunes of Continent. But none share Llywelyn's quarters, although many seek to do so. In his quarters, he is quite alone.

Llywelyn opens a hidden panel, removes a book, and places it on his desk. The book sits in a circle of light from the single lamp in the room. He reflects on the day's events and then writes.

Father named Telor to be Mentor to Garreth. I expected that, but not for three more years. Telor the teacher. A good role for him. But, why does Father give him that position now? I have never been named Mentor to my younger siblings, although Father would have done so had I asked. It is probably more work than it is worth.

Why does Father remind people Telor is a bastard by declaring him, once again, to be his son. This does not fool those who understand the importance of blood.

Telor saluted me, but his words were empty. They were not an oath. What are his ambitions? They remain hidden.

—Llywelyn Bleddyn, Private Journal

~~~~~

His father's salute to Telor during the banquet continues to trouble Llywelyn's thoughts. *What is Father thinking? And where is Father?* Llywelyn's calls to Aunt Aveta, his father's privy secretary and to Lieutenant Terrwyn, commander of his father's Praetorian Guard, are not returned. Two days later, Gens Bleddyn summons Llywelyn to his den. Despite the winter weather, the fireplace is cold.

"You wish to see me," Gens Bleddyn says. Llywelyn blurts his request and his father's face becomes colder.

Llywelyn's teeth are clenched; jaw muscles stand out below his cheekbones. Gens Bleddyn sees the anger, but ignores it.

9

"You are too young to be a father. You graduated from Academy less than three months ago. You are to be a soldier and a leader of soldiers. In a few years, you will command House Bleddyn's Home Guard. It is custom for those chosen for this role to remain unencumbered by children for some time."

"Father, I have heard you say the law is made for those who cannot think for themselves. How much more so is custom made?" Llywelyn had practiced these words, knowing he would need them.

Gens Bleddyn does not answer immediately. Llywelyn dares not interrupt his father's thoughts.

He has avoided his fraternal responsibilities to his siblings. He chooses to associate with the companions he assembled at Academy. They have graduated and are now the nucleus of a private army quartered in Fortress Bleddyn. They are an army that is learning the secrets and vulnerabilities of our home. This is my fault. I should have seen it sooner.

"Custom is interpreted in this house only by me," Bleddyn says. "You have a position in the house that requires your full attention."

"And if I reject this?" Llywelyn says.

"Then you will be rejected," his father snaps. "You will become no more than a common soldier in the house army."

Bleddyn's voice softens. "Do not challenge me, my son." he waves his dismissal.

He does not have the experience to rear a child, Bleddyn thinks. *Of all my children, he spends the least time with his siblings.* He closes the book on his desk. His mind is troubled and does not understand the injunction that works its way through the text: 'To live and work for the benefit of all.' He is unable to reconcile this with the oath he first took as a child – honor, valor, loyalty to Gens, to house, to sworn allies, and ultimately to the Res Publica.

That, Bleddyn thinks in a burst of insight, *may be the answer. Our first loyalty has been to our house, even after the*

10

houses united to destroy House Kaetween, to overthrow King Triumph Tarren, and to conquer the thralls of the Southern Continent. Perhaps there is a place for this.

He does not return the book to the shelf, but leaves it on his desk.

~~~~~

Llywelyn applies his anger to the dark stones of Fortress. His footsteps echo through the hallway. Thrall servants hear him coming and duck into empty rooms or stand with heads bowed and backs pressed to the wall until he passes.

He will replace me with the bastard, Telor, who he got on a whore from House Caerwyn. Llywelyn thinks. *He will replace me. Why? What does Telor have that I do not?*

~~~~~

Gens Bleddyn sits in the house War Room. Most of the screens and wall displays are dark. Controllers occupy only a few positions. The sensors of a reconnaissance satellite in synchronous orbit point toward Fortress. Bleddyn watches military floaters carrying Llywelyn and his companions depart. A satellite follows the floaters toward the Arista Mountains that line the equator. The mountains are ancient and mostly dormant volcanoes, formed when the southern part of the continent collided with the northern part two hundred sixty thousand millennia ago.

Floaters, individual anti-gravity sleds, are slightly larger than a toboggan. The pilots lie face down, navigating by a radar and video display. They fly along the treetops. Llywelyn disabled the radar transponders that would identify them to an enemy. It is an illegal but common practice in both war games and vendetta.

11

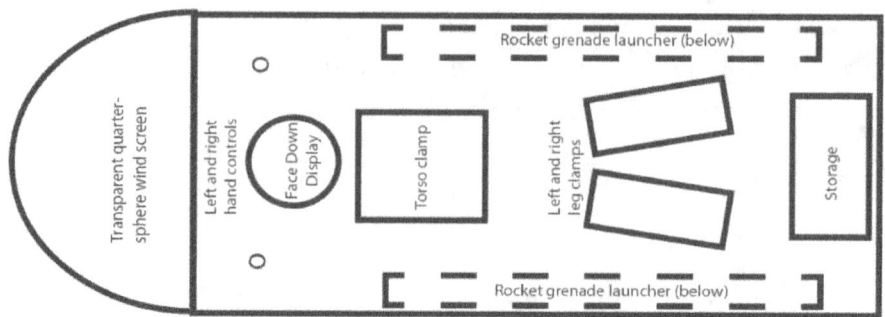

Gens Bleddyn snorts. *War games in the mountains. A camping trip. Play. Despite their age, they are still children. They are, however, children trained in warfare and armed. I must find an outlet for their energy and for Llywelyn's ambition.* He turns from his monitor and leaves the War Room. The duty controllers watch Llywelyn's floaters move northward. Another flight approaches from the southwest. The controllers trace them to their origin. They are from House Ellis, a Lesser House aligned with House Tarren.

The outcome of the encounter is a draw. The soldiers of Llywelyn Bleddyn and Ötsi, nephew of Gens Ellis, score nearly the same number of paintball hits. Ötsi was Llywelyn's chief rival at Academy. Although their houses have not sworn vendetta, the two young men did so, secretly and in violation of Academy rules. Their discussion after the exercise is muted; the agreement they reach electrifies their soldiers. The next exercise will be live-fire. Casualties are likely.

~~~~~

The day after Llywelyn returns from the exercise, his father summons him.

"You will begin life-extension treatment tomorrow," Gens Bleddyn says. "Today, you will fly to the hospital on Sehwa Island. Speak of this to no one."

Llywelyn struggles to hold his thoughts and emotions in check, to reveal nothing of what he feels. *Life-extension will allow me to live for tens of millennia, but will make me sterile. Father controls my seed that was harvested and frozen eight years ago when I reached puberty. Now, he takes the second step to make sure I will not have heirs to challenge him.*

"You seem pensive, Son," the Gens says. "This is an important step. In time, you will not only command my army but also have a place on my Privy Council. House Bleddyn's strength comes from two things – blood and the millennial thinking of those selected to receive these treatments."

Blood! He adulterates our blood by breeding with the Lesser Houses, Llywelyn thinks. *When I am Gens, I will have children only by Bethan, Delwyn, Aelwen, and other sisters.*

"And my children?" Llywelyn asks.

"Your seed has been preserved. After you complete an apprenticeship both as a soldier and as a councilor, we will select a suitable wife and surrogates."

I cannot challenge him, Llywelyn thinks. *But there is something I can do.*

"Yes, Father. I hear and obey." Llywelyn bows. It is the submissive bow of a child to its father, mother, or surrogate.

Bleddyn is not fooled. *The boy is resentful. He is full of anger. I must watch him.*

~~~~~

The morning after he returns from the hospital, Llywelyn seeks audience with his father. "Father, three of my companions wish to leave House Bleddyn's service and enter the mercenary auction at Cytgord. My other companions and I would accompany them if you allow this and will release the three from their vows."

"You have funds of your own, but do not bring back any mercenaries unless you are prepared to pay them, house them, train them, and feed them."

Gens Bleddyn chuckles. "Remember the adage, *Never invest in anything that eats.*"

"No, Father. I mean, yes, Father. We wish only to watch and to support our companions."

"Give the names of the three to Aunt Aveta and tell her and them in my name they are released without fault from their vows. She will send their new status to the auction computer."

The next morning, after arriving at Cytgord, Llywelyn speaks to his companions, hoping his words will seem unimportant. "I have private business in Cytgord. You may do as you wish, but do not follow me or seek me. Do not get into trouble. My father will learn of it."

It is easy for Llywelyn to find a thrall pharmacist. The woman is accustomed to dispensing drugs to young thralls and re-charging medical vambraces for young members of the Res Publica. She is puzzled when a soldier without a medical vambrace enters her shop. She bows, a courtesy bow, not deep but respectful.

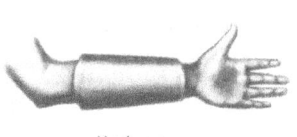

Vambrace

"How may I serve the Young Sir?" she asks.

Llywelyn is blunt. "I will soon embark on a dangerous mission. I wish my seed preserved in the event I do not return. This will require multiple ejaculations, a way to freeze the seed, and a powered container to transport the seed to my home. Can you do this?"

The woman thinks for a moment. "If you please, Young Sir, I must search for the equipment I will need."

14

Llywelyn nods. The woman operates a computer.

"I can have everything before evening. I will need payment in advance," she says.

A bargain is struck and payment made. Llywelyn rejoins his companions.

That evening, while his companions celebrate their three friends' contracts, Llywelyn returns to the pharmacy.

"Do you have everything?" he asks.

"Yes, Young Sir. Here is the freezer; here is the transporter. Its power supply will keep your seed frozen for at least three days without recharging. Please do not think me froward, but you said multiple ejaculations. I have also prepared drugs to ensure you can do that in one evening."

Several hours later, an exhausted Llywelyn accepts the transporter. It is well insulated and the cold he feels is only his imagination. *This is my future*, he thinks. *The life-treatment keeps me from creating new seed, but those already created? The ones hiding in my testicles and maturing in the epididymis? They are still alive. They are the seed that will impregnate my sisters when I become Gens. Father did not consider this. He did not think I knew about them.* Llywelyn draws his energy pistol. One burst is sufficient. The thrall doctor's blood seeps from the hole in her chest to form a puddle on the floor. *Blue*, Llywelyn notes. *Like ours.* He shrugs and leaves the pharmacy.

~~~~~

Llywelyn and his companions return to Fortress. News of Llywelyn's visit to the thrall pharmacist and of her death reaches Gens Bleddyn. *Llywelyn preserved the remnants of his seed so he can impregnate his sisters.* The House Patriarch frowns his displeasure. *This will not happen.*

15

Chapter 2: Stormtime

The equatorial continent is the largest landmass on World. It is about 9,000 km from east to west. World has an equatorial radius of almost 40,000 km, so storms have 31,000 km of open ocean to build strength. Coupled with an axial tilt of 37 degrees, the storms of solstice and equinox are especially fierce. Stormtime is a custom from the days when every able-bodied person was needed to prepare for the storms and make repairs afterwards.

Even in modern times, Academy, farms, and mines close four times a year, every 150 days, at Winter and Summer solstice and Spring and Fall equinox. House Bleddyn's merchant ships and fishers shelter in ports and the flow of trade is interrupted. Shuttles are moved into hangers. Starships in orbit around World may not land. Starships preparing for launch are held. People everywhere seek shelter. Gens Bleddyn opens Fortress to family and thralls.

Children of House Bleddyn enrolled in Academy are encouraged to bring friends to Fortress during stormtime. It is part of creating the alliances that make the house strong.

~~~~~

Gens Bleddyn stands alone on the battlements. Winds, precursors of Spring Stormtime, whip his cloak and spin pellets of sleet against his face, but he remains immobile. The shuttle bringing Bethan and her guests from Academy drops through low clouds, hovers, and then lands gently on the stones. Through the window, he sees his daughter in the pilot's seat. His smile does not reach his face.

Bethan and seven others, bundled in hooded cloaks, debark. Bethan, although an adult by all that matters, hurries to her father for a hug. The wind strengthens and howls through the crenels.

"Come, Daughter," Bleddyn speaks against the wind. "Bring your guests inside." He hesitates for a moment. "I assume you did not leave your pilot at Academy to walk home. He can move the shuttle to the hanger."

Bethan waits until the party is indoors before replying. "Father, I believe you made a joke."

Bleddyn's smile is brief. "Merely acknowledging your piloting skill. Now, who are your guests?"

Before Bethan finishes introducing her friends, little Sister Aelwen and Brother Guffudd mob her. The twins, Delwyn and Daffyd, nearly teens, are more restrained but still enthusiastic when they greet their eldest sister.

~~~~~

Gens Bleddyn is shoveling ash into a bucket when Bethan responds to his summons. She hands him lighter-pine kindling and small logs, which he stacks on the wrought-iron fire wolves before igniting the fire. Father and daughter stand on the hearth as the fire catches.

"I read your official report of the attempted assassination," Bleddyn says. "It was clear and concise – and incomplete. What did you not include? Start at the beginning."

Bethan hides her smile nearly as well as her father hid his when she landed the shuttle. "The two girls you assigned as my protectors keep close to me. I suspect others in my element learned the girls' role long ago. I am not the only scion of a Greater House who is guarded. There was some early resentment; however, Iona

18

and Tirion are both personable and professional and they won the respect and friendship of my element."

"Why is this information important?"

"Because it was they who saved my life. And you did say to start at the beginning." She ignores her father's grunt.

Bethan looks into the growing fire for a moment before speaking. "My group were to be defenders in an early round of *Botaoshi*, Pole pull-down. Iona was the monkey. She took her place at the top of the pole and clung to the projecting spike. My group surrounded the pole. When the referee's whistle sounded, Group XXXI ran toward us in melee formation. Before they reached us, their commander shouted. Still running, they formed an arrow for *chojeom*, a focal point attack. I was in the line of attack and went down, along with a dozen of the attackers.

"Iona, recall, was the monkey. She saw the two boys tackle me. She called to Tirion who was in the middle of the melee that followed the initial attack."

Bethan chuckles, before continuing. "Tirion was anything but gentle when she fought through the melee to me. The boy who held the force-blade was on the ground beside me. Tirion saw the boy draw the dagger and switch on the force-blade. She seized his hand and forearm and pushed the blade into the ground only inches from my side. She dislocated the boy's shoulder and may have broken his collarbone. She protected not only me but also everyone around me."

Gens Bleddyn nods and hides his anger.

"To aid Tirion, Iona dropped from the top of the pole, signaling victory for the other team. She forfeited the game. After the investigation, the record of the game was removed from the rolls. We replayed it – and won."

"You knew Iona and Tirion were your guards?"

Bethan chuckles. "From the first day at Academy. How could I not, Father? You are not nearly as clever as you think."

Bethan enjoys both the raised eyebrows and the smile that appears on her father's face. *He is marked more by gravitas than familiarity*, she thinks. *Therefore, I treasure his smile.*

Bleddyn's smile disappears when her father growls. "You forget yourself."

20

Her smile reappears. "But I am your favorite, eldest daughter, am I not?"

"You are my only eldest daughter," Bleddyn snaps. Then he relents. "Yes, and my favorite. Go now. Enjoy your friends' visit. And reward Iona and Tirion as you see fit."

~~~~~

The next morning, Gens Bleddyn summons Llywelyn, Bethan, and me to his den. When we arrive, he reveals the message he received at dawn. "House Hywel declared vendetta against House Fychan," he says. "It has become common knowledge Fychan is responsible for the unintentional killing of Gens Hywel during Garreth's elevation."

My siblings and I look from one to the other although Llywelyn avoids my eyes. Bethan speaks first. "Is it certain Gens Hywel's death was not intentional? He could have been a target. His death means Gens Tarren inherits the speakership early."

Father's face remains impassive. "A good thought, Daughter. We must not overlook that."

I speak next. "Father, has Hywel attacked Fychan yet?"

Llywelyn has never accepted my legitimacy, and frowns when I call Gens Bleddyn my father. Llywelyn asks, "What was the nature of the attacks, Father?"

"Hywel attacked members of Fychan's Home Guard who were engaged in maneuvers in the mountains. Hywel's soldiers killed a son of Fychan and wounded a daughter."

Llywelyn's voice pierces the brief pause in Father's words. "Hywel killed a member of House Fychan in justified vendetta. That restores Hywel's honor."

Now, both Father and I frown. *A fool can think only foolish thoughts*, I think.

Llywelyn does not notice our father's reaction. "Fychan will attack Hywel who will respond. Their vendetta weakens both houses while we grow stronger. Karmet told us, *The battle with our enemies is less bloody if our enemies are fighting with one another.*"

That is wrong, I think. *Strength comes from within us, not from others' weakness. Geraint told us that, but Llywelyn does not consider the teachings of Geraint. He thinks Geraint is soft, largely because Llywelyn does not understand him.*

Bethan speaks next. "That depends on whether both houses believe honor is satisfied." She seeks a rational consensus even though she knows Llywelyn will not follow that path.

Llywelyn confirms Bethan's opinion when he dismisses his sister with a wave of his hand and a puff of air through his lips. "Fychan will not think that way. They hope to become a Greater House. Their only route is to replace Hywel. Now, they have justification. Gens Hywel is an unaligned pacifist. A soft and rotting fruit to be torn from the tree and trodden. Especially if we help Fychan."

I am the only one who sees Father's disappointment as he dismisses his children. I surprise Father when I return.

"Rise, Telor. I know something troubles you."

"Father, why does Fychan continue this vendetta? Why does Llywelyn think House Bleddyn should come to the aid of Fychan who is aligned with Tarren, with whom we have declared vendetta?"

Father snorts as breath passes through his nose rather than through his mouth. "You find the heart of the matter," he says.

"Hywel is a Greater House, but unaligned. What does that suggest?"

"It means that having been attacked by an ally of House Tarren, Gens Hywel might be open to an approach by House Bleddyn."

"And Llywelyn's desire to aid Fychan?"

I think for several minutes. I know Father will allow time. "At best, it might wean House Fychan from House Tarren," I reply.

22

"At worst, it would escalate the vendetta between House Tarren and us. It could lead to war."

Telor is right, Bleddyn thinks. *He sees this correctly. Something his brother does not.*

"Speak of this to no one," Father commands.

~~~~~

Two days pass before Gens Bleddyn again summons Llywelyn and me to his den. "House Fychan acknowledged the vendetta declared by Hywel. They did that by attacking several of Hywel's military outposts near the northern coast. Fychan overextended himself. He lost a score of soldiers because he did not plan well."

Father looks from Llywelyn to me. "We will not make that mistake. Your oath is honor, valor, and loyalty. To that, I add *patience* and *planning*. We will secretly support House Hywel. I do not want to draw House Tarren to House Fychan's aid. Tarren is unlikely to attack Hywel, an unaligned Greater house.

"Llywelyn, you will develop covert plans to inflict harm on House Fychan. Not an attack on people but on property. A bite by the Wolf of Bleddyn, a bite to cause pain and perhaps to cripple."

House of Wolf Clan Salute

Father watches Llywelyn acknowledge this order with the military salute of House Bleddyn – right hand at shoulder level, palm forward, thumb tucked into the palm, four fingers extended and curved like the claws of the wolf.

Father returns Llywelyn's salute, then addresses me. "Telor, you will provide intelligence and ensure Llywelyn has equipment and more

23

soldiers as needed to supplement his companions. Llywelyn, I will review the plan before you execute it."

Take time to plan, but make your goal quick victory and not a lengthy campaign, I think. *Another of Geraint's lessons.*

~~~~~

Llywelyn's thoughts are different.

Fychan will be on their guard after Hywel's attack. They are a Lesser House, but strong. Is Father setting me up to fail? And why must I include Telor in my planning? I have enough expertise among my companions. Why does Father target Fychan? Fychan would be a stronger ally than Hywel. Why does he waste resources defending a weak, unaligned house rather than attack our real enemy, House Tarren?

—*Llywelyn Bleddyn,* Private Journal

Chapter 3: Vendetta

Llywelyn stands at the front of the War Room and uses a laser pointer to highlight the map. "We will infiltrate Fychan through House Ellis territory. Should we be detected, Fychan will not expect an attack from an allied neighbor's territory.

"We adopt a strategy from Karmet – to attack Fychan where he is unprepared and to appear where we are not expected. Fychan depends on three power turbines suspended in rivers that flow from the mountains. Our target will be the most central of those turbines."

Gens Bleddyn's face is in shadow. Llywelyn does not see his father's eyebrows rise nor feel his skepticism. Llywelyn changes the display to a satellite image of the central turbine. "My infiltration element will use low-power explosives to destroy the anchors of the suspension cables. The river is running rapidly following the rains of Spring Stormtime. It will appear one anchor failed followed by a cascade of failures of the others. Gens Fychan will lose half of his electricity until he can re-hang the turbine. It is likely the turbine will be damaged beyond repair and cannot be replaced in less than a year."

Llywelyn pauses.

"A good plan, so far. Show me the details," Bleddyn commands.

Show the details? Llywelyn thinks. *Does he not trust me with even this simple task?* He describes for his father the route, the explosives they will use to attack the anchor points, and their exfiltration plan.

When Llywelyn finishes, Bleddyn speaks. "A sound plan, Son. Remember, no plan ever survives contact with the enemy.

That is an apothegm, not a natural law, but something to think about. Avoid contact and withdraw should it be necessary. You are more important than the mission. No blame will attach."

The boy bows to his father and is dismissed. *He thinks I will fail. Otherwise he would not say that. But I will not fail.*

~~~~~

Two nights later, a shuttle carrying Llywelyn, ten of his companions, and eleven military floaters crosses the border between the territories of Houses Caerwyn and Ellis. It flies at nap-of-the-earth altitudes along a route that avoids even the smallest village. The shuttle's radar signature is masked. Clouds cover the sky. The new moon will not be visible even if the clouds break.

To avoid House Fychan's terminal defenses, the shuttle lands a hundred kilometers short of the generator. Llywelyn and his companions drag floaters and equipment from the shuttle and then fly below the treetops toward the generator. Dismounting from the floaters, they climb to the generator's mounts. They use rock drills to create holes into which they pack explosives. They emplace charges and set detonator timers before withdrawing. They plan to destroy only four of the eight anchor points. That should be sufficient for their first objective – to disable the generator. If the engineers' estimates are correct, the loss of four anchors will pull the remaining anchors from the rock and fulfill the second objective – to destroy the generator.

All but Llywelyn return to the shuttle. Llywelyn's floater hovers below the tops of nearby trees. Mist from the rushing water settles on him. The night is cold; the mist, clammy. Llywelyn's frequent checks of his chronometer betray his nervousness.

He is rewarded when the first charge blows. It is not spectacular, but Llywelyn sees the generator lurch, then lurch again as the second charge blows. Llywelyn does not wait for the last two charges, but returns to his shuttle. He skims the floater into the cargo door and lands it on the deck with an audible thump.

His shout is louder than the thump. "It worked! The first two charges disabled the generator. We'll know more when a reconnaissance satellite passes overhead tomorrow."

After Llywelyn's announcement, his shuttle flies southeast toward House Ellis territory. Before crossing the border between Fychan and Ellis, the pilot turns on the radar transponder with false signature and pops up high enough to be painted by Fychan's radar, then resumes the hidden path back to Fortress.

~~~~~

At high sun the next day, Llywelyn stands before his father. The boy is flush with victory. "Reconnaissance shows Fychan was prepared for an attack on the smaller generators near the marches, but not for my bold attack at the heart of his territory."

The boy is justifiably proud of his success. "Well done, Son. I look for similar success on your next mission."

~~~~~

Days later, I report to Father. "Fychan's people found evidence of explosives. Fychan, himself, called Dolffin and blamed her for the attack, but only because her territory is close to Fychan's and she is known to be our ally. Dolffin denied involvement and wishes to speak to you."

Father touches a button on his desk. On the wall opposite, the portrait of his father slides aside to reveal a communication screen. A symbol in the lower right corner shows the circuit to be secure. He stands when Gens Dolffin's image appears. He and she execute the bow of equals, a long tradition between Greater House Bleddyn and Lesser House Dolffin.

"Someone attacked Fychan. He blames us." Dolffin says when both are seated. Father sees her faint smile.

27

"Please deny all knowledge of the attack but tell me if Fychan makes any attack on you. He has no evidence. In fact, the only evidence he has is the attack may have come from Ellis." This is as close to admitting responsibility as Bleddyn will come, even on an encrypted circuit. Dolffin understands.

~~~~~

Twenty days later a cargo shuttle, registered to neutral House Eryr, lands at Fortress Bleddyn. No one notices me, in worn and dirty coveralls, when I step from the shuttle and join the workers unloading cargo. No one notices when I slip behind a stack of crates, discard the coveralls, and walk past the shuttle. After identifying myself to the guards, I pass through the warehouse and into the more secure hallways of Fortress. My steps quicken as I move toward Father's den.

"House Fychan plans a ground attack on Port Dolffin," I report to Father. He does not ask how I know. He never questions me about the intelligence network I created during my time as an Academy Cadet and in the years since.

Father does, however encourage me to explain. "Why a ground attack? And why the port?"

"Fychan has no warships and only a few unarmed merchant ships. Dolffin's islands are well guarded against attack from both sea and air. The only attack Fychan can mount is by land; the only ground target is the port. It's the only territory Dolffin holds on the mainland."

Father hides his smile. "Then, what should be our response?"

I do not answer immediately. When I do, I surprise my father.

"Should Llywelyn be part of this plan?"

Llywelyn hides his displeasure when he reaches Father's den. *Telor was here before me. He and Father are plotting something.* He pushes aside his enmity for the bastard who is his elder brother and listens to his father's explanation.

Father learned this from Telor, but how does Telor know? Llywelyn focuses his thoughts more on Telor than on the problem. Father's orders interrupt those thoughts.

"Llywelyn, you will command your companions and the Mountain Company of my Home Guard. Conceal them in the hills above Port Dolffin with fighters and military floaters to offer reinforcements, but only on my orders. Do you understand? You are not to engage unless I order it. This situation is delicate."

"Yes, Father," Llywelyn says. *He expands my command, but also chastens me in the presence of Telor.* Llywelyn thinks. *The only glory I can earn will be from engagement with Fychan. How can I engage without Father's orders? A communication blackout, perhaps. Perhaps Dolffin's forces will appear to retreat under an overwhelming attack. A well-planned flaw in my concealment? Is there a way to set this up? More important, will Father believe it if I do?*

~~~~~

Llywelyn and his soldiers depart early in the evening to reach Port Dolffin by dawn. After they leave, I enter Llywelyn's quarters and aim a modified energy pistol at the wall behind which Llywelyn hid a sub-zero carrier. The pistol's radiation destroys the frozen life held by the carrier.

Llywelyn will be guarding an empty dream.

I slip away through a hidden panel. My thoughts are in turmoil. *Father ordered the destruction of Llywelyn's seed collected years ago. I have destroyed the last chance of Llywelyn's line assuming leadership of House Bleddyn. Is this a good thing? I show loyalty to my father. No valor was required. But, have I acted honorably? It is Father's right to select his successor, but to do so in secret and in this manner?* Although my thoughts are troubled, I keep my voice calm when I report.

"It is done."

"I have erased the recordings made by cameras and sensors," Father replies. "There is no evidence except your memory and mine."

I cannot suppress my feelings; Father sees my eyes widen.

"You wonder if you have done the right thing," Father says. "You wonder if I will erase you."

"No …" I pause. "Yes, Father."

"Do you remember the pledge to you I made at the banquet following Garreth's elevation?"

"You named me son-of-the-blood and son of your heart. I will never forget that."

"I never saluted Llywelyn with those names," Father says. "Perhaps, if I had done so long ago, his mind would not have twisted his oath of *honor, valor, and loyalty* into *ambition, pride, and scheming.* You, Telor, remain both son-of-the-blood and son of my heart."

My heart continues to race as I complete the oath. "Father, I swear to live by honor, to be valorous in battle, and to be loyal to you, our house, and the Res Publica."

Gens Bleddyn nods. He turns to his desk in dismissal, but I carry his pride when I leave.

~~~~~

After a supersonic flight across the continent, Llywelyn stands on a bluff east of Port Dolffin waiting for Fychan's attack. He stands there the entire day, but his hopes of glory are dashed. Dolffin's forces are not in retreat. Master Sergeant Rhingyll, who commands the Mountain Company, maintains an open satellite link to Fortress Bleddyn and provides situation reports. The link is secure and Llywelyn cannot think of a reason to order him to maintain communication silence. Fychan's forces withdraw in the face of unexpected resistance. Casualties on both sides are light and the real loser in the conflict is Llywelyn, whose anger at being unable to earn glory for himself is palpable when he faces his father the next day.

"Son, because you were not involved in battle, you think your role was not important. You were not one of Geraint's cannons, a log painted black to resemble a real gun, a false threat. It was your presence and the knowledge Dolffin's forces could call upon you that gave them the courage to overcome their enemy. You should not feel lessened by this, but proud of your role."

Proud of standing aside? Proud of being thought of as an impotent weapon, one bereft of power? Geraint's cannons were impotent. Llywelyn thinks. *My father hints of my impotence after the life-extension treatments. Why does he do this?*

~~~~~

Llywelyn's sleep is troubled. After their return from Port Dolffin, he leads his companions in strenuous training, hoping the activity and fatigue will ease his mind and allow him to sleep. It does not work. After five days of foot soldiering in the mountains, he returns to his room and his journal.

I feel no different and my companions do not find me different. They do not know I have received the life-treatment. I have decades before we will separate in apparent age but I must be ready for that. At some point, I will have to discard them and create a new army. I must appear to cooperate in my father's plans for me. He continues the private teachings that began when I was six years old, but he allows me ample time to train my companions. Today, he summons me. I must be careful in my words and expression. His perception is uncanny.

—Llywelyn Bleddyn, Private Journal

Gens Bleddyn gestures Llywelyn to a chair facing the hearth. Although Spring Stormtime has passed, brisk winds pull cold air from deep in the southern hemisphere. Gusts that funnel down the chimney push the flames from side to side. Llywelyn's thoughts and feelings pulse as wildly as the flames. *What does Father want?*

"The medicos report complete success with your treatments. Instead of living a millennium or so, you have the potential to live for tens of millennia. That is a great gift; one whose cost must be repaid. You will begin by taking the Lieutenancy of the Second Company of the House's Home Guard. Your task will be to integrate your companions into that company. It is time they began earning their keep. Do you understand?"

"Yes, Father."

"Your companions are a stalwart team. They will serve as examples for the other soldiers."

Llywelyn's bow to his father barely conceals his displeasure.

Father tells me he plans for millennia longer than I will see, even with the life-treatments. Why should I plan for something I will not see unless it is for my blood and my seed? I will plan for the future, but it will be my future and the future of my children and my house, not his.

—Llywelyn Bleddyn, Private Journal

~~~~~

Llywelyn puts aside these thoughts and plans war games with Ötsi of Lesser House Ellis. Gens Bleddyn and Gens Ellis do not know of these plans, nor would they approve had they been aware. Ellis is aligned with House Tarren with whom Bleddyn has sworn vendetta. That is unimportant to Llywelyn and Ötsi.

"Father, you must see this." I kneel at my father's desk but speak without being acknowledged. I am sure my fear shows in the pitch of my voice, which is higher than normal. Father understands I am not only concerned; I am afraid.

He stands. "What is it?"

"In the War Room, Father. Llywelyn and a scion of House Ellis. They are fighting. In the mountains." I hurry behind my father to the War Room where screens display the battle.

"Those are not tag lasers, Commander," a controller says. "They're energy weapons. Pistols, from the signature."

"Both Llywelyn's soldiers and the Ellis forces are using them," a second controller adds.

"We recorded most of Llywelyn's challenge and the Ellis commander's reply." I press a button. Llywelyn's voice comes from speakers.

"… are agreed. Fifteen soldiers on unarmed military floaters, each soldier to have an energy pistol with five charges but no recharges."

"Agreed," a second voice says. "Swords, daggers, and grace knives."

"You will not need your blades; you will be dead." Llywelyn's blunt and emotionless words conclude the challenge. The channel dissolves into a static hiss.

"Contact Gens Ellis," Father commands. "No one other than the Gens and no time other than now are acceptable."

Moments later, Gens Ellis's face appears on the screen. "Gens Bleddyn, I—"

"Gens Ellis," Bleddyn interrupts. "Are you aware our sons are engaged in open hostilities with energy weapons?"

"No, Your Grace."

"Nor was I," Bleddyn says. "My War Room is sending a feed to yours." He sees Ellis freeze as he receives and understands the information, including the challenge and reply.

"Your Grace, I will accept the outcome of this battle," Ellis says. His agreement reflects his house's status as a Lesser House. Ellis knows his patron, Gens Tarren, would not challenge House Bleddyn over an incident involving a couple of youngsters.

"It appears both our sons have agreed," Father replies. "I will also accept the outcome. Honor demands this."

Gens Ellis sees in Father's agreement no insult, no reliance on power or position, but only Bleddyn's unquestioned definition of honor. He bows. "Gens Bleddyn."

Father returns the bow. Whilst not a bow of equals, it is deeper than protocol requires, especially for those on opposite sides of the eternal warfare that separates the Res Publica.

~~~~~

The time is halfway between midnight and sunrise. Llywelyn's armor bears several scorch marks. Immediately upon landing, he is summoned to his father's den. He knows the man is displeased. Llywelyn won a skirmish with Lesser House Ellis, aligned with Bleddyn's enemy, House Tarren. Llywelyn does not understand why his father is not happy with the outcome. *Although a soldier of Ellis was gravely wounded, he may recover. House Bleddyn shows supremacy in—*

"What was this about?" Gens Bleddyn's voice interrupts Llywelyn's thoughts.

He knows more than he is saying, Llywelyn thinks before he speaks. "It was an exercise, Father, not unlike those we conducted at Academy." Neither his voice nor his thoughts carry the assurance he once felt.

"An exercise using live weapons. An exercise involving a house aligned with an enemy with whom we have sworn vendetta. You did not consider the politics before you engaged."

Bleddyn paces. His face is bright with anger as blood rushes to his cheeks, and his lips are tight. "You are an officer in my Home Guard. Your actions are no longer those of an Academy cadet or an individual soldier. They are the actions of a claw of the wolf. I will not tell you how to train your soldiers. That is your responsibility. But you must plan more carefully and not repeat such an incident. Do you understand, Lieutenant?"

"Yes, Commander," Llywelyn says, using his father's military title. *He addresses me as Lieutenant. Not by name or as his son. His words do not join us; they separate us.*

~~~~~

Gens Bleddyn opens the windows and shutters of his den to the warmth of summer, moderated by the altitude of the mesa on which Fortress stands and by the forests surrounding it. He looks over the forest and fields, but he does not see them; rather, his mind fills with thoughts and plans. *Our society is hierarchical, but the hierarchy is fluid. My position at any instant is determined not only by my own strength, but also by the coalitions I build. A month has passed since Llywelyn's war games with Ellis. Is that enough time? Is now the time to strike?*

He turns. The door opens and Llywelyn steps in. *What does the Gens want, now?* Llywelyn wonders. His thoughts are sour; his lips, tight.

Bleddyn sees but does not acknowledge this. "You are aware of recent events."

"Yes, Father. Tarren experienced flooding; a volcano erupted in Ellis territory, creating earthquakes and pyroclastic flows of ash and boiling water. The volcanoes in Ellis territory are the only ones still active on the southern half of the continent. World attacks our enemies for us."

"Just as we can attract more ants with sugar than with poison, we can make more allies with cooperation than vendetta," Gens Bleddyn says.

"If I understand you, Father, we should send food to Tarren's thralls who are starving. We should offer to help House Ellis rebuild."

"Think, Son," Bleddyn says. *Think in reality and not in the fantasy of your mind.*

"No, we will not offer aid to Tarren," he continues. "Not now; perhaps never. Their betrayal is too old; the hatred, too deep. However, if we were to give aid to one of their allies, we might weaken that alliance and create a new alliance to strengthen our house. Gens Ellis and I reached an understanding during your war games with his nephew, Ötsi. I will contact Ellis and offer aid. You will provide this aid covertly. You planned well the secret attacks on Fychan. You will plan a secret aid mission to Ellis and execute it on my order. Suspend your training for the moment. Tell me your plan tomorrow."

When the door closes behind Llywelyn, Bleddyn returns his gaze to the window where clouds, heavy with moisture and lifted by westerly winds, pop up over Mesa, promising afternoon thunderstorms.

Llywelyn is smug when he faces his father in the War Room at dawn the next morning. "Ellis needs heavy equipment and operators. They lost their satellite ground station. They need to replace four bridges. They also need food, water, and medicine. So far, Tarren has not responded to their pleas, nor has Pugh, the nearest allied neighbor."

Llywelyn displays a map.

"The equipment and supplies will appear to come from Merrick and Caerwyn. I will funnel everything through Caerwyn's territory. If Tarren discovers our caravans, he will assume Caerwyn is the source. Tarren might complain, but not loudly. He depends on Caerwyn for access to the sea through their ports."

"Caravans?" Gens Bleddyn asks.

36

"Yes, Father. The first is loading now and will deploy from Fortress by mid-morning. Cargo shuttles will carry bulldozers, cranes, concrete pumpers, and building material. The operators believe they go to Caerwyn to build improvements to the port. I will divert them to Ellis. The first caravan with food and medicine will be dispatched from Caerwyn in an hour. I will fly there to coordinate. Additional supplies and equipment will be assembled and dispatched quickly. You will need to confirm this mission and ensure Merrick and Caerwyn will cooperate."

Bleddyn finds himself pleased by Llywelyn's speed and initiative. "Good work, Son. Keep me informed of any problems you encounter. I will contact Caerwyn, Merrick, and Ellis."

I will be on the first caravan to arrive in Ellis territory," Llywelyn thinks as he returns to his quarters. *Gens Ellis and Ötsi will know I am the benefactor.*

Ötsi is waiting when the caravan arrives. His bow to Llywelyn is appropriate for a junior member of a Lesser House when meeting the heir apparent of a Greater House. Llywelyn doesn't return the bow, not even with the nod due the least member of a lesser house or a thrall. *This is not good, Ötsi thinks.* "Welcome, Llywelyn, and thank you in the name of my Uncle, Gens Ellis, for your help."

Llywelyn closes the distance between them until he is sure others cannot hear his voice. "I am here only because my father ordered it. I have no love for you or your house."

"We swore vendetta while at Academy." Ötsi's voice is soft. "I awarded you the win in our exercise last month and have not returned your challenge because I know you have the stronger force. I would break our cycle of vendetta and—"

"No." Llywelyn's voice is firm. "I am here on my father's orders. I do not have to deal with you."

Ötsi will neither challenge me nor accept my challenge. Now, Father orders me to integrate my companions into the Second Company of the Home Guard. He keeps command of the First Company, his Praetorian Guard, the ones who guard the Gens and the family. I know what he is doing. He is trying to dilute my power, but I will use this to expand my power. My companions will not integrate with the Second Company; they will infiltrate it and control it.

—Llywelyn Bleddyn, Private Journal

Llywelyn and his companions graduated from Academy only a few years ago. Since then, they engaged in training including unsanctioned live-fire exercises not available to the ordinary soldiers of House Bleddyn's Second Company. Llywelyn uses this as reason to award his companions ranks and salaries as sergeants and corporals, and to place them as squad leaders and squad seconds. Most of the soldiers of the Second Company find it easy to accept the new leadership. Those who were squad leaders and seconds find it easy to transfer to other companies. There are few ripples.

~~~~~

The man who enters Gens Bleddyn's den wears the flashes of a private in the Second Company of the house Home Guard. He is, however, Sergeant Asant of the house intelligence corps and a nephew of the Gens.

Asant's report is brief. "Your son replaced the non-commissioned officers in the Second Company with his companions. He plans a live fire exercise against the forces of House Eryr in the unclaimed land between Eryr and Tylluan."

"How is the Second Company functioning?" Bleddyn asks.

"The company operates smoothly and the soldiers have accepted your son's leadership."

"Sergeant Asant, let me know the first sign of trouble, whether in the ranks or between Llywelyn's forces and an enemy, internal or external."

~~~~~

The relief convoys to House Ellis no longer need monitoring. Llywelyn turns his attention to more important matters. Eryr's lieutenant agrees to energy weapons, but Gens Bleddyn orders Llywelyn to limit the exercise to paintballs. *Father learned of our plans and forbade a live-fire exercise. He declared me to be a Claw of the Wolf, but he treats me as an Academy Cadet. How did he know it was to be live-fire? There must be a traitor in the ranks.* Llywelyn's thoughts are dark.

~~~~~

Eryr's territory lies among rugged mountains along the equator and near the eastern edge of the continent. The house's wealth comes from minerals extracted from ancient volcanoes and from tariffs collected at Port Aberwith. Llywelyn expects his adversary's defenses to take advantage of the mountains. He splits his forces into flights of floaters to slip through the Eryr *Mountain Eagle* defense easier than with shuttles.

Eryr's soldiers know their weaknesses far better than does Llywelyn. The Eryr commander sends his own floaters to intercept Llywelyn's forces before they can penetrate more than a few kilometers into Eryr territory. Llywelyn's forces are hard-pressed to maintain their frontal attack. By high sun, Llywelyn realizes he is out-maneuvered and calls a withdrawal. Floaters and soldiers, both well coated with paint, land in neutral territory west of Eryr's lands.

Llywelyn's closest companions sit on logs around a small clearing. Thick-needled pine trees block the last light of the setting sun but not the breeze that blows smoke toward them.

"Smoke follows beauty," a corporal says.

"Bite me," a sergeant snaps and wipes tears from his eyes. He pushes aside the soldier on his left and slides into her place, away from the smoke.

"Hey! Watch what you're—"

"Enough!" Llywelyn growls. *Somehow, not only Father but also Eryr knew my plans. There is a traitor in my ranks.* "Eryr anticipated our plan," he says. Although his voice is soft, those around him feel his anger.

"Their response was logical given what we know about them," Leiaf, a son of House Astin says. Leiaf is a junior member of an unaligned, Lesser House. Seeking advancement, he swore to Llywelyn in their third year at Academy.

"Logical," Llywelyn spits. His displeasure is scarcely hidden. "Logical, but unanticipated. Logical only if the plan is flawed. Who is responsible?"

None of his companions will answer, except Leiaf. "The fault is … somehow, Eryr knew. Eryr has spies." The boy sees the others draw back at the implied accusation and carefully thinks his next words. "None of us. But somehow, they knew."

Who knew? Llywelyn wonders. *A few members of my companions, including that one, Leiaf of Astin. He swore to me in our third year at Academy. Did my father know?* A new thought rises in Llywelyn's mind. *Was my father the source of the leak? If we had used energy weapons, I would have lost more than half my floaters. Some of my soldiers would be dead; many of the others wounded. Is this why Father ordered paintballs only? Did he have no confidence in me? Did he want me to fail?*

Llywelyn closes the meeting. "We will return to Fortress in the morning. Tonight, I will contact the Eryr lieutenant and accord him the win."

And I will seek answers.

The next morning, Llywelyn leads his soldiers on their floaters in a game of follow-the-leader through the trees. It is a test of both skill and courage. At the speeds Llywelyn sets, impact with a tree would be fatal. Llywelyn releases the clamps that hold his legs and torso firmly in the floater's cradle and rolls his body from left to right, sharpening the turns. None of his companions can keep up with him. His display shows him to be well in the lead when an alarm sounds. He pulls up. When he is above the trees, he reverses course. The display leads him to the wreckage of a floater. Others gather.

"Who …?"

"Where's the pilot?"

"Here!" Someone calls. "It's Leiaf. He must have fallen off. He's dead."

Llywelyn flips open his communicator, hoping a satellite is in range. He gets a signal and presses an icon to connect him with the house War Room. His report is brief. So are his father's orders. "Remain there. I will send help."

I don't need your help. I need a shower and a clean uniform.

Five days later, a technician reports to Gens Bleddyn. "Sir, the clamps on the boy's floater were open before the crash. We do not know why they were open. The flight computer was damaged, but we are confident the signal to open did not come from the pilot's controls."

"Sabotage?" Bleddyn asks.

"Likely, sir, but we cannot confirm that."

Bleddyn thanks the man. *Sabotage. By whom and why?* He summons Llywelyn.

"Llywelyn, the House Astin boy's floater was sabotaged. He did not release the clamps, himself. Your fleet, floaters and shuttles, is grounded until maintenance can check them all. Afterwards, they are not to be left unguarded, especially when on exercises.

"You will keep this information to yourself. The boy's death was an accident. It will remain so. You are dismissed."

Llywelyn returns to his quarters. His thoughts are troubled, but he is optimistic. *It worked. However, it will never work again, but I am clever. When I need it, I will find another way.*

~~~~~

Gens Bleddyn's thoughts are complex. *Tarren is not sure I am responsible for Llywelyn's attacks on Fychan, but he is suspicious. He knows someone helped House Ellis recover much faster than expected. Llywelyn left behind a damaged floater with House Maelon identification. He was clever to have stolen the floater. That will distract Tarren, who may think Maelon is gathering allies to challenge him. At the least, it may drive a wedge between Tarren and Maelon.*

Tarren's minions failed to assassinate Daughter Bethan or me during Garreth's elevation and Tarren knows I suspect his house is behind that. He will try, again. I have added defenses at Academy to better protect Bethan. However, I am the one he wishes to eliminate. Why? Is it because he knows Llywelyn is my heir and thinks he is tractable? How can I draw Tarren out without endangering my children?

I can remain in Fortress and be safe from attack. I can visit my territories and my people and lead them to believe I am safe from attack. The one approach preserves me. The other? The other strengthens the house but at great risk to me. My first duty is to the house. I cannot allow Llywelyn to inherit, but I have not yet positioned his heir. My father died too soon.

~~~~~

Some of House Bleddyn's holdings are safer than others. Fortress Bleddyn sits on the mesa that also holds Council House and Academy. It is the safest. Council House and Academy are open to all houses, but millennia ago House Bleddyn took responsibility to defend them. The weapons and soldiers positioned on Mesa are formidable. The hospital on Sehwa and the spaceport on Namhae are also secure.

I cannot, however, limit myself to these safe places. Bleddyn thinks. *I must also visit those places on the marches – a place like the open city of Aberwith.*

He flips open his communicator and presses an icon.

When I respond to Father's summons, I see in his eyes uncertainty that does not reach his voice.

"Telor, you are my chancellor in all but name." Father's words reflect a question to which both he and I know the answer. Llywelyn's jealousy and his enmity are reason enough. Naming me chancellor, the highest position in the house other than the Gens, would tip the balance between me as first-born and Llywelyn as heir, a balance Father struggles to maintain.

"Yes, Father."

"I will visit the seaport at Aberwith. The public reason is to inspect the harbor and its fortifications. Although Aberwith is an open city, all the eastern houses have a vested interest in a large, deep-water port on the Eastern Ocean. The private reason for the visit will be a meeting with Gens Eryr. I wish to discuss with him the exercises Llywelyn conducted and our responsibilities for the harbor."

"Our responsibilities?" I ask. "Aberwith is an open city in Eryr's territory. We have never had responsibility for the harbor except for the fees our ships pay."

"Never publically," Father says. "The harbor lies just north of the border between Eryr's territory and ours. We have long had an unofficial understanding that we would participate in its defense."

"You wish to make a public agreement to bring House Eryr toward House Bleddyn." I speak my understanding. "Toward, but not aligned. Eryr is a trusted neutral. The agreement should focus on trade and commerce, on fees collected from ships using the harbor, and on sharing the cost of the harbor's upkeep. Mutual defense should be clearly limited to the harbor and put in the agreement as if it were an afterthought."

Father nods. "This will be an important event. You will plan the visit and take my greeting and invitation to Gens Eryr. I will travel with only one element of the Praetorian Guard."

I do not think it necessary to tell Father I will order the Mountain Company of the Home Guard to shadow him.

~~~~~

A month later, minutes before dawn, I watch a shuttle land silently in the courtyard of an inn in Aberwith. Gens Bleddyn and eighteen of his Praetorian Guard, the Prime Element, walk down the ramp toward me. Father and the soldiers are in mufti – non-military clothes of a merchant or a sailor.

Father scans his surroundings. This is an ancient place. The flagstones are worn smooth by centuries of comings and goings. The grey of the walls, built from ballast stones discarded by ships in millennia past, is broken only overhead, where stars blaze through a light sea mist.

I greet my father. "The inn is secure. I reserved a private dining room. The inn remains open. Closing it would have drawn too much attention."

"You have done well, Telor," Father says. "It is nearly dawn. When will Eryr arrive?"

"Mid-morning, Father. Breakfast is ready for you and your guards."

44

Dawn winds driven by solar heating as the sun rises from the sea burble through the mountain terrain northwest of the city. The pilot of an unmarked floater curses as he tries to maintain level flight. The floater is old. Its batteries hold only a partial charge, but it is the best the pilot could find on short notice. Extra weight makes it sluggish. The floater is registered to House Dwyer. Its new owner has only a day to register electronic identification to his house. He will not need that time. Five hours later, the radar in his display pinpoints the inn at which Gens Bleddyn and Eryr are meeting. The boy points the explosive-laden floater toward the roof of the building.

My seed has been preserved. My line will be of-the-blood and will live with honor. That is his last thought before a missile intercepts his floater five kilometers from the inn. The fireball outshines the sun and the explosion rattles windows in Aberwith.

Some thousands of kilometers to the west, Gens Tarren receives a report of the failed attack.

"Destroy his seed," Tarren orders. "He was weak."

~~~~~

Bleddyn and Eryr have finished a lunch of fish taken from the nearby ocean only hours earlier. One of Bleddyn's guards is clearing the table when they hear the explosion. The guard drops the dishes, draws an energy pistol, and rushes to the window. Lieutenant Terrwyn, commander of the Praetorian Guard, knocks and enters the room.

"Sir, a floater with an invalid radar signature was moving directly toward the inn. The explosion was several orders of magnitude greater than it should have been."

"Who might have known we were here?"

"My soldiers and I; your pilot; Telor." Lieutenant Terrwyn does not add the obvious – Gens Eryr and anyone he might have told.

Eryr speaks. "No one knew our destination until after we left Fortress Eryr. I did not tell even the pilot until we were airborne."

"Thank you, Gens Eryr. Lieutenant Terrwyn, we will continue our meeting. The young man guarding the window may resume his duties."

Bleddyn's thoughts are murky. *One of Lieutenant Terrwyn's people? They did not know our destination until after we departed Fortress. A leak from Eryr's people or the innkeeper? There was no communication. Lieutenant Terrwyn would have said. Telor? No. Besides, I would have known. Llywelyn? He has access to the War Room and the Senior Controller knew my plans.*

"Gens Bleddyn, you seem preoccupied." Eryr's voice cuts through Bleddyn's thoughts.

"My apologies, Gens Eryr. We have much to discuss. Including the matter of ships' ballast. Too many ships are bringing in water ballast contaminated with invasive mussels. When they dump the water, they also dump the mussels. They are exterminating the native mussels, symbiotic partners in the reproduction of important food fish."

The conversation between the two men is more fruitful than Bleddyn hoped. Eryr agrees to a new treaty regarding harbor maintenance. He also agrees to the prohibition on importing invasive species and a mutual defense pact. "Our agreement to mutual defense of the port does not shatter my neutrality," he says, "and it is the right thing to do."

~~~~~

Father and I have returned from Aberwith when a call comes from the War Room. A message from Gens Astin, in the old language, asks for an *entente cordiale* and a meeting with Gens Bleddyn.

"He knows something about Leiaf's death, or he suspects something," I say.

Father nods. "How might he have learned?"

I think of the inspections and maintenance happening in the shuttle hangers and floater bays. "It's no secret our entire fleet is undergoing inspection, starting with Llywelyn's floaters. Gens Astin is clever."

Father hands me the message. "Prepare a response, with all courtesy, and invite Gens Astin to Fortress."

The next day, the War Room calls. "Gens Astin is fifteen minutes away. So far, his pilot is following our instructions precisely. An element of your Praetorian Guard in dress uniforms is at the landing pad," I say.

Astin's shuttle lands on the battlements. Gens Astin steps from the shuttle. No weapons are visible save dagger and grace knife. One soldier follows him. She appears to be armed similarly. Gens Astin and the soldier bow. Father and I return the bow.

Astin speaks first. "Please permit me to introduce my niece, Alicia, sister of Leiaf. It is she who wishes to speak with you."

Father, Gens Astin, Alicia, and I go to a corner of Father's den. Both hot tea and cold drinks have been served, but no one tastes them. The mood is strained. Father breaks the silence. "Alicia, sister of Leiaf and niece of Gens Astin, an *entente* exists between your house and mine. You are welcome to speak freely."

The young woman relaxes, but only slightly. "Thank you, Your Grace. My brother, Leiaf, was not a daredevil. He would never have released the clamps on his floater, no matter how important the race. Despite the design differences, our floaters are similar and use the same control system. Floaters have an interlock that requires two separate, deliberate actions by the pilot to release

47

the clamps while in flight. There is no record, anywhere, of a failure of these interlocks. Leiaf was murdered."

Father replies. "Your facts are correct and your conclusion about your brother's death is likely correct."

Despite Gens Astin's gasp and Alicia's frown, Father keeps talking. "We examined the flight computer, but it was badly damaged in the crash and yielded little information. My best technician concluded, however, the signal to release the clamps did not come from the pilot. We suspect either an unprecedented mechanical failure or sabotage, but do not know how or by whom."

Alicia absorbs this information. "Thank you for your honesty, Gens Bleddyn. Why were we not told this sooner?"

"We could not confirm sabotage," Father replies. "We could not determine who the target might have been. Admitting the possibility of sabotage would have created speculation. Speculation, as it always does, would sink to the lowest depth and find the worst possible conclusion – that there was a deliberate attack on Leiaf. Llywelyn's soldiers represent seven different houses, some allied with House Bleddyn, some unaligned, some aligned with House Tarren. The risk of inciting violence was too great. You now know the truth and have taken on a burden I once held. It is your decision whether to release that truth. I will support you, whatever you decide."

Before Alicia can reply, Gens Astin speaks. "Gens Bleddyn, I was angry when Alicia came to me with her words. I was angry when we reached Fortress Bleddyn. I am still angry, but only because you did not tell us the truth immediately. I am no longer angry because I suspect you of murder. Thank you for your honesty and your hospitality. We have a long trip home."

Astin stands; the rest of us rise as one.

When the door of their shuttle closes, Alicia challenges her uncle. "Why did you accept his words so easily? He offered no proof and his reason for not telling us earlier was specious."

"Niece, if there is one constant factor in the history of the Res Publica it is that the Gens of House Bleddyn have been clever, but they have always been honorable. He spoke truth as he knows it. If he learns more, he will share it."

~~~~~

Sergeant Asant of the house intelligence corps, wearing the flashes of a private in the Second Company of the Home Guard, is in the dojo practicing unarmed combat. The soldiers are adults and do not pull their punches. It is considered froward to injure another soldier, but injuries occur. Sergeant Asant is slow to dodge his opponent's leg. Asant's feet are swept from under him. He falls hard.

"By Karmet, I've broken my wrist!"

His opponent helps Asant stand and watches him leave for the medico, where I am waiting. The medico, a cousin, wraps the wrist and then leaves the examination room.

"Cousin Telor," Sergeant Asant says. "Serious news. Dirgel of House Reese, a member of your brother's companions, is collecting information about the defenses of Fortress. The War Room is actively monitoring his communicator. He has transmitted nothing, yet."

"You are certain." I say. It is not a question.

Asant taps his head. "I am certain." I understand the gesture.

"Is there any chance of turning him? Getting him to send false information?"

"Difficult. I have little contact with him and never any time alone."

"Any weakness we can exploit?"

"Like many of Llywelyn's companions, he is far removed in genealogy from his Gens, therefore of low status in his house."

"Strengths?"

The question puzzles Asant, but he says, "Better than average skill with weapons and unarmed combat, but not exceptional. Passable pilot and an excellent mechanic."

"Ambitious?"

Asant chuckles. "Since he swore to Llywelyn, I would say so. What are you thinking?"

I smile. "Offering him a position of importance in House Bleddyn, breaking him away from Llywelyn, and giving us greater access to him."

I summon Dirgel from the hanger, where he is working on a floater. He is nervous when he faces Gens Bleddyn. He bows deeply and waits for Father to acknowledge him.

"I believe I interrupted your work on a floater. I will be brief. I have been told about your skills as a mechanic. I need a Supervisory Floater Mechanic. That position comes with the rank of sergeant in my Home Guard. The only obstacle is you are a member of House Reese and sworn to Llywelyn. I offer an important position. I would require your oath of loyalty and agreement to be adopted into House Bleddyn." Father waits, silently, to give the young man a chance to think.

"Your Grace, I am the least of House Reese. My Gens made it clear he was disappointed I swore to your son and joined his companions. I cannot imagine him objecting to my accepting your proposal. However, I would not take a position where I would directly cause House Reese harm. With that stipulation, I accept."

"I have already spoken to Gens Reese. He was more than disappointed. He was angry. When he gave his permission, he severed his ties to you." Bleddyn says. "You are free to take another oath."

The ceremony is held in the Great Room. Father requires every member of the family present in Fortress to attend. A televisor signal is sent to House Reese.

Dirgel first swears the soldiers' oath of honor, valor, and loyalty to the House of Wolf. Then, he swears fealty to Gens Bleddyn. That oath has an extra line. Dirgel will never be called upon to directly harm his former house. Father returns the oath, "Dirgel ap-Bleddyn, scion of House Bleddyn, I swear loyalty to you. I swear to provide for you and to protect you, and to treat you as one of my own, from this day forward." Daggers are blooded and exchanged.

Llywelyn attends the ceremony, but only because Father orders him to. Llywelyn is sullen when Father requires him to release Dirgel from his oath and barely mumbles the words. *He took one of mine away from me, weakening me.* Llywelyn does not consider that he, himself, removed one of his companions – Leiaf.

Chapter 4: The War to Bring Us Out of Darkness

"The greater and more powerful
the motive for war,
the more it affects
the whole existence
of a people."
— Geraint of the Res Publica

~~~~~

"The Corvette *Gorlassar* was destroyed by an enemy – a hostile alien species. Caravel *Kobaya* and its crew are the only survivors of the attack."

Gens Bleddyn's face shows little reaction when his uncle gives him the message. He thanks the man who is in charge of house communication and walks to his den.

This is the time, Bleddyn thinks. *We have strong allies among the Greater Houses. We have resources from our islands and continental territory. This message triggers an opportunity House Bleddyn has sought for thirty millennia. It explains much of what my father taught me.*

Gens Bleddyn summons his Privy Council. Although I am not on the council, he expects me to attend and observe. I am the first to arrive, moving swiftly through the hidden passageways I discovered as a child and entering from a panel beside the fireplace. I kneel. "I am here, Father."

Father gestures me to rise. "One of our ships encountered an alien species, a species which may be dangerous to us. I will use this encounter to advance the fortunes of House Bleddyn. Tonight, I want you to be silent. Watch and learn."

"Yes, Father." I move to stand at one end of the room farthest from Father's seat.

Llywelyn arrives next. I watch him count the number of aunts, uncles, and elder cousins as they enter. *He is hoping one will be absent so he may take a seat at the Council Table,* I think. *Even though he is not a member.*

Llywelyn is disappointed. The table is filled. Llywelyn moves to the back of the room, to the corner opposite me.

The news is understood and debate is short. This is too large for House Bleddyn.

"We will lose one of our advantages over the other houses. Nevertheless, we will gain other advantages," Father concludes. His council agrees.

Gens Bleddyn's message to the rest of the Council of the Res Publica carries a code-group that has not been used since the War of Conquest – *The Res Publica is in danger. Come immediately.*

Father takes a shuttle across the twenty kilometers that separate Fortress from Council House. The Prime Element of the Praetorian Guard, Llywelyn, and I accompany him. Even at supersonic speeds, it will take hours for western Gens to reach Council House. Father is surprised to find Gens Tylluan already present. I recognize one of his sons.

"Gens Tylluan," Father says. "Well met."

Gens Tylluan's bow is appropriate to Father's higher station. Father, however, executes the bow of equals. I hear in the voice of Tylluan both gratitude for the courtesy and some curiosity. "Your Grace, may I present my sons?" Tylluan asks.

The two lads step forward and bow more deeply than had their father. We exchange names. Llywelyn's greeting to Tylluan's sons is brief. His eyes are elsewhere and he seems disinterested in

54

these scions of a Lesser House. I ignore Llywelyn and greet Martyn Tylluan, who was an element-mate at Academy.

"I am surprised to see you here so quickly," Bleddyn says to Tylluan after the young men have moved away.

"We were here to arrange the elevation before Council of my newest child when we received the summons, Your Grace."

His politeness seems genuine. Bleddyn feels no threat. After congratulating Tylluan on the birth, Father gestures him to an electronically screened alcove where they will not be overheard.

"One of my ships reported contact with an alien species, one that has starflight and which is hostile," Father says. He looks for Tylluan's reaction. The man's eyes widen. Then, his face becomes impassive.

"I am not aware any ship arrived," he says.

"The ship which reported is equipped with an experimental communication system that operates at faster-than-light speed," Bleddyn says. "This system will be shared with every house when it is proven. I expect that to be soon."

Tylluan is more amazed by FTL communication than the discovery of another species. "We expect intelligent life to evolve in a galaxy with more than two hundred thousand million stars, many of which possess planets suitable for life," he says. "However, genuine faster-than-light messaging? That is something thought impossible."

Father opens his mouth to respond, but Gens Lagon enters the anteroom. Protocol demands they accept his greeting. Hours pass as other Gens arrive. Father politely refuses to say the reason for his summons. The usual feelings of suspicion among the Council are heightened. When the gong sounds for Council to assemble, Father take Tylluan's arm and walks with him.

"There is more news, even stranger. There will be anger, animosity, and antipathy. I depend on your support," Bleddyn says before they separate.

~~~~~

Thirteen Gens of the Greater Houses sit behind a massive slab of ancient oak on a dais that elevates and separates them from the Lesser Houses. Gens of the Lesser Houses and onlookers sit on benches along the walls to the left and right of the high dais.

"Well, Bleddyn, you have called us here at a most importune time," Gens Tarren, who holds the office of First Speaker, opens the meeting without the usual ceremony. "Harvest time is upon us. I hope this is important."

Father stands. "One of my ships made contact with an alien species, a species that has starflight. A species that is hostile. My ships are equipped with an experimental communication system that operates at faster-than-light speed without the constraints of the emergency tachyon system. Contact was made 8,000 light-years from World."

Bleddyn pauses while murmurs run through the houses' representatives. He interrupts the rumble to speak loudly. "A corvette of the *Vishnu Nerada,* my fleet, reached a system with an inner planet suitable for colonization and an outer planet useful for mineral exploitation. The corvette launched a caravel to explore the inner planet and continued to examine the outer planet. It detected a ship with an unknown power signature. The alien ship's path was toward the inner planet. The caravel hid behind the inner planet's larger moon. In an attempt to gather information, the corvette pushed an asteroid out of orbit. It would have crossed the orbit of the inner planet, well above the ecliptic and at a safe distance from the planet. My ship hugged the asteroid as it fell inward, watching only with passive sensors.

"They misjudged the hostility of the alien ship. The caravel watched as high-power energy weapons and torpedoes destroyed the asteroid and my corvette.

"The alien ship entered a polar orbit around the inner planet and sent shuttles into the planet's atmosphere and later, to the

56

ground. After four local years, the ship left. The caravel remained undetected behind the moon and then resumed exploration.

"What they found was remarkable. Before the arrival of the alien ship, life on the planet was limited to primitive sea creatures, insects, and grasses. After the alien ship left, life on the planet included amphibians and reptiles, birds, mammals, and shrubs and trees that weren't there earlier.

"The aliens had seeded the planet."

Bleddyn pauses to allow the Council to digest this information. Their reactions range from shock to suspicion.

"Scientists aboard the caravel examined samples of the new plant and animal life. Both flora and fauna have eukaryotic cells, true cells, with many organelles. We are familiar with that. Our own cells contain organelles that respond to instructions from the nucleus but which contain their own controlling molecules – DNA. When the cell divides, these organelles divide—"

"Gens Bleddyn," Gens Maelon interrupts. "You have already presented the problem, an alien species that does not hesitate to destroy one of your ships and which you presume to be unfriendly. We do not need an Academy biology lesson."

"This biology lesson is perhaps more important than the discovery of the aliens or the existence of faster-than-light communication." Father clips each word. "Among several species of mammals, we found extra organelles that seem to serve no purpose. They divide when the cell divides and so perpetuate themselves. Because they are so different, we examined them closely.

"These organelles contain human DNA. I say human because these molecules are within a few points of exactness of our own. They wait for a signal we do not understand, a signal to begin creating and propagating the species of the Adversary – the Adversary who seeded our planet.

"We have never understood how life on our planet first came to be. We now have the answer. Life on our planet including us – the Res Publica – is descended from seeds planted by this Adversary."

The First Speaker is too stunned to demand silence. Bleddyn waits for a moment and then speaks over the babble.

"There is more," he says. His cold voice sweeps over the gathering. The room quiets. "The evidence is clear. We are their creation. They seeded this planet and then abandoned us to happenstance. Moreover, the DNA in these organelles codes for blood in which haemoglobin, iron, carries oxygen. This is like the blood of our cattle, the blood of the beasts of the field and forest. It is not our blood, in which copper-based haemocyanin carries oxygen. The Adversary is not-of-the-blood. They seed planets with creatures that are not-of-the-blood. This is intolerable. The Adversary must be annihilated."

This is what House Bleddyn's Privy Council agreed. House Bleddyn will benefit most from war with this Adversary. The house has the largest shipyards, access to the most raw materials, and the greatest labor force. Even the least of the Lesser Houses will want to be a part of the war with this Adversary; they will be drawn to us.

Gens Tarren stands to speak. The babble stills. "One hundred forty millennia ago, the Res Publica began equipping starships with a tachyon-burst system that sends a signal if the ship is destroyed. That system can be operated only once, since it requires the collapse of a ship's power reactor. Once the message is sent, the reactor is dead and the ship and its crew will die unless they are already dead. The tachyon message is short, containing only the ship's designator, its location, and the number of life pods, if any, launched.

"In the past sixty millennia we have received seventeen such messages. We have considered accident, natural disaster, and failure of the engine fission chamber. We have also considered attack by another ship."

Tarren looks at Bleddyn, but his glance does not linger long enough to make his words an accusation. "We speculate the attackers might belong to another house."

Another hubbub rises from the assembly. It quiets when Father does not take offense at Tarren's remark.

Father speaks, again. "A battle among the stars between ships or houses of the Res Publica does not make economic sense. The galaxy is large, more than eighty thousand light years in diameter with more than two hundred thousand million stars. There is room enough for all houses."

Father looks to the ranks of the Lesser Houses and repeats his words. "Enough for all houses. It seems, however, the Adversary does not think there is room for both them and the Res Publica. They are claiming worlds not by planting a flag, but by planting their seeds ... seeds of creatures that are not-of-the-blood. Seeds of themselves."

For three days the Council debates. Messengers from the Lesser Houses on benches along the sides of the chamber carry their questions and comments to a Council member. Bleddyn watches closely. The movement of messengers reveals a great deal about house loyalties. He sees that I watch, too. My younger brother, Llywelyn, stands in a corner and talks with others his age. *More banter than discussion,* I think. *Although perhaps that will be useful.*

By the third day, the Council is saying nothing new but hoping by repeating a point often enough and loudly enough it will be believed. I bring Father a data chip. He inserts the chip into a slot on the dais and projects its contents on screens throughout the chamber. The room falls quiet when he stands.

"I believe this is a fair summary of our discussions and resolutions," Father says. "We have agreed to establish a military command with authority to commandeer in time of emergency the armed starships of all houses.

"The military command will consist of one representative of each Council member and ten representatives selected from the remaining houses. Each appointee will select his or her own staff. The expenses of the military command will be born in the same manner we support other common projects including the Council staff, our occupying force on the Southern Continent, Academy, and the tachyon communication system.

"The military command will be charged with developing more powerful weapons with which to arm our ships." He then deviates from the script. "The torpedoes that attacked my ship might be the model for those weapons."

Father reads again from the proposed agreement. "All new starships and returning ships will be equipped with House Bleddyn's faster-than-light communication system once it is operational. We will be reimbursed the cost of creating and installing the system in ships, in house communication rooms, and in the military command communication room. We will not, however, reveal the manner by which the system operates. Nor will we profit from this."

Then, he says the most important words. "The Res Publica herewith declares war upon this Adversary. Like locusts, they spread. They are not-of-the-blood. They are anathema."

Gens Tarren, the First Speaker, asks for a vote on the resolution.

The Council Scribe holds a deep bowl. He bows to each member, who draws a numbered token from the bowl. The tokens specify the order in which the Council will vote.

The vote is unanimous although Tarren's assent is grudging. The previous night, Father sent uncles and aunts, Llywelyn, and me to visit other Houses, reminding them of Bleddyn's words and his commitment to include all houses in the exploration of the galaxy. Father, himself met with Gens Tarren.

60

Gens Tarren seethes inwardly. Fortress Bleddyn is on the mesa that holds Council House and Academy. Tarren knows Father will have great influence on this new military command. The argument that the galaxy is big enough for all houses, plus access to our FTL communication system, while not winning Tarren's loyalty, sway him for the moment.

~~~~~

At Fortress two days later, Father scowls at the screens in the War Room. Llywelyn and his cohort are engaged in exercises with other units of the Home Guard. *He has not integrated his cohort well. Perhaps my instructions were not clear. He challenges the other company commanders; he creates conflict rather than cohesion. This is something—*

"Father, we have a visitor. She awaits in your den." I interrupt Father's thoughts.

"In my den? Alone?"

"Bethan returned from Academy for Fall Stormtime and accompanies her."

~~~~~

"This is the Fourth Gens Bleddyn…" Bethan stands below one of the many portraits in her father's den.

Her guest knows Bethan is more guard than guide, but responds politely. Both women turn when the door opens and Father and I enter.

"Gens Hywel, be welcome," Father greets the woman and executes the bow of equals.

"Gens Bleddyn, thank you for your welcome." Hywel returns the bow. "Your children are the only ones besides my pilot who know I am here. I would like to maintain that secrecy."

"On my honor," Bleddyn says. He does not need to add that his oath binds Bethan and me.

61

Moments later, the two Gens sit in comfortable chairs in front of the fire. I serve tea and demitasse glasses of *dŵr y bywyd.* Bethan and I leave the room. Father senses Hywel relax although she remains alert.

"Despite the new enemy, the real business of the Res Publica continues. Vendetta may likely become even more important." Hywel chuckles. "It appears a wolf nipped at Fychan. The bite of the wolf is an ancient tactic. This one was well planned and executed. Masterful."

"Indeed it was," Bleddyn says. "Although Fychan has no idea who perpetrated this attack, he is willing to blame anyone. Following the attack on his generator, Fychan was more rabid than any wolf could be. He blasted messages to Tarren and to Council. He is especially angry he was attacked without vendetta having been declared and demands Council intervene.

"I am something of a student of history," Father adds.

Of course, you would be, Gens Hywel thinks. *Your ancestors ruled for centuries and your house was first to use life-extension not only for the crews of starships but also for the Gens and key offspring. You were also the first to offer the treatment to leaders of houses who could not otherwise afford it. Longevity has done a great deal to stabilize the Res Publica, although it also means vendetta lasts longer.*

Father frowns for a moment before continuing. "My son, Telor, found the record of a Declaration of Vendetta by Bleddyn against Fychan 140 millennia ago. Relationships between Fychan and Bleddyn have become somewhat normalized; however, the Declaration of Vendetta was never withdrawn."

"There are rumors I was behind the attack," Gens Hywel says. "These rumors increased respect for my house." She indirectly acknowledges her debt to House Bleddyn. "I have neither confirmed nor denied we were the source."

"My son, Llywelyn, has a talent for operational planning and execution," Father says. His words admit without admitting the attack on Fychan's generator was, indeed, carried out by his house.

The dance of point and counter-point continues. Although nothing is said directly, after an hour the two Gens agree. Hywel will support Bleddyn while officially remaining neutral.

This is one of the victories I have sought. Houses Bleddyn and Tarren have been evenly balanced in Council until this moment. Now, when I need it, I will have the stronger position. I still need other allies among the Greater Houses to win a supermajority. That will come.

~~~~~

As soon as Hywel's shuttle departs, Father summons me. I make my way from the library to his den and kneel. "I am here, Father." I know my father knows that. I also know he appreciates the ancient forms.

"Telor, I have an assignment for you." He gestures and I rise.

I listen. The more Father says, the weaker my knees get. *Only four years ago, I graduated from Academy. Five days ago Father told Council our ships have faster-than-light communication and encountered an alien species. Three days later, the Council declared war on that species. Father offered to install an FTL communication system in every ship of the Res Publica, a system that has until now been the greatest secret of the house. Today he appoints me to oversee that project.*

"Father, if I am to manage this, I need to know exactly how the system works. There may be something about its operation that will give away the secret."

Father accepts my explanation and hands me a data key.

"We invented this system sixty millennia ago," he says. "We have kept it secret for that long. The fewer who know a secret, the longer it may be kept. But you are right. You should know.

"Insert the key in my private elevator. It will take you to the laboratory."

~~~~~

The laboratory is deep in the rock, hundreds of meters below Fortress. My ears pop as the air pressure changes. I wiggle my jaw and swallow, a technique I learned as a pilot, parachutist, and under-sea diver.

Uncle Grigor waits for me in an anteroom with rock walls. He takes me through a pair of massive doors with copper fingers on the edges. The laboratory walls are lined with a fortune in copper, making it secure against electromagnetic radiation and snooping. Aunt Chooli and Uncle Tahoma greet me. The room smells of ozone. Tables hold computer terminals and other, unrecognizable, electronics.

"Do you understand the limitations of the tachyon system?" Uncle Grigor asks.

"Yes, Uncle. Although it operates nearly instantaneously, the message is short and weak. In order for a message to reach World, it must be relayed."

"Do you know the inverse square law?" Aunt Chooli asks.

I nod. "Yes, ma'am. The tachyon signal radiates from the transmitter in an expanding sphere. The strength of the tachyon signal is reduced by the square of the distance from the source. At some point, it becomes too weak to be separated from the noise that surrounds it. That is why the Res Publica builds relays in orbit around brown dwarf stars."

"That is correct," Aunt Chooli says. "What we have created is similar. Our messages are digital. It is different in that it is not subject to the inverse square law. It does not require relays. It does not require any more energy than a light bulb and the messages are not limited in length like the tachyon system."

~~~~~

64

The manufacturing apparatus is contained in a vacuum chamber. The 10^{-7} meter beam of a particle accelerator, barely visible through the heavy glass, is split when it passes through a crystal. My uncles and aunt do not tell me of what the crystal is made; only that it separates paired particles creating sets of entangled particles.

Aunt Chooli describes what happens next. "Each entangled particle set is manipulated by magnetic fields to become part of a carbon atom, a stable isotope with six protons and six neutrons. These atoms are further manipulated to create spherical molecules containing sixty atoms of carbon. These are deposited, one from each stream of entangled particles, in a precise, regular crystalline structure to create two cubes," Aunt Chooli explains. "The cubes are less than 0.01 millimeter on a side."

"Forgive me, Aunt Chooli, but carbon atoms are electrically neutral, with an equal number of protons and electrons. They cannot be manipulated by a magnetic field."

Uncle Tahoma laughs. "You caught us there, Telor. The atoms do not respond to a magnetic field, but the quarks that make up the protons and neutrons in the nucleus do respond to … let us say, forces we control. Is that sufficient understanding?"

"Yes, Uncle. I do not need to know more."

Aunt Chooli continues her explanation. "Our ability to harness the creative forces in the laboratory and the nature of the crystal that creates the paired particles are the greatest secrets."

"Until developed in our laboratories, this force only existed in the initial singularity that created the primordial universe and in the nuclear furnaces at the core of stars," Uncle Grigor adds.

"Originally, it required months to make a pair of cubes," Aunt Chooli explains. "We have improved the process. Now, we can create a pair of cubes in less than twenty days. That has been sufficient for the *Vishnu Nerada* – the House Bleddyn fleet. We have begun assembling more devices to meet the new demand."

"But, I still don't know how the system works," I say. "That is what I need to know."

"The cubes are entangled at the sub-atomic level, the *quantum* level. What affects one cube is reflected in the other, no matter how far they are separated. Instantly and without energy loss. One cube is installed in a ship, the other in our communication room. To send a message, we modulate a beam of gamma rays of wavelength 10^{-12} meters and pass it through one cube. An un-modulated beam of the same frequency is continuously passed through the cube's partner which modulates it. Detectors convert the modulations into a signal that is interpreted by algorithms to display the text of the message, an image, or a televisor signal on a viewscreen."

That much I understand, but I feel there is more they aren't telling me. "And all this is in the component we will install in ships of other houses?" I ask.

"This and more." Aunt Chooli confirms my suspicions there are other secrets to be learned.

~~~~~

Uncle Grigor takes me to a secure room near the War Room. "From these consoles, we exchange isoquant messages with each ship of the *Vishnu Nerada* daily when they are not at light speed. By then, of course, everyone on board is in cold-sleep."

"Isoquant?" I interrupt. "From the Old Language for *same* and *quantum*. Do we not reveal too much by using that name?"

Uncle Grigor pauses to think. "Already you find a problem," he says. "From now on, we shall call it only the *FTL system*. The transceivers will be made in our shipyard, but a place will be left for the cubes which are the heart—"

"Uncle," I interrupt again. "The weakness of the system is that communication exists only between a pair of cubes. If ships in an element are separated, they cannot communicate except by

66

electromagnetic signals, which take hours to cross interplanetary distances."

"That is correct. However, this console," he gestures, "allows instantaneous ship-to-ship communication. The switching is done, here. That is how Corvette *Gorlassar* was able to alert Caravel *Kobaya*."

"Then in addition to building transceivers for ships, we must build the consoles for each house's War Room," I say, "and those for Military Command, so others do not discover this aspect of the system. We will keep that secret for the moment, to continue our house's supremacy in this matter."

I think for a moment and then add, "We must also include a fail-safe, self-destruct against tampering in each console. One that will utterly destroy the console and the cubes should it be opened. It will not be necessary to kill someone trying to penetrate a console, but collateral damage is acceptable. We should probably make this clear to everyone."

I think what I say next surprises my Uncle. "Finally, we must be able to overhear all messages whether sent by ally or enemy. That, of course, must be secret."

Uncle Grigor recovers quickly. "We will have a design for your review in … um, five days."

≈≈≈≈≈

While I am with Uncle Grigor, Llywelyn enters Father's den. Before Llywelyn can speak, his father asks, "Why are you here and not exercising with your cohort?" Llywelyn spends most of his time in the training rooms, dojo, and firing range with the young men and women he brought with him when he graduated from Academy. When they are not at Fortress, they are engaged in war games and exercises on the rugged terrain of the mountains, without the rest of the Second Company. Gens Bleddyn's plan to dilute Llywelyn's power by integrating his companions into the house army has failed. The boy continues to create a private army.

"Father, the war with an Adversary will be important to our House. I wish to be part of it, but you have not taken me into your confidence nor given me an assignment."

Bleddyn answers quickly. "Llywelyn, I know your interests are in the art of war. There is always need for that, but no urgent need at the moment. Otherwise, I would have summoned you." He pauses and looks at his eldest son. "Planning for this new Adversary leaves me little time for house business. There are many opportunities for you to serve. You will ensure the continuation, indeed, the survival of House Bleddyn in these turbulent times. I will soon open you to details and challenges.

"That will not be today, however. I will summon you."

Not today, he says. Llywelyn thinks as he walks away. *I will be summoned, he says. Yet Telor, my bastard brother, visits him without being summoned. There is more to this than meets the eye.*

~~~~~

The Gens enters the family dining room. All rise. He looks around. His eyes stop briefly on each of his children and their surrogates, then move to the aunts, uncles, and cousins.

"Be welcome, my family, and be seated." Clothing rustles. All sit except the Gens. A few are puzzled until he speaks.

"Dinner will be served in a moment. In a few days, we will celebrate the Third Year of my son Garreth's elevation. I see he is here at family supper with his surrogate, Nana."

Garreth blushes; his face pales and he ducks his head into Nana's breast. Father smiles before he continues. "That is good news. You all know the bad news. The Res Publica declared war against an unseen and unknown Adversary. House Bleddyn has both support and resistance in this matter. However, we will be in the forefront of preparation and, likely, the vaward of war when it comes. For now, I ask you all to remember your oaths to House Bleddyn during these times."

Uncle Dewi stands and lifts his glass in response. "My brother, I salute your courage in facing the Council and the Adversary, and I pledge my support. 'My blood is your blood, unto death.'"

Everyone present, even the children, stands and holds glasses high. "Unto death."

When we all sit, Father raises his glass and responds. "To my family. My blood is your blood, unto death."

After dinner, Bleddyn's communicator beeps.

<<Llywelyn moved his companions, but not the soldiers of the Second Element, to Sehwa Island, where they engage in fighter pilot training. I cannot get close enough to him to understand his plans.>>

Bleddyn touches an icon on the communicator. When the call is answered, he asks, "Can you safely get away and meet me on the archery pitch?"

The answer is short. "Yes, Commander. Tomorrow. Immediately after first meal."

Morning mist swirls across the field that holds the archery pitch. Gens Bleddyn steps from his Praetorian Guard and toward the firing line.

"Your bowstrings will be damp, Your Grace," the Range Master, a thrall, says.

"Not these," Bleddyn replies. "Single strands of hemp, waxed and then braided with two similar. Then, braided in bundles of three, also waxed. Today is a good day to test this bow."

Sergeant Asant, wearing the flashes of a private in the Second Company, stands at the next firing position. Bleddyn dismisses the thrall and turns toward the sergeant.

"My Lord, I am having difficulty understanding what is in Llywelyn's mind. It is as if he were blocking me—"

"You must not say that, even here," Bleddyn says. "Thank you for your report." He hands the private a communicator. "This is cloned from your personal communicator, except for a direct link to me. The link is disguised as a pornographic feed."

The spy smiles. "Not a problem, My Lord."

Chapter 5: House Tylluan

The message I am about to send will be cryptic. I keep it innocent while trying to pique Martyn Tylluan's interest. Martyn was in my element through most of Academy. House Tylluan is unaligned. Martyn and I never showed animosity toward one another. Neither did we show close friendship. I am taking a chance with this message.

<<TO: Martyn Tylluan. It's been years, but we never held our promised shuttle race during Last Form at Academy. Weather looks good on Namhae for another twenty days. Will you join me on Day 560 for a match? Shall we say best three out of five? Telor Bleddyn>>

Martyn takes the message to his father, the Gens. "Father? Telor and I did race shuttles, but we did not plan a challenge our last year. He wants me on Namhae."

Gens Tylluan takes little time to reply. "Son, you were present when Gens Bleddyn extended a courtesy, the bow of equals, when we met three years ago on the day the Council declared war on the Adversary. I supported his position in Council. Now, he seeks an alliance and chooses to open negotiations using our sons as intermediaries. Of course, you must go."

~~~~~

The sun is only halfway to the zenith. I am alone on the tarmac when Martyn's shuttle lands. I whistle my astonishment. A red dragon is painted on the side of the shuttle. The door opens. The instant Martyn steps out, I execute the bow of equals,

71

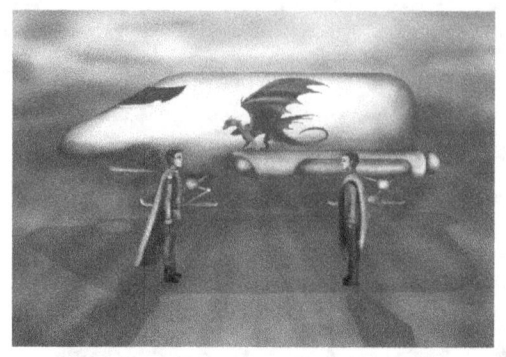

surprising him. Martyn bows. Then he smiles. "Telor, you always were polite. More, you were always sincere. Thank you for your invitation and courtesy."

"You are welcome."

I watch a dozen young men in utility jumpsuits leave the shuttle and stand in ranks behind Martyn.

"You brought your own maintenance and recharging crew. Good. May the first race be tomorrow morning? When the air is cooler." A current from deep in the equatorial ocean warms Namhae. The island's weather is clement except during Stormtime, when the warmer current feeds energy to storms.

Martyn agrees, and tugs take his shuttle to a hanger where I introduce his crew to their counterparts. "Lunch and planning the race course?" I offer. I sense Martyn's discomfort; however, I also sense his thought. *Telor has always been honorable.*

After lunch is served and the thralls dismissed, I speak. "We will, of course, conduct the races. One every second day, I think. We will finish a few days before Winter Stormtime. The schedule will leave time for us to talk."

"I know there is no unfulfilled challenge hanging over us," Martyn says. "So does my father. He thinks your father is honorable. I think you are both honorable and clever. Father is happy for me to meet with you."

"I will be as candid as you," I reply. "My father wishes a formal alliance with yours. What I hope to do these next few days is explain what it would mean, so you can take it back to your father. If he agrees to a meeting, my father will come to him at Fortress Tylluan."

The offer surprises Martyn, but he hides his emotions well. "I will listen and I will be an honest broker to my father."

The shuttle races are anticlimactic, not because of the discussions of alliance, but because I take Martyn through the production plant where house members and thralls labor to make not only a corvette, but also the twenty fighters and two caravels it will carry.

"Your fighters are built on a shuttle frame," Martyn observes.

"Yes, stretched and narrowed, and equipped with both reaction engines and anti-gravity engines."

Martyn points to the wings. "Why wings in airless space?" He answers his own question. "Of course. You're planning to operate in a planet's atmosphere. Brilliant, and somewhat frightening."

"Yes, it is. I mean brilliant. And, I mean the part about fighting in atmosphere, too. The control surfaces on the wings make these fighters more maneuverable than a regular shuttle or the older fighters." I signal a technician. The wings slide into slots in the body of the fighter. "But do not hinder flight when they are not needed."

"I don't suppose there's any chance I could fly one," Martyn says. He chuckles at his joke.

"Oh, yes. But not until tonight when we will be masked by darkness. You and I. There's not enough time for you to solo, but someday you will have a fighter of your own."

After four races, the young men are tied, two-and-two. They laid out the last race over a complicated course that requires precision navigation plus speed. Martyn finishes less than a tenth of a second ahead of Telor, but clips a pylon at the finish line. The judges penalize him. The boys' agreement to declare the race a tie scandalizes the judges.

"It gives us reason to meet, again," Martyn says. "Thank you for suggesting it."

"It was the right thing to do. Another race and an opportunity for you to solo a fighter."

Three days later, Martyn sends a message to me.

<<TO: Telor Bleddyn. Father agrees we might hold a rematch, this time over the mountains around Fortress Tylluan. We will see if you can navigate rocks as easily as the sands of your beaches. Martyn Tylluan.>>

I take the message to Father. "Gens Tylluan agrees to a meeting. We will have to travel in my shuttle with only a few guards and my race crew. We need a reason for your absence from Fortress."

"I believe I need some time to … contemplate things," Father says. "Officially, I will be at my cabin on Soando. I don't do that often enough."

~~~~~

Tylluan's fortress is smaller than Bleddyn's. In fact, every Fortress is smaller than ours except perhaps those of Hynafol and Emrys, two of the oldest houses. I land my shuttle in a small courtyard. Only Martyn and his father await us. I step from the door onto the gray slate paving stones. I bow to Gens Tylluan and accept Martyn's handclasp. When I step aside, Father exits and offers Gens Tylluan the bow of equals.

As host, Tylluan speaks first. "I remember the honor you bestowed when we met at Council some years ago. My sons were most impressed that you honored their father." He ruffles Martyn's hair. Martyn grimaces, but then smiles at this gesture.

"I honor one who deserves honor," Father says. "And not because of rules and ritual created millennia ago. I wish to

74

associate my house with your house's reservoir of honor in the hope that together we can achieve greatness."

They dismiss Martyn and me to plan the races, the official cover for the visit. Father and Gens Tylluan spend the days discussing, negotiating, and finalizing the treaty between them. On the eighth day, with Martyn and me once again tied at two-and-two, Martyn creates an opportunity to talk to his father.

"Why would you ally with Bleddyn rather than Tarren?" Martyn asks. "Telor and I are friendly and the races are a fun and not-too-dangerous way of establishing dominance, but...?"

"Your question is good," Tylluan says. "What answers can you think of?"

"We are hundreds of kilometers closer to Bleddyn than Tarren. If we were attacked, they could respond faster than Tarren."

"True, but not the most important reason," his father replies.

Martyn is silent while he thinks. Then, "Surely, not the honor of a bow of equals," he exclaims. "I know you are not that shallow."

"Thank you for the vote of confidence, Son," Tylluan says, and then chuckles. "What you think of me is very important."

"Telor has proven to be honorable and I think his father is, too," Martyn says.

"A very important point."

"That's it," Martyn exclaims. "Bleddyn shows confidence in your judgment and honor..." His words slow. "Just as Telor has always shown confidence in my judgment and honor in our relationship, although we are not aligned. At Academy and when we designed the racecourses for our competition, in his insistence our last race on Namhae be a tie because it was the right thing to do."

His father smiles at this. "Geraint told us, 'There is a tide in life which taken at the flood, leads to greatness. If taken at the ebb, it leads to oblivion.' I intend this house shall come to greatness, but only through honor. House Bleddyn offers honor."

Martyn's father sips from the cup of hot tea poured from a pitcher left by thralls. "It is because I believe House Bleddyn has honor and House Tarren does not. Tarren pushes the boundaries of vendetta and seems to conflate vendetta with vengeance. They are different."

"How, Father?" Martyn asks.

"That, son, is for you to learn."

~~~~~

Martyn and his father are the only ones in the courtyard to watch the departure of my shuttle.

"It is done," Gens Tylluan says. "We are aligned with House Bleddyn, although we are not declared enemies of House Tarren. A perilous precipice, indeed. On the other hand, your fighter will be delivered by month's end."

"Father, you know it was a gift given freely and not a bribe," Martyn says.

"Yes, son," Tylluan says. "Moreover, the terms of the alliance are fair. Bleddyn will sell us the corvette under construction, including the fighters and caravels. He will train our people to be crewmembers. They will undergo life-extension at his hospital before the ship launches in mid-summer.

"We will share with House Bleddyn wealth from minerals or colonies until we pay the cost of the ship. Bleddyn was generous in setting the cost in today's currency and not inflating it over the millennia. When I showed curiosity, his answer was, 'It is the right thing to do.' You have heard me say that, often."

Gens Tylluan watches the wind ruffles his son's hair. Martyn, unaware of his father's attention, stares as if seeing through the gray stone walls that protect Fortress Tylluan and guard the courtyard. In his mind, he sees future greatness for his

76

house, but his dream is muddled. The sun is much too yellow and the forest holds strange plants and trees. He shakes off this vision in time to hear his father's words.

"We have made a fine ally. Telor is likely to continue as Bleddyn's senior advisor. He and you will implement the alliance. My first duty is to House Tylluan, which I think is best performed as an ally of House Bleddyn."

~~~~~

Fortress Tarren sits southwest of the Pass of Perdition, site of several ancient and bloody battles. The winds of Spring Stormtime are especially fierce and their whistle penetrates the most inner rooms, including the room at which Gens Tarren is at breakfast with his three eldest sons. His chancellor brings him news of the treaty between Bleddyn and Tylluan.

Tarren slams his cup on the table, splashing hot tea from which clouds of steam rise. "House Tylluan's defection is the first of an unaligned house in history."

In recent history, Aaron thinks. With brother Huw about to enter Academy and brother Cadfael not yet graduated, Aaron at age eleven will be the eldest of Tarren's male offspring to remain at home. *And, it's not a defection. Father exaggerates.* "It is not surprising," Aaron says, "given the geography. Tylluan is closer to Bleddyn than to us."

Tarren bares his teeth and challenges the boy. He snarls. "But what can Bleddyn offer we cannot?"

The boy is adept at the dance of power and politics that pervade his father's court. "Nothing, Father, except an empty promise. Huw? What do you think?"

As usual, Huw's answer is neither useful nor confident. Aaron conceals his smile at his father's frustration with his second son.

At Gens Tarren's right, his eldest son, Cadfael watches and thinks. *Aaron seeks to undermine his elder brother. In time, he will seek to undermine me.*

~~~~~

Sixteen days after Father and I return from Fortress Tylluan, I bring the private elevator to his den.

"We are ready, Father. May I show you?"

In the laboratory, Father listens as I describe plans and safeguards. "We will be able to charge for the FTL consoles installed in ships, at Military Command, and in each house's War Room. We will buy some material from other clans – steel and plastics – thus sharing the wealth. Our books will be open to inspection. Some of the houses will complain, but most will agree the price is fair. The future financial benefit to them is tremendous."

"Very good work, all of you," Father says. He turns and speaks to me. "Ensure the first console is installed in the ship Tylluan purchased and the second in his house's War Room. His crew will finish their training and life extension by mid-summer when the ship is completed."

Father gave Tylluan that ship, I think. *He sold it for far less than its worth. What besides loyalty does he expect from Tylluan?*

Father understands my question. "Besides their loyalty, Tylluan will share with us the discoveries made by the ship. We will continue to monitor without Tylluan's knowledge their communication with the ship and colony."

Trust but verify, Geraint told us, I think.

To live and work for the benefit of all; to create something bigger than one person, perhaps bigger than one house, Father thinks. *This is the beginning.*

78

~~~~

After Father and I return to the den, he quizzes me on my second mission. "Have you maintained contact with the Lesser Houses I identified to you?"

"Yes, Father," I reply. "None of the lesser houses can afford to build or buy their own ships. None know the details of the arrangement you brokered with Tylluan. Unaligned Astin, Eryr, Griffin, and Itan are eager to add their people to our crews. Ellis, although aligned with Tarren, is cautiously interested. Dolffin, Dwyer, and Mynydd are very eager to reap the benefits of exploration and colonization. They all would like to have an independent way to communicate with their people and they all want a presence on future colony ships."

I pause. "That's a knot to unravel."

Father lifts an eyebrow in question.

"What will be the relationship among multiple houses in a single colony?" I ask, then answer my own question. "All the colonists will fight the new planet for survival. They must not also fight among themselves and must see the common good as more important than house loyalty. That is against everything our heritage teaches us to believe."

"That is a good question, Son and one we will need to answer soon. Create a schedule for bringing these houses one at a time on board our exploration and colony ships. Put them under blood oath to the mission commander. Offer the houses a basic FTL base station at cost. We will get our reward through loyalty and future trade."

Father stretches his arm and takes a book from his desk. He hands it to me. "This book has thoughts that might be helpful."

I look at the title, "To Live, to Work, to Benefit All." I raise an eyebrow in question.

"Read it," Father says. "We will discuss it at another time. Telor, you have managed two critical assignments well. You conducted yourself with confidence at the Council meeting when we declared war on the Adversary. You directed the FTL communication project in a way that advances the house and keeps our secrets. None of my children could have done any better."

"Thank you, Father. I..." I hesitate. *Is this the time?* I ponder the question and then decide: *It is.* "I know the law and I know my place. I know I will have at least another score brothers and sisters of your blood and each one diminishes my place in the house. I am content, Father. I am content because you have given me your trust."

As soon as I speak, I am afraid. Father's face becomes immobile. His eyes fix not on me but on a point on the wall, perhaps on something well beyond the wall. I fear what father might be seeing.

He turns his eyes to me. "I know the law, too. The first Gens Bleddyn was instrumental in its creation and adoption by the Res Publica. The law is for those who cannot think for themselves. And nothing can diminish you. Think on that."

Father turns to his desk. I am dismissed with a new puzzle.

Chapter 6: Delwyn and Daffyd At Academy

"Father." Daffyd, third son and fifth child of Gens Bleddyn, kneels before his father. The man extends his hand; the boy stands.

"Daffyd, tomorrow you will report to Academy."

I know this, Daffyd thinks. *I am about to take the second step toward adulthood.* He glances at the medical vambrace that covers his left forearm, the symbol of the first step. *Why does Father tell me what I already know?*

"Also in your element will be Huw Tarren."

"Father, I—"

"Do not interrupt," Bleddyn says.

"You will work with him and show the respect due the scion of a Greater House. You will not trust him, but you will behave as if you do. He will not trust you, but will behave as if he does. You will not become friends – you both know the historic enmity between our Houses. You will, however, nurture a cautious mutual respect that may serve your house. Do you understand?"

"Yes, Father," Daffyd says, even though he does not understand. *Why would this be? There are rumors Huw Tarren called to the field one of his companions and killed him in a duel, and—*

Bleddyn is still talking. Daffyd missed something. *Is my vambrace working properly?* The boy pulls his attention back to his father.

"… and a bastard. The bastard is female, natural-born of a Lesser House. Her mother would not name the father. Therefore, her blood is assumed to be impure."

Academy Calendar	
Day	**Event**
1	New Year begins
7	Winter Stormtime ends
8	Academy year begins
125	Spring *Bo-taoshi* competition
139	Recognition of First Form cadets
140	Spring Stormtime begins
147	Spring Equinox
155	Spring Stormtime ends
287	Summer Stormtime begins
294	Summer Solstice
302	Summer Stormtime ends
425	Fall *Bo-taoshi* competition
435	Fall Stormtime begins
442	Fall Equinox
450	Fall Stormtime ends
581	Graduation Ceremony
583	Winter Stormtime begins
590	Winter Solstice

"Why was she allowed into Academy, much less in an element with two scions of Greater Houses?" his son asks.

"Three," Bleddyn says. "Your sister Delwyn, Huw Tarren, and you. Aurin of Ellis, heir of a Lesser House, will also be in your element. Were you not paying attention?"

"I'm sorry, Father, my mind drifted when you mentioned the feud. I do not understand why I must pretend to like someone who has been our adversary for a hundred and fifty millennia."

Bleddyn frowns. "Have your vambrace checked when I dismiss you. The bastard is there because House Helygen sponsored her. Now do you understand?"

"Yes, Father." Daffyd feels alert. His vambrace must be functioning and injected the proper drug.

"Enrolled and assigned to your element. Her name is Soosong. You will not disrespect her, but will treat her as a companion-student without embracing her as an equal. Over time, you will get close to her, but you will keep this secret from everyone, especially those who support House Tarren. You will win her loyalty and her trust. Huw Tarren likely will attempt to do the same. I will give your sister these same instructions. You will work with Delwyn and under her direction in this matter. Do you understand?"

82

"Yes, Father. You want Soosong as an ally, without that being known. You do not want her to become allied with House Tarren," Daffyd says. He is sure, now, his vambrace is working. The drugs it controls and injects into his arm are in balance. He feels clear-headed and excited. And he feels proud his Father, Gens Bleddyn, the House Patriarch, entrusts him with an important task. Even though he will be subordinate to his sister. *Just because she was born a few minutes earlier than me.*

~~~~~

Winter Stormtime passes, leaving snow and ice on the grounds of Mesa that holds Academy, Council House, and Fortress Bleddyn. Flight Control directs scores of shuttlecraft to one of the Academy's five landing pads. First Form cadets hurry off the shuttles. The youngsters wear unmarked utility jumpsuits and carry only a small duffle bag. There will be little room for personal possessions. One shuttle scarcely departs before another lands. The line of shuttles will continue until after dusk.

Each element of eighteen cadets is assigned a pod with sleeping rooms, toilets, bathing rooms with mob showers, and a common room where they will study and spend free time. A Forth Form cadet, a member of the cadre, leads Soosong to an empty sleeping room. All the bunks are unclaimed. Surprised she is the first to arrive, she tosses her duffle bag onto a top bunk. In the crèche where she grew up, top bunks were the least desirable. Surely, as a no-blood, she will be required to take a top bunk if she does not do so voluntarily.

The door opens and another cadet enters. She scans the room and sees Soosong's duffel. "I'm Delwyn. You really want the top bunk?"

"It's warmer in winter when the hot air rises," Soosong repeats the story she used in the crèche to justify her choice and avoid conflict.

"And hotter in summer," Delwyn says. "My home is in a hot place and I enjoy the heat. Perhaps we could switch. You take the top bunk in the winter and I'll take it in summer."

"I know who you are. And you know who I am." Soosong's voice is sharp. "You know I am a no-blood, a bastard."

"And you know I am a daughter of a Greater House. But neither of us knows the other's heart. In fact, other than our birth and name, neither of us knows a bloody thing about the other. I am willing to learn. Are you?"

Although shocked by Delwyn's candor and language, Soosong agrees.

In late afternoon, the new cadets assemble in their common room. A lieutenant who wears the crest of House Lagon on his breast pocket enters the room. All the cadets know to stand at attention, although not commanded to do so. Delwyn and Daffyd exchange brief glances. House Lagon is neutral in the vendetta between Houses Bleddyn and Tarren. *His appointment as our Tactical Officer is no accident,* Delwyn thinks. *I wonder what his orders are? Will he remain neutral? I must watch him.*

The man addresses the assembled cadets. "I am your tactical officer for the First Form. You will address me as 'Tac' or 'Sir.' My task is to begin your training and education as warriors."

The man keeps his eyes away from Huw Tarren and the Bleddyn twins when he continues. "You will take an oath to treat one another as companion-students, with amity, courtesy, and respect. Academy has no time for house rivalries. If you are here to engage in vendetta, you should not be here tomorrow. The doors of Academy will open to you and you may depart without prejudice. If you engage in vendetta, you will be found out and expelled – if you survive. This, on the authority of the Compact and orders of Council. There is no recourse. Do you have questions?"

The other seventeen cadets mirror Delwyn's wide eyes and raised eyebrows. *Father has always protected my siblings and me*

84

from our enemies, she thinks. *House Lagon is truly neutral; Tac will not be our protector. Daffyd and I must be our own protectors.*

Daffyd, who stands somewhat apart from his twin, has a different thought. *Delwyn already contacted the bastard. Our enemies will try to separate us – Delwyn from me and both of us from her new friend. The Academy motto of 'Cooperate and Graduate' is for those who cannot think for themselves. Which of these classmates should I cooperate with? Which ones can I trust? How can I ensure Delwyn's safety and her friend's? Father is a good judge of character; so is Telor. I wish they were here.*

Soosong's understanding is different from Daffyd's. *Cooperate and Graduate. Tac said it was designed to spur teamwork. I think what it really means is don't make waves and don't call unnecessary attention to yourself.*

~~~~~

Daffyd and Delwyn are accustomed to being tutored privately or with only their companions, in familiar spaces, and by familiar people. They are uncomfortable in the stark classroom and its ranks of desks to be filled by their element and members of the three other elements in Group XII.

I do not know why we study biology, Delwyn thinks. *I am a warrior. All I need to know of biology is how to bind a comrade's wounds, or mine. Yet I must endure—.* Her thoughts shut off abruptly as the instructor enters the room and the cadets stand at attention until told to sit.

"You all have heard Gens Bleddyn's claim at Council that an Adversary seeded our world with DNA from which we evolved. For this next quarter, you will learn enough about our genetic history for you to determine for yourself if this is true."

The other cadets avoid looking at the two Bleddyn scions.

The instructor begins with a reminder of the deep-time history of World. "You know our sun is one of a cluster of young stars in a spiral arm on the fringes of our galaxy. You all know World was formed about four million millennia ago. Most of you are from agrarian houses. You understand how we mate animals to improve the herd, whether cattle or horses."

Daffyd and Delwyn exchange glances. Their house is breeding wolves to domesticate a breed with the ferocity of their ancestors but which will accept human companionship and domination. They are close but—

The instructor's words interrupt.

"You have studied evolution, the science that shows how random mutation of the DNA of plants, animals, and humans coupled with competition for resources and natural selection, creates new species. You know we, ourselves, are the products of evolution.

"You also know when the Equatorial Continent and the Southern Continent separated, it isolated two groups of this species, we, the Res Publica, developed bronze skin, which protects us from the sun. The thralls lost the melanin in their skin so they could absorb more sunlight. We are still the same species and inter-fertile, as a few youngsters have found to their everlasting shame."

Two of the cadets are unsuccessful in suppressing giggles at this. The instructor frowns. Then, he continues the lecture. "The science of evolution is supported by everything we know about life on World, by biology, embryology, comparative anatomy, and other sciences. There remains, however, two great questions, two serious problems.

"Who will identify those problems for us?"

Now, the cadets do look at Daffyd and Delwyn, but only for a moment before looking away. A girl from another element raises her hand and is acknowledged.

86

"Many scientists, but not all, say there has been enough time for hominids to evolve and for humans, the Res Publica and the thralls, to evolve. Other scientists say we evolved more quickly from DNA planted by the Adversary. The first question is, 'Which is correct?'"

"Good." The instructor points to another cadet.

"The second question is 'What is the first origin of life on World?' Is it the chemical bonding of atoms into replicating molecules, or is it the seeds Gens Bleddyn says were planted on our world?"

"Gens Bleddyn must be drinking his bath water to believe that." The muttered voice of one of the students is loud enough for the instructor to hear.

"Cadet Aurin of House Ellis, stand!" the instructor demands.

The boy rises. His face pales with embarrassment, but his posture is resolute. He stands straight, head erect, shoulders back, eyes focused on the instructor.

"Cadet Aurin, do you wish to modify your outburst?"

The boy's eyes flicker from side to side as he thinks. "Yes, sir. Gens Bleddyn's conclusions are unsupported by both fact and science, sir."

"That is what we shall examine. You will serve one punishment detail for interrupting my class."

Punishment detail. Daffyd thinks. *The instructor punished him for interrupting, but not for calling Father a liar. For that, I can call him to the field, challenge him to a duel—*

The instructor's voice brings Daffyd back to the classroom.

≈≈≈≈≈

The sun has not risen when the bugle call to Punishment Detail sounds. Cadets assigned to detail and those with excess demerits assemble in the quadrangle. They wear utility jumpsuits and sandals. Neither provides adequate protection from the cold wind that sweeps across Mesa and swoops through the sally ports.

Daffyd, with fifteen demerits, is paired with Aurin. Under the eyes of an older cadet, they and six others trot at double-time to one of the exercise fields. Their task is to dig new pits for the outhouses and fill the old pits with dirt.

"This isn't too bad," Daffyd says. "I'll be released in time to clean up before lunch."

Aurin, who is shoveling next to him, hears. "Easy for you to say, Bleddyn. You're working off demerits. I'm on detail. I'll be here until the job is finished and that will be after sunset. No lunch or supper." The boy jams his shovel into the ground and turns to face Daffyd. "You're like your father … you talk without thinking and never mind who you hurt."

Aurin stands, feet apart, hands clenched by his sides, eyes fixed on Daffyd. He raises his arms to his waist and presses his fists together in challenge.

Before Daffyd can respond to Aurin's challenge, some of Telor's advice reaches his consciousness. "Treat your enemies with kindness," his brother said. "It will mess up their minds and may give you advantage."

Daffyd drives his shovel into the ground where the new cesspit is to be dug. "Come on," he says. "If I help, we'll finish by supper." He turns his back to Aurin and digs.

Aurin frowns at this unexpected reaction. He unclenches his fists, retrieves his shovel, and resumes work.

"I'm sweating from digging, but my toes are frozen," Daffyd grumbles. "Who decided punishment detail uniform should be sandals?"

The Challenge

"Tradition." Aurin grunts and lifts a shovel of dirt. "Common hardship creates common bonds. At least, that's what Father says."

Daffyd feels he must respond and blurts, "Why did you say my father drank his bathwater?"

"I was repeating something I heard. I thought it was funny at the time."

"Actually, it was," Daffyd admits. "When you said it, I wasn't sure whether to laugh or challenge you. Sometimes I wonder about some of the things Father tells us. My elder brother, Telor, always has an answer, though."

"No talking, Cadets!" The voice of the detail supervisor reaches them from across the field.

Aurin's body continues the task, but his mind is elsewhere. He is his father's eldest child. He has no older brother in whom to confide. He wonders about Daffyd's elder brother, Telor.

Daffyd's prediction of finishing before supper is wrong. Neither boy is fed. When released from the detail, they immediately go to the empty mob shower. Their words echo from the tiles covering the floor and walls, attenuated by water falling from adjacent showerheads.

"At least they let us shower," Aurin says.

"The kitchen is closed," Daffyd says. "You know what that means."

"Yes. No supper."

"It means there's no one there to stop us."

"Stop us?" Aurin says.

"Come on, I know you're smarter than that." Daffyd grins.

The lock on the kitchen door opens to the two thin strips of metal Daffyd uses, and the cooler yields eggs, grated cheese, and a bowl of ground meat and chopped onions. Daffyd hesitates, unsure what to do.

Aurin chuckles at Daffyd's confusion. "You may be a great thief, but I don't think you're a cook. How did you know to open the lock, anyway?"

"One of my companion-guards was a thief. Guild member," Daffyd replies. "He was trying to enter … well, somewhere important. He was caught, but he'd penetrated several levels of security. I don't know if he was more afraid of Father or embarrassed he was caught, but he swore loyalty and became a member of the Home Guard. He taught me some things."

Filled by the omelet Aurin prepared, Daffyd leans back, pats his belly, and burps. "Should we wash the dishes?"

"They're going to know someone's been here," Aurin says. "If we clean up, they'll never believe it was cadets."

~~~~~

Only Delwyn notices the next morning when Daffyd enters the classroom with Aurin at his side. The cadets find their seats barely in time to stand when the instructor enters. He offers no introduction, but begins the lecture.

"A ship of House Bleddyn discovered a planet with life whose DNA is much like our own. Gens Bleddyn, with the support of much of the scientific community, tells us World was seeded by members of an older species, a species perhaps thousands of millennia older than we, and we are descended from *already evolved DNA*, the Adversary's DNA, planted on World."

All of the cadets know this, but none except Daffyd and Delwyn have ever heard it said so bluntly.

Father made it quite clear. So did Telor, and in more detail, Daffyd thinks. *We are the children of the Adversary, but we have changed. We are no longer the same species. We are the Res Publica!*

90

Daffyd looks at Aurin, but the boy is focused on the instructor.

After the morning lecture, the cadets are released to the library to research and determine the truth of the matter for themselves. Daffyd finds Aurin at a terminal and sits beside him, uninvited.

"Aurin, our houses are not aligned in vendetta, but are aligned against the Adversary. My brother, Llywelyn, told me about an enmity between himself and your cousin, Ötsi. Yet you and I are not part of either disagreement except as bystanders—"

"And sworn members of our houses," Aurin interrupts.

"Our houses are not in vendetta. Can you and I be, if not friends, at least not adversaries?"

Aurin sits silently. *A scion of a Greater House asks me to be his friend. Our houses are not sworn in vendetta, but have been traditional enemies. My house is sworn to Tarren, which is in vendetta with Bleddyn. Is there a way?*

"Friendship, like trust, must be earned," Aurin says. "But like trust, friendship must be offered before it can be returned."

Aurin pauses while he thinks. "I am willing to hope we might become friends."

That will be sufficient for the moment, Daffyd thinks.

≈≈≈≈

Academy has been in session for 75 days when Grach finds Soosong and Delwyn in the element's common room.

"The gloves come off tomorrow," Grach says. Soosong and Delwyn look up from their studies.

"We have been protected until we entered Academy. Tomorrow is the first *Bo-taoshi* competition," Grach explains. Seeing puzzlement, she adds, "The pole is taller than we used as children – five meters. It's heavier and not padded. If the pole hits you, you could be hurt. We will wear helmets, but not pads. And the pole must be brought all the way down … not only part way as in children's games. The monkey will likely fall off before that."

Soosong looks at Delwyn "I guess we knew that," she says. "It didn't sink in until now."

The pole pull-down competition pits Group XII against Group VI. From among the volunteers, Aurin is smallest, and selected to be the monkey. He grins when he is boosted to the top of the pole. He grabs the meter-and-a-half spike projecting from the top of the pole, and signals he is set. On the ground below, Daffyd grimaces. They are barefoot in the snow … not even the sandals of punishment detail.

Bo-taoshi (pole pulldown) attackers in *chojeom* formation (overhead view)

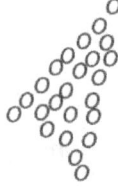

x – defender
m – monkey
o – attacker

Group XII forms concentric circles around the pole and waits for the Group VI attack. The referee's whistle sounds, and the match begins.

Group VI's strategy is easy to see. It is *chojeom* or 'focal point' attack. The seventy-two cadets form an arrow, with their strongest and heaviest members at the point, and run toward the Group XII defenders. Aurin immediately calls signals, and Group XII moves to reinforce the aim point.

The instant the point of Group VI's arrow reaches the defenders, the cadets in the back of the arrow break away and surround Group XII. This is a standard maneuver, and Group XII moves quickly in response to Aurin's calls. Attack and defense

92

soon reduce to scrums surrounding the pole. Aurin shifts his weight, helping keep the pole vertical. At one point, he is holding the spike with both hands while he flies from the spike like the pennant atop a ship's mainmast. He quickly regains his position, shifts his weight, and calls new signals.

After two tenths of an hour, the referee's whistle sounds. The pole is erect, and Aurin stands atop it, his face shining in victory. Group XII defended long enough to win the match.

Three roommates make their way back to their pod. "I'm too beaten up to shower," Delwyn grouses.

"Then you won't be sleeping in our room," Soosong snaps, and then pales with embarrassment when she realizes what she said and to whom.

"I second that," Grach says. "There's a nice couch in the common room. You may take a pillow and blanket from your bunk."

Delwyn's mind races. *I have been insulted by a bastard, but she's the one Father told me about. Grach stood up for her, and Grach is a member of an allied house.* The answer comes in a flash.

"You win … the two of you … and rightly so. Lead on."

In the boys' mob shower, Aurin is congratulated repeatedly, until his face pales in embarrassment. "Come on, guys, it was simple … standard attack in *chojeom* formation and standard defense … until they split their forces. That was their undoing. Every attacker does it, every defender anticipates it, and it's the wrong move."

At Fortress Bleddyn, Dirgel slowly adapts to his new role as the senior floater mechanic. Llywelyn's companions shun him because he achieved something they coveted but did not receive – adoption into House Bleddyn.

"Dirgel," My voice interrupts a task he is performing on one of the shuttle's anti-gravity drives. He ignores the call, completes the task, and then turns and bows.

"Please forgive me," he says. "The task could not be interrupted."

"Dirgel, Brother. Please do not bow to me, well, unless we are in some formal ceremony," I say. "You are my brother, and while the *bow of family* is appropriate, it has fallen out of use. We have ten brothers and sisters, and countless aunts, uncles, and cousins we encounter every day. If we were to stick to protocol, we'd get nothing done.

"There is a staff meeting in a few minutes. Would you attend with me, please?"

Dirgel has been uncertain and uneasy from the time he agreed to swear loyalty and fealty to House Bleddyn and its Gens. Although he was an unimportant member of House Reese and was offered a position of honor in House Bleddyn, he is unsure of himself. On this wintery day, I, whom he knows to be the Gens' eldest son and *de facto* aide-de-camp, invite him to a staff meeting. I sense his uncertainty.

Before we enter, I hand him a tablet. "The information from your communicator about the defenses of Fortress is all here. I hope, today, to understand what you have learned."

Dirgel's face darkens as blood rushes from it to major muscle groups in the *flight or fight* reflex. I see, but pretend not to notice. Dirgel takes several deep breaths.

Dirgel suppresses the churning in his belly and takes the tablet. "While I was one of Llywelyn's companions, I began collecting information about the defenses of fortress. Since I was adopted, I have continued. I told no one of this. My actions are those of a spy." He looks at me. "You should kill me, now."

I laugh, which frightens Dirgel more than a knife at his throat might have.

"What?" Dirgel demands.

"Brother, I am sorry. Someone should have told you, but it wasn't mine to tell. Your actions are known. You did not betray House Bleddyn, and I want to know what you have learned."

"I hear your forgiveness for my stupidity—" Dirgel begins.

"Not stupid!" I interrupt. "You have looked at something we take for granted. You have a fresh perspective and you may have discovered flaws we could not see. Moreover, we do not believe you are or ever were a spy."

~~~~~

At Academy, Delwyn and Caitlan return from a study session. They are alone in a hallway when Caitlan whispers. "There was a strike against my house. An attack on Port Dolffin. A cousin who is a Tac told me."

Delwyn pulls the girl from the hallway into an empty classroom. "Tacs aren't supposed to have contact with—"

"I know," Caitlan anticipates Delwyn's objection. "But he is afraid for me."

Delwyn nods. *Caitlin is a member of House Dolffin, one of Father's allies. If she is in danger, Daffyd and I are obliged to defend her.* "What did he tell you?"

"There was an explosion in the harbor at Port Dolffin. One of our fishing vessels was sunk. There is no reason for an explosion on a wooden sailing vessel unless there is a bomb … or a torpedo. We think it was a torpedo, 'cause we know House Ellis has torpedoes and their ships were nearby. None of our sailors survived."

"Ellis is aligned with Tarren," Delwyn says. "An attack by them on your house is an attack on my house. Did Tac say you might be in danger, here?"

"He said to be careful."

"Come, we will tell Daffyd," Delwyn says. *And I will tell Soosong. I will ask her to help protect Caitlin. If she agrees, and I know she will, it will put me under obligation to her. Perhaps she will accept an invitation to Fortress Bleddyn next Stormtime – to satisfy that obligation.*

≋≋≋≋

The monotony of the classroom is broken by more *Botaoshi* and, after hours of safety instruction, a visit to the firing range. Delwyn and Daffyd's element stands behind firing positions. A metal canopy that stretches forty meters from side to side shelters them from the bright, spring sun. All the cadets and the instructors wear earmuffs and yellow-tinted glasses. A slug rifle, a clip, a box of ammunition, and a spotter scope lie on a table in front of each cadet. Beyond the tables is a grassy field. One hundred meters away are targets, silhouettes of human figures. An escarpment of red earth topped by thick forest stands behind the targets. On command, the cadets load their clips, pick up the rifles, insert the clips, and point the rifles downrange.

Before the order to fire is given, a figure jumps from among the trees, slides down the scarp, and runs toward the cadets.

"Hold your fire. Safe your weapons. Signal 'range safe.'" the range commander calls. All the cadets obey, except one. Grach lifts her rifle to her shoulder, sights carefully, and fires. The runner stumbles, falls, and explodes in a great cloud of fire and smoke more than seventy meters away. Shrapnel, robbed of force by distance, peppers the canopy. The stunned eyes of her element-mates and the instructors turn toward Grach.

The cadets are marched to their pod. Tac leaves them in the common room with instructions not to speak of the incident to anyone. "An investigation will be conducted. You will be questioned. Eyewitness accounts are notoriously inaccurate. If you discuss the incident, you may create further inaccuracies."

Moments after Tac leaves, Delwyn opens the door. She slips into the hallway and walks to the Academy War Room. When she enters, she is neither gentle, polite, nor subservient.

"You have no right. Just because you are a scion of House Bleddyn—" a captain says before Delwyn's words silence him.

"Do you not understand the difference between right and privilege?" Delwyn hisses in the ancient language.

"Queue the recordings from the firing range," she orders one of the watch-standers, using the modern tongue. "You," she points to another. "Open a secure channel to Fortress Bleddyn."

The watch-standers look at the captain, who nods.

Gens Bleddyn is summoned to the house War Room. There, he watches the recordings. His face is impossible to read. His words, however, are clipped; neither inflection nor pitch change when he gives orders. "The cadet who fired on this assassin is not to be punished in any fashion. If any entry is made in his record—"

" 'Her' record, Father," Delwyn says over the comm link. "It was Grach."

"… her record, it is to be a commendation. My representative will arrive at Academy in less than an hour to join the investigation. Gens Tarren should be invited, since his son was endangered. And Gens Dolffin, since it was one of hers who killed the assassin."

How does he know Grach is of House Dolffin, Delwyn wonders before more important thoughts take her mind elsewhere.

97

"The bomber was a thrall." I return from Academy and report to Father. "A toxicological examination of the remains shows high levels of several drugs, including adrenalin and a hypnotic. It is likely he was programmed, brainwashed. It is likely he did not know he would die. It is very difficult to program someone to take his own life. The target is presumed to have been scions of Houses Bleddyn or Tarren, or both.

"That's the official report," I say. "The report does not address the motivation of Cadet Grach. Delwyn told me Grach 'felt danger' the moment she saw the bomber. The committee accepted Grach's explanation that she intuited danger from the man's movements and appearance. Delwyn is unaware Grach was placed in her element to protect her, and does not suspect Grach is an empath. Her empathic talent allowed her to convince the committee her actions were based on her observations.

"The committee skirted around assessing blame, assuming since scions of two Greater Houses were at risk, the vendetta between us and Tarren is not a factor."

"I do not doubt Gens Tarren would kill Huw if he could also kill two of mine," Bleddyn says. "You have more, though."

I nod. "I did not mention this to the investigators, because I did not want to give anyone ideas, but millennia ago, during the War of Conquest, the Abrahamic sect among the thralls is said to have created suicide bombers by promising them an eternal paradise if they died in service to their god. When their leaders were exposed as charlatans and their message failed to withstand the light of reason and logic, the sect died out. Could it have been revived?

"We will investigate," Father assures me.

~~~~

After the element members are interrogated and dismissed, Delwyn, Grach, and Soosong grab towels and walk to the mob shower.

"Grach, thank you for saving our lives, but how did you know?" Delwyn asks when the door is closed.

"The way he ran. The bulges in his clothing. He was carrying and hiding something."

"What if you were wrong…?"

"Then I would have killed a thrall and be expelled. But I wasn't wrong. 'What-ifs' have no place and no meaning in combat. If you live, you are right; if you die, it's no longer important." She paraphrases the words of Karmet.

Delwyn shakes her head. "You were amazing, and saved the lives of at least a dozen cadets including me and Huw Tarren. The bomber was running toward me."

I knew, Grach thinks, *and factored it into my decision. But I cannot tell you, nor of the danger I felt even before the bomber appeared at the top of the scarp.*

~~~~

Tac announces the time on the rifle range will be rescheduled. Today, however, the element is back in class.

"The second great question of biology is *how did life come about from non-life, and why is life so rare?*" The instructor looks over the classroom. He doesn't expect any of the cadets to venture an answer and is surprised when Aurin raises his hand.

"We have found many of the chemicals necessary for life on comets and asteroids, and in clouds of interstellar gas," the boy says. "We know chemicals seek to form bonds that conserve energy. Many of these bonds can be found in our DNA and the proteins that make up our cells. The proper question is not how life originated, but *why isn't there more of it?"*

Aurin pauses and glances at Daffyd. "On the other hand, there has not been sufficient time on World *both* for these chemical bonds to have formed *and* for evolution based on random genetic modification and natural selection to have taken place." He does not add that Gens Bleddyn's claim World was seeded by the Adversary is therefore validated. He doesn't have to. All the cadets and the instructor understand.

"Why did you change your mind?" Daffyd asks. He and Aurin have completed a session of *Jaryeondo*, unarmed combat, and are walking from the dojo to their pod for showers before supper.

"Telor explained it," Aurin says. He holds his breath while Daffyd processes that statement.

"Telor? My brother?"

"Yes. I wanted to understand what your father said. Telor accepted my call."

Aurin laughs. "Telor wouldn't say why your father had spoken, but he was happy to talk about the science behind it."

Aurin is more than he seems, Daffyd thinks.

~~~~~

The line in the mess hall moves quickly, although it leaves time for conversation. "Caitlan, something is wrong," Delwyn says. Soosong, who is behind Delwyn, pays close attention.

Caitlan shrugs. "Nothing, really. Just nerves. We have a test, tomorrow. That's probably it."

"More than that," Delwyn says.

Caitlan bristles. "You always seem to know. Yes, my cousin warned me, again. I'm afraid. I'm afraid I will draw an attack on those to whom I am sworn and those at Academy who have become my sisters."

100

Soosong breaks into the conversation. "Then, let your sisters help."

Delwyn nods. "She is right."

"After lunch," Caitlan says. "We have study time this afternoon and will not be missed."

After placing their trays on the conveyor that leads to the scullery, the three girls leave Academy and take a path toward the forest. When they are deep in the forest, Caitlan sits on a log and gestures to the others.

She speaks without preamble. "It should be safe to talk, here."

"Not in our room?" Soosong asks.

"Not in any room of Academy," Delwyn says. "Everywhere there are annunciators there are also microphones. Caitlan, what was the warning? Who endangers us?"

"Tarren leads them, and sits in the center of a web of connections that includes Fychan and Mynydd."

"But Mynydd is sworn to Father," Delwyn says.

"It is my cousin's belief some of the raids on Port Dolffin were led by Mynydd. He is afraid there will be another attack at Academy. Tarren's cabal is more powerful than any single house. They are stronger than even House Bleddyn." She looks at Delwyn when she speaks.

"But not stronger than the three of us united, and others we can bring to this battle," Soosong says.

"I will contact Father and relay this information," Delwyn says. "It's only fifteen days until Spring Stormtime. Both of you please join me then at Fortress Bleddyn. We will meet with Father. Meanwhile, I will tell Daffyd to enlist his friends in mutual defense."

Soosong is slow to respond. A member of a Greater House has invited a bastard to visit her house's fortress. This is contrary to every story she heard in the crèche.

Caitlan speaks while Soosong's thoughts are muddled. "I must return to Fortress Dolffin to talk with Mother. I know she has secure communication with your War Room. I will contact you. Thank you for the invitation. Another time, perhaps."

Soosong's thoughts settle enough for her to answer Delwyn. "Thank you. I accept."

~~~~~

Five days later, the cadets of Academy march onto troop shuttles. Meanwhile, shuttles with infrared and radar sensors crisscross the beaches and sand hills south of Aberwith. Soldiers sworn to Academy are augmented by ground-based sensors to protect the perimeter of the eighty thousand hectare training ground. The sun has barely broken the eastern horizon and is rising into gray clouds that will obscure it for the rest of the day.

"Worst weather I've seen in years," one guard says. "Academy must be crazy to send cadets out in this."

"Who would be on the beach in this weather, anyway? There isn't a threat."

Their lieutenant, an Academy graduate, smiles to herself. It is a soldier's right to complain and this soldier is correct. The cold, damp wind from the sea makes this duty miserable. It is a soldier's right to question orders not given in the heat of battle, but she has no doubt of these soldiers' loyalty. *Every one of the cadets, barely older than children, is someone's daughter or son,* she thinks. And then thinks about the life stirring in her womb, and wonders if she, herself, will earn an honorable place so her blood will—

"The first shuttles have arrived," a soldier interrupts. "Cadets are deploying."

The lieutenant turned her attention to her duty.

Delwyn, Caitlan, and Soosong stay together when they jump from the hovering shuttle onto a sand dune. Daffyd, Folant, and Aurin follow a few yards behind the girls. Their element is

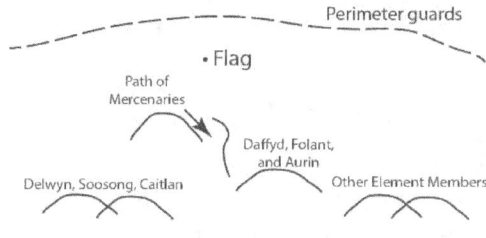

part of the defending force and will have an hour to establish positions before the exercise begins. On the southern edge of the range, half the cadets are deploying as the attacking force.

"The flag is planted," the commander of Group XII reports. "One hundred meters inside the northern boundary and two hundred meters behind us. We will be the last line of defense." He directs his four elements to take cover on the north slope of a series of parallel sand hills.

"*Ilja-jin* formation – one line," Delwyn says. "It exposes us to attack from the north if the enemy flanks us." Neither she nor the Group Commander sees Daffyd and the two other boys crawl through the sea grass and take positions on a dune twenty meters northeast of the girls. From there, the boys can cover the flanks while technically not disobeying orders.

At midday, laser tag bursts reflect from low clouds to the south. "Looks like the front line has engaged," Delwyn says. She peers through waist-high sea grass. "Can't see anything except the reflections. Must be at least ten kilometers away."

The boys see the same reflections, but keep their attention focused behind them.

"Movement. Northwest. Thirty meters," Folant's whisper is barely loud enough to penetrate the sighing of the wind through the sea grass.

Aurin picks up his binoculars. "Three men in desert camo … no, it's armor … crawling. Those aren't laser tag rifles. They're energy rifles. They're up to no good."

Daffyd puts down his laser tag rifle and draws his dagger. "Then they are fair game. Are you with me?"

Aurin and Folant nod, and draw their own daggers.

"Their best path is through that break in the sea grass. Slowly, melt into the grass," Daffyd orders. "Be silent and invisible. I will attack first; then, reveal yourselves."

The first man comes abreast of Daffyd's position. Confident of his companions, Daffyd yells and seems to fly from the grass onto the man's back. The boy pushes his dagger between plates in the man's armor and into his right kidney. Daffyd rocks the blade against the armor, shredding the man's guts before withdrawing the knife. A bolt of energy from the second man's rifle flashes overhead, nearly singeing him.

"Sorry about that," Aurin whispers. "He had the safety off and finger on the trigger. He's dead, now."

The body lying under Daffyd shudders once and is still. "This one is, too."

"So is the last one. Are there more?" Folant says.

"No, but the energy rifle drew attention. Academy guards on floaters approach."

"Put down your weapons. Lie flat, face down, arms outstretched." An amplified voice interrupts. The boys obey. A whistled signal from the Group Commander demands an emergency recall.

Daffyd laughs. "Game over."

"We win," Aurin adds.

~~~~~

The war game is suspended, to be rescheduled. Cadets return to Academy. After showering and dressing in clean uniforms, Daffyd, Aurin, and Folant are called to face a hastily organized Board of Inquiry.

"Group XII was in *ilja-jin* – one line formation – aligned east-west, two hundred meters south of the flag. The terrain dictated that Cadets Folant, Aurin, and I were about twenty meters behind the main line. Something behind us caught Cadet Folant's attention. We—"

"Can he not speak for himself?" Provist Myrmidon interrupts.

Before Daffyd can respond, the chamber door opens. Gens Bleddyn accompanied by guards, enters.

"Please, do not let me interrupt," he says, although his voice is hard and his attitude contradicts his words. "I am here only to determine why my son, daughter, and their element-mates were placed in danger and to learn how you plan to reward my son and his two companion-students for saving the lives of their comrades."

Myrmidon stutters. His patron, Gens Tarren, ordered him to punish Daffyd Bleddyn, even though Tarren's son Huw had also been in danger and was likely saved by Daffyd's actions. Folant and Aurin, scions of Lesser Houses, would become collateral damage. Myrmidon shudders. Gens Tarren will not be happy, but he is not present.

The board's questioning falters. The recordings made by guards are played. Less than an hour after Gens Bleddyn enters, Myrmidon gives the board's summary and decision.

"Three mercenaries with no record of having been hired positioned themselves in the exercise area at least four days before the exercise. They were concealed from both radar and infrared detectors by insulating blankets. In future the exercise area will be swept at random intervals and guarded for at least ten days before exercises. Cadet Daffyd Bleddyn and his companions acted correctly and honorably. A commendation will be entered into their file. This board is adjourned."

The slam of Myrmidon's gavel covers Gens Bleddyn's snort.

~~~~~

"You failed." Gens Tarren does not sound pleased.

It was your assassins who failed and were killed by children, Myrmidon thinks, but dares not say. "Gens Bleddyn was in the room. With his Praetorian Guard," Myrmidon whimpers. "At least I ensured the boys would not become heroes, only a commendation—"

"This is the first time you have failed me, Myrmidon. Let it be the last." The connection breaks.

~~~~~

The inquiry had lasted into the night. When Daffyd, Folant, and Aurin return to their element's pod, they quickly shower and don sleep pants. Daffyd jumps into his bunk and closes his eyes. Aurin stands with his hand on the light switch. "Daffyd, we fought well together. You have been a friend." Remembering the first of many night raids on the kitchen, he adds, "And a fun companion. Our houses are aligned with those who are sworn enemies. Even so, you have offered trust and friendship. I would swear amity with you."

Daffyd's eyes pop open. *I was supposed to get close to Soosong. But an alliance between Aurin and me? He is scion and heir of a house sworn to Tarren. I know Father wants to get closer to Ellis. He would approve. But ...* "It cannot be a blood oath without permission from both our fathers. I will ask permission of my father when I can speak to him. For now," he sits up and looks at Aurin. "For now, I swear amity with you, Aurin of House Ellis. Let there never be strife between us."

"Thank you. I swear amity with you, Daffyd of House Bleddyn. Let there never be strife between us."

"Now, turn out the light, please. Morning will come quickly."

The next afternoon at their studies, Daffyd and Aurin share a carrel and computer terminal. Their task is to plan a sea battle, pitting warships against warships. The battle is set among the Free Islands northwest of the Equatorial Continent, and the ships are armed with arrows and cannon.

They are deep in their planning when Aurin speaks. His voice is soft, but Daffyd senses a quiver. "I know amity does not mean we have to share house secrets, and I would not presume to ask you to do so, but I've heard rumor that Dolffin is blaming my house for a torpedo attack on one of their ships."

Fear? Anxiety? A little of both, Daffyd thinks. "That story is more than the gossip sailors swap around the scuttlebutt. It is true. I was warned House Ellis … you … might … Oh! I don't know! Cause trouble?"

"Why did you not say anything?" Aurin demands.

"I do not see enmity in your eyes or in your behavior. I believe I can trust you."

"It's more than scuttlebutt." Aurin pauses. He seems encouraged by Daffyd's words. "I know my house's ships have torpedoes, but only to use against the pirates of the Free Islands. Those are Father's standing orders. It was not my house."

"Amity does not mean sharing house secrets, but honor and truth are more important than secrecy. I will find out what my house knows and tell you what I may."

Chapter 7: Hidden Evil

There are only a few places other than Council House and Academy where the houses mix without open hostility. One is the city of Cytgord, home of the Mercenary Auction. The Peace Bond is enforced by guards under the command of Houses Bleddyn and Dolffin. In the port city of Aberwith, even house rivalries are set aside for commerce and profit. The third place where houses mix easily is the Free City of Ocsiwn.

Llywelyn plans an exercise between his companions and the forces of House Merrick in the mountains west of Ocsiwn. While his companions set up camp, Llywelyn flies a shuttle without markings and with a false radar signature to Ocsiwn. Four of his companions accompany him in the shuttle; however, Llywelyn orders them to wait. "The next step is for me, alone."

Llywelyn wears a jumpsuit without insignia. His weapons are sword and energy pistol plus dagger and grace knife. Llywelyn's dagger does not bear the head of a wolf, but an innocuous green stone that marks him to be without house. Even that does not attract attention. His appearance is like the mercenaries, hard men and women, who walk the streets and inhabit the bars and hiring halls.

Ocsiwn is where clandestine deals are made, where drugs and slaves are bought and sold, where assassins are hired, and where trade among enemies is conducted.

Llywelyn's business is none of these. He is responding to a message from a woman who was an Academy element-mate. A woman of the Second Rank of House Tarren. She hints at information important to Llywelyn and asks him to meet her on this day at a particular place.

Bars, pharmacies, slave pens, and the offices of Procurers – people who offer their services to satisfy unusual requests – line the main street. Alleys a block or two long lead away from the main street. They offer access to boarding houses, warehouses, and places less savory than those on the main street.

Llywelyn walks until he sees the sign identifying the meeting place – an apothecary. Llywelyn's gut tightens. This could be a trap. An assassination. A kidnapping. Despite his weapons, Llywelyn is afraid.

I demolish my bridges behind me leaving no choice but to move forward, he thinks and pushes the door. A bell chimes and startles him for an instant. Strange odors fill the air. The dim light reveals shelves lined with glass bottles and ceramic jars. Bundles of herbs hang on racks. A young man sits behind a counter. He grinds something with a mortar and pestle. The bell startles him, too. He looks at Llywelyn, and then turns back to his work.

Llywelyn's eyes narrow. Behind the young man a curtain shifts, revealing a doorway. A woman of Llywelyn's age steps into the shop.

"Well met. Will you follow me?" She gestures to the doorway. "My cousin wishes to speak with you."

Llywelyn recognizes the woman as his former element mate. His gut loosens. *She is of Second Rank in House Tarren. The Gens is her cousin. Is he truly here, or is she offering me cheese in a rattrap? She did not ask me to surrender my weapons. The opportunity is worth the risk.* These thoughts flash through his mind. He does not hesitate. "Well met. Yes, I will follow."

In the next room, Llywelyn faces a solitary figure. He wears only a sword, dagger, and grace knife. Llywelyn unclips his energy pistol and hands it to the woman. She accepts the weapon and then leaves the room.

110

Several hours later, two shuttles leave Ocsiwn. One moves toward the territory of House Tarren. The other, east to the mountains where Llywelyn's companions wait.

Llywelyn takes many things from the meeting, including a sealed container and instructions for using its contents.

~~~~~

Before breakfast, Gens Bleddyn summons Llywelyn and me to his den. I kneel. Llywelyn, Heir Apparent, does not kneel. I know he sneers inwardly at me until I rise at Father's command. Llywelyn and I stand side-by-side in an uneasy silence.

"I need to show myself to both the house and to the rest of the Res Publica. I need to get away from Fortress. This winter is especially cold."

Cold? He's getting old, Llywelyn thinks.

He's creating a reason to expose himself to danger, I think. *Why does he need a reason?*

"I will inspect my farms on Sehwa," Father says.

The island is bathed by a warm ocean current. Even the winter weather is mild. Volcanic soil, suited to growing both grapes and olives, covers most of the land. The wine and olive oil are so good even House Tarren is a buyer although they make purchases secretly through agents in the Free City of Ocsiwn.

Sehwa, Llywelyn thinks. *An exercise while Father is there will show him my prowess as a commander. I have little time to plan.*

~~~~~

Three days later, Gens Bleddyn lands at the first farm and is discussing grape varieties with the manager when Lieutenant Terrwyn hurries from the shuttle.

"Sir, Llywelyn preceded you to the island, and commandeered the communication net," Lieutenant Terrwyn reports.

Why would Llywelyn do this? Bleddyn wonders before giving orders. "Use the comm system in the shuttle to set up a link with the War Room at Fortress. Then, penetrate the island's net. What traffic is being carried?"

"An exercise, Your Grace. Lieutenant Bleddyn's forces are engaged in an exercise with a company from House Lagon."

"Live-fire or laser tag?" Bleddyn demands.

The lieutenant understands the rules may be flexible. "Laser tag at the moment, sir."

"Tell me if that changes."

~~~~~

Llywelyn conducts the exercise on the southern reaches of Sehwa Island. Satellites capture battlefield images. The House Bleddyn War Room forwards them to Bleddyn's shuttle. Lagon's forces stand in *Ilja-jin*, one-line formation. Llywelyn uses a focal point attack, *chojeom,* to penetrate the line and reach the goal: the flag of the opposing house. If the Lagon commander reacts fast enough, his forces can swing and flank Llywelyn's in *hajik-jin*, crane-wing formation, putting Llywelyn's forces in a killing zone. Llywelyn accepts the risk.

Ilja-jin defense against attackers in *chojeom* formation

x – defender
o – attacker

*Defense folds into
hajk-jin (crane wing)
formation*

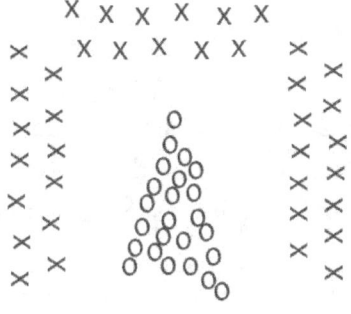

*x – defender
o – attacker*

Gens Bleddyn and Lieutenant Terrwyn watch Llywelyn's forces surround the flag. A red arrow appears on Bleddyn's display. It points to a floater from Llywelyn's forces moving northward toward the farm. "One individual, on a floater," the lieutenant says after giving an order to his soldiers. "Five minutes until intercept."

"You will not likely take him alive," Gens Bleddyn says.

"Twenty coppers say we will," the lieutenant replies. He pitches his voice for only the Gens' ears.

Bleddyn's smile does not reach his face. His soldiers are well paid, but twenty coppers is a lot of money. The offer from his lieutenant is a measure of the man's confidence in his soldiers and his devotion to his Gens. A lesser person would not have dared make the bet. "I'll match your twenty," Bleddyn replies. "And will add a bonus for your soldiers if they succeed."

The lieutenant nods understanding while keeping his eyes on the screen.

The attacker is Brawin of House Pugh. She was for two years a member of Llywelyn's Academy element. She used their relationship to secure an invitation to participate in the war games.

"She fought strongly against difficult odds," Lieutenant Terrwyn reports, "and then tried to kill herself when capture was inevitable. My soldiers stopped her. Her injuries are being treated at the Sehwa hospital."

"What guided her to us?"

"Just as we could see Llywelyn, his forces could see us. They had a feed from the War Room at Fortress."

~~~~~

Llywelyn wears combat armor with laser-tag sensors when he enters his father's shuttle. Gens Bleddyn sits behind a desk in his private compartment. Screens around the desk and on the walls of the compartment display the terrain. The largest screen plays and replays Brawin's capture.

"You are aware Brawin left your exercise and sought to assassinate me."

Llywelyn shrugs. "A nobody, Father. She was not part of my command, merely an acquaintance from years ago. I assume she is dead and Telor will notify her house."

He is too casual about the death of someone under his command. He is too casual about the threat to me. For whom was this soldier from House Pugh acting? For her Gens, or is there something darker at work? Llywelyn's face is a mask and Bleddyn cannot penetrate what should be the boy's most obvious thoughts.

"How should we respond, then?" Bleddyn asks.

"Pugh is a Greater House only because it is one of the original houses. It is weak and unimportant. It would raise their standing if House Bleddyn declared vendetta against them," Llywelyn answers. "We should act through another house."

"Who, then? And what would be their reason?"

"Our ally, House Caerwyn," Llywelyn replies. "The border between Pugh and Caerwyn has been in dispute for centuries. Gens Caerwyn would be happy to strike at Pugh, especially if you were to send some soldiers from House Dolffin's school. Gens Dolffin has a class ready for positions."

114

"A satisfactory plan. I will contact Gens Caerwyn. Telor will transfer the soldiers and ensure Gens Tarren learns of the vendetta between Caerwyn and Pugh. He should know one of my allies is attacking one of his allies. Caerwyn will send Brawin's ashes to House Pugh. You are dismissed." The door closes behind Llywelyn.

Bleddyn stares at the closed door. *Llywelyn is revealing less and less of his feelings. He has learned more control than I expected. Does he suspect? Does he know? He's blocking with more than strength of mind. There's something else at work here.*

In the hallway leading to his quarters, Llywelyn's thoughts are smug. *Telor will arrange transfer of the soldiers; Telor will send a message to Gens Tarren. Trivial tasks, suited to a clerk. He thinks he is my father's favorite, but he is a fool.*

Llywelyn returns, alone, to his quarters. From a concealed panel, he withdraws a book. Taking a pen, he opens the book and writes.

Gens Tarren gave me a drug that muddles my thoughts and hides them from Father. It emboldens me. Perhaps too much, for should Father learn about the drug, I am undone. Should he discover this journal, I am undone. But I must have some place to record my thoughts and my plans, for I find it difficult to keep them organized otherwise. Is it the lack of a vambrace that blurs my thoughts? Nine years ago Father ordered my vambrace removed. I no longer receive the drugs that temper the fires of puberty. Was that decision correct? By Karmet, I hope so! It would be devastating to wear a vambrace at my age. It would be a sign I am flawed.

—Llywelyn Bleddyn, Private Journal

~~~~~

Two days later, I report the result of the woman's interrogation to Father. "She acted independently and was not

115

ordered by Gens Pugh to attack you. However, Pugh made it clear to his soldiers he would like to see you dead. Pugh is not directly responsible; he may not have known her plans."

Father chuckles, but it is dry and ironic, more a snort than a chuckle. "Telor, you have delved too deeply into the law. Was Pugh responsible or not?"

I look into my father's eyes and speak with confidence. "Gens Pugh is responsible, Father. Like the ancient despot Triumph of House Tarren, his words created the conditions in which his soldier acted. He is her commander. He is responsible for her actions."

~~~~~

In their common room, the Prime Element of the Praetorian Guard stands at attention while Gens Bleddyn hands their lieutenant twenty coppers and an additional copper per soldier. "You and your soldiers served exceptionally well. I know neither you nor they will grow overconfident because of this. 'Exceptional' is the least thing expected of those who hold your positions."

Chapter 8: Recognition and Brotherhood

Daffyd and Delwyn's classes and training in weapons and *Jaryeondo* continue unabated. An early winter storm has piled snow on the ground around Academy. The classrooms are too warm and encourage torpor. Soosong pokes Caitlan to wake her. The instructor sees, but ignores.

"Thousands of millennia ago, World underwent a time of intense cold that lasted two hundred millennia. It was then blood employing haemocyanin to transport oxygen became a survival trait. One line of Primates evolved in that direction. We and the thralls are their descendants.

"Today, our equatorial continent is too warm for us. The heat encourages torpor. Perhaps in another thousand millennia we will develop blood that uses haemoglobin to transport oxygen in red blood cells. Perhaps our technology, the vast systems that cool Academy, Council House, and your houses' fortresses and homes, will defeat further evolution. Perhaps the climate will change again. It has done so in the past, and will likely…"

Now, Soosong drifts off, but she learned in the crèche to appear awake while she naps.

~~~~~

At Academy, the spring *Bo-taoshi* is more than a competition between groups. It is a rite of passage for First Form cadets. After the competition, First Form cadets will be recognized as individuals by older cadets, and welcomed into aeons of Academy traditions.

More than as individuals; as humans, Soosong thinks, recalling the degrading punishments inflicted on her by older cadets. *How many will offer their hand in friendship to a bastard, even after this?*

Group XII, which includes the element of Daffyd, Delwyn, Soosong, Huw, and Aurin, plus three other elements, performs well. Their score is in the top five percent of First Form cadets. After the final competition, the seventy-two cadets of the group stand in line, backs against the outer wall of Academy, facing nearly three hundred older cadets of Squadron Raptor.

These cadets will conduct the recognition ceremony. Soosong looks for faculty, but sees none. *This could be bad.*

The Cadet Squadron Commander's eyes rake the line of First Form cadets. "Group XII petitions to become members of Squadron Raptor and assume a mantle of history." She pauses long enough for the First Form cadets to understand the importance of her words. "Who among you knows our history?"

Her question surprises the cadets of Group XII. Soosong's voice surprises them more, when she takes two steps forward to stand in front of the line. "During the House Wars of 60,000 C.E., when Academy became a prize to be won, Group XII, although not yet recognized as a member of Squadron Raptor, held the western sally port against overwhelming odds. No member of the unit survived, but the sally port did not fall.

"During the Thrall Rebellion of 80,000 C.E., when sent to defend the Pass of Perdition, Group XII fought with honor. These two encounters are why the flag of Raptor Squadron – and no other squadron – bears two battle streamers."

Soosong pauses only briefly. "We are the heirs of Group XII. We demand your recognition." Before the Squadron Commander can respond, Delwyn steps forward to stand beside Soosong. Aurin who was on Soosong's left follows. Others, seeing what is happening, step forward all seventy-two cadets of Group XII stands in line.

Soosong is not the only cadet who fears the hazing said to accompany recognition. Delwyn knows her position as scion of a Greater House will not protect her from what generations of cadets – including her father and older siblings – consider tradition. She watches the face of the Squadron Commander, trying to discover what she will do.

Soosong has impressed her, Delwyn thinks. *We all have.*

At a word from the Squadron Commander, her adjutant calls Raptor Squadron to attention. What the commander says next surprises nearly everyone. "Advance the colors." The adjutant echoes the command.

From behind the older cadets, screened until this moment, a color guard lifts seven flags. The flags of six groups – including Group XII – flank the Squadron flag with its two battle streamers. The presence of their flag with the others, more eloquently than any words the Squadron Commander might have said, tells the cadets of Group XII they are now, officially, part of Raptor Squadron.

Commands are given. The Squadron, now complete, assembles in parade formation and marches through the main sally port into the quadrangle. Once in position, the colors are retired, and the cadets dismissed to be welcomed with clasped arms by the older cadets. *No hazing, no harassment.* Soosong isn't the only one who is relieved.

Once back in their pod, Soosong's mates, forgetting for a moment her status, congratulate her knowledge and courage. *It will not last,* she thinks. *They are speaking from emotion and not from depth. Still, it feels good.*

~~~~~

A few kilometers away but only moments after the ceremony, I stand before Father's desk. "Group XII was accepted

into Squadron Raptor without the usual hazing and harassment, thanks to Soosong." I summarize the recognition ceremony.

"She is more than we expected," Father says. "Continue to watch her."

A few days after recognition, Academy closes for Spring Stormtime. Most of the cadets and faculty will return to their homes. The departing cadets line up at shuttle pads and gossip. Gens Bleddyn's personal shuttle, emblazoned with the house crest – the wolf couped in black against an orange moon – draws attention.

Delwyn escorts Soosong into the shuttle for the short trip from Academy to Fortress Bleddyn. The girl is uncomfortable and struggles to control her emotions when the Gens, himself, greets the shuttle.

"Father, this is Soosong, a member of our element and a friend," Delwyn announces.

"Thou art welcome, friend of my daughter," the Gens says in the ancient language. He does not seem surprised when Soosong replies with her thanks in the same tongue.

The two girls bow to the Gens before Delwyn leads her guest away. Everyone's attention is on Soosong. Daffyd's guest, Aurin of Ellis, passes without notice.

~~~~~

Daffyd and Aurin turn toward the men's quarters. Delwyn leads Soosong through hallways and doors toward her quarters.

120

Delwyn sees the concentration on Soosong's face as she memorizes the route.

"Quarters are often full during Stormtime," Delwyn says. "Usually, I would have to share my bed with two young cousins, but they are such chatterboxes I'd not get any sleep. And I do so tire of their talk of the boys with whom they are most recently enamored.

"I did not invite you here only so I could cast aside my cousins. I hope we can continue our training. I have an uncle who trained as an assassin. He promises to teach us some of his techniques."

Soosong halts abruptly, forcing Delwyn to stop. "You would allow me to learn this? Do you not know how great a target your family is? How much danger you invite?"

Delwyn faces the other girl. "Father taught me while trust must be earned, the beginning is offering trust." Delwyn turns away and puts her hand on a plate beside a door. The door opens. "Here are my quarters. If you will put your hand on the plate, the computer will register you and the doors to the family quarters will open to you. All the doors except others' bedrooms. That is an offer of trust. My uncle's training is another."

~~~~~

Years before she entered Academy, Delwyn received her own quarters, separate from her surrogate. Father summoned her to his den. It was the first time she had been there and despite her nervousness she took a moment to look around.

The stone walls were not covered with tapestries and banners like the anteroom. Rather, they were filled with bookshelves or adorned with portraits. *The old Gens,* Delwyn realized. She knelt and lowered her head in front of her father's desk – a massive slab of oak, polished so it gleamed in the light of the many fixtures on the walls and ceiling.

121

"Rise, Daughter Delwyn," Bleddyn said. "Come, sit by the fire. Our evolution made us equipped for the cold, but our temperament needs the warmth of a fire."

After Delwyn sat, her father pressed a button on his communicator. A screen above the mantle displayed a map of Fortress. "What do you see, Daughter?"

Delwyn looked at the diagram. "It is a concentric defense. The quarters of the Gens, surrogates, and children are in the center. Older siblings surround them. They would be expendable if hostile forces penetrated Fortress."

Delwyn faced her father. "But that is not the way it is."

Bleddyn nodded, but concealed his smile at his daughter's understanding. "Now, look at how the quarters are organized today and select the ones you want from those available."

Delwyn looked at the changed image. "It's different. Children's quarters are in the center. There are empty rooms near them, rooms you want me to claim. Uncles, Aunts, older cousins, and soldiers occupy the outer rings of this circle. You protect something other than what the ancient Gens hoped to protect. You seek to protect House Bleddyn rather than Gens Bleddyn."

"Correct, Daughter. Think on this, but keep it to yourself."

~~~~~

Soosong presses her hand on the plate at the door of Delwyn's quarters, while thinking. *Huw was disappointed when I turned down his invitation. I know of the enmity between Bleddyn and Tarren. Is Delwyn offering me trust or is she trying to tie me to her? Can I separate those two thoughts? Does it matter? Are they different?*

~~~~~

Gens Bleddyn's den is too large to be considered cozy, despite the fire that fills the hearth. The heat of the fire is barely

122

able to hold back the chill rolling from the ancient stones and the bay windows. The Gens and his eldest daughter sit before the fire. The Gens pulls a poker from the fire and quenches it in a pitcher of wine. A cloud of steam, laden with spices, rises. He pours cups of the mulled wine for Bethan and himself.

"You have earned much honor, Daughter." Bethan sits quietly as her father speaks those words. He did not ask a question; no answer is required. He stated a simple truth; no acknowledgement is required. Bleddyn approves of the girl's silence. His face relaxes. It is not quite a smile.

"What assignment do you want after Academy?" he asks. "Space? Home Guard? A position with one of our allies? A husband?"

"Instructor at Academy, Father," Bethan says. "I was on cadre, training First Form cadets, for four years. I have led my element for three years. I like bringing others to knowledge. Do you understand?"

"I am not surprised," Bleddyn says. "You have found your calling. I will arrange the appointment. It will be announced after you graduate at the end of this year."

~~~~~

Father's talk with twins Daffyd and Delwyn is neither straightforward nor simple. He directs his first question to Daffyd. "How are you getting along with Huw Tarren?"

"Inconsistently, Father. I have never argued with him and have occasionally supported his position in class – when he is correct, which isn't often. I have helped him on the training field and in the dojo. He seems either hot or cold. One day he will return my favor, the next he is sullen and obstinate."

"Sometimes he retreats into himself," Delwyn adds, uninvited. "I look into his face and see blankness, as if he weren't conscious. It lasts only for moments. I wonder if his vambrace is functioning properly."

"That would explain his behavior toward your brother," Bleddyn says before changing the subject. "Your Tactical Officer?"

"Rigidly neutral," Daffyd says. Delwyn nods.

"Any pushback, any animosity from others in your element or group?"

Delwyn speaks. "One girl from House Maelon seemed determined to harm me during our games. I am sure she deliberately tripped me more than once. She's clever and agile, and no one notices."

"Are you in danger?" Bleddyn asks.

"Not any more," Delwyn says. "Not since she broke an arm. It was a nasty break. She will be out for the rest of the year, and will always be a year behind us."

The Gens raises an eyebrow, but Delwyn says no more. Bleddyn does not press her for details.

"There is another matter, Father. The cabal that Caitlan of Dolffin described. She was twice warned by an instructor that she might be in danger."

"The most distressing news," Bleddyn says, "is Mynydd's treachery. Others have reported it. It is, however, not widely known and it will remain that way until I am ready. You will be cautious around cadets and faculty from House Mynydd. The longer Tarren thinks us ignorant of this cabal, the more easily we can penetrate it.

"Gens Dolffin and I met with Gens Caerwyn. Dolffin opened her fishing grounds to Caerwyn, whose ships are armed. In return, Caerwyn will defend Dolffin against attack. You will not discuss this, either."

The twins' father dismisses them with a nod.

~~~~~

After showing Aurin to their room and keying doors to him, Daffyd leads him to the library. I am sitting in a nook with broad windows. Garreth sits in my lap while I read to him. At fourteen kilograms, he is almost too big for my lap but we both take comfort from our closeness. The library is comfortably cool, but the nook is warmed by sunlight streaming through a break in the clouds.

"Telor, you know Aurin," Daffyd says. "We have sworn amity and we have a question for you."

"Welcome, Aurin, and welcome home Brother. Aurin, you and my brother have sworn amity. Therefore amity exists also between you and me."

Both Daffyd and Aurin relax when I say those words. They sit facing the windows and let the sunlight warm them. The warmth is comforting although they must struggle to stay alert despite the drugs their vambraces inject.

Daffyd leans forward in his seat. "An explosion destroyed a ship of House Dolffin. There is tension between cadets from House Dolffin and House Ellis, because Dolffin claims Ellis launched a torpedo. Ellis acknowledges they have torpedoes on their ships, but denies the attack. What is the truth? If anyone in the house knows, it would be you."

Rather than answer Daffyd, I address his guest. "Aurin, Daffyd will take you to our War Room where you may use a secure channel. Please tell your father what I am about to say. You may tell him I said it. Ask him to keep it close to himself until Dolffin makes it public. That will be within days, perhaps within hours. Daffyd, you may speak of it to no one until Dolffin does. Do you both agree?"

The boys nod.

"A submerged mine caused the explosion. House Fychan has long wanted control of Port Dolffin, the only part of Dolffin's territory on the mainland. Fychan thinks it would be easier to take control of Port Dolffin than to build their own port and cut roads through the swamp and jungle lying between them and the coast.

"Fychan mined the harbor to destroy Dolffin's ships and weaken them. They hope to show other houses Dolffin is not capable of defending the port. Maelon backs Fychan directly; Tarren backs them indirectly. Dolffin is, as you know, allied with Bleddyn. However, no one wants to force a confrontation between Tarren and Bleddyn. The harbor at Port Dolffin is now clear of mines. The only Fychan ships allowed into the harbor are merchant ships, and they are searched before passing the breakwater."

Both boys absorb this latest information about house rivalries and vendetta. Aurin is first to speak. "Thank you, Telor. I am the oldest of my siblings, and Father's heir. I want to become a good elder brother. You are a fine example for me."

Gens Dolffin makes the announcement through Council channels two days later. Dolffin also announces the destruction of three Fychan merchant ships past the breakwater. The ships were deploying mines.

~~~~~

The next day, Daffyd and Aurin wait in an anteroom to be summoned to Gens Bleddyn. Daffyd will ask if he and Aurin may swear blood oath. Gens Ellis gave his permission to do so, hoping it would counter the long-standing enmity between Ötsi of Ellis and Llywelyn.

The anteroom is designed to intimidate. The walls are covered with weapons, trophies of the hunt, banners with the arms of defeated enemies – some blotched with what might be dried blood – and tapestries depicting millennia of battles. The boys sit on a bench of hard, polished wood. It is tilted toward the front; they must brace their feet against the floor so not to slide off.

126

Despite the spring storms that rage across the continent, this room is over-heated, inviting torpor.

Daffyd tries to convince himself his father will grant the request. "My father and surely yours have had life-extension. They will live longer than any amity or vendetta declared by children at Academy."

Aurin's reply is scarcely louder than the whispers the boys exchanged in the darkness of their Academy room. "Ötsi's vendetta with Llywelyn, you mean. The amity we swore. You know, don't you, when Llywelyn brought aid to us after the volcanoes erupted, Ötsi offered an honorable end to their vendetta and Llywelyn refused."

"No. Llywelyn never told me. And what they had wasn't vendetta. It was vengeance over some imagined slight. I never knew what."

Aurin snorts before answering. "Llywelyn and Ötsi's groups were in final competition for the annual pole pull-down. Llywelyn's group won, but Ötsi claimed they had too many cadets on the field. The judges upheld Ötsi's claim. Llywelyn lost his victory. He blamed Ötsi and never forgave him. You are right, though. Llywelyn seeks vengeance. Vendetta is legitimate only when the grievance is just and when a person or a house is defending its rights."

"Or defending that which is right," Daffyd adds. Before Aurin can answer, the boys are summoned to Gens Bleddyn's den.

Because he is accompanied by Aurin, the scion of a Lesser House, Daffyd does not kneel. Both boys halt in front of Bleddyn's desk and bow deeply. They wait for the Gens to speak.

"Your father sends his greetings, Aurin, and gives permission for you to swear blood oath with Daffyd. What form shall your oath take?" Gens Bleddyn looks from one boy to the other.

Daffyd is the first to respond. "Aurin and I talked about the enmity between Llywelyn and Ötsi. It has eaten at both houses for years. That canker needs to be healed. I would, if he agrees and you permit, swear brotherhood with Aurin of Ellis."

Aurin's head snaps toward Daffyd. This is much more than he expected.

"And what will your brothers say?" Gens Bleddyn asks Daffyd.

"Llywelyn will say nothing. What I do is unimportant to him. Telor will support me. I am sure of this."

Aurin's voice is firm; his answer, short. "This will please my father and Cousin Ötsi, Your Grace."

The ceremony is held in the Great Hall. Fortress is filled with family, retainers, guests, and thralls seeking shelter from the storms, and all are invited – Delwyn and Soosong, Brothers Guffudd and I, Sister Bethan, Delwyn and Daffyd's surrogate, uncles, aunts, and cousins. The thralls who are tutors – Sani and his brother – stay in the background until I urge them closer. Llywelyn, although invited, has found something else to do.

Gens Bleddyn, Daffyd, and Aurin of Ellis stand beside a small table in the center of the cavernous room. The boys place their daggers on the table. They are too tense to notice the televisor camera, which carries the scene to Fortress Ellis.

The Gens speaks. "We assemble, family and friends, to witness blood oath."

Daffyd takes his dagger from the table, looks at the wolf head on the hilt, and then bloods the blade on his arm. "By my blood, I swear brotherhood with you, Aurin of Ellis." He offers the dagger to Aurin, who bloods his own arm, and places the dagger in the sheath at his belt.

Aurin takes his dagger from the table, and looks at the deer with golden horns. He bloods his arm with the dagger. "By my blood, I swear brotherhood with you, Daffyd of Bleddyn." He

128

hands the dagger to Daffyd, who bloods it and places it in the sheath.

Gens Bleddyn closes the ceremony with a phrase in the ancient tongue, "Mae ewyllys da'r ddau Bleddyn Ellis gyda chi. The good will of Houses Bleddyn and Ellis rests upon you and your bond."

Chapter 9: Exploration

Two months after the twins and their friends return to Academy, Father summons me. I find him at the Privy Council table with four of his siblings – two brothers, my Uncles Maddox and Dewi, and two sisters, my Aunts Chooli and Aveta. Father gestures for me to sit, and then signals Aunt Chooli to begin.

She slides her finger across a tablet and an image appears on a display screen.

"You know three years ago the Caravel *Kobaya* reported finding a planet with life limited to primitive sea creatures, insects, and grasses. After an Adversary ship visited for several years, life on the planet included amphibians, reptiles, birds, shrubs, and trees. The Adversary seeded the planet.

"Based on reports from other ships, we have concluded the Adversary seeds planets in five waves. First, cyanobacteria—"

"What?" Uncle Maddox asks.

"Blue-green algae," she replies. Then she laughs. "Think 'pond scum.' What you waded through as a child chasing frogs. The algae create an oxygen atmosphere to support later seedings. The five waves are shown on the screen."

1-Cyanobacteria
2-Fungus, simple sea life
3-Simple vegetation, insects
4-Birds, reptiles, complex plant life, amphibians
5-Mammals

"We have found nearly a hundred planets in one stage of seeding or another. I've sent a summary to your tablets. By estimating the age of the DNA, we have determined the Adversary began seeding and then mysteriously abandoned more planets than they completed seeding. Further, based on variations in the DNA of mammalian species, we believe the Adversary completed seeding many planets and then abandoned them."

"Thank you, Sister," Father says. "Why would they operate this way and will they someday revisit their creations, including World?"

"Any answers we might come up with would be pure speculation," Uncle Maddox protests.

"True, but we must have a basis for our planning, even if only speculation," Father replies. "Please think on this, and be prepared to present it to the Privy Council tomorrow."

The Privy Council meets for two days. At the first break, Llywelyn leaves and does not return. With Llywelyn gone, Father invites me to sit at his desk rather than stand in a corner. I use his computer to take notes.

Shortly before evening meal on the second day, Aunt Aveta notifies Father the council reached consensus. Uncle Dewi presents the report. "It is the opinion of the Privy Council that the Adversary's governance is similar to the Res Publica – loosely organized into factions which compete with one another or are allied in bonds somewhat easily broken. Further, in the forging and breaking of these bonds, and the warfare which likely results, records are destroyed, ships are lost, and planets are forgotten. Further, the resources devoted to warfare may preclude follow-on missions."

"And our response?" Father asks.

Uncle Maddox's answer is not surprising. "More ships, more missions, more exploration, and more colonization."

"That shall be our plan," Father commands.

~~~~~

A rain shower stops just as Uncle Maddox's shuttle lands. He and Uncle Grigor, who was on Namhae since the Privy Council

132

met six months ago, rush to Uncle Grigor's laboratory, deep under Fortress, where Father and I wait.

"We have broken the code of the universe," Uncle Grigor announces. The high pitch of his voice and the frenetic waving of his hands show his excitement. "Our scientists have determined our universe is one of many. Although each universe has three spatial dimensions, the scientists describe them as sheets of paper in a stack. The new stardrive allows a ship to duck *below* our sheet, travel in an inter-sheet void at great velocity and then duck back into our sheet at its destination."

"You said *velocity*," I say. "Velocity is a vector – it has both speed and direction. So, the ship needs to know where it wants to be when it ducks out."

"Yes. This will require precise calculations to account for the destination star's motion relative to the ship's starting point. Fortunately, the stars in this arm of the galaxy tend not to move very far relative to one another, even in a millennium."

"What happens if the ship has no velocity when it ducks?"

"Nothing. It will not go anywhere. With this drive, it will be possible to reach any point in this arm of the galaxy in a century or less," Uncle Maddox says. "The only disadvantage is it cannot be used within about 100,000 astronomical units of a star. The ship must be approximately that far from a star's gravity well. We still need anti-gravity engines for takeoff and landing, and to maneuver away from the star. The ship must still accelerate toward the speed of light in order to reach its destination, but that adds only a few years at each end of the voyage."

"We are keeping secret not only how this works but also that it exists. At least, until after the first colony ship reaches its destination in only a few years and reports," Uncle Grigor says.

I ask if we could use this to explore neighboring universes. Uncle Maddox laughs and says he asked the same question and spent the next two days with a headache trying to understand Uncle Grigor's explanation of why it is not possible.

The spring sun is bright on the plateau of the Namhae spaceport. Most of the plateau is glassy – not from ancient volcanic action, but from the flames of hydrocarbon-fueled ships of millennia ago. Martyn and I squint only briefly when we step from our shuttles. The epicanthic folds of our eyes, evolved when World was a place of ice, snow, and glare, protect us. The bronze skin of the Res Publica workmen, who seldom wear more than a loincloth, shrugs off the sun but the pale skin of the thralls would have burned except for the clothing that envelopes them.

Martyn and I walk to the *Breuddwydio Tylluan*, the "Dream of Tylluan." The starship carries two caravels for exploration and a score of fighters for defense. What very few people know is the ship also holds a hundred colonists in cold-sleep. "It is too small a gene pool or a talent pool for a permanent colony," I explain to Martyn. "But Father promises to send one of the larger colony ships when this one finds a suitable planet."

"I know," Martyn says. A breath that might have been a sigh escapes his lips. "That is where I want to be. On a ship exploring the stars, finding a planet on which to plant a colony, being a part of a colony."

"I, too. Yet we stay here while cousins, aunts, uncles, and someday brothers and sisters, go to the stars. Come on, at least we can see it before it leaves."

"The fighters are packed tightly together," Martyn observes. "Will that slow their response?"

"See the mechanism from which they hang? It's a rotary thing, like an ancient powder pistol. It will launch a fighter each second when needed."

"This, I understand," Martyn says. We have reached the largest chamber in the ship where blue-green algae in a brightly lit maze of transparent tubes eat, excrete tailored molecules including

134

oxygen, grow, and provide raw materials for food. "But what happens when the crew goes into cold-sleep?"

"Automatic systems will slow and stop the algae. It will form cysts to survive until conditions are right for growth. When warmth and light are returned, the algae will break from the cysts and grow again."

"The cold-sleep canisters ... they're in rotary racks, too," Martyn observes. "But not for speed."

"No, only for convenience. Look, each one has a compartment for personal things."

Martyn spreads his fingers and puts them against a compartment to get an estimate of size. "Not much room to store everything needed for a lifetime on a new planet."

We look at the artificial wombs in which cattle, horses, and other important animals will be nurtured from frozen eggs and seeds of their species. "We cannot create a biosphere as diverse as World's. We will plant the colony only on a planet seeded by the Adversary and forgotten. They are doing much of our work for us."

Martyn sees my blush. "Something troubles you."

"Martyn, we believe the Adversary has seeded and then forgotten many planets. It is those planets we hope to colonize. Your father is aware of this. So is your colony leader. They accept the risk that the Adversary might return. It is something you must never speak of."

Martyn sees my fear, but quells it. "Telor, this is a secret of both my house and yours. I will keep it secret."

After our walk-through, Martyn and I sit in the command chairs of my shuttle. We have dismissed our guards, and are alone.

"She's a lot bigger than an older corvette, but smaller than a regular colony ship." Martyn tries to keep his voice emotionless.

I am not fooled. "You are wondering why. You are wondering if my father will keep his bargain."

Martyn blushes, his features become pale.

"It's okay," I say. "There are several reasons for the size. First are the colonists and the cargo needed to get them started on a new world. Second, are the caravels. After the *Gorlassar* was destroyed, and her caravel left stranded without FTL drive, Father swore that would never happen again. The two caravels on the *Breuddwydio Tylluan* have an FTL drive and power supply."

Martyn nods his understanding. House Bleddyn is building not one, but three nuclear fission engines on Namhae. He knows we did not inform other houses or Council. I cannot tell Martyn the other secret. Uncle Maddox's people worked without pause to remove the second-generation stardrive engines and replace them with the third-generation, inter-sheet drive. The ship should reach its destination at the far edge of our arm of the galaxy in only seventy years.

Chapter 10: Failed Attack

"You have news." Father says.

"An agent has penetrated House Mynydd." I name a third cousin. "I overwrote Aderyn's origin and training in the mercenary guild's database and sent her to an auction. House Mynydd bought her contract as a probationer. She—"

"A single mistake, and her life is forfeit," Father interrupts.

"She knows, Father. So do I, and I agonize—"

"I assume her eggs have been preserved and she knows it?"

"Yes, Father. Before she left, she quoted Geraint, 'Do not look back when the only path is forward.' She went with open eyes. It will be some time before we learn anything from her."

"And the cabal?" Bleddyn asks.

"We have identified those we believe to be members. All except Mynydd are publically sworn to House Tarren – Greater Houses Maelon, Cythrual, Helygen, Pugh; lesser houses Fychan, and Reese. There is evidence House Ellis, sworn to Tarren, may be – 'dragging their feet' were the words I heard."

~~~~~

Less than a month passes since Aderyn was emplaced, but the agent at House Mynydd has not reported. She is still alive and not under suspicion. Now, something more important demands my attention.

News a Lesser House will launch a starship from House Bleddyn's spaceport spreads throughout the Res Publica. Several of our allies and two non-aligned houses have approached us about joint ventures. The visitors to the spaceport on Namhae see not only the Tylluan starship, but also the scores of people building additions to the shipyards.

"Gens Hynafol, be welcome," Father says, and executes the bow of equals. I stand behind Father with my siblings. Llywelyn chafes at the formality and need to be polite to those he considers lesser than him.

"Gens Bleddyn, thank you for your welcome." Hynafol briefly shields his eyes from the sun and looks around the spaceport. "Very impressive – both the starship and the new facilities. Have you thought about my last message?"

"I have. We will discuss the details soon." Father forces a smile and a chuckle. "Not today, though. As you can see..." he sweeps his arms in a gesture encompassing the spaceport and the line of shuttles waiting to land, "...there will be little time."

Father continues to greet guests, invite them to take refreshment under one of the marquees, ensure their armed guards are escorted by his own soldiers, and introduce their children to be entertained by his own.

The invited guests are present when, less than an hour before the scheduled launch, Gens Tarren's shuttle arrives.

Our agents have reported Gens Tarren is pale with anger that Bleddyn is launching a starship for a Lesser House, especially one whose territory borders Tarren's. Father is not surprised when Lieutenant Terrwyn relays the message that Gens Tarren is inbound. "He brazenly announced his intentions. You will allow him to land?" the Lieutenant asks.

Father almost smiles. "A very impressive honor guard should meet him. Ceremonial swords, braid and brass – and your usual weapons." *A heavily armed honor guard will confirm that I do not trust him, although he and everyone else knows that.*

Lieutenant Terrwyn salutes, turns, flips opens his communicator and gives orders as he trots away.

His mind is blocked, Father thinks as the man leaves his shuttle. *Like Llywelyn's.* His voice carries none of these thoughts, and is low, audible only to Tarren. "I welcome you in the name of the Res Publica."

"Gens Bleddyn!" Tarren cries, loudly and heartily. "Thank you for your welcome." He continues more softly. "I have won this episode. I won't dignify it by calling it a battle."

Moments later, a brief summer shower sends people scurrying to the shelter of the refreshment marquees. Father and I escort Gens Tarren.

~~~~~

The rain stops. Visitors empty the tents to stand on the tarmac. Loud speakers announce the imminent launch of the ship.

Although the new ship's propulsion is silent and invisible, the force of the antigravity raises blinding clouds of mist from the wet tarmac. It is then the attack comes. The first signal is a massive explosion that destroys Gens Tarren's shuttle and several others parked nearby. In the confusion, Tarren's guards attack their escorts.

Gens Tarren reaches for his dagger and turns toward Father, but I am faster. I step toward Tarren and rest the point of my dagger on the cloth of his uniform above his navel. "Oops!" I say. "Looks like both of us had the same idea. Do not draw your dagger. No one sees. They are all enraptured by the explosion. That is your plan, isn't it?"

Tarren blanches as blood rushes to his face. He snarls. And draws his grace knife. I anticipate this, and seize Tarren's wrist. "Naughty, naughty." Tarren's face pales even more at this childish chiding. I take the grace knife and sheathe it at Tarren's waist. "Keep this close. Your second will need it some day. Soon, I think."

139

Tarren is both embarrassed and afraid. *Bleddyn is a demon who can look into others' minds. Is this boy, also a demon? Can he foretell the future?*

Within minutes of the initial chaos, the Mountain Company, held in reserve, fast-ropes from shuttles hovering close overhead. At my signal, one element surrounds Gens Bleddyn and Tarren, guarding but not obviously threatening.

Father, fully aware of what transpired, turns to Tarren. "It seems your shuttle malfunctioned and exploded. I'm sure you will compensate those whose shuttles were damaged. It's a shame we missed the launch."

Tarren snarls. "If it had not been for the rain shower, we would have won. To Ahnwyn with you, Bleddyn and your spawn. Another shuttle is on the way. I trust you will allow it to land." Without waiting for an answer, he stalks from the tent and onto the tarmac.

"That went well, Father," I say. My voice reflects my smile. "The *Breuddwydio Tylluan* reports it is in orbit around World completing final checks before departure."

Father stares at me. He frowns. "Telor, I dare not laugh now. There is chaos to control and damage to repair. Remind me of this after we are home. I do need to laugh."

You do, indeed, I think, but keep it to myself.

~~~~~

Gens Bleddyn, confident his family on Namhae will continue to expand the shipyards and spaceport, returns to Fortress. He stands behind his console in the rear of the house War Room as he often does, monitoring activities and intelligence reports on the screens. I am on the floor of the War Room, moving from position to position, looking for patterns.

The sound of a bell in one corner of the War Room draws everyone's attention. A teletype chatters and then falls silent. The

140

machine is a fifty-millennia-old relic from a time when Houses Bleddyn and Ellis were aligned. The watch officer sees Father's nod and tears a page of yellow paper from the ancient machine. He hands me the paper and I scan the message.

"The message is from House Ellis. Ellis is a mouthpiece for House Tarren. The true source of this message is Tarren."

Father reads the message, and then nods. "The message is long and contains many assertions, some true, some not. What is the real message from House Tarren? And why is Ellis the messenger?"

His words prompt me to read the message more closely. I parse phrases, shuffle them into mental compartments and watch as they cancel or reinforce one another. At last, only two thoughts are left. I look up from the yellow foolscap. "Gens Tarren is angry Tylluan received their FTL communication console earlier than House Tarren. Ellis is clear he is speaking for Tarren, and not for himself."

I hand the message to Father. "Tarren knew this would happen, of course. He would have sussed that Tylluan's ships and caravels carry FTL systems. He does not have ships ready to launch, so he doesn't yet need a console. He's turning this into the Academy game of pole pull-down – *Bo-taoshi* – with House Ellis as the token monkey, exposed to the most injury."

"You see the heart of the matter," Father says. "How do we respond?"

"Father, not only is the monkey exposed to the most injury but also to the most honor."

"Then send an acknowledgement to Gens Ellis. Make it clear we thank him for acting as intermediary and we don't blame the messenger. Put that in diplomatic language. What about Tarren?"

"It is not our fault House Tarren is slow to reveal their ships' schedules. I suggest we make a public ceremony of the first delivery to House Tarren, perhaps when their ship launches in two months. We should praise his accomplishments and wish the expedition well."

"Why?" I sense puzzlement from my father.

"To confuse your enemies, praise them in public," I say.

Father lowers his brows. "That's not from either Karmet or Geraint." He cites the two most important influences on the Res Publica civilization.

"No Father, it's from me."

~~~~~

Once each month Father dons a black robe over his uniform and sits in judgment at the *Banque d' Bleddyn*. The first call this day is unsettling both to the Gens and to those present, whether physically or via televisor.

Father's sister Aveta, his Privy Secretary, serves as Clerk of Court. She announces, "Telor of Bleddyn brings charges against Medrus, eldest son and heir apparent of Gens Mynydd."

She does not say Medrus was brought unwillingly, kidnapped last night and flown, hooded and bound, to Fortress.

Father sets the rules for the court. "We know people's first impressions are the most lasting. We know once an opinion is formed, it is surrounded in the mind by walls that prevent opposing opinions from entering but which allow supporting opinions to penetrate. Some houses take advantage of this by detailing the accusation before the defense. House Bleddyn does not. The first to speak will be Medrus of Mynydd."

The young man stands. He knows why he is here – I told him the charges, but did not give him any evidence. I gave him an opportunity to clean himself and put on a soldier's jumpsuit. He is surprised to see the crest of his house on the breast pocket and the flashes of his rank on his shoulders. *They honor me, even though they accuse me,* he thinks. His thoughts solidify.

142

"Your Grace, the televisor signal ... is it being sent to my house?"

"It is, although we do not know if anyone watches," Father replies.

"I hope my father watches," the young man says. "For this day I forfeit my life for honor. My house, although sworn to Bleddyn, sent soldiers against House Dolffin, an ally of House Bleddyn. I led some of these forays. I planned others. My father chafes under House Bleddyn's yoke, and wants more for his house, his children, and..." He pauses. "... and for himself. That is all I will say." He sits.

Father looks to me to speak for House Bleddyn. I stand. "Your Grace, Medrus of House Mynydd states our case. Under the circumstances, we recommend clemency for the witness."

I look at the televisor camera. I know my image and words are being carried to the entire Res Publica. "We recommend execution of the accused."

Even though forewarned by my declaration, Gens Mynydd does not escape. Two days later, he is brought to the courtroom. Cousin Aderyn, who I had positioned as a spy in House Mynydd, was instrumental in the operation.

In the courtroom, Gens Bleddyn addresses Gens Mynydd. "You have seen and heard the testimony."

Gens Mynydd responds. "Trying and failing is failure. Not trying because you are afraid is both failure and disgrace. I elect the former."

"You quote Karmet." Father frowns. "His aphorisms are not necessarily truths, and I think you misinterpret him. You have broken your oath of fealty and violated the rules of vendetta. By my right of High Justice I sentence you to death. Your son, with our support, will become Gens Mynydd. He will take a new name, Anrhydeus, from the ancient language meaning 'honorable.' He agrees House Mynydd will remain neutral from this day forth."

143

Father pauses. "At least, for the present. Given the long history of the Res Publica, it would be foolhardy to expect an eternal oath."

Anrhydeus returns his father's ashes to his home. He declines Father's offer to send soldiers to support his claim to the title of Gens. "I will succeed or fail on my own, but I am not afraid to try."

Chapter 11: House Itan

Summer passes uneventfully; the harvest is gathered and thralls prepare for the annual Harvest Festival. Father sits in the War Room while I present details of current operations and projections of long-range plans. "The expansion of the shipyards on Namhae continues. In less than a year, we will be able to launch one colony ship accompanied by a corvette holding two caravels and twelve fighters every year."

Then, I delve into the details of current events. "Anrhydeus succeeded in becoming Gens Mynydd. At the next Council meeting he will be recognized and will pledge the house as unaligned.

"House Itan is in war mode because one of their children is missing. This morning, a boy named Niniwed was playing in a fountain with other children when his mother realized he was no longer there. She summoned soldiers, but they found nothing. Rumors are that agents of House Maelon kidnapped the child."

"*Innocent*. The child's name in the ancient language is *Innocent*," Father muses. "Maelon is a blot on the Res Publica. Take command of the War Room. Assemble all possible information on this kidnapping. Your first mission is to find the child and ensure his safety."

I bow. "Yes, Father."

Father watches me give orders, delegating tasks to the most appropriate station in the War Room. When I finish, I turn to my father. I say nothing, but Father understands the question in my mind.

"This is the first and best opportunity we have had," Father says. "Maelon has been suspected of child slave trafficking for decades, but we have never found a direct link."

Father leaves the War Room. His thoughts, while bleak with the knowledge of the event, look for opportunity with honor. *House Itan was open in their desire to have a place on our colony ships, even after they were told their colonists must swear fealty to House Bleddyn. I need more of the Greater Houses to side with me in Council. Gens Itan leads a lesser house, unaligned although known to be leaning toward House Maelon. Can I sway Itan? Is this the time for me to take on House Maelon?*

Two days pass before I call Father to the War Room. "Father, we have found the child. I ... I had to buy him. Even though it was a rescue, I felt incredibly dirty after the experience. He was in a slave market at Ocsiwn. I took him to the infirmary, where medicos examined him. He is healthy and uninjured. A vid link to House Item is set up on your console."

I hear my father's approval in his words to Gens Itan. "My son, Telor, found your missing child in Ocsiwn. The boy is at Fortress Bleddyn in good health and unharmed. Do you wish to see him before we fly him to Fortress Itan?"

Gens Itan finds it hard to speak. "How? ... How did he get there? How did you find him? By Geraint ... No. I mean, I don't need to see him. May I send a shuttle? How can I thank you?"

"If you will agree, Gens Itan, I will bring the child and his rescuer. You may thank him in person. We will arrive at sunset."

Father and I step from the shuttle to face Gens Itan and two soldiers. The parties exchange bows, although my bow does not meet the demands of protocol because of the child in my arms.

"Gens Bleddyn, may I present Niniwed's parents. They are Captain Anja and her husband, Captain Joyhan."

146

I give the sleepy child to Captain Anja. "I think Niniwed would like to be held by his mother."

"Perhaps after the child is put to bed, we could talk more," Father suggests. Gens Itan leads us to a conference room.

Minutes later, Captain Anja tiptoes from an adjoining room and softly closes the door. "He is asleep, exhausted. A nurse is with him."

Captain Joyhan holds a chair for his wife who sits beside me at the table with the two Gens and a young man introduced as Itan's chancellor. At Gens Itan's urging, I explain how we located the child. "We suspected the slave market at Ocsiwn. We focused resources there. Our agents located your child at a slave market dedicated to children…" I cannot complete the sentence.

Father fills the void. "The town, while considered independent, lives under the thumb – and protection – of House Maelon. We have linked this auction and the kidnappers to House Maelon."

"Geraint told us slavery destroys both the slave and the master," Gens Itan says.

"And the Compact outlaws slavery," Itan's Chancellor adds.

"Something must be done," Captain Anja says.

"The Council?" Gens Itan looks at Father.

"Would do nothing," Father replies. "Maelon is strong, as is his master, Tarren. They control enough votes to stall any action we might propose.

"This is not often spoken, but every house, including mine, has an interest in the free city of Ocsiwn. We have allowed it to exist for millennia as a place for clandestine meetings, secret trade between enemies, and a place to recruit assassins.

"Gens Itan, you look shocked, but you know it is true. Consider the contracts made there for your minerals. Consider the sales there of my medicines derived from seaweed. We both sell to houses with which we are not aligned and with those we consider enemies. We justify it by saying our customers need the goods, but the real reason is profit. We now can serve the greater good."

The discussion continues well into the night before a wide-ranging agreement is reached. The slave markets of Ocsiwn will be destroyed. It will be a joint effort with House Itan. House Bleddyn will recruit soldiers from among allied houses. They will mount simultaneous attacks on Ocsiwn and a symbolic attack on the property of House Maelon.

"We will destroy the slave markets and execute anyone tied to them. Even though the attack on Maelon will be covert, the timing of the attacks will signal the attack on Maelon is linked to the slave trade in Ocsiwn," I say.

"And Gens Tarren?" Itan says.

"I will deal with Tarren," Father says.

The final point of the agreement is that House Itan will align with House Bleddyn and we will provide training and life extension, and places on our next colony ship for a contingent of Itan's people.

Gens Itan urges Father and me to stay overnight at Fortress Itan, but we decline. "We need to plan."

House Alignments c. 200,373 C.E.

Bleddyn Faction	Tarren Faction	Unaligned
Bleddyn	Tarren	Emrys
Dolffin Itan Tylluan	Reese Ellis	
	Maelon	Hywel
Marredudd	Fychan	
		Lagon
Hynafol	Cythrual	
		Astin Eryr Griffin Mynydd
Caerwyn	Helygen	
Merrick	Pugh	
Dwyer		

It is not yet day-break when our shuttle lands at Fortress. Father summons his Privy Council and Llywelyn.

Llywelyn is already awake, roused by one of his companions when the shuttle appeared on house radar. *Father and Telor visited Gens Itan after Telor brought a mysterious passenger*

148

from Ocsiwn. Who was the passenger? Assassin? Spy? Why else would Telor go to Ocsiwn, and why would Father then visit Itan? Again, they plot without me – and perhaps against me.

~~~~~

The Privy Council assembles. Most are somewhat bleary-eyed, but all rise when Father enters the room. They become alert when I describe my mission to Ocsiwn and the meeting at Fortress Itan.

Father begins with a proverb. "The smell of a cesspit cannot spread against the wind, but the odor of dishonor taints the air on every side." He then explains his determination to strike Maelon and the slave market. Even his announcement that Itan swore alignment with House Bleddyn does not calm the queasy stomachs and racing thoughts of the Privy Council.

"Llywelyn, you will use the same skills you used to nip at Fychan to prepare a clandestine strike on Maelon – property, not people and not Fortress Maelon. You will lead the strike. Your strike must be precisely on time and completed quickly."

"Yes, Father. Who will lead the raid on the slave market?"

It is not your concern, Father thinks before answering. "Lieutenant Terrwyn."

Llywelyn hides his disappointment and anger. *I will be tilting at windmills or blowing up a dam while Terrwyn takes troops into combat. Father's excuse for this? The kidnapping of some child? Does the child exist, or is he a figment of Father's imagination – or of Telor's?*

Father turns to the Privy Council. "I am determined to do this, but please assess the risks of the plan. Assess the willingness of our allies to take part. Assess the likely reaction of the houses that do not take part. Plan our political and military strategy to deal with any problems. The attacks will take place in fifteen days.

"And Gens Tarren?" an uncle asks.

"I will deal with Tarren," Father says.

~~~~~

Twelve days later, both Llywelyn and Lieutenant Terrwyn report readiness. Llywelyn's soldiers will destroy a crucial road bridge over a mountain gorge. They will attack from floaters armed with high-explosive rocket grenades. An engineer studies the bridge and provides aim-points. Llywelyn's report to his Father and the Privy Council is terse.

Lieutenant Terrwyn's task is more complex; his report, longer. "Infiltration elements from all four allied Great Houses and allied Lesser Houses including House Itan have joined us. Most have arrived in Ocsiwn. Some are disguised as wealthy citizens who are accompanied by armed guards. Others appear to be out-of-work mercenaries seeking employment – but not eagerly or actively. Others blend in with the detritus of humanity on the streets. By tomorrow, we will have two hundred seventy soldiers in the town, itself, and another eighteen in fighters loaded in the rotary launchers of a corvette we borrowed from the Namhae spaceport."

"Fighters? Ocsiwn is a crowded city. No matter how accurate their aim, there will be collateral damage." A cousin, a lieutenant in the Home Guard, says.

"Our soldiers on the ground will guide the fighters' targeting. They have planted transponders and will activate them at the moment of the attack. They will supplement transponders with laser target designators," Terrwyn says.

"Other than the slaves, there are no innocents in Ocsiwn," Father says. "Rescue and removal of the slaves will be the first order of battle."

"You will destroy the city?" an aunt asks.

150

"After the initial attack, our ground forces will withdraw," I reply. "Our forces will give any surviving residents opportunity to flee before the corvette turns its weapons on the city."

"And Gens Tarren?" an uncle asks.

Father answers the question. "Gens Tarren agrees to meet with me at Council House. We will block communication from Ocsiwn and Maelon from the moment the attack begins until the city is destroyed. Lieutenant Terrwyn assures me this will require only four hours. When communication is restored, Tarren will learn the attack was conducted by an army from many houses, and will do nothing except perhaps complain." His lips tighten in a slight smile. "Tarren is very predictable."

~~~~~

Lieutenant Terrwyn's soldiers raid the slave pens long before daylight. By mid-morning, they confirm all slaves have been removed to safety. Terrwyn signals Llywelyn and the corvette. Exactly ten minutes later, Llywelyn's floaters fire on the bridge. The bridge falls instantly, to become rubble at the bottom of the gorge. The primary land route to Ocsiwn is cut and Llywelyn's floaters return to their shuttles.

I have accomplished my mission – at Terrwyn's command. Floaters and rocket grenades. He commands a force of fighters with torpedoes a hundred times more powerful than my grenades.

The instant Llywelyn's soldiers fire their rocket grenades, fighters from the corvette pop up from behind a mountain ridge. Terrwyn's troops activate transponders and light up targets with lasers. Torpedoes strike with precision. The aerial bombardment lasts only a few minutes and reduces half the town to rubble. Allied ground forces attack individuals who escape the initial strikes. Loud speakers, mounted on armored vehicles, urge people to flee the city where more soldiers meet them. After three and a half hours, the corvette rises over the city and fires masers on what remains. Four hours after the attack began, there is nothing left of the City of Ocsiwn but glassy rock and a great deal of smoke.

At Council House, Gens Bleddyn watches Tarren as reports reach him. Tarren's face darkens with shock, then glows when anger pushes blood to his cheeks. He snarls at Bleddyn. "You … you were behind this."

Bleddyn's lips barely move. "I have won this episode. I won't dignify it by calling it a battle.

"It was too easy," he adds.

~~~~~

Father stands, as he often does, at the rear of the War Room, watching reports flash on the status screens. Winter Stormtime rages over the continent. House Bleddyn's people and those of our allies are safe, so far. The operations building on Namhae loses a roof to the wind, but the hangers and dry docks and six ships under construction are secure. Dolffin reports one sailing ship, late in arriving to port, sheltered in a cove. The crew is safe on shore, but the ship will probably be lost. A red icon calls Father's attention to the central screen. *Communication intercept – Maelon to Tarren.*

<<Gens Tarren. It is imperative we mount a counterstrike against Bleddyn.>>

Father steps toward the Senior Controller. "Captain, turn the closest satellite to this. I must hear Tarren's response."

The answer comes quickly.

<<Maelon, this is not the time to attack Bleddyn. He stands on a success that unites his supporters. Your failure is not something on which House Tarren wishes to stand.>>

152

"A real slur, Commander," Lieutenant Terrwyn says. "Gens Tarren addressing Gens Maelon without his title. Accusation of failure."

"Can we be sure these messages are legitimate and not counter-espionage?" Father asks.

"Yes, Commander." The speaker is a Lieutenant in the house intelligence corps. "We have made sure every house learned of the slave market and trafficking in children. Maelon is the only house which endorsed slavery. Niniwed's parents and Gens Itan allowed the child's image and story to be broadcast. At the moment, we believe Maelon stands alone."

Llywelyn has been watching and listening. He speaks for his father's ears, only. "If Maelon is alone, would he not be interested in an offer of alliance from us?"

"Not now, Son, and not in my lifetime. I will not ally with evil."

Not in his lifetime, Llywelyn thinks. *Father offended two powerful houses. Fychan has long been aligned with Maelon, but seeks to take Maelon's place as a Greater House. Will they see this as their opportunity? How can I use this to my advantage?*

Chapter 12: Conspiracy, Challenge, Celebration

His father's words run through Llywelyn's mind. He parses them, trying to wring from them every possible meaning. At the end, only a few thoughts remain.

The boy who Father installed as Gens Mynydd summoned home the only member of my companions from his house. Father cut off a key line of communication with others whose ambition is greater than their place in their houses. One slip and I am discovered. Who among my companions is the most ambitious?

—Llywelyn Bleddyn, Private Journal

It is easy for Llywelyn to arrange for Slade, member of House Maelon of the 7th Rank and one of Llywelyn's companions, to be his sparring partner. They are evenly matched. Slade scores only one point fewer than Llywelyn. After three matches, Llywelyn dismisses the rest of his companions. "One more match," he challenges Slade. "The two of us. Alone."

Slade watches the others of Llywelyn's companions, the trainers, and the medicos, leave the dojo. He raises his saber, and addresses Llywelyn in the old language. "*En garde.*"

Llywelyn returns the salute, and the round begins. After several minutes it becomes clear they will not settle today who is the better swordsman.

"Pax!" Slade calls. "I have not your stamina—"

"But you have skill," Llywelyn replies and agrees, "Pax."

The two remove their masks and wipe sweat from their faces.

Slade is startled when Llywelyn changes the subject. "Gens Mynydd recalled Afon – with my father's blessing and connivance.

Two years ago, my father hired Dirgel and adopted him into House Bleddyn. Less than a year ago, he executed Brawin. He is eliminating my companions one at a time."

"Did not Afon's house plot against yours? Did not Brawin try to assassinate him?" Slade says.

"Gens Mynydd was the plotter, but not the only plotter. The cabal includes all houses sworn to Tarren. Even yours. Someday, the cabal will rise up against us. House Bleddyn has the power to destroy them when this happens, but it will be a pyrrhic victory. The cabal will destroy us unless we are better prepared."

"I don't understand," Slade says.

"I think you do," Llywelyn replies. "Your house, Maelon, is second only to Tarren in that axis of power. Until my bastard brother, Telor discovered them, it included Mynydd. Think as Gens Tarren does. At some point, he will lead his allies to attack this house. He will either destroy us or render us so weak we would become a Lesser House. I would rule a strong House Bleddyn."

"There is a fine line between honor and betrayal," Slade says. "Why do you tell me these things?"

"Think!" Llywelyn yells, and then lowers his voice, even though the two are alone in the dojo. "Think. Your house is under the thumb of Tarren. You are of the seventh rank in your own house. The odds of you rising under normal circumstances are slim. Your chances of advancement are much greater as my ally. You, too, walk a fine line between honor and betrayal. We are not so different."

Llywelyn watches Slade's face as he considers this statement. Finally, Slade speaks. "I understand. What do you want me to do?" Llywelyn sees in those words Slade's declaration of loyalty.

"Arrange a secret meeting with your Gens." Llywelyn puts his saber in a rack, and takes Slade's arm. The two walk down the stone passageway linking the dojo and Llywelyn's quarters. "You

156

will set the time and place, and ensure no one except you, your Gens, and me know of it."

I have taken a step on a path that will lead me to glory or doom. I have offered Slade trust, but also have bound him to me in conspiracy by demanding he take responsibility for this meeting. He accepts the task willingly. My assessment of him is correct.

—Llywelyn Bleddyn, Private Journal

≈≈≈≈≈

Half a month later, Llywelyn's companions gather in the mountains above the Pass of Perdition. They plan, with forces of two lesser houses, to repeat one of the ancient battles for the pass, using tag lasers. Llywelyn's companions are there, but Llywelyn is not. Nor is Slade of Maelon. They leave by shuttle to Fortress Maelon the moment the battle begins.

Gens Maelon's greeting to Llywelyn is barely sufficient for a Gens to the heir of a Greater House. Llywelyn's bow is just as perfunctory. *Gens Maelon seeks to intimidate. Since I know his motive, I can overcome it.*

"I am surprised," Maelon says. "Your father did not message me that you would visit."

"My father knows I am here only to discuss with your Lieutenant the terms of our war game. My father does not concern himself with my training of my troops."

Gens Maelon cuts through the fog of Llywelyn's words. "You sought to speak with me. That belies what you say."

Time for some butter. "No, Your Grace. What I said about my father's interest – and knowledge of this meeting – is true. However, my interest is wider than his."

Maelon gestures, and all except Llywelyn leave the room. "You may speak freely."

Llywelyn explains his concern he would become Gens of a House that was a vassal of House Tarren. "Tarren would offer that after a revolution, an attack by his axis of power. I might someday rule House Bleddyn, but only under Tarren's thumb."

Llywelyn pauses before he adds, "I would rather the revolution be on my terms, not his."

"You speak frankly," Gens Maelon says.

"I have only scratched the surface of frankness," Llywelyn says. "Your house is powerful, yet you have been shunned by former allies. There is a saying Father is fond of repeating, 'A rising tide lifts all boats.' I believe you and I can create such a tide, which will lift not only our houses but many others who will follow us."

"You know the reason for our isolation," Maelon says.

"Yes. You were exposed. Both my father and Gens Tarren made you the scapegoat for all that occurred at Ocsiwn," Llywelyn says. He and Maelon share a long silence. Maelon understands what Llywelyn means. Llywelyn does not say Maelon did wrong, only that he was caught.

"I believe," Llywelyn continues, "you chafe at the yoke of Tarren, as I would. I believe you would rather an equal partnership." *With me.* Llywelyn does not complete that thought, but Gens Maelon knows what he means.

"You must return to your war game before you are missed, but visit again, soon. We have much to discuss." Maelon's words are sufficient to assure Llywelyn agreement will be reached. The blood seal will come later, but Llywelyn does not doubt it will come.

Llywelyn returns to the war game in time to order floaters into the defenders flank and win the battle of the Pass of Perdition. *It is an omen,* Llywelyn thinks. *An omen of my future successes.*

~~~~~

Father is preoccupied when I enter his den and kneel. After a moment, he recognizes me.

158

"Telor, rise. You said you had an important message."

"Yes, Father. House Tarren will launch three ships from the House Reese spaceport in one month. Two ships are large fighters. They call them corvettes, but they are larger than ours. They are equipped only for destruction. The third ship is equipped for exploration, but they do not use caravels, but send shuttles to examine planets with potential. They have requested three FTL comms systems for the ships, linked with one another through their house War Room.

"They blame us for the delay in launching their ships."

"No one is fooled by that," Father says. "We will follow your earlier plan, making this launch a cause for celebration. Can you arrange a surprise for Tarren's launch? Not an attack, but something impressive?"

My smile conveys my understanding. "Yes, Father."

~~~~~

A late winter sun and a cloudless sky greet Tarren's allies and non-aligned houses, all professing congratulations. The visitors all think what none will say. *It's too bad Tarren doesn't have his own spaceport, but must build and launch from the island of an ally – and a Lesser House, at that.* They also see Gens Bleddyn's shuttle. The house symbol of a wolf couped against a full moon is unmistakable. Father, surrounded by his Praetorian Guard, stands near Gens Tarren. The only weapons visible are ceremonial swords, daggers, and grace knives, but no one doubts their uniforms conceal other, more deadly weapons.

The crews of the three ships stand in ranks and salute Gens Tarren. After a brief speech, Tarren dismisses them. As they return to their ships, but before they can board, Father moves to stand beside Tarren at the podium. The microphone picks up his words. "House Bleddyn wishes to honor House Tarren for this accomplishment." He turns to face east. The eyes of the crowd follow. A series of black dots moves closer. In only seconds, the dots become fighters – dozens of them. Two caravels and a colony ship that dwarfs the largest of Tarren's ships follow them. When the fighters reach the island, they release smoke, which trails behind them in the black and gray colors of House Tarren.

Father turns and offers his hand. Quietly, he says to Tarren, "I have won this episode. I won't dignify it by calling it a battle."

~~~~~

Father's show of power at the launch of Tarren's ships, Helygen's vote in Council helping defeat Tarren's proposal, last winter's coordinated attack on Maelon and Ocsiwn, and Father's execution of Gens Mynydd have weakened the bonds of the cabal. My spies report the houses are no longer planning coordinated attacks on the House of Wolf or our allies. We remain vigilant, but I can spend more time with Garreth and Rodric. The two boys are three years apart, but have become fast friends.

—Telor Bleddyn, Journal

~~~~~

Volcanoes, now dormant, uplifted the mountains of the Arista Range along the equator. *Dormant* is what we think until the western-most mountain erupts in a spectacular and devastating explosion. Nearly a hundred members of House Griffin are killed in the first few hours. The sulfur dioxide and ash blown into the stratosphere will linger for years, cooling World. Our blood might rejoice in the cooling, but our crops, including seaweed and marine creatures, will not.

The explosion is sensed by one of our reconnaissance satellites, and information is sent to the War Room. Although it is past the middle of the night, Father and I are summoned. Father arrives before I do. His uniform is immaculate. Mine is rumpled, but Father does not call attention to that.

160

He challenges me. "What should be our immediate response? What should be our long-term response?"

"Immediate response. Assemble relief teams and fly to Griffin. Continue relief efforts depending on what the first responders find. Long-term response. Seed clouds over the Equatorial Continent with silver iodide to wash the nitrogen oxide and particulate matter from the air. The volcanic material will enrich the soil. And, this will ensure we do not face another 'decade without a summer' such as happened after the volcano on Chindo Island exploded five millennia ago."

Father is happy with my grasp of history and quick response. "It is the right thing to do," I say, and bask in his approval.

~~~~~

We have much to celebrate this year at Harvest Time. Lesser House Griffin, although initially devastated by the volcano, recovered, and is grateful to our house for its help. Griffin is unaligned, but Father believes we can count upon them for support. The cloud seeding projects were successful and weather across World is returning to normal. A surrogate is pregnant with my Brother-minus-twenty-three, and she and the fetus are healthy.

At the Harvest Banquet, Father recites ancient words. "Like a tree, encompassing the earth, the air, and the sky, the house represents the past, the present, and the future. The house is the embodiment of the continuation of the Res Publica." He raises his glass. "I salute the House of Wolf."

Family, guests, and thralls stand. Their response echoes from the vaulted ceiling, "To House Bleddyn."

The moment Father sits, his and my communicators beep. The message from the War Room includes a code meaning an important message requires the Gens' personal and immediate attention.

Uncle Grigor stands at the same time, signaling the message was received on the FTL system.

By the time we reach the room in which Uncle Grigor and his staff intercept FTL messages, the emergency is over. Three ships of House Tarren encountered one of our corvettes outside the cometary cloud of a promising system. Rather than stand off, the Tarren ships attack. There is a reason Father does not give away all we know of starflight. When they saw torpedoes launched from Tarren ships, our ship ducked into inter-sheet space before popping back into our universe and annihilating Tarren's ships. Father reviews the messages, and chuckles. He seldom does that. I wait for his explanation, but he says only we must prepare carefully for the next Council meeting.

~~~~~

The last Council meeting of the year is supposed to be routine and unexciting. The Council has already dealt with requests for help following Fall Stormtime. During the winter, by tradition, every house stands down from the usual vendettas and petty attacks. This year, in an attempt to erase his loss at the first meeting of the year, Gens Tarren accuses House Bleddyn of … actually, no one is quite sure what the accusation is. Tarren asserts one of our ships attacked three of his ships as they approached a star system. Tarren offers several messages from his ships as evidence, and demands reparations.

Father is First Speaker this year, and his position is awkward. He solves the dilemma by handing the gavel to Gens Emrys, seated on his left.

Gens Emrys understands. He stands, raps the gavel, and announces, "Gens Tarren enters a request for reparations from House Bleddyn under the rules of vendetta. Gens Tarren will proceed with his request."

162

The heart of Tarren's charges is our ship "disappeared" and then reappeared to launch torpedoes against the House Tarren ships.

"As far as our ship disappearing and reappearing, I can only suggest faulty sensors on House Tarren's ships – or perhaps an overabundance of ethanol," Father says. "And you know we have shared our torpedo technology to all houses. Further, we can produce copies of messages from our ship reporting that it was attacked, first. Of course, there is no way to authenticate those messages – or the ones Tarren offers."

Father stops short of calling Tarren a liar. Tarren knows he will not get the supermajority he needs. Rather than face that, he withdraws his request, and Emrys returns the gavel to Father.

~~~~~

A ten-day later, Father summons me to his den. Through the huge windows, I see Winter Stormtime raging. Although my blood relishes the cold, the fire Father laid in the hearth calls to something within me. He gestures me to rise and join him in front of the fire.

"Telor, a few days after Stormtime ends, the council will meet. By tradition, Gens Maelon will become First Speaker. Despite his perfidy, despite the evil he created at Ocsiwn, he will be first of the Res Publica to speak in Council and will set the agenda."

Father pauses long enough for me to know he wants me to say something. "Yes, Father. But the rotation of the First Speaker is much more ancient than any current evil. Are we not a people of law, and is not this rotation one of our earliest laws?"

I feel Father's pride when he replies. "You are correct, Son. Therefore, you will sit in the seat of House Bleddyn, in the place of honor to the right of the First Speaker. You will say those words with conviction, and ensure even our allies agree."

163

Fifteen days later, I am seated on the dais with eleven other representatives of the Greater Houses when Gens Maelon enters and walks toward the First Speaker's seat. Rumbles with an undercurrent of anger swell from the benches. Gens Emrys, long unaligned, exclaims his objection. Gens Hynafol and Helygen follow.

Before Maelon can sit, I stand. "House Bleddyn shares your extreme discomfort and understands your objections; however, this Council is ruled by law. The law says Gens Maelon is now First Speaker."

The law also provides a way to remove a First Speaker, but it is unlikely anyone other than me has delved so deeply into history. I remain standing until Gens Maelon takes his seat. I sense his appreciation, and surprise, and think, *Kill your enemies with kindness. At least, it keeps them off balance.*

Chapter 13: Garreth

Winter Stormtime passes. The days which follow are bright and clear but icy cold, and our blood rejoices. Nana brings Garreth to me and I take the boy, now three years old, onto the battlements of Fortress. I point to Academy, fifteen kilometers away, where his older siblings – twins Daffyd and Delwyn and brother Guffudd –

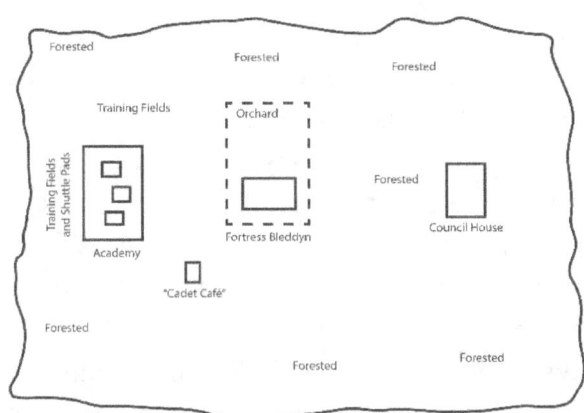

Not to scale. The three elements (Academy, Fortress Bleddyn, and Council house are separated by about 20 km. The mess on which they sit slopes steeply on all sides to forested land broken by farm fields.

are students, and Sister Bethan is an instructor. Council House is too far away to see, even though most of the trees have lost their leaves, and only gymnosperms – those with "naked seeds" – show any green.

I point to the Keep – the tallest and strongest tower in Fortress. "In olden days this is where the house would mount a last defense if Fortress were overrun. Today, the Keep is a museum."

Garreth is eager to learn. He tires climbing the stairs to the top of the Keep, but struggles not to let me know. My brother is growing up. I remember the meaning of his name, brave and modest, and wonder how that will guide his life. He is good at behaving during formal ceremonies. I am glad to see Garreth does not fidget during Alaw's elevation. Had he done so, it would have reflected badly upon him – and me. After the ceremony, I tell him

165

how proud of him I am. A few days later, a surrogate from House Tylluan arrives. She will bear the next child of Father and his wife. Then, she will bear a child of her own egg and Father's seed. Garreth stands with the family during the welcome and acts quite the little soldier during the banquet.

—Telor Bleddyn, Journal

~~~~~

Gens Maelon, First Speaker of the Council, calls a meeting for the second month of the year. Father instructs me to represent House Bleddyn. This meeting is scheduled every year and traditionally attended by young representatives of their houses rather than by the Gens. The significant exception this year is the presence of Gens Tarren. Most of us assume it is because he is afraid what his official heir, Cadfael, might say or do. Gens Tarren is rude and snippy toward the rest of us, until the heir of Gens Maelon, who holds the speakership for his father, silences him. *That took courage*, I think. *Maelon is Tarren's closest ally, but he stood up to him – and he was right to do so.*

The Council's discussions are limited to things relatively unimportant. We discuss regulation of population to prevent overtaxing World's natural resources. We talk about efforts by houses along the seacoast to expand tidal marshes where important fish and shellfish breed. We agree each house with forestlands will increase tree replanting by ten percent to help control soil erosion, and, in a surprise motion by the Heir of Caerwyn, we vote – with Tarren nay-saying and Maelon abstaining – to affirm our resolution to defend World against the Adversary.

~~~~~

Attending Council is not as challenging as the next task Father gives me. He commands me to provide a horse for Garreth. Given Garreth's size, the horse will be more a pony than a horse. I

166

am pleased when Garreth first sees the horse and names it for a woman warrior in one of the stories I read to him. He is much more interested in the horse, itself, than in the house's millennial-old efforts to breed such horses from their smaller ancestors.

The first time Garreth rides Rhiannon, the horse shies at a snake in the path, and scrapes her flank and Garreth's leg against a rock ledge. I must explain to Garreth the difference between his blood and Rhiannon's – and the other beasts of the field. I am not sure he understands, but he accepts my explanation that he is of-the-blood and Rhiannon is not.

~~~~~

I am present to greet my younger siblings and their guests from Academy when they arrive for Spring Stormtime. The day after they arrive, Father sends me to Namhae. He wishes me to learn more about the ships we are building. The weather becomes too treacherous to return to Fortress. However, Uncle Maddox has no trouble finding work for me. He is Father's brother, a senior member of the house, and has responsibility for the house's shipyards and spaceport on Namhae.

Uncle Maddox began life as a sailor. His face is wrinkled and most of his hair is gray. His eyes seem to look through me and the wall behind me as if he were looking toward the horizon for an enemy ship to approach. He is also my favorite uncle, the man who taught all the Bleddyn kids to sail in little two-person boats with a tiller and a single sail. I meet him on the battlements of Fortress Namhae and get one of his strong hugs before he puts me to work.

We build two kinds of ships – wooden sailing ships to ply the oceans, and starships to ply the emptiness of space. Both kinds of ships make up the *Vishnu Nerada*, the fleet of House Bleddyn.

Uncle Maddox takes me to a hanger where a colony ship is under construction. The ship is metal and has antigravity engines rather than sails, but is built using lessons from millennia of sailing ships. The keel is flat, and 350 meters long. Sprouting like flowers from the keel, elements of the ship are assembled – framing struts, strakes, deck beams, bulkheads to separate compartments, and outer plating. Its cross-section is rectangular, 80 by 50 meters. The edges of the rectangle and the bow and stern are rounded although more for aesthetic reasons than for streamlining. The ship will not see atmosphere after it leaves World until it lands on the colony planet. It will then be disassembled for raw materials.

"Talk to the workers, the architects and engineers, the chandlers. Learn all you can while you are here," Uncle Maddox commands, and leaves me standing in the bottom of the cavernous hull, while workers scramble around me.

≈≈≈≈

Stormtime is over and the cadets have left for Academy before I return from Namhae. I fly my shuttle into the hanger, where Garreth waits. When I step from the shuttle he takes my hand and drags me to his dojo. "Come see what Soosong taught me!" he exclaims.

Garreth joins his playmates as their instructor takes them through third and fourth katas of *Jaryeondo*. Then, in pairs, they perform gymnastic routines. Garreth's partner is the tallest boy among his mates. The boy is a scion of Dolffin, fostered to House Bleddyn. I wonder at the disparity in their height, but Garreth is adept. I see his pride in what he learned in so short a time.

Chapter 14: House Eryr

Three days into Spring Stormtime, Gens Bleddyn summons Llywelyn. "There is a break in the weather. Gens Eryr and his son, Sawel, will arrive in minutes. Come with me to the battlements to welcome them. You will entertain Sawel and join his father and me after lunch."

House Eryr has been a nuisance for years, Llywelyn thinks as he follows his father toward the battlements. *Not this son ... he's still a child ... but the house's lieutenants. Father interfered with my war games against Eryr. He doesn't understand the exercises strengthen us, harden us. This may be a chance to score against this house.*

Gens Bleddyn, Llywelyn, and three of the Praetorian Guard stand on the battlements. The sky is overcast. Gray clouds scud with the wind, tokens of Spring Stormtime.

"Your guards carry only ceremonial swords." Llywelyn shouts over the whistle of the wind through the crenels of the battlements. "They will not likely want to blood them. House Eryr is unaligned and an unknown. We are in danger. I should have at least an energy pistol."

At least he knows of Eryr's official status. But he cannot see further, Bleddyn thinks. "I have worked for decades to link Eryr more closely to our house. Gens Eryr and I will seal the pact, today. Sawel knows this. Keep in mind the history of the relationship between Houses Bleddyn and Eryr; more important, understand we are offering an alliance and our trust."

By our Blood! Llywelyn thinks. *Eryr is a Lesser house. We debase ourselves with this alliance.*

Gens Bleddyn sees the boy's distain in his sneer and narrowed eyes. *Llywelyn does not see Eryr's market for our medicines. He does not see a house that wishes to rise in prominence through trade and wants to purchase starships from us – ships Tarren will not sell them. Llywelyn does not see that elevating Eryr will also elevate Bleddyn. He does not see the complexities of this bond. Ah, well, a son who is a soldier is better than—*

The crunch of the shuttle's skids on the stones of the landing pad interrupts Bleddyn's thoughts.

~~~~~

A burst of cold and heavy rain interrupts the formalities of the welcoming ceremony. Bleddyn leads Eryr in one direction; three guards of each house, armed only with ceremonial weapons, follow. Llywelyn escorts Sawel, eldest son of Eryr, to his quarters. Llywelyn's companions, fully armed, await them. Sawel doesn't react except to say, "We are both soaked, and the rain was cold. A hot shower and dry clothes would be most welcome."

What is he doing? Why does he say this? Llywelyn wonders. *Is he trying to place himself above me by demanding hospitality? Is he showing he is weak to give me a false impression of his strength? Why does Father give me charge of a fifteen-year-old cadet? He is a child!*

Sawel, a boy more than a decade younger than Llywelyn, has none of these things in mind. He is wet and uncomfortable, and his father told him Llywelyn was to become an ally and friend. Sawel sees no need to play games.

Dressed in dry clothing, Sawel and Llywelyn sit at table while thralls serve lunch. Llywelyn now wears an energy pistol. Sawel wears not even the ceremonial sword he wore when he arrived, but which he dried and oiled before his bath.

170

~~~~~

After their lunch, Eryr and Bleddyn sit by the fire in Bleddyn's den. "Bleddyn, I have entrusted my son to yours," Eryr says.

Bleddyn sees the undercurrents of Eryr's thought. "Your son is much younger than mine. Llywelyn will not harm him. He will not even tease him. At worst, he will ignore him. You and I will set the terms for our alliance. I will impose them on my son. I suspect you will find it easier to impose them on yours."

"House Eryr never blindly followed anyone and we will not do so, now. I offer alliance only because it will benefit my house."

Bleddyn nods. "I understand. You know House Bleddyn began as sailors and fishers. Our heritage is the sea. We have a saying, 'A rising tide lifts all boats.' It is an apothegm, and although the analogy is not firm, I expect our alliance to lift both houses. The words of the treaty confirm this. The only modification I would make is your heir need not be in the company of my eldest son after today. Their meeting is the only ceremony needed. Do you understand?"

Eryr takes a moment before answering. "No, Bleddyn, I do not. But I accept it."

Bleddyn touches a button on his communicator. "Summon Llywelyn and Sawel to us."

Llywelyn is not happy when he and Sawel reach the den.

Ah, his father thinks, *Lieutenant Terrwyn relieved him of his energy pistol. Why did he wear it? Fear of Sawel or a dominance game? Certainly not the former; therefore, the latter.*

"Llywelyn, you and Sawel will implement our treaty. It is necessary you be part of this discussion." *Eryr was concerned for Sawel's safety. Now the boy is here and safe, Eryr is more relaxed. Good. That will serve me well.*

171

The discussion is tedious, delving into details of the treaty. Llywelyn grows bored. *He will not make himself a part of this,* his father thinks. *Telor understands the treaty. He will be the son who implements it.*

Sawel, seated across the conference table from Llywelyn, sees his boredom. *Does he understand the treaty so well? No, he is truly uninterested. He tried to dominate me by donning an energy pistol as soon as we were alone. He is a bully.*

As he crafts this thought Sawel glances at Gens Bleddyn. The man smiles at him.

"Are we in agreement, then? Does anyone have questions?" Bleddyn asks. "Gens Eryr?"

"No, Gens Bleddyn. The treaty is sound."

"Llywelyn?"

"No, Father. Are we finished here? I'm late to practice."

"Yes, we have finished, and you may leave. Sawel will remain."

Llywelyn is up and out the door before the echoes of his father's words die.

"Sawel, do you have questions?" Bleddyn asks.

"No, Your Grace. Thank you for allowing me to speak."

Bleddyn smiles at the young man, then turns to Gens Eryr. "Now do you understand my earlier question?"

"I do."

The two Gens do not sign the documents. Instead, Gens Bleddyn and Gens Eryr exchange blooded daggers. Then, Bleddyn takes another dagger from the table. "Sawel, since my son chooses not to be part of this, will you accept a dagger with my blood and your father's, knowing your oath to your father and the blood you share with him will always be preeminent?"

Bleddyn sees understanding and agreement in the mind of Gens Eryr. Pride nearly blinds Sawel's eyes as he pricks his arm with the dagger and mixes his blood with his father's and Gens Bleddyn's.

The rain has stopped, but the wind whips the cloaks of Bleddyn, Eryr, and Sawel. The wind is too loud for speech. Bleddyn and Eryr clasp arms before Eryr and his son enter the shuttle. Bleddyn stands alone and watches the shuttle until it disappears into the low clouds. *It will rain again, soon. Eryr has a fine heir.*

Eryr is an unaligned house, and neither Gens Eryr nor Father is obligated to notify anyone of their alliance. They transmit the treaty through Council channels. Tarren fumes, but there is nothing he can do.

~~~~~

Rodric, my Brother-minus-sixteen is to be fostered to House Dolffin. He will leave Fortress Bleddyn before Fall Stormtime and be away for three years. Llywelyn is happy Rodric will be absent from Fortress. It is hard for me to understand Llywelyn's thoughts, but I think he is glad one of his younger siblings is no longer at Fortress and under Father's protection. Garreth and Rodric have become close, and Rodric's impending absence weighs heavily on Garreth.
—Telor Bleddyn, Journal

Chapter 15: Vendetta and Betrayal

Llywelyn and his companions are relaxing in a pool of water heated to several degrees above body temperature by a thermal spring. The haemocyanin in their blood evolved aeons ago during a two-hundred millennia glacial age. The warm water not only relaxes muscles, but also impedes the flow of oxygen to their brains. It encourages torpor. They counter this with a drug.

"Garreth and Telor are becoming a nuisance," Llywelyn mutters.

"Yes?" someone says.

"Yes! They block my succession as Gens Bleddyn … and your advancement." Llywelyn has taken a second drug. Despite its effect on his mind, his eyes are sharp when he looks from one member of his coterie to another. "I cannot bypass them, or remove them."

~~~~~

Father calls Llywelyn and me to his den. That is surprising. Usually, he tries to keep us apart. Llywelyn is uncomfortable when I am in the same room with him, especially when we are together in Father's presence. Father does not seem to notice. "I received a call from a member of the academy faculty. A son of Gens Maelon called to the field the seventh daughter of Gens Reese. The boy won the duel – by killing her."

Father stares at Llywelyn and me, silent for several minutes as if deciding how much to tell us. "There was enmity between them at Academy for several years. The children took to the field four hours ago. After killing the girl, the Maelon boy savaged her body with his broadsword. Gens Reese is furious but stopped short of declaring vendetta with Maelon."

"Both Maelon and Reese are aligned with House Tarren, Father," I say.

"Yes, and Academy is in turmoil. The Provost summoned two elements from the Home Guards of unaligned Houses Emrys and Hywel. How might we gain advantage from this?"

"Side with Reese," Llywelyn says, instantly.

"Why is that not practical?" Father asks Llywelyn. I know the reason, but do not speak. If Reese were to favor us, then we would control all the Eastern Islands, including the one holding Tarren's spaceport and shipyard. Tarren would never accept that. He would defend Reese and attack our house's islands, shipyards, and spaceport.

Rather than answer, Llywelyn suggests a covert, surgical strike on a Maelon target. I know he is disappointed he only got to blow up a bridge in the attack on Ocsiwn. I think Llywelyn has fallen in love with destroying things.

Father asks Llywelyn how such an attack could be tied to the duel, but my younger brother cannot to answer.

"'Sometimes we must let evil run its course,' Geraint taught," I say. "Perhaps he was right."

"Thank you both for your counsel," Father says. "I will send a message to Reese. I will not tell him we are shocked or appalled. He will not believe it, but he might believe a simple expression of the House's sympathy." *And, someday, at a critical moment, he may remember it, and will hesitate or stay his hand to benefit House Bleddyn.*

~~~~~

Father embarrassed me in the presence of Telor. Was that his intention? Telor's answer was smug, an aphorism from a weak philosopher. Was that, too, deliberate?

176

I have watched Telor for more a decade since I graduated from Academy, just as I watch my other siblings — and Father. Father and Telor are good at concealing their talent, but both have made mistakes. They both know things they cannot know except they are demons, telepaths. Delwyn and Daffyd are drugged. Something extra in their vambraces hides their telepathy, but after their vambraces are removed, they will reveal their talent. Guffudd, too, I think. I suspect Rodric, and am not sure of Garreth, so I watch them all.

The greatest strength of House Bleddyn is this secret talent. I know Father will not allow me to become Gens since I am not a telepath.

—Llywelyn Bleddyn, Private Journal

≈≈≈≈

Yesterday, our soldiers foiled an attack on Garreth. Today, Father summons his Privy Council. Llywelyn and I stand, as usual, in opposite corners of the room and pretend to ignore one another. In truth, we constantly study the other's reaction to what is said.

"A floater strayed from a safe-passage lane and menaced Garreth and his companions. The controllers in the War Room cannot determine whether the floater was destroyed by one of our missiles or by a rocket grenade from a house floater. There was little left to examine, however our forensic team found a slug rifle in the wreckage. The serial numbers were filed off, but x-ray crystallography revealed the numbers that had been stamped into the metal. The numbers link the weapon to a mercenary. We cannot determine who might have hired him. Who might have ordered this attack?"

"Brother, the question is broad," Uncle Dewi says. "However, none of the enemies of House Bleddyn would do such without Tarren's orders — at least, without his knowledge and approval. The real question is, 'Why would someone attack Garreth, who is only a child – and eighth in line of succession?'"

"Perhaps he was a target of opportunity when the attacker realized he couldn't get closer to Fortress." Someone suggested.

The questions continue without answers. After an hour Father thanks the council and dismisses it. *There is more to this. Why would Tarren target Garreth? Why would anyone?*

~~~~~

Llywelyn enters the workroom where his companions are cleaning their weapons. Disassembled weapons, cleaning rods, brushes, and files cover the tables. The room stinks of ozone from the energy pistol chargers and naphtha used to dissolve old grease.

"Where is Bugail?" Llywelyn asks. One of his most loyal followers has been absent for several days.

"He took a floater to Cytgord," one answers. "Five days ago. He said he would observe the mercenary auction."

"Where is he, now?" Llywelyn asks.

No one can answer.

Was the Privy Council's first guess correct? Did the attack come from Tarren? Was the attack against Garreth or Fortress? Was Bugail the pilot, and did he get the gun and explosives in Cytgord? Or did Bugail hire a mercenary to pilot the floater? But then what happened to Bugail? Where is he? Why did he not return? I dare not make inquiries lest Father have the same questions.

—Llywelyn Bleddyn, Private Journal

~~~~~

"You are inviting Huw Tarren to visit during Winter Stormtime?" Delwyn's face and voice express her disbelief.

"Father said to get close to him, but Telor told us we are not to visit Fortress Tarren. This is the only way, and the first—"

178

"You are right, Daffyd," his twin interrupts. "But we must be careful he does not learn—"

Daffyd's laugh interrupts his sister. "He won't learn anything from us. He's not learning anything at Academy. Huw is eager to accept the invitation – on some days, at least. I think his vambrace is still out of synch."

The twins learned long ago that visits to Fortress during Stormtime are more intense versions of Academy training. Most of their friends appreciate this. Huw, however, doesn't want to join them in sessions at the dojo or firing range. They despair of finding ways to entertain him until they learn he attached himself to their second eldest brother and his companions.

~~~~~

Huw Tarren accompanied Daffyd to Fortress for Stormtime. Like a lost puppy – the runt of the litter – he injects himself in my activities and among my companions. I struggle to avoid him but am not always successful. Besides, he may offer me secret entrée to his father.

—Llywelyn Bleddyn, Private Journal

~~~~~

Daffyd gives Huw key-lock permissions to the family's common spaces, which include the hot soak where Llywelyn is relaxing. The boy opens the door, sees only Llywelyn, drops his towel, and slides into the tub next to him.

At first, Llywelyn does not understand what Huw is saying and almost misses the boy's whisper. "The drug you take. It's the same one Father takes before he meets with your father. It's also the best thing for—" Huw's hand reaches toward Llywelyn.

Llywelyn jerks his mind back to reality. *By Karmet! This is the final proof Gens Tarren knows Father is a demon.*

179

Before Huw's hand reaches its target, Llywelyn stands, steps from the tub, and leaves the room.

Chapter 16: Soosong

Fall Stormtime of Garreth's seventh year promises to be mild. The sun is bright when Garreth and I stand on the battlements to welcome the shuttle from Academy. I see his disappointment when Soosong is not among the passengers. She trained him for several years, and he is looking forward to continuing that. Soosong and I, Delwyn, and Father are the only ones who know the reason. I may not share it with Garreth.

~~~~~

The day before this, in an Academy bedroom, a young woman packs a duffle with a few clothes and some weapons not on the Academy's approved list. Her thoughts are muddled.

Fall Stormtime approaches, she thinks. I will graduate from Academy in 150 days. I will graduate with honors – athletic, scholarship, and military – but I am still Soosong the bastard, and I do not have a position or a future. I hoped Delwyn would invite me to Fortress Bleddyn where perhaps something would be offered. Daffyd and Delwyn invited me often in the past, but neither did so, now. When Huw Tarren, the boy who pretends to be enamored of me, invites me to spend Stormtime at House Tarren's Fortress, I feign reluctance. "You know I am without family and without honor."

"Soosong," Huw replies. "Honor comes not from blood, but from deeds. I these past years taught me you have honor."

I know then he is lying. Blood is the most important thing to all Houses, more so to the Greater Houses. What I learned about House Tarren and their commitment to primogeniture suggests bastardy is especially repugnant to them. However, I accept his invitation. And then, careful not to be observed, I seek Delwyn.

"Thank you for your trust in telling me this," Delwyn says. "This may be the opportunity we have sought for years. Are you willing and prepared?"

We have never spoken of it directly, but I know what she means. I take several minutes to consider her question. Delwyn is not anxious, but allows me time.

"I am prepared. I have the tools I need. I am willing," I say. Then, I laugh. "I would like some help escaping, though."

Delwyn smiles. She takes me secretly to her brother, Telor. "This is what we shall do," he says.

~~~~~

No matter how important and how well guarded a person is, he or she can be killed if the assassin is not afraid to lose her life. I am without House. The only honor I have is what I earn at Academy, but it will matter little when I graduate. Even if I win a place at a mercenary auction, I will always be a bastard without family.

I do not wish to die, but I am no longer afraid of death. During the previous Summer Stormtime, Delwyn took me to a hospital. It was a short journey and without risk, for the hospital belongs to House Bleddyn. After the procedure, Gens Bleddyn visited and assured me my eggs had been preserved. He swore formally at least one will be fertilized by one of his sons, making my child a blood member of House Bleddyn. Tomorrow I might die, but my blood will live with name and with honor.

Gens Bleddyn's promise was neither a bribe nor a reward. I believed him when he said it was offered because of the love and loyalty I showed his children, especially Garreth whose training I continued during my visits. I understood then how much more than blood binds those loyal to House Bleddyn.

I cannot bring a weapon into Fortress Tarren. My only tools will be my skill and the spider-silk thread that holds fasteners on my blouse. On the night of my arrival, Gens Tarren will hold a banquet celebrating the elevation of one of his children. It was during the elevation of Garreth that House Tarren's secret allies attacked Gens Bleddyn and his family. The irony is not lost on me, although it seems overlooked by House Tarren.

Huw escorts me through the gate of the fortress. For six years I have played the coquette and pretended to return his affection. I know he and his father hope to sway my loyalty toward House Tarren – at least, away from House Bleddyn. I know I must continue this charade for at least a day before I can get close to Gens Tarren. I know will likely suffer the father's groping and worse. He will take me to humiliate his son and me.

After the banquet, Huw accompanies me to my room. "Soosong, I will change from my uniform, and return in an hour," he says. He uses my name, knowing its meaning – a bastard, a person of low status. I am accustomed to the slur and do not let my feelings show on my face.

I pull him into a brief embrace and offer a kiss. "I will be ready, Lord of My Heart." I say, knowing my next visitor will likely be the father, not the son.

After Huw leaves, I work quickly. I remove one fastener from my blouse and then another. Spider silk connects them. I know how to hold them so the silk will cut the throat of my victim without slicing my own fingers. It is a lesson from Delwyn's uncle, another irony that does not escape me.

I am right. When the door opens, it is not Huw but his father, Gens Tarren. He is a little bit drunk and not at all subtle. His robe is open. He is naked beneath it.

"I know you would prefer a man to a boy," he says. "You would rather the child of this union be the child of the Gens and not of a son."

"Your Grace is as perceptive as he is strong," I say. I open my gown and watch his strength rise. I allow the gown to drop to the floor. *This will be easier than I thought.*

I hold one fastener in each hand. The spider silk is invisible in the dim light. I stretch my arms across Tarren's shoulders and behind his head as if to bring him close to my nakedness. It takes only an instant to loop the spider silk from the left fastener over the right to form a noose. It takes only an instant to pull the noose tight. The spider silk slices through the flesh of Tarren's throat. It does not stop until it reaches the bones of his neck. I cannot avoid the blood pouring from him.

His heart stops instantly. Volemic shock. His brain continues to function for several seconds. His mouth opens to speak, but there is no air to form words. His eyes blink twice, and then stare at me. I push him onto the bed and see in his eyes the knowledge he is dead, killed by a bastard invited into his home by his son. The light fades from his eyes. The crimson sheets, soaked with his blue blood, are like a purple-gray. His strength lies flaccid, bereft of blood.

I wash the blood from me and change into a black jumpsuit. How much time do I have? Gens Tarren would not have stayed the night. When will he be missed? Unknown. Would Huw visit later? Unlikely, despite his parting words. I decide speed is important, although stealth is important, too.

A blouse held the spider silk garrote; a skirt made of a knitted fabric unravels to make a rope of carbon fibers, thin but strong. A broach becomes a carabineer; large, loop earrings complete the ensemble. After rappelling down the fortress walls, I work my way through the forest.

The body is discovered. Careless steps, flashing lights, and loud voices warn me of the approach of searchers. I fear they will hear the heavy beat of my heart. Then, I feel the slight pressure of its anti-gravity engines as a floater passes above me. It lands silently. "Ruger," a voice whispers. It is the safe word. I have no choice but to believe my rescuer. I roll onto the two-person floater. I cringe as the safety clamps lock my legs and torso to the cradle. I am well and truly captive, at the mercy of the floater pilot. The floater rises and moves south, holding to the treetops.

My rescuer speaks aloud. "I will take you to Cytgord." I recognize Delwyn's voice and relax. I committed to her, and I trust her.

"The auction will be in three days," she says. "The town will be full of mercenaries; you will not stand out. The Bond of Peace will protect you. Because of your youth and lack of a record, you will not be selected at the auction. If someone enters a bid for you, our agent will enter a higher bid. After the auction, someone will contact you and bring you to a shuttle. The safe word is, again, *ruger*. You will be taken to another destination. You know you cannot return to Academy. You will be taken to a hospital where your DNA will be modified. Then, you will become a crewmember on a starship of the *Vishnu Nerada* – the Gens Bleddyn fleet. Do you have any questions?"

Delwyn risked her life to rescue me and bring me this far. How can I doubt her? I cannot. I understand the trust she offers is not only to bind me to her and her House but also to protect me. I nod and say, "I understand."

We land an hour before dawn. I change into the armor and cloak Delwyn provides. The weapons do not appear to be the best, but they are substantial. *Of course. I am a mercenary candidate without record. These weapons appear no better than what I could properly afford. Delwyn thought of everything.*

Delwyn and I eat from field rations and then nap. At dusk, we take off again and continue eastward. At the next dawn, we arrive at the town of Cytgord. We do not stand out among the shuttles and floaters that bring mercenaries and bidders to the auction. Delwyn surprises me. She kisses my cheek, then gently pushes me toward the town. Her floater rises and turns east. I am alone, but I am armed and unafraid.

Cytgord is like the town of the crèche in which I was reared. A broad mall stretches from east to west. Stone buildings, none more than three stories, hold shops on the ground floor and lodgings on upper floors. The façades display garish signs offering food, drink, clothing, armor and weapons, and less savory things promising pleasures for the mind and the body.

The mall is full of people. Bronze-skinned Res Publica barely outnumbers the pale, well-covered thralls. Armor and weapons identify mercenaries. Guards accompany bidders. Thralls walk briskly, careful to keep out of the way of mercenaries, some of whom are already drunk. The Hiring Hall, a huge circular building with a domed roof, is my first destination.

The Registrar of the Auction does not laugh when I give him the memory stick holding the sparse and fictitious record of my training and skills. I hear his snort and see derision in his face. It means the data on the memory stick passed screening at the central computer.

As I leave the Hiring Hall, a woman thrall steps toward me and bows. "There is a room over my husband's shop. One silver for the night."

"Bath included?" I ask. "And can the door be bolted from inside?"

She nods, likely accustomed to both questions. "And no vermin."

The room is adequate, and her husband's shop is a café where I take my supper. It, too, is adequate.

~~~~~

The morning of the auction, I wake early and stroll the mall looking for a better-than-adequate place to have breakfast. Today will be an important day and I don't want hunger or bad food to distract me. I see a man scrubbing the stone stoop of a building whose sign declares it to be a café. At least, it may be clean.

The café is clean – and crowded. Talk hums as the men and women exchange thoughts and gossip about the auction. I slide among them and find a small table in a shadowed corner. The smells pique my appetite. Unasked, a waitress delivers a cup of hot tea.

"Breakfast?" she asks. There is no menu and only one choice.

I nod and thank her for the tea.

"Aren't you kind of small for the auction?" The man who asks is at least 30 cm taller and 50 kg heavier than me. He and two companions sit at a table near mine. I am not sure I should answer until one of his companions speaks.

"I don't remember you always being so big." The speaker's voice holds humor and not derision.

"Or so loud," the woman companion says. She turns to me. "Come, sit with us. This bear's name is Arth but his growl is much worse than his bite."

The town is under a truce for the auction. There are stories though – stories of fights that end in death and of mercenaries being maimed by rivals. *Is there any reason for me to believe they have ill intentions?* I wonder. Only seconds pass while I think.

"Thank you, Mistress." I slide into the fourth seat at their table, making sure the waitress sees me.

"You call me Mistress? You are a polite one." She lowers her voice. "Academy trained, I'd guess. Call me Crëyr."

"Why do you say *Academy trained*?" I ask. "Is that a bad thing? My name is Soo—" I close my lips.

"Soo, and more," Crëyr says. "You are more cautious than others your age; you sat where you could see the room. You hesitated before sitting at our table with your back to the room; you relaxed after I gave you my name. And, you have a napkin in your lap."

Crëyr laughs. It is a happy laugh. I see she is not laughing at me. "You may want to skip the napkin. After all, sleeves were invented before napkins." She laughs again. The two men chuckle.

I am surprised and gratified by the camaraderie during our meal. My breakfast arrives first. I put the plate in the center of the table and invite the others to scoop bites with the flat bread. When their food arrives, they share it with me.

Crëyr seems to know this is my first auction. She tells stories of past auctions. I understand they are teaching stories, and she is telling me how to present myself, how to make the best impression, how to recognize those who would make the best masters, what to look for in a contract. Even though I don't plan to be hired in this auction, I remember the words of Geraint: *Before I know it, I will be a thousand years old. I must not neglect to learn. Life is never long enough to ignore the quest of the mind.* I listen carefully to Crëyr's stories.

Crëyr and her companions have scheduled interviews with potential employers. After breakfast, we wish one another good fortune and go our separate ways.

~~~~~

It is early morning when I leave the café. The streets are crowded. Sounds coming from doorways tell me many mercenaries are already in bars. The day is warm and I throw my cloak over my shoulders. I feel a touch at my left hip, stop, and spin in time to catch the hand that holds one of my throwing daggers.

188

The hand belongs to a thrall child. *She seals her fate. It is a death sentence for a thrall to touch, much less possess a weapon.* I look around. Thralls surround me. They stand quietly. They are not threatening. One speaks.

"You hold a life in your hands, Mistress." She bows as she speaks. *The girl – her daughter,* I think.

There is a bench within the circle of thralls. I pull the girl-child toward the bench, sit, and gesture for her to sit beside me.

"You have something I want," I say. "I would buy it from you." There is money in my purse, quite a lot of it. More than I should need. *Was this for a contingency, or has House Bleddyn abandoned me?* I shake off the question.

"Will you sell it for a silver?" I hold up the small coin. The girl's eyes widen, and then narrow.

"It is worth more," she says.

It is worth your life. She knows, and is asking me to assess the value of her life. I take a heavier and more valuable coin from my purse. The coin is copper – treated as valuable because copper is in our blood. "Your life is worth many, many coppers, but I have only one. Will you sell the dagger for one copper and my name?"

The girl nods. I hear the sighs of the thralls that surround us. I take the dagger from the girl. When I give her the copper, I say, "My name is Soosong."

The girl knows what my name means. She grins. Then her face hardens. "My name is Emlyn. I thank you for your name and my life."

In the next instant, the thralls move away. The girl stays on the bench.

I wonder if I did the right thing. I rewarded the girl for breaking the law, a law against which there is no appeal. I have both the right and obligation to execute her, in public, even in front of her mother. I did not do so; I lost the high ground.

"Emlyn, whose name means *industrious*, your life is worth far more than one copper, and even more than a small throwing-

189

knife. The next time you steal, take something of greater value and lesser risk, won't you?" I smile. The girl's face freezes for a moment. She nods, and then slips away.

In the crèche I was told all relationships in life are the result of a connection made in the past and are formed in the present because two people are meant to meet each other. I wonder how this meeting might affect my life.

~~~~~

Delwyn's prediction I would not be selected at auction is correct. I watch the three I met in the café place themselves together.

After the auction, those not selected walk toward the cafés and bars. I move with them, but stay at the fringes of the crowd. I hear a voice near me. "Ruger." A hand touches my arm and guides me away from the crowd. It is a woman, dressed as I am. Embroidered on her breast is the crest of House Dolffin – a sleek fish leaping from a green sea into a blue sky. She does not speak again until we reach a shuttlecraft. I am the only passenger. The shuttle rises and turns toward the setting sun.

"Our flight will be a long one," she says. "Here is food and drink. After eating, you may nap."

I understand. Her house fortress is on a western island. We will cross the entire width of the Equatorial Continent to reach it. Hours later, mountain-wave turbulence from Ellis' volcanoes buffet the shuttle and wake me. I fall asleep quickly, though.

~~~~~

Telor Bleddyn greets me when we land.

"You risk greatly to be here," I say.

"In truth, your risk was the greater," he says. "There are many blood ties between Houses Bleddyn and Dolffin. They will

190

not betray you or me. Father has selected a surrogate and promises me your child will also be mine. I hope that pleases you."

"Yes, it does, My Lord. Very much."

"There is a name in our House that has not been used in millennia. It is Gwenallt. I give it to you and ask you to call me Telor."

This offer is more than a name. Besides fathering my child, Telor invites me to be come a member of his house.

~~~~~

A month later, the control segments and key genes of my DNA have been modified to prevent aging and senescence. I have been injected with nanobots to supplement those modifications. I am a crewmember on a ship – the *Yosok Maru*, a corvette. My primary position is weapons; secondary, astrogator. When I sign the ship's articles, I see my name listed not as Soosong, but 'Gwenallt ap-Bleddyn' – Gwenallt, adopted into House Bleddyn. It is an honorable name.

As we accelerate toward the speed of light, time outside the ship will pass much faster than inside. Telor will certainly receive the modification to his DNA that grants near-immortality, but I wonder about my friends from Academy and about Crëyr and her companions. I wonder about my promised child.

Before we slip between universes, the FTL console chimes. The captain brings the message to my quarters. "Born to Telor and Gwenallt by surrogate, a son elevated before House Bleddyn as Selwyn, child-of-the-blood."

Selwyn. From the ancient language meaning Friend.

The captain explains. "Your son is blood-of-the-Gens by his son Telor and as of the time we departed World, 11th in the line of succession. You are the mother of a very important boy."

I remember my oath – to serve with honor, valor, and loyalty. "Sir, I will not be able to see my son grow up. I hope he becomes an honorable and courageous man. I hope he will be loyal to his father's house. I entrust his upbringing to his father and his father's family. Please do not share this message with anyone and please do not treat me differently because of it."

"You have the right of it, Lieutenant," my captain says, and closes the door behind him. *Lieutenant? The rank of his second in command. It begins.*

We are approaching the speed of light when the message is received. In the few minutes it takes the captain to deliver the message, years pass on World. Before the captain returns to the bridge, my son will have grown to manhood. I will not see him grow up. I will never know what he looks like. Will his features be mine or his father's? Will his teeth grow crooked, like mine, or will he be handsome like Telor?

Because I am a crewmember, my DNA was modified to ensure I will live for millennia. Will my son Selwyn find a place of honor and importance? Will his DNA be modified? Has it been modified? It is difficult to think in this mix of inside and outside time. Will he be assigned to a ship? In the infinity of time and space in which we live, will we ever meet?

Chapter 17: Transitions

The house War Room is deep under Fortress and insulated from the winds of Fall Stormtime. Screens on three walls and at the controllers' consoles display global weather systems imaged by satellites. Communication systems are busy with reports of damage and recovery. A red light flashes on the Senior Controller's console. He answers, presses a single button, and connects to Gens Bleddyn's communicator. "Commander, Cadfael Tarren reports the death of Gens Tarren and declares himself to be Gens. It happened last night."

"You have already put our forces on alert," Bleddyn says rather than asks. It shows his confidence in the Senior Controller.

"Yes, Your Grace."

"May his days be few; and let another take his place," Gens Bleddyn quotes Karmet. *We have repaid Tarren in vendetta for the attack on us at Garreth's elevation. Almost eight years ago, but the plan was executed flawlessly. Honor, valor, loyalty – patience and planning.*

No one comments on the transition of power in House Tarren. Assassination is traditional in that house. At Fortress Bleddyn, everyone's focus is on the graduation of Delwyn and Daffyd.

~~~~~

Nearly every member of the family living at Fortress will attend the graduation. Both the Praetorian Guard and the Mountain Company provide security. Caitlan of Dolffin is a member of the twins' element. Her mother, Gens Dolffin, is a guest at Fortress.

Aurin of Ellis is another member of the element and swore brotherhood-by-blood with Daffyd. However, House Ellis is sworn to Tarren. It would not be politic to host Gens Ellis.

The day before graduation, Father summons me to his den. "Telor, Llywelyn will be at play in the mountains during the graduation. You are to be in uniform. Mingle with cadets, the graduates – newly commissioned ensigns – and the faculty."

"What am I to look for, Father?"

"Focus on House Tarren. It is only a few months since his father was assassinated and Cadfael became Gens. He has no children, yet. The house is so inbred there are already rumors of monstrous embryos not allowed to live. His heir is Huw. You know what I think of him. Cadfael is building up his land and air forces, but he does so in a studied and deliberate way. Aaron, the third son, is a hothead and ambitious. Watch him, closely."

The next morning, I accompany Father, Gens Dolffin, and Delwyn and Daffyd's surrogate on the brief shuttle flight to Academy. I remember little of my graduation. My element's farewell party the previous night had involved a considerable amount of ethanol. I'm sure Father knew I was groggy the next morning, but I'm also sure he understood.

I attended Llywelyn's graduation, and Bethan's. The form has not changed – not in the past ten years, and probably not in the past ten millennia. The commandant invites Father to sit with him and turns the rest of us over to staff and faculty who take us to our seats. Father sits at the commandant's right – the singular place of honor. The commandant does not seem happy Father brought with him the Gens of a Lesser House, but seats Gens Dolffin at Father's right. The new Gens Tarren sits on the commandant's left, the secondary honor seat. I focus more on him than on the ceremony.

Soosong, a member of the twins' element, vanished while visiting Fortress Tarren during Fall Stormtime. Some people speculate it was she who assassinated Gens Tarren. It is universal knowledge that Cadfael Tarren suspects our house was behind his

194

father's death. A few cadets, who do not know Huw's limitations, speculate that he killed both Soosong and his father. Soosong's rebirth as Gwenallt ap-Bleddyn is a closely held secret in Houses Bleddyn and Dolffin.

Even from twenty meters away, I feel the chill in Cadfael Tarren's greeting to Father.

~~~~

I give the twins a day to recover from their own celebration before summoning them to the library.

"You both look sharp in your uniforms; however, the Ensign flashes are inappropriate. Here are your commissions as Lieutenants in the House Home Guard."

I hand them the ornate documents, relics of an ancient tradition. "The stipend Father gave you since you were six years old ceases and your salary as lieutenants begins. You must reevaluate your finances and live within your means."

"But, Telor!" Daffyd's voice projects his anguish. "My laboratory, the research, I've barely been able to pay for it, and my salary is less than my stipend. Years of research will have been wasted."

"Your laboratory now falls under the house. One of your cousins will assume day-to-day responsibility. You will continue to control the research. House Bleddyn will pay for it. The only difference is you will have to ask for any additional funds for the new DNA sequencer you want, for example."

I watch Daffyd's face go from pale to dark and back to pale. "You knew?"

"Yes, Brother. I have watched your research with great interest."

I turn to Delwyn. "Sister, do you have questions?"

"Yes. Lieutenants in the Home Guard are in command positions. Which company of the Home Guard will be mine?"

I manage not to smile. Delwyn has always been a warrior, and wants to lead warriors. I almost say that, but do not. "Sister, Father wants you to learn from several commanders. For a while, you will rotate among companies as deputy to the commander, starting with the Mountain Company. I will pull away the commanders often enough for you to experience command. They will be present often enough to share their knowledge and wisdom with you. After this apprenticeship, Father will award you command of whichever company you wish, except the Mountain Company."

"I understand, Brother. I also understand why I may not command the Mountain Company. Master Sergeant Rhingyll has refused to be commissioned for how many years, now?" She chuckles. "I'm looking forward to being his deputy."

"Daffyd, you will take command of the Training Company from me. Father thinks your skill as an instructor will best serve the house and its Home Guard there."

Daffyd nods his acceptance. Unlike his sister, he is not ambitious.

Delwyn does not mention money. I don't ask her why. I know she saves most of her stipend. *One twin saves for the future; one invests in the future. Which is right? Are they both right?*

It is not long before Llywelyn learns of the twins' assignments. His reaction is muted. I think he is pleased Daffyd commands only the training company and Delwyn will not have any command. I do not ask if he wants to join them in training their younger siblings. I know Llywelyn has no interest, other than watching to ensure one of his potential rivals does not become too powerful.

~~~~~

Cadfael Tarren moves quickly to quell the confusion that follows his father's assassination. Supported by allies among his

196

father's Praetorian Guard, he rallies the house to accept him as Gens. He requires most residents of Fortress Tarren, including other siblings and cousins and all members of the Home Guard, to swear blood oath. Cadfael does not need to swear any aunts or uncles. His father eliminated them long ago. Cadfael's stamina when he returns the oaths, blood-for-blood through scores of dagger pricks to his own arms, appeals to ancient ritual and loyalty.

With Cadfael's elevation to Gens, Huw Tarren becomes heir presumptive until Cadfael fathers a male child. The ambition of Aaron – in line after Huw – does not fade, but becomes more immediate and urgent. As soon as Cadfael has an heir both Huw and Aaron will be expendable. Rumors reach us that Cadfael's potential offspring are flawed.

Aaron is careful not to appear threatening to Cadfael. Rather than pursue a military position, he asks to supervise the herds and spends much of his time keeping breeding records, selecting strains of fodder, constructing silos, and mucking out stables and barns.

No one notices the intense loyalty Aaron creates among the younger members of the house who traditionally perform these tasks. No one realizes the maneuvers Aaron teaches for gathering the herds from pasture might have a military application. No one remarks that in defense of the herds against the saber-tooth cats and other predators, the herders now carry slug rifles. No one measures the barley crop to find there is a surplus used to brew beer. Nor does anyone see mess stewards of the house Home Guard receive both beer and choice cuts of meat for the soldiers' meals.

~~~~~

In mid-winter, Cadfael Tarren orders Aaron to join him and Huw on a hunt through the mountains. Aaron is not surprised. The hunt has long been House Tarren's way of proving its children's

mettle. Aaron prepares himself with armor, winter clothing, and weapons appropriate to hunt homotherium.

The hunting party assembles. Two soldiers who have been Huw's companion-guards since his childhood stand beside him. Aaron exchanges brief glances with the two men. They show no sign, but Aaron is certain of their loyalty – not to Huw, but to him.

Cadfael assigns Huw, Aaron, and Huw's guards to a blind on the west end of the line. Huw whines. "Aaron is a poor shot. He will miss and scare off the biggest tom! I want his pelt." The thrall beaters who will drive the animals up the slope toward the hunters in the blinds report a huge male homotherium with black-spotted golden fur. Huw decides it will be his.

"Brother, I will go where you assign me, if you would rather I not be with Huw," Aaron says. There is a touch of subservience in his voice and manner.

Huw huddles in his heavy coat. "See? He doesn't want—"

No," Cadfael interrupts. "Huw, you have a duty to your younger brother. Would you rather I give you one of the children? Their squealing would frighten away the entire pride."

Huw grumbles, and then orders Aaron to take up a second pack of rations. Aaron quietly obeys. He feels Cadfael's eyes on them as they strike the trail to the west.

Homotheria are carnivores, apex predators. They are hunters, but not reluctant to eat someone else's kill. There will not be enough of Huw's body left to find any mark of the dagger that ended his life. Aaron wipes the blade on Huw's coat and sheathes it. He faces the two lieutenants, the only people who accompanied Huw and him. "You know I am like neither of my brothers! You seek power, and you will follow power. On your oath! Now!"

198

The two officers kneel. "By our blood," they say. "We follow and obey."

Aaron takes their hands, one after the other, and lifts them to their feet. "Within two years I will be Gens and you will become Captains. The delay is a simple deceit, which will mislead no one of any intelligence, nor is there anyone I need to mislead. I will rule by power; you will wield power on my behalf."

"Yes, Your Grace," they reply.

Chapter 18: Vengeance, Honor, & Dishonor

Llywelyn knew Cadfael Tarren long before Cadfael became Gens. They were the same age and had attended Academy at the same time. Their elements were in competition, but only in the normal schedule of element against element and group against group. They were neither friends nor – until Cadfael became Gens Tarren – enemies. Llywelyn sends a message to the new Gens Tarren through Slade of House Maelon.

<<I will be at the Parrot Bar in Port Lagon early on Day 29>> *No more and no less*, Llywelyn thinks.

Six days later, Llywelyn enters the Parrot Bar. His companions are uncertain, but accept his orders to stay outside the bar. Three patrons who seem watchful do not surprise Llywelyn. They look hard at him then turn their eyes away. *Cadfael is here, and early. So are his guards. Does that mean he is eager for this meeting, or simply cautious?* Llywelyn puts those thoughts into his decision matrix, and then looks for Cadfael.

Even in early morning the bar is busy. None of the patrons are interested in breakfast even though it is offered. Most are drinking shots of ethanol followed by beer. Llywelyn sees Cadfael and walks to his table. He sees men at two nearby tables watch his movements. *Not all of Tarren's guards are on the street. Neither are mine, and they are more careful than these not to reveal themselves.* He makes sure Tarren's men see his hands do not stray toward his weapons.

"Cadfael, well met," Llywelyn says and sits at the young man's table.

"Llywelyn, well met, indeed," Cadfael replies. "A fortuitous meeting, and—"

"Neither fortuitous nor without risk," Llywelyn interrupts. "I am jamming electronics including recording and outgoing communication. Your father gave me a drug that masks my thoughts from demons. Huw let it slip that your father used the drug because he thought my father was a demon. I use the drug for the same reason. I have no proof, but have the same suspicions your father had."

"And I," Cadfael says. "Father thought your father was able not only to see his thoughts but also to foretell the future. He thought the same things of Telor. He wasn't sure, but suspected the drug masked his thoughts. Is that true?"

Llywelyn's laugh attracts attention from Cadfael's guards. "If it were not true, I would be dead."

Llywelyn's face no longer holds laughter when he says, "Your father said I would become Gens Bleddyn long before my father died of natural causes. What say you?"

The rest of the conversation is quiet. When it is over, both Cadfael and Llywelyn understand the next step in their alliance.

An hour later and unseen by anyone, two shuttles rise into the low clouds above Port Lagon. The pilots turned off the radar beacons and fly low to avoid detection. One moves toward Fortress Bleddyn; one, toward Fortress Tarren.

~~~~~

The first month of summer arrives and with it, the usual problems that warmer weather and summer storms bring. Winter wheat was harvested, but the summer crop is vulnerable to weather. Without enough rain it will not grow. Too much rain and it will rot. Hail from summer storms might beat it to the ground. I have climbed to the top of the Keep to watch for the rapidly rising cumulous cloud turrets that signal the formation of hail cells.

Father surprises me when he joins me atop the Keep. "You watch the weather," he says. "Are not our satellites adequate?"

"They are, Father, but there's something visceral about watching storms develop, something the satellites do not capture."

Father nods his understanding, then hands me a message. "One more thing to concern you," he says.

Fishing boats on the largest inland lake, which lies between Bleddyn, Merrick, and Lagon and which the three houses share by treaty, report a massive fish kill. I thank Father, and return to my duties.

House Merrick is my best source of information. Although they do most of their fishing at sea, they have several boats on the lake. And, Merrick is committed to sustainable fishing and carefully records water conditions, location, and size of the catch. When I call the Merrick War Room, I am connected with a woman whose hair is tightly tied back, enhancing an already stern expression.

"Nitrogen fertilizer washes down the river from Tarren territory and creates an algae bloom. When the algae consume these nutrients, they die and fall to the bottom where decay leaches oxygen from the water. The fish kill resulted from un-oxygenated water."

"Are we sure the source of the fertilizer was Tarren and not House Emrys?" I ask after calling up a mental map.

She snorts. "Emrys has only forests on the banks of the river, and they do not fertilize trees with artificial nitrogen fertilizer."

"Artificial?" A memory tries to come forth.

"Artificial. The substance is ammonium nitrate, $N_2H_4O_3$. It occurs in nature, but in nature the oxygen component has an atomic weight of 16. In what we found, the O_3 component is oxygen 18, which would exist in those quantities only in a chemical laboratory."

I understand. The fertilizer was manufactured by Tarren. The next question is whether over-fertilization was deliberate or accidental.

Father, Gens Merrick and his staff, and one of my aunts spend hours on the televisor debating details, proofs, and strategy. When Father ends the conference, he calls me.

"We will register a complaint at Council and ask for restitution. We will not get it since Helygen is First Speaker and in league with Tarren. Nor will we get a supermajority of votes."

Father is correct, and our complaint is dismissed. After Council, I offer Father a somewhat convoluted calculation of calories – what Merrick, Lagon, and we lost due to the fish kill and the equivalent number of acres of Tarren's wheat crop. Father consults with Merrick and Lagon. Four nights later, shuttles from House Bleddyn fly over some of Tarren's wheat fields at an altitude of fourteen kilometers, seeding storm clouds with silver iodide. We create rain and hail to destroy part of Tarren's wheat crop. No one will starve because of this or the fish kill. Tarren would have spotted our shuttles on radar, and his people will find evidence of the silver iodide. He will know; he will fume; he will file a complaint in Council; and, he will lose his complaint by the same eight-to-five vote that dismissed ours. *Anatol's equivalent retaliation strategy. It may not win, but it's the best way to deal with Tarren.*

~~~~~

Six days ago, my son by surrogate was born. I am, of course, excited – and worried. His biological mother, Soosong, was a bastard until adopted into House Bleddyn and named Gwenallt ap-Bleddyn. She is on a starship, approaching the speed of light before dropping into inter-plane space on a journey that will last at least a century. Today, Father will elevate and name the boy who is Gwenallt's son and mine. I scheduled the birth so I could tell her before her ship reaches 0.7 C – nearly the speed of light – and loses communication with the house War Room.

First, however, Summer Stormtime arrives, and Fortress is crowded. Nearly three thousand people gather in the Great Hall for the elevation and celebration. Even though Father acknowledged me at my birth, a few members of the house do not accept me. Many do not accept Gwenallt because she was adopted – and they do not know her history or family. Only Father, Gens Dolffin, Delwyn, and I know she is the assassin who killed Gens Tarren. Among family who witness Selwyn's elevation, even those who hear Father's words, some will not accept him.

The ceremony is simple. My father, Gens Bleddyn, holds my infant son in his outstretched arms. "Son of Telor Bleddyn and of Gwenallt ap-Bleddyn, I name you Selwyn, child-of-my-blood, child-of-the-blood of House Bleddyn."

The last words are the most important, and should have settled any of the questions of our family.

I take the boy from my father's arms. *Selwyn, meaning 'Friend.' Father selected the name, himself. It is a sign of his approval.* I do not have to look at Llywelyn to see the anger and hatred in his face.

Llywelyn does not stay for the celebration, but orders food sent to his room. He sits at his desk. His only company is his journal, which he thinks of as his alter ego – his other self.

Fortress teems with poor cousins and thralls. Stormtime howls through the crenels. Telor fathered a child by surrogate and the egg of that bastard the twins brought home. My bastard brother fathered another bastard by a bastard. Father elevated the thrice-bastard child before what he thinks of as family – the hundreds who shelter in Fortress and the caverns below it, who eat the food grown and gathered by House Bleddyn, who treat Stormtime as a celebration of their indolence at our expense. Yet Father tells me I am too young to father a child, even though my seed was harvested, and a proper wife and surrogates selected. I am only two years younger than Telor. Father's excuses have worn thin.

  —Llywelyn Bleddyn, Private Journal

~~~~~

  Llywelyn is my younger brother, but he will be Gens should my father die. He graduated from Academy years ago and is a member of Father's Home Guard. We were playmates as children, but I no longer know him. He spends his time with his companions in the dojo, at the firing range, or in the mountains on camping trips he calls war games. The only time the family sees him is at banquets when he sits at the head table near Father.

~~~~~

  Gens Bleddyn summons Llywelyn to him. The young man reflects on the recent past. *I have done nothing to win either his contempt or his approval. Why does he summon me?*

  "Llywelyn, I said I would task you to deal with House business. Do you know what is happening on Soando Island?"

  "Yes, Father. Some trouble with the thralls."

  And that's probably all he knows. Some trouble. "The miners are threatening to strike unless we meet their demands for safer working conditions. Their own people, the shift supervisors, have not been honest with me. I believe they have misused or stolen funds intended for ventilation and safety equipment.

  "I want to learn what is happening without anyone being able to conceal evidence. You will travel alone to the island. You will discover the root cause of this problem, and solve it.

  "The Garrison Commander, Captain Tywyll, will meet you. She will assemble the shift supervisors. You will determine what happened and why they have not kept me informed. You will solve the problems identified by the miners. Remember, we rely on the

206

thralls, but do not hesitate to punish or replace any who have neglected their duty."

Bleddyn turns to his desk, his usual and abrupt way of dismissing visitors.

~~~~~

Llywelyn's shuttle skirts the plume of smoke that rises from one of Soando Island's volcanoes and lands in the courtyard of the military post. Three sides of the courtyard are ten-meter stone walls. A heavy gate breaks the southern wall. Single-story barracks, armory, mess hall, offices, and storerooms form the base of the north wall. Llywelyn's uniform boots crunch bits of ash and glass fallen from the volcano's cloud. The wolf of House Bleddyn in gold thread embellishes his left breast. Although Captain Tywyll outranks Llywelyn, who wears Lieutenant's flashes, she salutes.

"Where are the soldiers?" Llywelyn demands. "Why are they not assembled?"

"Sir, the message from the Gens said you are not on a military mission," she says. "I have assembled the supervisors as he ordered. They are waiting for you in the conference room."

Father gave me this mission, Llywelyn thinks, *but he sent instructions to her?* He keeps his voice low and tries to mimic his father's expression of anger when he answers. "I am Llywelyn Bleddyn, heir apparent of House Bleddyn. I am now in command of this post and this island. I will inspect my forces. You will assemble them, now."

"Yes, sir," she replies and takes her communicator from her belt. In seconds, alarms sound and soldiers rush from the buildings. Some are still buckling their armor. The element leaders pass through the ranks before reporting to Captain Tywyll.

Twelve minutes after the alarms sound, Captain Tywyll turns and salutes Llywelyn. "All present or accounted for, sir."

Llywelyn walks through the ranks. Seven elements, one hundred twenty-five soldiers. Well armed, too. He sees grenade launchers and energy rifles. Element and squadron leaders wear swords. A few uniform buttons or flaps are unfastened. A few soldiers are missing a piece of armor. The look in Llywelyn's eyes as he stands before each soldier makes it clear this is a formal inspection. *Marginal performance*, Llywelyn thinks.

He addresses Captain Tywyll. "Twelve minutes, and a third are not properly armored. I expect five minutes and perfection. Dismiss them and take me to the thralls."

Twenty-five thralls sit around a table in the conference room. They stand when Llywelyn enters. Their clothing completely covers them except for faces and hands. Broad-brimmed hats, which protect their faces from the sun, and gloves are on the table. Captain Tywyll introduces them. "Sir, the man on your left is the senior supervisor, Glöwr."

"Sit." Llywelyn orders. "I am Llywelyn Bleddyn. My father, your Gens, sent me to assume command of the garrison and to take charge of the mines. There are rumors the miners are dissatisfied with their working conditions. There are rumors money for safety equipment and ventilation was misspent. I will understand this and you, the senior thralls, will help me. Is that clear?"

He placed his cards on the table too soon, Glöwr thinks. *And he played a hand he was not dealt. Those were not his orders, not according to the message sent to the garrison commander.*

"Yes, My Lord," Glöwr says. "Your instructions are clear. I will order an immediate audit of funds and will call meetings of the miners to learn their concerns."

Whatever Llywelyn might have said is interrupted when the room shakes. Dust falls from the ceiling. Captain Tywyll grabs Llywelyn and pulls him to a doorway. "Earthquake," she says. "Or

208

an explosion in a mine. Or both. The doorway is the safest place at the moment."

~~~~~

Llywelyn paces. Hours pass. He is alone. Video screens show the rescue operations. Helmet-camera images of smoke and dust weave and bob as rescuers move. Growing tired of the cries and moans of the injured, Llywelyn mutes the sound. The status bar on the main screen flashes an update: twelve miners are dead; another seven are missing. Captain Tywyll is leading a search team into the affected mine.

The room shakes again. Dust falls from the ceiling. Cups that rolled off the table during the first quake jiggle and bounce on the floor. Llywelyn darts for shelter in the doorway, but the shaking stops before he reaches it.

Llywelyn's communicator trills. The call is from a sergeant.

"Sir, part of the ceiling of Mine Two collapsed. Captain Tywyll was caught. She was removed but is unconscious. She will be airlifted to the hospital at Sehwa. Command will be assumed by Sergeant—"

"No," Llywelyn interrupts. "I will take command of the garrison. Notify the element commanders and have them report to me."

A day passes since the last tremble of the ground. Glöwr returns. "There were two explosions in Mine Number Two," he says. "Almost certainly from a buildup of methane. We have removed fourteen bodies. Five are still trapped behind the rubble. I have mobilized all available people and equipment to rescue them. Captain Tywyll reached the hospital but is still unconscious. The other mines have been shut down until—"

"Shut down?" Llywelyn slams his fist onto the table. "Certainly you cannot have every miner and all your equipment working on a rescue. There is no reason to shut down the other mines."

"My Lord, the shutdown is temporary while we search for the cause of the explosion. It may exist in the other mines, and—"

"Cause of the problem? May exist?" Llywelyn's whining voice mocks Glöwr. "Your contract calls for full pay during a stand-down. You are picking my pocket to pay lazy miners."

Surprised that Llywelyn knows so much about the contract, Glöwr is reluctant to answer, but he does. "Yes, My Lord, and the contract also calls for ventilation to ensure—"

"Enough!" Llywelyn slams his fist on the table again. "The miners are engaged in a work-stoppage. Assemble the supervisors in the courtyard."

~~~~~

"What happened?" The narrowband circuit is encrypted and renders Gens Bleddyn's question flat and robotic.

Captain Tywyll reports from her hospital bed. "Sir, your son acted in anger. He lost it."

"More," the Gens demands.

The Captain describes the incident. Llywelyn ordered the thrall supervisors assembled in the courtyard. Twenty-five men and women stand against the outer wall. The day shift, including those recalled from the rescue work, wear their gear – headlamps on helmets, heavy gloves, and boots. The others wear their usual gray, long-sleeved shirts, trousers, and broad-brimmed hats.

Those clothes may have protected them from sunlight, but not from the energy weapons Llywelyn orders turned against them. Most have no time to scream before they die. Llywelyn leads the soldiers who step among the bodies and use their grace knives on the few survivors.

"Twenty-five dead, sir," Captain Tywyll reports. "All the supervisors. Your son is on a shuttle returning to Fortress."

"Captain Tywyll," Bleddyn orders, "you will take a shuttle to Fortress. Report to me upon landing. Do nothing of significance until we speak. Do you understand?"

"You order me not to kill myself in dishonor, Your Grace," Captain Tywyll answers. "I will obey."

≈≈≈≈≈

The Praetorian Guard allows Captain Tywyll to keep her dagger and grace knife but takes her energy pistol.

Bleddyn sits behind his desk. The Captain stops three meters away, kneels, and bows her head.

"Stand," Bleddyn orders. "My son exercised legitimate authority over your soldiers. The soldiers who followed his orders acted with loyalty, but not with honor. That is not your fault or theirs. It is a fault of our traditions." He gestures, and a guard gives Captain Tywyll her energy pistol.

The Gens ignores the woman's surprise as she holsters the weapon, but he sees her stand taller.

"It would be awkward for you to return to your former post. There is another place you can serve. I will not punish your soldiers. However, their new commander will teach them a different understanding of honor."

≈≈≈≈≈

Less than a day later, Llywelyn stands in front of his father. *I have done my duty. It's not my fault the thralls and the garrison commander could not do theirs. I am sure my father will—*

"You executed twenty-five supervisors," Gens Bleddyn says. "Why?"

"Father, they led the miners in strike. They were in revolt. The law is clear," Llywelyn answers.

"The law is clear. What is not clear is whether they were in revolt," Bleddyn says. "The house will pay death benefits to the families of those who died. By doing this, we acknowledge you may have acted wrongly. We will pay higher wages to the new supervisors. The cost to the House is significant, but not crippling. Learn from this before your next assignment."

Bleddyn turns to the computer display on his desk.

This is not an assignment as he calls it, Llywelyn thinks as he walks away. *It is my patrimony. I know to the penny the wealth of the house, the wealth I will inherit upon his death. The money he is worried about is trivial compared to that. My father blames me for the miners' rebellion. He demands obedience to my oath of honor, valor, and loyalty, but he no longer honors me.*

~~~~~

I have little time to understand what happened on Soando before I learn my brother Rodric is dead, fallen from the rigging of one of House Dolffin's sailing ships. Garreth is hard hit, since he eagerly awaited Rodric's return after three years and to hear stories from his fostering.

The morning after Rodric's remembrance, Father summons me to his den. His words are abrupt. "I received more information from Gens Dolffin. A sailor from the ship on which Rodric died, disappeared. The ship's captain found part of the rigging had been weakened.

"You will fly to Fortress Dolffin and investigate. Your first task is to ensure Gens Dolffin knows we have no cause for enmity between us, and our long ties of blood and loyalty are intact. If her house is responsible for Rodric's death, they must not believe we know or suspect. Do you understand?"

"Yes, Father. The alliance of Bleddyn and Dolffin is more important than revenge."

"For the moment," Father agrees. "Perhaps longer. Do what you must to find the truth and if possible, this sailor." His words are a dismissal, but I do not leave.

212

"May I take Garreth?"

Father looks at me. One eyebrow lifts. "Why?"

"Garreth thinks there is a mystery to be solved. He will pursue it and may discover and reveal things he should not know. Making him a part of the solution will ensure his silence. Also, bringing a youngster will clearly signal Gens Dolffin that House Bleddyn trusts her and her people."

"You are correct," Father says. "Use all haste; Fall Stormtime approaches."

Less than an hour later, Garreth and I are in Father's shuttle en route to Fortress Dolffin. I explain the reason he accompanies me. "You think there is a mystery to be solved. I want you to be part of that, so you will understand why you must never speak of it. In addition, if I am accompanied by a child—"

"I am not a child! I am eight years old."

"Of course not. I am sorry. You are more than my brother. You are a symbol of family and house. You will help maintain the bonds of friendship that join our houses." Garreth accepts this – and my apology.

Two of Gens Dolffin's sons, Gawain and Marwin, meet us. They have located the missing sailor – on a floater headed for the territory of House Maelon. They provide military floaters and supplies for the chase. I try to dissuade Garreth from accompanying us because of the danger, but he wins the argument. Besides, I know Father included jungle camouflage jumpsuits in Garreth's size in our shuttle. I allow Garreth a slug rifle, with which he is qualified, but not an energy pistol. I do not tell him the floaters are equipped with rocket grenades, but sense his smug delight when he realizes he commands four of them.

A stern chase is a long chase. That is an aphorism from House Bleddyn's sailing days. The chase is halted at dark when a windstorm – too strong for floaters – is predicted. We stay overnight on a hummock in the middle of a swamp. Companions of Gawain and Marwin who are shadowing us bring clean jumpsuits and supper.

At high sun the next day, we catch up with the sailor who dives into the trees to avoid us. Garreth follows. And does something he should not do. He releases the clamps that hold him securely in the floater, enabling him to roll from side to side in tighter turns. After some few minutes, the sailor, who also released his clamps, falls from his floater. Garreth dives toward him and uses his bolas to trip the sailor. I land beside the man and pull him from the ground, avoiding a Sarcopterygian which climbs from the river looking for lunch.

Sarcopterygian

After we return to Fortress Dolffin, and knowing the psychology of the interview, I enjoy a hot shower and put on a clean and pressed uniform before Gawain and Marwin join me to interrogate the sailor. Despite my probing, I learn only he believes a man from House Astin hired him. He cannot identify the man or confirm his House.

Gawain and Marwin watch, emotionless, when I execute the man and accept my interpretation of the interrogation. "House Astin is firmly neutral, and has no cause to do this," I say. "The man revealed to us what he was led to believe. We should assume the man was from Tarren's orbit."

The interrogation lasts until the late hours of night and it is mid morning when I wake. Garreth is waiting for me.

"The man … he killed Rodric."

My best answer is the simplest. "Yes."

"Why?"

I am surprised Garreth asks that question. I assume he would ask *how*, but more important, *Who sent him?* I am not prepared to answer Garreth's *why*, but I do my best.

"Because Rodric was a scion of House Bleddyn. He might have discovered something about the attacks on ships of House Dolffin. Because he knew—"

"Because he knew a secret you are not telling me!" Garreth exclaims, before running to me for a hug. I remember he is only eight years old, and understand – he does not blame me.

"Garreth, Brother, I promise to tell you all I know, but only when I may do so. Do you understand?"

Garreth looks up. He nods. "I do, Brother."

After supper the next day, Gawain and Marwin ask Garreth and me to their Great Hall. There, they invite us to swear brotherhood-by-blood in memory of Rodric. The ceremony is short and simple. I am very proud of Garreth, who participates correctly and with honor.

The only problem I see is that Llywelyn will learn of the ceremony, and it will increase his animosity toward Garreth – and me.

Chapter 19: Villainy

A door opens. Two figures step into a dark room. Heavy curtains block all but a little light from tall, narrow windows. A platform about three meters square and covered with black cloth lies along one wall. In a corner, barely visible, is a mannequin wearing a suit of ancient armor. A plain desk and wooden chair sit in an alcove.

"What is this place?" one figure asks. A hood shadows his face; a black cloak hanging from his shoulders matches the color of his clothing.

"The bedroom of Gens Bleddyn," the second, uniformed figure replies.

"His bedroom! Are you insane?"

"No. It is one of few places with no cameras or microphones. He attends Council. We may speak freely."

"You risk our lives bringing us here." The first man pulls at his cloak as if to conceal himself from the non-existent cameras.

"Trust me. We are safe, here. You said you would assassinate the boy. How will you do that?"

"One of the boy's tutors is a thrall. He would be familiar with the flame weapons used against us in the War of Conquest."

"You can create one?" the uniformed figure asks.

"In the boy's schoolroom. He always enters first. The fire will be extremely powerful. There may be collateral damage. The device will be triggered by the door."

"I am neither interested in the details nor concerned with collateral damage, only your assurance it will work. And how you will escape suspicion."

"The trail will lead to the boy's tutor, the thrall, Sani. Bleddyn trusts him too much because the boy adores him. Once the boy is dead, there will be no reason to trust or protect Sani. A few hints will lead the investigation to evidence prepared and planted."

"Sani must be killed before he can be interrogated," the uniformed figure says. "Else Bleddyn may believe his denial."

"That is a complication…"

"You must deal with it."

The first figure nods his head, although the gesture is scarcely visible. "It is a simple matter to kill one old thrall."

~~~~~

The attack on Garreth fails. "The fire only scorched his toes," the uniformed figure says. "However, there was an attack, and we must divert attention away from me."

Two figures, one in a black jumpsuit and cloak and one wearing a uniform enter the quarters assigned to the thrall, Sani. The pale man stands and bows in time for a bolt from an energy pistol held by the man in the jumpsuit to pierce his head. His body falls. A pool of blood turns blue and spreads over the floor.

"Where is the evidence you planted?" the uniformed figure asks.

"Inside the second book in the stack. Now, we must summon the guards. And I must turn off the scrambler before someone realizes no signals are coming from the cameras in this room."

The man in uniform raises his energy pistol. A bolt ends the assassin's life. Another pool of blood spreads. The surviving conspirator removes the book and scans the papers folded inside.

That no-blood bastard! My name is here! He would have taken me with him. This was his insurance.

The man stuffs the papers into a pocket before the door behind him opens. Members of the Praetorian Guard push into the room.

"Lieutenant," their commander says, when he sees who stands there. "Sensors reported energy weapons discharge."

"That should be obvious to anyone with an iota of intelligence," Llywelyn replies. "He killed my brother's tutor without provocation. I executed him. Cleanse the room, by fire."

~~~~~

Gens Bleddyn looks up from his desk. Moments later, a hidden panel opens and I enter the den. My face is drawn; my uniform, torn. Blue blood, becoming black as it coagulates, seeps from my right shoulder. I tremble as I kneel.

I speak before being acknowledged. "Father, Llywelyn betrayed you. Sani would never—"

Father stands so abruptly his chair slams into the stone wall behind him. His face blazes with anger, then becomes implacable. "You fear me. You think I will not believe your message. Do you not trust me?"

Father turns and retrieves his chair. He gestures to a chair beside his desk. I support my weight on the arms of the chair and sit, hard. I relate to Father what I learned.

"I have long suspected Llywelyn cloaked his thoughts, but how?" Father asks.

"A weed, Father. It is kin to the hemp grown to make rope for our ships. The weed contains a chemical Llywelyn learned to distill. The chemical blocks certain electrochemicals in the brain – the ones that create the signal telepaths sense. Had Llywelyn been wearing a vambrace, it would have injected adrenaline to counter this chemical."

"How were you able to see his thoughts?"

"His own anger betrayed him. I caught him alone, accused him and threatened him. The natural hormone generated by my threats and our fight were enough to break the barriers in his mind. I disarmed and arrested him."

"I will summon Llywelyn. You must not be present."

I leave the room through another panel. Moments later, Lieutenant Terrwyn brings Llywelyn into Father's den, under guard and unarmed. Llywelyn stands before the desk. At a gesture from the Gens, the guards depart.

"What does this mean?" Llywelyn asks. He holds his face immobile, but his thoughts race. *There must have been other evidence. It is my word against the bastard Telor. I must remain calm. They have taken even my grace knife. Can I overpower him?*

"Llywelyn, you conspired to kill your brothers Rodric and Garreth, to whom you swore loyalty and love. You killed their tutor, Sani, and your sworn companion who was your accomplice." Bleddyn's voice is soft, but is steel wrapped in velvet when he demands, "Why?"

Llywelyn's thoughts of attacking his father vanish. His face darkens as blood rushes from it. *My only crime is that he has discovered me,* he thinks.

"You should not need to ask, Father. I acted as I should have, as you taught me by example every day of my life. I acted to advance myself as you act to advance yourself."

Llywelyn ignores his father's gathering anger – the man's clenched teeth and taut jaw muscles, the darkening of his face as hormones divert blood to muscles, the unblinking eyes.

"You denied me children of my blood. You defy law and custom because you are a telepath – a demon. You know when someone lies to you. You know who is loyal. It is logical to believe the power of House Bleddyn comes from this. I am not a telepath." Llywelyn paces from side to side. His arms and voice tremble.

Gens Bleddyn gestures for Llywelyn to continue, even though the young man needs no encouragement.

220

"You would have found reason to pass over me and would have selected a telepath as your successor. I arranged the death of Rodric and tried to kill Garreth, as I would kill any telepath – or anyone else – who stands in my way."

The Gens nods. "You are correct. I am a telepath. My father, his father, and your brother Rodric were telepaths. But how do you know this?"

He didn't admit Telor is a telepath. Perhaps I can get out of this. "Telor isn't the only one who knows the secrets of Fortress, Father."

Llywelyn does not see Bleddyn flinch when Llywelyn calls him "Father." Llywelyn continues what has become a tirade. "While Telor contents himself with wandering through dusty passages and exploring ancient texts, I have wandered through the recordings made by cameras and microphones. There is little I do not know."

The bolt from Gens Bleddyn's energy pistol takes his son's life.

Bleddyn stands. He puts the pistol on his desk and watches Llywelyn's blood pool on the ancient, gray stones. *How much blood have they seen,* he wonders.

He sits, and then stares at the silent portraits of his ancestors. Ancestors dead thousands of millennia and his own father dead less than thirty years. Women and men, the Gens of House Bleddyn. *If only you could speak,* the present Gens thinks. *I need your council. My son is correct. I created him in both body and mind. I am responsible for his flaws – for the murder of the mining supervisors on Soando, for the risks he took in his war games, for the deaths of Rodric and Sani. I am responsible for his failures and for his death.*

He stands again. He stares at his son's body. *Llywelyn, I am sorry.* He pauses for a moment, and then presses one button to summon his Praetorian Guard and another to summon me.

~~~~~

With only two hundred family members present the Great Hall seems empty. Father stands atop the thirteen steps leading to the high dais.

Father raises his hands for silence, and then lowers them. "Llywelyn is dead. I executed him for treason against family and house. Daughter Bethan is now Heir. Bethan asks that we forego the customary celebration. We will also forgo the customary remembrance.

"House Bleddyn has a bloody history. But the blood we spilled has always been blood of our enemies. This is the first time we have known a traitor who was of-the-blood. I trust it will be the last."

Father's face is immobile, his posture rigid, and his steps measured as he walks through the great hall. His family moves aside, bowing and making a path for him.

~~~~~

Hours later, I respond to Father's summons, kneel, and rise at his gesture.

"My Praetorian Guard arrested Llywelyn's companions minutes after I executed Llywelyn. The guard isolated them and relieved them of weapons except daggers and grace knives. You will treat them all with courtesy but you will question them. You will determine their complicity in the plot to kill your brother, Garreth."

"And Rodric?" I ask.

"And Rodric," Father confirms.

Deep in Fortress, the members of Llywelyn's coterie are called one by one into a small room where armed guards and a medico in a white lab coat wait. Two straight, wooden chairs sit across from one another at a plain wooden table.

"Llywelyn was executed for treason against House Bleddyn," the medico says. "You were sworn to Llywelyn. The Gens wishes to have no doubts about your loyalty. He requires you submit."

The man gestures to a computer sitting on the table. "This machine will measure your blood pressure, respiration, and other body responses to stimuli. You will keep your eyes open and on the screen at all times. Do you have any questions?"

These words are recited to each of the young women and men in Llywelyn's cohort. They are attached to the computer with sensors and multi-colored wires. They do not know I stand behind a window where I can hear and see without being seen. It is not a machine, but I who will pass judgment. I can see much more than truth or lies.

~~~~~

What seems an eternity later, I report to Father.

"Do any of them know about the chemical?" Father asks.

"Only one. Slade of Maelon. I scanned each of them while they saw images and heard words that would cause them to think of the drug and of Llywelyn's..." I find it impossible to continue.

"His treachery," Father says the word. "Do they know anything about the plot against Rodric?"

"None responded with any hint they did. However, Slade of House Maelon knew Llywelyn had approached both Gens Tarren and Gens Maelon. Llywelyn was trying to position himself to come out ahead no matter which of those two won. Slade confirms Llywelyn was part of Tarren's cabal."

Father's face darkens as adrenaline draws blood to the large muscle groups in the flight-or-fight reflex. He draws in a heavy breath, and his normal, bronze complexion returns. "I failed to see that," he says.

I am stunned by Father's words but say nothing.

"Did you learn more?"

I am uncomfortable. I had entered the interrogation room to question Slade more closely. He was strong, and I had to use all of my abilities, including those to inflict pain, to wrest the truth from Slade.

"Yes, Father," I whisper. "Slade knew Tarren had offered Llywelyn command of House Bleddyn after you were assassinated and the house subjugated. It would not be a normal succession, but the aftermath of a great battle."

"Was this the product of Cadfael or of his father?"

"The genesis was his father, but Cadfael renewed the promise shortly after he became Gens Tarren. Slade also knew the old Gens Tarren was the source of the drug Llywelyn used to keep his thoughts hidden."

"That is troubling. It means Tarren believes we are telepaths, and knows a way to block us," Father says. "We must assume Cadfael has that same belief – and access to the same drug."

He thinks for a minute. "We will return Slade's ashes to House Maelon with honor. We are sad his guilt led him to use his grace knife on himself. Neither Gens Maelon nor Tarren will believe us. Return the others of Llywelyn's companions, alive, to their houses. None are to remain here, and all are to be escorted by armed guards until they depart."

Chapter 20: Promotion, Planning, and Vendetta

Two days later, Father summons his Privy Council. I stand in a corner of Father's den while the members file into the room.

The uncles, aunts, and cousins wear formal clothing according to their station, whether soldier's uniform, teacher's robe, medico's white coat, scientist's smock, or nurturing mother's blue pinafore. As each enters, he or she executes the bow of family to the Gens, who returns the bow. They take their seats even though Father remains standing behind his chair. The privilege to sit while the Gens stands is a mark of their station.

When the last chair but his own is filled and the door closed and sealed, Father nods to his brother, Maldwyn, who takes a chair from the hearth and places it beside the Gens' chair at the head of the table. None of the council are surprised. The chair means only that the Gens will add a member to the Privy Council.

Father turns his head toward me. "Telor, there is a place at the table for you."

My face darkens as blood rushes from it, but my step is steady. I have seen this happen once before and know to stand facing my father. What happens next has not happened in my lifetime.

"Do you swear by your honor and your blood to execute the duties of Chancellor of House Bleddyn to the benefit of only the House?"

That raises eyebrows. Not since the death of his father three decades ago has Father named a chancellor. I see Father struggle to conceal his pride when I answer without hesitation.

"Yes, Father. I do."

"Take your seat."

There have been four important events in my life. The first was my elevation and naming before the family. That required a dozen words from Grandfather. Of course I have no memory of that. I was only six days old. The next event was at the banquet celebrating Garreth's elevation, when Father used ten words to declare me son-of-the-blood and Mentor to Garreth. The third was when Father elevated my son, Selwyn and named him a child-of-the-blood, the blood of the House. That required only twenty-one words. Today, with only three words, "Take your seat," Father names me to the most powerful position in the house except his own.

After Father and I sit, he speaks. "It has been nine years since the Council of the Res Publica declared war on the Adversary. When something involves vendetta, we have long memories. When something involves the Adversary, memory is fleeting. The declaration of war advanced the fortunes of House Bleddyn; however, that is not our goal. The Adversary is real and capable of doing great harm to the Res Publica. It falls upon us to keep the threat and preparations for defense alive. How can we do that?"

The eyes of the Privy Council either twitch in confusion or stare at Father. They have never faced such a great and important challenge.

Great-uncle Grigor is first to respond. "Your Grace, your father and grandfather knew this day would come. Their instructions still serve us."

Father nods and fills the silence with his own words. "By now, you all know that Grigor, Tahoma, and Chooli maintain and monitor our faster-than-light communication system. Grigor, please continue."

"For one hundred forty millennia," Grigor says, "House Bleddyn has been communicating with our ships through the FTL comm system."

That brings surprise to many faces. Until now, the age of the FTL comms system has been secret.

"A species we label Adversary attacked one of our ships ten years ago. They are not the first sentient species we have encountered. One was a species of felines – descendants of creatures like our saber-toothed cats. They are intelligent, walk erect, use tools, and have a language. Their blood uses haemoglobin to transport oxygen. They are *not-of-the-blood*. They are, however, our brothers and sisters in every other way. And, they have legends of someone from space who attacked them without provocation. We believe the attacker was the Adversary.

"They are not the only species we have encountered. Our ships have focused their missions on this arm of the galaxy in which the stars are dense and close together. We have encountered four species. We landed, studied, and sampled them. All but the cats are primates. The DNA of all these species – including the cats – is within a few points of exactness of ours. All, however, are red-blooded.

"Do you have questions?"

I wait until it is clear no one else will speak. "What was their level of technology and how old is this information, please?"

Grigor fiddles with his communicator. The portrait of an ancient Gens slides aside and a chart appears.

Species	Technology	Discovered
Primate I	Early stone tools	7,000 BP
Primate II	Flaked stone tools	5,000 BP
Felines	Bronze tools	2,500 BP
Primate III	Bronze tools	1,500 BP

"Primate I, II, and III are our designations of three primate species. They are very much like us, physically, although their blood is red. 'BP' is 'before present' in real time; not the compressed time of starflight." Uncle Grigor sits and looks around the table.

"It took us five hundred millennia to advance from the first flaked stone tools to metalworking," a cousin observes. "But only ten millennia to progress from metalworking to nuclear fission and then to stardrive. These species will visit us some day."

"How long has it been since the Adversary last visited these planets?" an aunt asks.

Another aunt, a biologist answers. "Our scientists can estimate the age of a species' DNA based on changes in parts of the DNA that are not expressed – that do not do anything. They cannot do this with great accuracy. We estimate the Adversary seeded these planets approximately three hundred thousand millennia ago with DNA designed to create hominid species. The Adversary seeded World at the same time. We evolved in ways not intended by them, so did the cats."

"Please remember," I interrupt, "The question on the table is how to use the information we have to keep the threat alive in a way that not only protects the Res Publica but also advances House Bleddyn."

A brief hush falls. Eyes turn to Father. His silence both endorses me and gives direction to my elders. He says nothing while I conduct the meeting, summarizing ideas to ensure common understanding, and keeping the discussion focused.

After an hour, I stand, bringing silence to the room. "Gens Bleddyn, your Privy Council proposes you provide all evidence we have of these four species to Council. We recommend you order ships with physical evidence to return at the best possible speed.

"The new Gens Cadfael Tarren, like his father, is without honor. We recommend you send agents to penetrate House Tarren to learn if they, too, have encountered alien species. We recommend you remind the Council of the Res Publica it is likely someday we will encounter another civilization more advanced than ours. It may be one we have not contacted."

I feel Father's approval when he speaks. "My father anticipated one of your recommendations. He ordered those ships to return as soon as he learned of their discoveries. All the ships have older, slower stardrive, but the first will land in about a year.

228

Thank you all for your excellent advice and counsel. The Privy Council is dismissed." He does not need to add that I should remain.

Father stays seated at the council table. Moments after the last member of the Privy Council has left, a young man and a young woman enter through one of the secret panels and bow. I am less surprised by Father's introduction than by learning others know the secret panels and passages which I think of as my own.

"Telor, these are your cousins Ardeth and Gwydion. Like you, they are telepaths. You may greet them."

I overcome my surprise to respond, then turn to Father. "I have never met them, nor are they recorded in the house records. For their protection, I suppose."

"You are correct. They have lived with House Caerwyn since their initial training as telepaths. They are key members of our intelligence corps. I believe you have a mission for them."

Startled by Father's display of confidence, I shift in my chair, stare at the two spies, glance at my father, and speak. "House Bleddyn reported first contact with the Adversary. I'm sure you know that. Our ships also contacted four other species, one Feline and three Primate. They were, when discovered, some few millennia less advanced than the Res Publica in both evolution and technology. It is likely House Tarren also contacted other species. We need to learn more about what House Tarren knows of other species. Is this a mission you can undertake?"

Gwydion replies for both cousins. "We can, and we will. When do you need this information?"

I turn to Father who answers. "In time for a Council meeting before Spring Stormtime."

The two spies bow and depart – through the secret panel. Father answers the question in my mind. "Yes, they are the only ones other than you who know the secret passages."

A cargo shuttle with the crest of House Caerwyn carries the two spies to Port Caerwyn where they load several crates before joining a flying caravan. They travel to Fortress Tarren as merchants bringing fish, dried seaweed, and other products of the sea from House Caerwyn's fisheries. They have made the trip many times. Tarren's guards recognize the two and know there will be special cargo for them.

The guards are not disappointed. Ardeth and Gwydion unload crates from the shuttle and stack them in a corner of the warehouse. Guards take the crates to their mess hall where Ardeth and Gwydion join them. "Some of the finest ethanol from the distillery," Ardeth says. "Filtered through peat and then aged five years in ancient oak. Better than what the Gens is willing to buy, for certain."

Prompted by a few drinks and well-chosen words, plus some gentle disparagement of Gens Bleddyn's notions about the Adversary, the minds of Gens Tarren's Praetorian Guard – men and women who would never consciously betray their Gens – reveal to the two telepaths conversations overheard and secrets spoken in their presence.

Two days later, Ardeth and Gwydion report their findings to me. I enter Father's den. As House Chancellor, I no longer kneel, but bow.

"What have you learned?" Father asks.

"Tarren's people have encountered other Primate species but not the Adversary. The first contact was about 65,000 C.E. The old Gens Tarren received the information about ten millennia ago, but did not know how to use it to advance his house. Now, Cadfael Tarren cannot reveal it without supporting your position, and he will not do that."

Father snorts his derision. "Thank Ardeth and Gwydion in my name, and ask them to continue their visits to Tarren."

~~~~~

Father summons his Privy Council. Uncle Blevins, Garreth's new tutor, brings the boy to the Council Room and tells him to stand in a corner and be silent. Uncle Blevins sits at Father's desk. Father glances at them before standing at the head of the council table.

Despite the urgency of the meeting, the members observe the formal choreography of the Privy Council. Gens Bleddyn's most trusted advisors enter, bow to him and one another, and take their designated seats.

Father addresses them. "House Bleddyn is wealthy. We have been hoarding our wealth both in goods and in alliances until they will be needed. I believe that is today."

The aunts, uncles, and cousins of the Privy Council sit straighter. I feel their excitement, and a little fear.

"You all have seen the evidence this spiral arm of the broad galaxy of stars is home to more than a few sentient species, including at least one other which has space flight and is hostile. I ask you to consider the validity of my opinion, the truthfulness of the underlying information, and the likelihood and degree this threat may pose to the House and the Res Publica. Having done so, make recommendations for action."

Father stands and leaves the room. That is my cue to speak. "Our Gens wants no hint, even from a nod or a grimace, that he is influencing your deliberations. He did not tell me what he wants, so I cannot influence your decision – even if you all weren't my elders."

I wait for a few chuckles to subside. "Please, Aunt Belisiama, you are the most senior of the Privy Council. Would you begin?"

Aunt Belisiama is more than an aunt. She is my great-great aunt, sister of a former Gens. Despite life extension treatments, she appears old, wizened, and short. Her teacher's robe is like a purple-gray. On her left breast is a badge – the Wolf of the house couped and surmounted by a cloud of stars, symbols of decades of honor. "Thank you Telor. You always were a good boy," she says. My face pales with embarrassment, but the Councilors pretend not to notice.

Aunt B begins. "For millennia, the Res Publica were isolated from other sentient species. It was only two hundred millennia ago we discovered the thralls – and found despite their complete lack of melanin we are the same species. One hundred and fifty millennia ago, we developed stardrive and cold-sleep, and explored stars near us.

"One hundred and forty millennia ago, we discovered other life among the stars. Not sentient, but creatures who might evolve sentience. In our paranoia, we created the tachyon system to warn us if any ships were destroyed. As our exploration expanded, we added relays."

Although her words are common knowledge, the members of the Privy Council sit, enraptured by Belisiama's voice. As if understanding, she smiles before continuing. "Not long after, we developed the technology to give starship crews and other individuals near-immortality through genetic manipulation and later, nanobots in their blood."

She chuckles. "As you can see, this technology is not perfect although it continues to improve. Near-immortality is not immortality. I, for one, am grateful. But, I wander.

"One hundred twenty millennia ago, our first exploration ships returned from the nearest stars. They brought reports of planets with coal and petroleum, fossil fuels we had exhausted on

232

World. At first, there was joy at the possibility of remaking our early industrial civilization. We discovered it was not economically possible to tap these far-away resources. Our exploration turned from energy to rare-earth minerals and to colonization."

The members of the Privy Council exchange glances and nod to one another while Aunt B sips from a glass of water. "Sixty millennia ago, we received the first tachyon signals from ships destroyed. We did not know if they encountered an unknown enemy, an accident, or another house." She frowns at a mutter of "House Tarren."

"Ten millennia ago, we developed a second-generation stardrive. Missions that took millennia required only centuries. Soon after, one of our earliest exploration ships encountered an Adversary ship and defeated it. That ship is bringing evidence of the Adversary. They were an early ship with the early stardrive and will not reach World for at least another five years. House Bleddyn has always planned for the future, the far distant future. Today, we are being asked to assess the current plan and recommend changes."

Aunt Belisiama sits. Uncle Grigor speaks. "What do you recommend?" he asks.

"My goodness, Grigor. You don't still expect me to do your schoolwork, do you?" Belisiama sits and folds her hands in her lap.

The discussion draws on the centuries of experience and broad knowledge of members of the Privy Council. After four hours, I am able to summarize their recommendations. "This is what we will recommend to Gens Bleddyn. First, we will increase our investment in shipbuilding – corvettes and caravels for exploration, fighters for defense, and colony ships to settle known worlds and new worlds. Until now, we established colonies to expand the reach and power of House Bleddyn. From today, we will establish colonies so if an adversary destroys world both

233

House Bleddyn and the Res Publica will survive elsewhere. The number of colonists and their skills must reflect this new understanding, including possible isolation from World.

"Second, we will arm the ships we send to the stars with the most powerful masers we can create plus torpedoes with nuclear fission warheads. We will defy, in secret, the Compact."

I look around the table and meet the eyes of every councilor. I see affirmation. It is time to brief my father. But first, I dismiss all but six members of the Council for lunch. I tell those six they are a sub-element, and assign their task.

After lunch, I face Father and the Privy Council, once again assembled. They know what I will say. Most are glad they are not in my place. I present the recommendations of the Privy Council. Then, I describe some challenges.

"The members of your Council understand the implications of these recommendations. These colony ships cannot depend on resupply and reinforcement from World. They must be equipped to survive on their own. For example, there are no sheep on our continent. It's too hot for them except in the mountains, and they can't live there. They keep falling over cliffs. I think that's why we call them sheep." I wait for the chuckles to subside.

"We have not sent sheep to previous colonies, and depend on trade with the thralls of the Southern Continent for the wool to make most of our clothing. The thralls of the Southern continent grow and ship to us almonds and sunflower seeds, both sources of the copper in our blood. There are other examples.

"There are no weavers, save a few hobbyists, among the Res Publica. Thralls run our mines, smelters, and forges. From weaving to metallurgy, we depend on the thralls. Future colony ships must include both thralls and sheep. There are many more challenges. Sub-elements of the Privy Council will address these issues."

234

I pause, hoping Father will speak. He does not disappoint me. He thanks the Privy Council for their advice and counsel. "It seems World and our place in it are undergoing a great change. You are addressing that change, and you have created a strong start. My chancellor will continue to lead this effort. Please give him your fullest support."

Startled their Gens had said, *please*, the Privy Council responds as one with a pledge of loyalty.

≈≈≈≈≈

"Telor, you left much unsaid." Father sits behind his desk. It is less than an hour since the Privy Council adjourned.

"Yes, Father. And much is unknown. A dozen or more sub-elements will discuss even the haziest and most unlikely questions." I chuckle. "Uncle Blevins thinks in a way different from most of us and is a rich source of ideas."

≈≈≈≈≈

There are things I have not revealed to the Privy Council. The science of the Faster Than Light comm system is one of those. On the day after the Council met, I insert the key into Father's elevator and descend to the laboratory where uncles and an aunt create the linked cubes that are the heart of the house's FTL system.

Uncle Grigor meets me. "We know why you are here. The weakness of the house's FTL comm system is it exists only between pairs of entangled particles, the cubes we produce. We use consoles to link our ships, but those consoles are here. If we lose Fortress to an adversary, if we lose World to the Adversary, our ships and colonies will be isolated. We must overcome that weakness and plan for a future without Fortress and without this laboratory."

"There are three challenges. First, creating hundreds of extra cubes to form a robust and survivable FTL system. Second, delivering those cubes to colonies and ships already launched. Finally, providing the secret of this system and the ability to create cubes to the leaders of selected colonies. This challenge, which must pass your father's scrutiny, may prove the most difficult."

I describe what my father and I discussed. "Father's thought is for caravels with our third generation stardrive to become messengers among house colonies. I think he will understand the need for faster communication than the caravels can provide."

Then, I reveal something not even the Privy Council knows, yet. "Father places great reliance on what he calls *The Last Starship*, a colony ship holding the leadership of House Bleddyn and its allies and the FTL communication technology. That is not sufficient. I will tell him this. I do not think he has given enough thought to preserving your technology. I will also tell him this. Meanwhile, please continue your mission and ensure all ships departing have consoles with the extra cubes linking them to other ships and colonies."

~~~~~

Spring Stormtime is only days away, and already the air is tense with the electrical forces that reveal themselves as lightning. The tension at Council House is a strong reflection of the weather.

Gens Caerwyn, who is First Speaker, recognizes Father.

"During the past one hundred fifty millennia we have sent starships to explore other worlds. They have returned with massive amounts of data. Our focus was at first, energy – coal and petroleum. When we learned it was not practical to bring these to World, our focus changed to minerals – rare-earth elements critical to our electronics. In a third wave which began seven millennia ago, House Bleddyn stopped merely raping worlds for their minerals. We colonized worlds.

"We assume House Tarren did the same."

236

Several Gens squirm in their chairs on the high dais. Father is offering elementary history, taught to children in their first years of school. Father understands this and bursts their disinterest with hard facts. "For months, we have been scouring archives of voyages of exploration. We have found records of life on dozens of planets. We expect someday to encounter other species with technology as good or better than ours."

Father offers visuals of creatures, plants, and their DNA to support his claims. He does not convince Gens Tarren. Despite his youth, Tarren speaks confidently. "These are claims without proof. Dreams. Propaganda designed to create disharmony. Nor do we believe House Bleddyn has colonized other planets. The task is too difficult. The risk is too great."

Father continues, ignoring the boy's objections. "I assume other explorers, House Tarren and their ally, House Maelon in particular, also encountered life. We urge them to examine their records and share what they find. We offer our help in evaluating ancient records."

Gens Tarren and Maelon both seem polite when they agree to examine their records, but they reject our offer to help. The Council is adjourned and we return to Fortress

≈≈≈≈

Gens Bleddyn responds to one of the few people who can summon him preëmptorily – Uncle Grigor.

"Another message, Nephew. Another attack on one of our ships by the Adversary. Our ship won the battle. This is the third such message we have received. I plotted them." He displays a three-dimensional image of the local arm of stars. "See, they are in a line in space and time, a line pointing to World."

"How long?" Father asks. "More important, is their path deliberate – do they know where we are?"

Grigor understands the question. "Impossible to say, Nephew. Only three data points. It may be coincidence. If it is deliberate, we can expect them no less than two hundred years and no more than five hundred years. That is only an estimate."

"Thank you, Uncle." Gens Bleddyn returns to the elevator, and selects a location open only to himself and three others.

This shielded laboratory is less far below fortress than Grigor's. Gens Bleddyn greets his aunt, Calenda. "Time is against us. What progress have you made?"

"Atomic fission is easy. Controlled fission powers our starships. It is easier to create an explosion. Put enough isotope 235 of Element 92 together and it will explode in a fission reaction. Isotope 235 is rare, and must be separated from the much more common isotope 238 and then brought together at the right time. It must be small enough and light enough to fit in a missile warhead. The separation and assembly have their own dangers. We moved this to a laboratory deep under Kosong. If there is an accident, we can blame a volcano."

Aunt Calenda's description is convoluted. *Something else for Telor to understand*, Bleddyn thinks.

~~~~~

Bethan finds her father on the battlements. He is watching summer cumulous clouds move northward toward the equatorial mountains where they will rise and drop their moisture. Although the fields and farms of House Bleddyn will not receive the rain, rivers from the mountains will irrigate them. Other clouds hide the sun, but the southern sky is clearing. Gens Bleddyn does not turn when Bethan approaches, but she knows he is aware of her presence. "You summoned me, Father," she says.

Bleddyn turns and leans against a merlon. "Daughter, someday – with my death – you will become Gens. There is another option. I offer marriage to someone you knew at Academy,

238

the young man who will become Gens Caerwyn. You would be the mother of the heir of that house."

Bethan hesitates. She knows her father expects more than platitudes and speaks as if thinking aloud.

"Since graduation from Academy, I have been an instructor and tactical officer for First Form cadets and a mentor to my younger siblings. Although I have not been a mother, I have had a nurturing role. If I become Gens Bleddyn, I will be distracted by the business of the house, by vendetta, and by war. If I become wife of Gens Caerwyn and mother of his heir, I can fulfill what I see is my role – nurturing mother. I accept. Thank you."

Bleddyn is pleased with the arrangement. He will have grandchildren of-the-blood of both Houses Bleddyn and Caerwyn, including one who will someday be Gens Caerwyn. The bonds between the houses will be secure for at least another generation.

Five days later, the house assembles for a celebration and a banquet. The heir of House Caerwyn accepts Bethan as his wife. Father and Gens Caerwyn exchange blood oaths. The mood is joyous, perhaps too joyous as people try to forget the assembly at which Father announced the execution of Llywelyn. He names Delwyn, the eldest of the twins by an hour, heir apparent of House Bleddyn.

Let Delwyn enjoy her position, Bleddyn thinks. *Neither her telepathy nor her brother's is strong enough to rule. When Guffudd graduates from Academy, I will assign the twins to starships where they may discover other telepathic species. Through them, the house will forge alliances among the stars.*

Satisfied his plans are working, Father signals for a glass of *dŵr y bywyd* with which to salute his daughter and her husband.

~~~~~

Garreth is too impetuous. I have said this to myself and to Garreth often enough. The summer of his ninth year it becomes too obvious to ignore and I am sad Garreth must be drugged.

He is playing at war-games when he strikes out at a toy soldier. His reaction is far beyond reasonable. His blood is no longer governed by the chemicals of childhood, but the more powerful chemicals of puberty – including testosterone.

I am reluctant to do so, but I inject a soporific into his arm, and take him to the medico's chamber where he is fitted with a medical vambrace.

Father explains to Garreth the vambrace's function – to monitor health and inject different medicines when needed. Garreth knows there is more to the vambrace than Father says. It will be my responsibility to fill in the gaps and to make sure Garreth not only understands but also accepts the vambrace. After all, he will wear it for perhaps six or eight years.

~~~~~

The late-summer meeting of the Council of the Res Publica is usually routine, with nothing of importance to discuss. Gens Caerwyn, the First Speaker, recognizes Father, who breaks routine with three words.

"The Adversary approaches." He displays the map with three encounters and a line pointing to World.

"They will likely reach here in two hundred to five hundred years. We must prepare to defend ourselves."

He proposes the Res Publica build battleships and station them at the libration points of our World-Moon system. He proposes a fleet of picket ships, equipped with the house FTL comm system, placed outside the cometary cloud that surrounds our sun-system.

Gens Tarren objects. "You would turn World into a fortress in which to hide. You propose a force to hang over us like a sword on a thread and which can attack any house without warning. What will it cost? Who will profit? More important, who will control it?"

Father responds calmly. "The Adversary's attack, when it comes, will not be a child's game of hide-and-find where the prize is candy or a dessert. It will be a war, and a war of annihilation with the prize being World and our colonies. At best, the preparations I propose will ensure our victory and leave us able to take the battle to the Adversary's home world. At worst, we will slow the Adversary long enough for some of our people to escape to new worlds. It is an intelligent option."

Tarren sneers. "It is the act of a coward."

Gens Bleddyn's face is immobile. "You know what you said. You force my response. I call you to the field."

"The Council will retire to the field," Gens Caerwyn announces before most of those present realize Gens Tarren called Gens Bleddyn, *coward* and Father

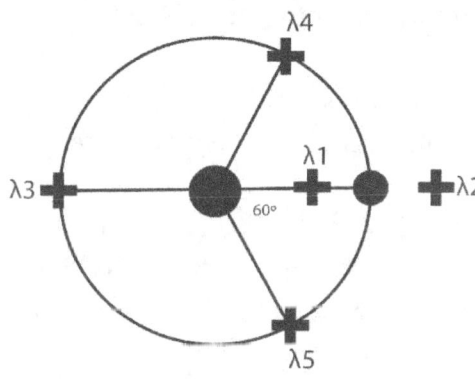

Libration Points (Lagrangian Points or Stable Points) in a two-body system (sun & planet or planet & large moon). Points λ4 and λ5 are stable without expending energy. A ship that drifted slightly away from one of those points would be pulled back into equilibrium.

challenged Gens Tarren to a duel.

Aaron Tarren is his brother's second. "You know our ancestor lost to the sword of Bleddyn's ancestor. He will be prepared for a blade. You should choose energy pistols. Get this done quickly."

"No. I want to see death in his eyes. I will hack him to bits in front of his bastard and the Council. Bring the rapiers."

Aaron carries a box with matching rapiers to Gens Bleddyn, who selects a blade, and whips it about, testing the balance. He slams the sword into the block of wood placed for that purpose. The blade is sound. He nods to Aaron who takes the box with the remaining sword to his brother.

Bleddyn and Tarren exchange salutes, raise their swords, and step toward one another. Tarren attacks first. Bleddyn blocks, then strikes. Tarren retreats; Bleddyn advances and strikes again. Tarren counters. His sword slides along Bleddyn's and catches in the guard of Bleddyn's sword. The two struggle to free their blades. Tarren sweeps his blade wide. In that moment, Bleddyn strikes. His sword penetrates a dozen centimeters into Tarren's gut. Tarren falls, then struggles to rise.

Aaron approaches. Tarren sees his brother, grace knife in his outstretched hand. "No! I am not done! Bleddyn waits for me to rise—"

Aaron's knife flashes across his brother's throat. A gasping gurgle replaces Gens Tarren's words. Aaron stands by his fallen brother and calls, "Gens Bleddyn has won the field." *And House Tarren has a new Gens.*

Gens Caerwyn announces, "The Council is adjourned."

~~~~

An encrypted message from Gwydion comes in an invoice for ethanol. *Tarren will act within a ten-day.* Coupled with earlier warnings and reports of a military buildup, Father believes the action will be an attack. He orders the War Room to be fully staffed. He takes the day shift. I am proud he assigns me to command the night shift.

Eight days later, at the hour between midnight and dawn, a satellite detects fighters coming from the west. Most of Fortress is asleep. Alarms are replaced by the sound of running feet. The War Room seizes televisors and loud speakers throughout Fortress and gives orders.

"Fortress is under attack. Enemy thirty minutes away. Twenty fighters from the west. Soldiers to duty stations. All civilians to the caverns."

I see more fighters coming from the west. I order a squadron of our fighters to intercept.

The initial attack is well coordinated. Only seconds after I launch our fighters, shuttles pop up on radar. They come from the north, across unclaimed land between Tylluan and Eryr and are likely filled with soldiers. A third wave of shuttles comes from the southwest; a fourth from the east.

"Floaters have broken away from the northern attackers. Floater Squadron Six, launch as each element is ready."

"All weapons released, fire at will."

I am standing behind Father's command position when he arrives. It takes only a few words to fill him in on the situation. He nods. It is a mark of his approval. Moments later, Garreth bursts through the door.

Father turns, sees the boy, and gestures to him. "Sit here," he points to his command position. "Watch the screen. Tell me what you see.

Garreth slips into his father's chair. I turn my attention to the ongoing battle.

"Unlock the Academy and Council House defenses," Father tells me. I move to the Senior Controller's position and enter commands.

The attackers did not scout or plan well. They seem unaware of the defenses of Mesa. House Bleddyn takes seriously its responsibility to defend Council House and Academy. Those weapons are unmanned, but the controls are in our War Room. I launch two volleys of anti-aircraft missiles and nearly annihilate the attackers from east and west. Our forces seem to be dealing with those from north and south, but I watch closely.

Our shuttles are armed with rocket grenades, but those are quickly expended. I am about to order the now unarmed shuttles to retreat when a controller grabs my attention. "Our shuttles in the north? They're firing masers."

That is a dangerous tactic, especially so close to the ground. The masers are integral to the antigravity modules. Each time a pilot fires a maser, he loses AG and drops one or two hundred meters of altitude. The tactic is effective. I watch our shuttles drop briefly below radar and then return. The enemy shuttles hit by the masers aren't as lucky. It takes satellite imagery the next day to show them littering fields and forests.

Behind me, Father and Garreth are monitoring the battle. After some whispers with Garreth, Father tells me to send reinforcements to the forest south of Mesa. "They will encounter both floaters and ground troops."

After I issue those commands, I order our fighters to reinforce the north. The enemy commander is slow to react. When he does, it is to order a retreat. His few remaining forces spin and fly away at best speed.

Some are still in range of our missiles. I feel Father's hand on my shoulder. "Let them go. We have achieved a great victory."

Father's next words surprise me. "Although most of the attackers were Tarren's, there were others not in vendetta with us, but who joined the attack in violation of the Compact and custom. Our forbearance today will be important later."

I turn the War Room over to the Day Shift Commander. Less than half a day has passed since the initial warning.

~~~~~

Lieutenant Terrwyn immobilizes a prisoner in a cell deep under Fortress. I draw wires and sensors from a computer on the table and attach them to her body, then turn on the computer.

"The computer will display and record your body's reaction to my questions and your answers. I will know if you are telling the truth. What is your name?"

The woman's eyes flicker from me to the door. "I will not answer. You have no right—"

"You are a prisoner of war," I interrupt. "It is my right to execute you, at this moment and in this place. It is also my right to grant clemency and perhaps trade you to House Tarren for something of value.

"You wear the crest of House Tarren. Are you a soldier of that house?" I pause and switch my eyes to the computer screen. The woman remains silent. "Are you a mercenary in the hire of that house?"

She continues her silence while I ask question after question.

"Are you of-the-blood? Are you adopted?"

"Who planned the attack? Was it Aaron Tarren?"

I narrow the questioning without any answers from the woman other than what I sense from her mind. The images and numbers on the computer screen are irrelevant. After a hundred or so questions, I stop and disconnect the wires and sensors from the woman's body.

"You are a member-by-blood of House Tarren under the direct orders of Aaron Tarren. You led a squadron of floaters from

245

House Tarren and three houses not in vendetta with House Bleddyn. Aaron Tarren ordered the attack. I will not call him Gens because I was present when he murdered his brother. Aaron was not with his soldiers, but safe at Fortress Tarren. That delayed his response to our tactics and cost him the battle.

"Since you failed, Aaron will kill you if you return. You know too much about our methods of interrogation to be allowed to live."

I put the woman's grace knife on the table and use my dagger to cut her bonds. The moment I close the door behind myself, the woman takes the grace knife and draws it across her throat. I feel her death and signal a thrall to clean the room.

~~~~~

Every house knows of the battle. It is impossible to pretend ignorance, even by those of Tarren's allies who claim not to have taken part, but who send messages to us expressing shock, dismay, and their innocence. Father orders un-redacted recordings of the battle transmitted by televisor from our satellites. The signal blankets the continent. Even the thralls know there was a battle, which House Bleddyn won.

~~~~~

Gens Caerwyn is an ally of House Bleddyn, but Caerwyn is also the First Speaker in a rotation dating back hundreds of millennia. It is Caerwyn's right to summon the Gens of the Greater and Lesser Houses. When all have arrived, the Council assembles.

Caerwyn stands. "Gens Tarren attacked Gens Bleddyn in vendetta." Before the whispers become rumbles, he continues. "We are not here to discuss that. The rules of vendetta are older than even the oldest of us. The attack fell within the rules. No, we are here to determine if others, not sworn in vendetta but in allegiance to Tarren, broke the rules of vendetta. We are here to

246

determine not the past, but the future of the Res Publica. Gens Emrys asks to speak."

Gens Emrys rises. "My house sits on the high dais with others of the Greater Houses because we are one of the original thirteen houses. We are not, however, powerful either militarily or economically. Our only strength lies in our honor. *Honor is a coin hard to earn but easily spent.* So Geraint told us. If House Emrys has earned that coin in your eyes, let us spend it, today."

The chamber falls silent. Not only the Gens of Greater Houses but also the Gens of Lesser houses, the members of the audience, the soldiers who stand in ranks at the rear of the chamber – all wait with abated breath.

Gens Emrys takes their silence as assent. "We have seen proof that houses aligned with House Tarren but not in vendetta with House Bleddyn joined the recent attack on House Bleddyn. In its defense, House Bleddyn destroyed not only equipment but also people from those houses, soldiers who flew under the banner of House Tarren.

"House Tarren remains a Greater House by birthright, but is no longer worthy of the fealty of others. I call upon all houses to renounce their allegiance to House Tarren."

This is not the first time such an action was proposed. It failed a hundred fifty millennia ago when Gens Bleddyn defeated Gens Tarren to win Fortress. It failed more than two hundred millennia ago when Gens Bleddyn led a revolt against the despotic Gens Triumph Tarren who had made himself King of the Res Publica.

It fails again, today. While Gens Emrys' plea is passionate, and while his cause is just, it does not overcome the web of deceit and power by which Gens Tarren binds other houses to him. This becomes another incident in the wars of vendetta and the changing tides of loyalty among the houses.

~~~~~

Most of the rest of the month is spent planning and executing our retaliation against Houses Pugh, Reese, Fychan, and Cythrual. Father remains closed when I ask what we will do about House Tarren. I understand he takes responsibility for that. Other events, including the work of our Mountain Company and Gens Marredudd's people in replanting northern hardwood forests are quickly overshadowed by immediate concerns.

Only a month passes before we hear the results of our plans. Messages arrive. Aaron Tarren is dead. Murdered by a Captain of his Praetorian Guard, who declares himself to be Gens. Gens Pugh is found floating in his bathtub, face down. His throat was cut while he dozed in warm water after a tryst. The Commander of House Reese's Praetorian Guard, who is Reese's heir apparent, and who led the forces that attacked Mesa from the north, is dead. A training accident, it is said. Gens Cythrual is dead. Something he ate disagreed with him, according to his heir. Gens Fychan, puppet of Maelon, dies when his shuttle falls from the sky, burning, into a mountain meadow. A battery, overcharged, and which caught fire is blamed.

Father orders all our shuttle and floater batteries and their chargers be inspected. Then he summons Delwyn and me. He is standing in the middle of his den, staring at portraits of his ancestors, when we arrive.

"You know," he says without looking at us, "four Gens and one heir have recently died. Everyone assumes we are responsible. They are correct. Do you understand why we did this?"

Delwyn is always the warrior and thinks like a warrior. "Aaron Tarren cost us and his allies lives. The others are responsible for troops who fought with House Tarren in his attack on us, but are not in vendetta with us. They acted outside the law of the Compact and were fair targets."

"Partly correct, Daughter. Telor?"

248

"We are in vendetta with Fychan. It was declared more than 140 millennia ago and never withdrawn. That made him a legitimate target. Otherwise, you are correct."

Delwyn succeeds in hiding her annoyance when I correct her.

~~~~~

Near the end of Fall Stormtime, Father asks Gens Caerwyn to assemble the Council as soon as weather permits. Both Gens know the attack on House Bleddyn by Tarren and the recent deaths of five persons of High Blood will be foremost in people's minds. The meeting will prove, in Father's words, "most interesting."

He and Caerwyn spend hours discussing the agenda with me and Caerwyn's chancellor. When they are satisfied, the call goes out to the houses.

I sit in the benches, trying to keep my protégé, Garreth, quiet. Caerwyn disposes of routine business quickly and, in some eyes, peremptorily. Then, he recognizes Father. "Gens Bleddyn has the dais."

"Two months ago, you sat here when I encouraged defending World against the approaching Adversary. You all saw how that debate ended – with the death of a Gens and the subsequent decimation of his house. I say *decimation* advisedly. It means the destruction of only *a decile*, a tenth-part. I do not doubt the remaining strength of House Tarren – or its allies. Vendetta was expanded.

Then, Father says the most important words. "House Bleddyn offers to withdraw vendetta with House Tarren and its allies. Will Gens Tarren agree?"

I know Father means what he says. I also know he is sure Gens Tarren will not agree.

The new Gens Tarren stands. "The roots of the enmity between our houses are too deep. We do not withdraw vendetta."

Father nods, very slightly, in the direction of Tarren. "Nevertheless, today, I renew the call for the Res Publica to build defenses. Picket ships in the cometary cloud 100,000 World-radiuses from the sun. Battle ships in libration points of both World and Moon and World and Sun. And, production of weapons."

Father continues to outline the steps he recommends. I see the Gens of the Greater Houses become ... nervous? Unquiet? I am not sure. I see the Lesser Houses and visitors in the benches becoming almost afraid. They remember Gens Tarren's concern – that this force would become a sword hanging over them.

Father knows others will resist his proposal. "I see your concerns. There is only one way to relieve them.

"Lagon's neutrality has been unquestioned for millennia." Father then proposes investing the keys to the defense system with House Lagon.

It is obvious from the expression on Lagon's face he is not expecting this. His reaction makes it easier for Father to sell the proposal.

There are arguments about funding. Father waves them aside with assurances that current exploration will return the dividends necessary. There are arguments about the command structure, which Lagon – waking to the challenge – promises to answer before the first part of the system is built. Gens Tarren tries to mount an argument, which is little more than bluster.

In the end, the Council votes to create the defenses, with only Tarren and Maelon naysaying.

~~~~~

The Res Publica can move quickly when united in a common cause. Only Gens Tarren is reluctant to cooperate in building the defense system. His attempts to delay and obfuscate are easily overcome. Gens Caerwyn, First Speaker, reminds Tarren he risks his status as a Greater House if he does not, in Caerwyn's words, "...pay your bills to Council." With Caerwyn and Lagon handling the creation of the planetary defenses, Father is free to address other plans.

Today, the table where Father's Privy Council usually sits holds the Gens of allies and their heirs, Privy Secretaries, and Chancellors. Present are Marredudd, Hynafol, Caerwyn, Merrick, and Lesser Houses Dolffin, Dwyer, Tylluan, Itan, and Eryr. House Hywel is unaligned, and Gens Hywel's presence piques the curiosity of the others.

"Friends," Father says, "I salute you and thank you for attending. Ten years ago, I called a meeting of the Council of the Res Publica using the ancient code group that the Res Publica, itself, was in danger. I no longer can do that without facing resistance from Gens Tarren and those who cling to alliance with him. The threat is still valid. The future of the Res Publica and of World is in jeopardy.

"I intend to face this in three ways. Two, you know. The first is the defense system being built despite foot-dragging by Tarren and those aligned with him. Second, our colony ships are already taking members-of-the-blood of other houses to planets we believe will be hospitable to colonies."

"I propose that every future colony ship will carry representatives of all our houses. The colonists will also include thralls who have the critical skills to reconstitute our civilization. These thralls will not be servants, but partners. They are the craftsmen upon whose skills we built our civilization. They will become the foundation of the next."

Some of his audience seems uncertain, but he challenges them. "Could you forge a sword – or a plowshare? The Res Publica have lost many of the old skills and become dependent upon the thralls."

Gens Bleddyn looks at the eyes of his audience. He sees the beginning of understanding. *Perhaps the notion of 'service to all' is not completely lost from our collective memory.*

"The ships will hold people in cold-sleep." He seems to smile, but only briefly. "We are very good at preserving seed and eggs of humans. The ships will carry these and the eggs and seeds of herd animals. We will focus on planets seeded but lost by the Adversary, planets which will have other plants and animals useful to us.

"The third step will be to preserve the leadership of our houses should World be destroyed by our Adversary."

The room hums with murmurs of disbelief. No one has ever spoken of the defeat of the Res Publica or of World's destruction. Father does not flinch, nor does he smile. Silence falls.

Father then calls upon Uncle Maddox who stuns the assembled Gens and their advisors with his description and diagrams of a massive colony ship to evacuate the leadership of our allied houses. When Uncle Maddox finishes, Father stands. His speech holds both an offer and a commitment.

"I am building a ship to carry my heir, my immediate family, and the heirs and family of allied houses who wish to join us, to a new world. This is more than a standard colony ship of 5,000. Colony ships know we will send reinforcements to join them. This ship will not have backup. It will be *The Last Starship.*

"Five caravels with fighters will accompany it. Even they may not be enough to ensure its survival."

"This ship, how will you protect it from House Tarren – and, when needed – from the Adversary?" Gens Merrick asks a key question. A few others nod in sympathy. They know Father is asking them to gamble the future of their house and their blood on his plan.

"A good question, thank you," Father replies. "We will keep this ship in a dry dock on Namhae. We will admit it failed

252

because a design flaw renders it useless. That lie is extremely secret.

"Rather than destroying this mistake, we will make it a training ship. Crews of future colony ships will live and work on this vessel for months. We will keep it stocked, with all systems operational and a trained crew ready to accept passengers and launch instantly."

"When will the Adversary attack?" Although no one cheers the question, many hope for an answer they can understand. Bleddyn disappoints them.

"I cannot answer," he says. "My house plans for the future, but we plan for a future we understand. The Adversary creates a future we cannot understand." He displays again the chart showing three encounters in a line leading to World, and the estimate of 200-to-500 years.

"The earlier colony ships – how many people will there be on each ship? And how will you allocate slots to other houses?"

Father turns to me. "Neither I nor House Bleddyn will allocate slots. Telor will explain."

I remind them that each regular colony ship will have room for five thousand people including crew. "The colonists will be selected primarily to ensure the colony has the skills necessary to survive on its own, should we not be able to reinforce it with a second or third ship as we do, today. That will be the first criteria."

I invite each house to send a representative to Namhae to form a team to select colonists from among those submitted by the houses. "That team must understand the importance of skills, and must be granted autonomy by every Gens."

Eyes widen, eyebrows raise, mouths open, necks stiffen as each Gens greets this announcement in his or her own way. Before anyone can object, I ask Gens Hywel to provide the team's first speaker.

Father seals the matter. "By my blood, this team will have complete authority and their decisions will be final." The neutrality of Hywel and the honor of Bleddyn are sufficient to get agreement.

"And how many ships will there be?" Caerwyn asks, even though he knows the answer.

"We plan to launch one colony ship per year," I say.

"Five thousand colonists per year for 200 years … One million people. Can we find that many with the qualifications needed – and who are willing to become colonists?"

"By including thralls, and by changing the focus of our house training programs and the School of House Dolffin, we believe we can."

Father refers the rest of the questions to me. I invite them to expand the custom of fostering children and heirs at Fortress Bleddyn to include Fortress Namhae. I propose the houses' Home Guards begin joint exercises to prepare for integration. "This will be the situation on all future colony ships – children and adults, caregivers, mentors, medicos, thralls, and soldiers from every house. They will swear blood oath to the leader of the colony. Leaders will be drawn from all houses. Every colony ship which launches from this day forward will be a rehearsal for *The Last Starship*."

Chapter 21: House Ellis

Father's summons surprises Daffyd, especially when he is told to wear his flight suit and prepare to remain away for several days. *Stormtime begins tomorrow,* he thinks. *Already, the winds are brisk. I'll be flying home in storms.*

He kneels and rises at his father's command. "Have you kept in contact with Aurin of Ellis?"

The question is Daffyd's second surprise. "Yes, Father. I last saw him at the House Emrys Harvest Festival. We met at a neutral—"

"Is your relationship good?" Father interrupts. "Do you trust him? Is he honorable?"

"Yes, Father, to all three questions." Daffyd smiles. He remembers their first meeting at Academy, digging holes for latrines, and breaking into the kitchen afterwards. "Our first encounters were rocky but we became fast friends and then brothers."

"Good. You will seek an invitation to spend Winter Stormtime at Fortress Ellis. You will seek audience with Gens Ellis and in my name ask for a meeting to discuss the defense of the Res Publica. I would like that meeting to be at Fortress Ellis and as soon as Stormtime is over."

Daffyd has no trouble understanding this order. Now that Llywelyn is dead, the enmity between Llywelyn and Ötsi of Ellis should no longer prevent an alliance. Daffyd knows Tarren continues to make Ellis the token monkey in a political game of *Bo-taoshi.*

Father seeks an alliance, and I am to speak for him. "Yes, Father, I understand." the boy says.

255

News from House Caerwyn overshadows the elevation and celebration of Eurion, my Brother-minus-thirty-years. A caravan returns from delivering wine and medicines to House Tarren with word my cousins, Ardeth and Gwydion, are dead. A soldier who felt his bribe wasn't enough betrayed them. They killed themselves before they could be questioned.

Their suicides would confirm to Gens Tarren they were spies, I think, until I heard the rest of the message which comes from a third agent placed to watch and, if possible, protect Ardeth and Gwydion.

"They ignited a fire which killed them and the soldier when his ammunition belt exploded. It is being treated as an accident. Given this, it will not be possible to return their ashes."

That night, at family supper, Father commands the fire to be lit on the battlements. "Do not question this. Do not speculate among yourselves, but know heroes have died."

≈≈≈≈≈

The volcanoes at the heart of House Ellis's territory are quiet, although the snows of winter do not stay long on the slopes warmed by World's internal fires. Aurin of Ellis clears a shuttle to land at Fortress Ellis. The shuttle's radar transponder shows it belongs to House Caerwyn. It has no external markings, although it carries the Gens of two Greater Houses.

Gens Ellis, who meets the shuttle with Aurin, is surprised when both Gens Bleddyn and Caerwyn, and a youngster in a jumpsuit with the Caerwyn crest and lieutenant's flashes, follow Daffyd from the shuttle onto the landing pad. Daffyd breaks the tension with his greeting to Aurin. "My father was telling Gens Caerwyn there's some pretty good fishing in the mountains around here. When it warms up, anyway. They thought maybe, after the protocol and stuff, they might convince your father to invite them back for a visit."

"And I thought you were here to plan a race, Brother," Aurin says. The Caerwyn youngster's eyes widen when he hears Aurin, scion of a Lesser House, address Daffyd as 'Brother.'

"That, too, Brother, but we should let the adults talk before they get too impatient."

That is Gens Ellis's cue. His bow is suitable to the status of the two Gens. Both Gens Bleddyn and Gens Caerwyn reply with the bow of equals. *Off to a good start,* Daffyd thinks as he senses Gens Ellis's reaction.

Aurin greets the young Caerwyn soldier, whom Daffyd introduces as Marchant, son of Caerwyn.

"Daffyd spent the entire flight assuring me you would welcome me despite my age," Marchant says. "I know my father expects me to represent the house to you and Daffyd. I hope that will be acceptable to you."

"Depends on how well you can race a shuttle, Marchant," Aurin says. "Daffyd and I built our relationship entirely on racing."

Marchant does not hesitate. "Youth and cunning will defeat old age every time. I accept your challenge – when I can bring my own shuttle and not this rattletrap of Father's."

Daffyd snickers. Aurin grins. "I like you, lad. May we put aside protocol, and will you join Daffyd and me to plan our next competition? A third shuttle will make it more interesting."

While the young men talk, Gens Ellis escorts Gens Bleddyn and Cacrwyn to a room where a quickly reacting staff provides hot tea and biscuits for three.

Bleddyn starts the discussion. "Gens Ellis, please forgive me for being abrupt, but Caerwyn and I cannot be gone long before we are missed and face questions we'd not want to answer. Only the three of us, our sons, and those of your people who see us know of our visit."

After Ellis assures secrecy, Caerwyn picks up the thread. "House Bleddyn offers alliance with House Ellis. However, we know Gens Tarren would not accept that. He would cause difficulties for Ellis. Caerwyn offers alliance with Ellis on fair terms with the understanding Caerwyn is aligned – more inextricably than Tarren knows – with Bleddyn. The alliance includes mutual defense, including war games between Ellis and Caerwyn – with non-fatal weapons and with soldiers of Bleddyn secunded to Caerwyn. The alliance offers free access by Ellis merchants and ships to Port Caerwyn. Free, except for standard port fees paid by everyone. It includes the free, mutual exchange of intelligence information among all three houses. What have I overlooked, Bleddyn?"

"Free trade without tariff between Ellis and Caerwyn and thus with Bleddyn."

Bleddyn continues. "What say you, Gens Ellis?"

"The war games? Where will they be held?"

"At least some would be east of your volcanoes, near the border with House Pugh. It would let them know Ellis has strong allies and likely stop some of their incursions into your territory. Your merchant sailors may want to join some of our fleet exercises, especially if you ever arm your merchant ships."

The discussion delves deeply into details, but is amicable. After an hour, and mindful of the deadline, Gens Ellis agrees to the alliance. The three Gens blood their daggers, sealing the agreement.

"I believe our sons will easily plan their shuttle races. If we agree, Caerwyn will prepare documents of this alliance for them to formalize with their blood at their next race."

"I must under ancient protocol notify Tarren, immediately," Ellis says. "And under modern protocol, record his reaction. It should be interesting."

The shuttle carrying Gens Bleddyn and Caerwyn barely clears the trees when Gens Ellis and Aurin meet in the house War Room. Gens Ellis gives brief instructions to his son, and then sits at a terminal to compose a message to Gens Tarren.

The message is in the ancient language, the language of oaths, treaties, and vendetta. Ellis is careful to read over the message several times to ensure it is precise and accurate – and to give his son time to complete his task.

No one in the Tarren War Room speaks the ancient language, and there is more delay before a controller takes the message to Gens Tarren. He stumbles through the first four lines, and then hands the message to his Constable. "Read this."

The Constable takes the document and scans it. "Aloud, fool!" Tarren shouts.

"Sorry, Your Grace." The Constable clears his throat. He skips the meaningless formal language that troubled Gens Tarren and goes to the heart of the message. "'To Gens Tarren, Father and Progenitor of House Tarren, from Gens Ellis. By the terms of our ancient treaty, House Ellis herewith dissolves all bonds between us, whether by trade, or by defence, or by amity, and advises that House Ellis is now allied in trade, defence, amity, and law with House Caerwyn.'"

"There's more, Your Grace, dealing with terminating existing trade agreements and protocols to protect one house's people within the lands of the other house. Would you like the details?"

Gens Tarren sweeps his arm across the desk, pushing papers and writing instruments to the floor. "No, by Karmet, I do not. You take care of them, but first, arrest every member of House Ellis who is in our territory."

"Your Grace, the law forbids that."

"I interpret law in my territory. Do it."

Aurin's task is more difficult than his father's. He is to contact every member of House Ellis who is in Tarren territory. The message is brief. *Hide-and-find. Return home. Do not be seen.* Aurin sends the message to the last person on his list and looks up to see his father beside him. "Message sent to everyone. A few responses, more coming in. I will tell you when they have replied."

"Let us hope they all reply," Ellis said. "And return safely."

~~~~~

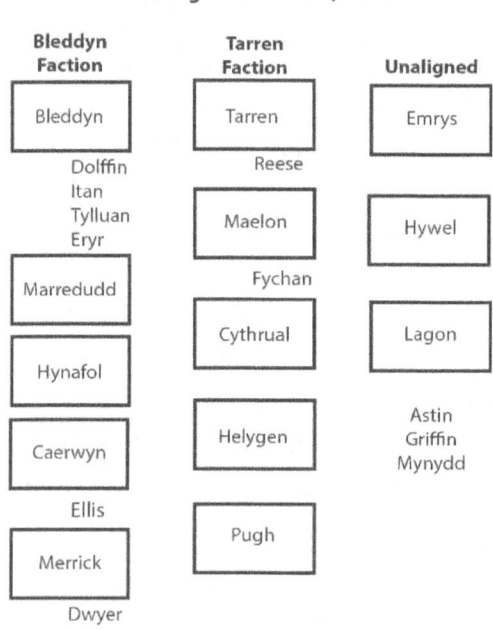

House Alignments c. 200,379 C.E.

Bleddyn Faction	Tarren Faction	Unaligned
Bleddyn	Tarren	Emrys
Dolffin Itan Tylluan Eryr	Reese Maelon	Hywel
Marredudd	Fychan Cythrual	Lagon
Hynafol		Astin Griffin Mynydd
Caerwyn	Helygen	
Ellis	Pugh	
Merrick		
Dwyer		

A few days have passed. The weather is far from clement. A winter storm left ice on tree limbs. The temperature rises and dribbles of icy water from above make the forest a miserable place. Tom of Ellis leads his mother and two sisters on a dirt track. "Why do we go in this direction?" Sister-minus-three protests. "Our home is to the west. Father would want us to—"

"Quiet! Be silent!" Tom commands, and then lowers his voice. "Please, be quiet. Father is dead. We saw him killed. I am sorry, but that's the way it is. I am now head of the family by law and by custom."

"You're only eleven years old," Sister-plus-six says.

260

"Twelve! And it is the law," Tom replies. "Besides, don't you think Tarren will search more closely to the southwest, toward our home? I seek the lands of Emrys, an unaligned house, and one known to be honorable."

"Daughter, listen to your brother," their mother says. *Tom takes on a burden not his. Under the old law, as eldest male, he is the head of the family. Under the new law, I am. But, Tom has the courage to lead us, and his sisters need his surety and confidence. I will follow him in this.*

Tom calls a halt, and then urges his mother and two sisters to seek shelter in a dense copse that rises alongside the track. "Someone follows us," he says. "Be still and silent." He pauses a moment to sprinkle something from a pouch onto the path.

The sound of hounds gets louder as the hunters approach. The hunters move toward the thicket where Tom and his family hide when the hounds bark. Thinking the hounds have closed upon their prey, the hunters loosen swords and energy pistols from their sheaths. The hounds mill about the path, baying at one another, refusing their handlers' instructions to search and find.

After minutes of this, the leader of the hunting party orders it forward. "Something in the trail. A long dead skunk, perhaps. Move on. The hounds will pick up the scent," he says. "Move!"

~~~~~

"Stand and deliver!" The ancient challenge of the highwayman rings through the woods. Tom's mother and sisters freeze. Tom draws his only weapon, the dagger his father gave him on his twelfth birthday – less than a month ago. "Never, on my life!" he replies.

A figure steps from the trees. She is armored and carries not only an energy pistol and rifle but also a broadsword, dagger, and grace knife. None of these are in her hands. "Sorry, lad. That was an old joke and, I am afraid, a bad one. I am Sergeant Markham of the House Bleddyn Home Guard. Who are you?"

"Tom of Ellis, and my family who I will protect with my life," Tom replies. "Wait. You said House Bleddyn? But we are in Tarren territory. I do not believe you."

"You have reached the lands of House Emrys. They are unaligned, and officially we are not here," Markham says. "We were sent to meet you. Well, not you, specifically, but refugees from Tarren territory."

Tom's mother and sisters accept his decision to stay with Sergeant Markham while they are flown to safety. "I will be all right," Tom says. "Sergeant Markham offered her protection and a position in the Home Guard of House Bleddyn. She assured me you will be treated well and cared for and I will receive arms and training. That is all I can hope for as head of our family. Do you understand?"

"Go, find your destiny," Tom's mother says, then kisses his forehead. "We will be safe, and we wait for your safe return."

~~~~~

The meeting of the Council in the Second Month of Year 200,380 C.E. is not cordial. Tension begins when Gens Pugh, the First Speaker and ally of Tarren, fails to call the meeting, claiming there is nothing to discuss. Tension mounts when Gens Bleddyn, with the support of eight of the Greater Houses, demands Pugh call the meeting. Tarren remains silent, but he is sullen when he arrives at Council House.

I attend with Garreth and several of our companion-guards. Father tells me Caerwyn warned Pugh that Caerwyn would cut off his access to the sea if Caerwyn is not first to be recognized. Meanwhile, Merrick approaches Pugh offering to expand trade between their houses if he will cooperate with Caerwyn. Father

262

orchestrated both moves. Although Pugh does not agree to anything, after opening Council he recognizes Caerwyn.

"Compères," Caerwyn begins, but his courtesy is short-lived. "Soldiers of House Tarren executed members of House Ellis who were in Tarren territory when Ellis's change of alignment was announced. This is both reprehensible and a violation of the Compact. I call Gens Tarren to defend himself."

"And why does Gens Ellis not speak for himself?" Tarren says.

Without being recognized, Gens Merrick stands. "You would elevate House Ellis to a Greater House so Gens Ellis might speak at Council? Merrick supports the proposal."

Gens Pugh calls for order, and the babble that swamps the chamber subsides. Pugh calls on Tarren.

"It is not a proposal. It is a joke. So are Caerwyn's charges. We should adjourn."

Before Pugh can raise the gavel, Merrick speaks. "No. Caerwyn brought charges against the Compact. They must be substantiated and answered."

Pugh dithers. He looks first at Tarren, but sees no support. Bleddyn fixes unblinking eyes on him. Emrys, his unaligned neighbor, frowns. Pugh yields. "Gens Caerwyn will present his evidence."

Caerwyn calls Tom of Ellis to the chamber. A boy-child enters to a susurrus of whispers. The whispers increase when people realize the boy is wearing the uniform of the House Bleddyn Home Guard. Tarren sits up. "He is a tool of Bleddyn. You know he will lie. Besides, a child?"

Tom does not wait to be recognized. His voice is loud, but controlled. "A child of House Ellis who saw his father murdered by your soldiers. A child who led his mother and sisters through the forest, evading dogs and your soldiers, until they reached safety. A child who was allowed by the Gens of two honorable houses –

Ellis and Bleddyn – to swear a new allegiance. A child who accuses you of murder."

Tarren shrugs. "What else do you have to entertain us, Caerwyn?"

Gens Caerwyn calls person after person to the chamber. Each tells of soldiers in the uniforms of House Tarren taking members of House Ellis prisoner – or killing them.

"We have sent inquiries about those known to have been taken prisoner," Caerwyn says. "Tarren claims to have no knowledge of them." He spreads his hands, palms up, at his waist. "I am finished."

"Gens Tarren may respond," Pugh announces.

Tarren stands. "I am shocked by these accusations. There were some disturbances after Ellis reneged on our treaty. Some followers of House Ellis trying to flee with stolen property were arrested. Some may have been killed resisting arrest. I know nothing of any murders, but I assure the Council I will investigate and any of my soldiers who are found guilty will be severely punished."

~~~~~

Father and I have returned to Fortress and are in Father's den with hot tea and a crackling fire. Father asks if I have questions about the meeting.

"You know I do, Father. Gens Tarren violated the Compact and the law. But Ellis could break the treaty by notifying Tarren. Didn't he?"

"Yes, he did," Father says. "Tarren lied. He hopes people will believe the lie because he said it from the High Dais. Some will. Others will believe it when Tarren repeats the lie, which he will."

"Repeating a lie doesn't make it true," I say. "Saying a lie loudly doesn't make it true."

264

At that moment, an ember pops from the fire and lands on the stone hearth. I rise to push it under the grate but father stops me. "Watch and learn," he says.

I watch the ember release a puff of smoke and die. *What is the lesson? What does Father see that I don't? Ah, ha!*

"Isolated from the fire, the ember burns weakly and dies. Isolated from the Res Publica, House Tarren may burn for a while before it dies."

Father smiles. He doesn't do that often. "You understand, Telor, son-of-the-blood and son of my heart." His words and smile are the highest praise I could receive. But I have questions.

"Tarren said he would punish any of his soldiers found guilty. But he is High Judge of his house. Will he find any guilty?"

I don't think Father expects that question. "Probably not," he says. "Unless ... unless there are soldiers he wishes to execute, in which case he will charge them, find them guilty without evidence, and execute them."

"Tarren is vicious," I say. "Ruthless."

"He is without honor," Father says, and changes the subject. "Ellis is our ally. We are in vendetta with Tarren; Tarren wronged Ellis. Do we have cause to attack Tarren?"

"We do, Father, both in custom and in law."

Our discussion is brief. Father sets out the rules of this encounter. Tarren caused deaths. Tarren seized property. Our response will be against both property and Tarren's forces.

It is simple to find something of Tarren's to destroy. Attacking the Captain of the Praetorian Guard who killed Tarren before declaring himself Gens – that is impossible. The only blood-of-Tarren remaining are Cynwrig and Bräu, who the new Gens keeps alive as figureheads – or pawns. They are youngsters. Attacking them would not be honorable. After I discuss this with Father, he commands me to plan an attack on property, only. Collateral damage to soldiers is acceptable.

A former Gens Tarren built a fortress that overlooks the Pass of Perdition. I suspect his goal was to control the flow of trade between the north and the south. The fortress is a relic of the Middle Ages when the Res Publica depended on ground transportation or sailing ships for trade. The fortress is, however, an important symbol of Tarren's power in the region, and is an easy choice.

For one moment, while I plan the attack with Master Sergeant Rhingyll, I wish Llywelyn were here. I catch my thoughts and set them aside. Llywelyn and I were nearly the same age and were playmates as children. He was my younger brother, and although he became heir, I don't think I was ever jealous. He did not become distant until we both were at Academy where he was two years behind me.

"Are you all right, sir?" Rhingyll's words pull me back to the present.

"Yes, Master Sergeant. I was daydreaming and not paying attention. Please, continue."

Master Sergeant Rhingyll's plan is not to destroy the fortress guarding the pass, but to capture it. "And then, turn it over to House Dwyer."

His words confuse me. "How can House Dwyer hold the fortress? Their territory is far to the east, and Tarren is closer."

Master Sergeant Rhingyll speaks to me as if I were a child. I bristle until I realize it is the way I speak to Garreth. *He's not denigrating me, he's teaching me.* I listen more closely.

"Dwyer claims land up to the pass, including the mountain on the east side. The mountain on the west lies in unclaimed territory. Tarren's holdings are south of the pass. From a geographic perspective, Dwyer has the best claim on the pass. Further, during the Thrall Rebellion of 80,000 C.E., it was an army from Dwyer, reinforced by First Form Cadets from Academy, who held the pass and protected the entire northern half of the continent.

266

"Tarren claims the pass only as a symbol. He hopes to tie his house to the honor won by House Dwyer and the Cadets. His motive lacks honor."

I repeat something Father often says. "Tarren lacks honor. What can we do about the fortress?"

Master Sergeant Rhingyll outlines a plan that includes elements of the Mountain Company and companies of Ellis and Dwyer's Home Guards fast-roping from shuttles into Tarren's fortress. "There is no sense attacking from the ground. It is too well built and defended. But, even as the old Gens Tarren thought of this as a Middle Ages fortress, he thought only to defend against Middle Ages attacks."

Chapter 22: *Vishnu Nerada* Ship *Twysog*

Spring Stormtime is close and the early winds buffet the corvette as it approaches the spaceport on Namhae. The corvette is the *Twysog*, which discovered the planet with the species we have named Primate II. It was closest of four exploration ships and is first to return. The instant it touches down, tugs rush to tow it to shelter. I swoop over the hanger. Even in the rain, the black wolf against a yellow moon marks my racing shuttle. I land beside the corvette, grazing its side as a gust catches me. *That's going to mess up my paint.*

The Port Commander's mind is bright with anger and his voice on the radio is stern. "Telor, I told you to wait. You can—"

"I am truly sorry, Cousin. Father demands all haste. Please have a tug – in these winds, two tugs – lock down my shuttle and bring charged batteries. I used a lot of power to get here, and I'll need full batteries to return." I chuckle, and then add, "And tell them not to worry about scratching the paint."

The crew of the corvette is listening. They extend a boarding ladder and drop a safety line. I clip the line to my utility harness before climbing the ladder. At the top, hands reach from the airlock to lift me into the ship.

"Your father said you would meet us," one calls over the wind. Silence falls when the thick airlock closes and seals.

"Thank you," I say. "You must be Aunt Carson."

"I am. Your Uncle Justin is in a lower cargo lock loading boxes on a pallet. We couldn't risk damage from buffeting and waited until we landed. He will signal when he is ready to transfer to your shuttle. Would you like to meet the captain?"

Aunt Carson leads me through narrow corridors toward the bow of the ship. The air seems odd until I realize it carries not only the odor of people living in close quarters for millennia but also the smells of new worlds.

I bow to the captain. "In my father's name, welcome home. You must feel a great deal of pride in your success."

"We do. Thank you for acknowledging it. Of course, the important information was long ago sent to the Gens. This disk holds the details. Perhaps you will take it to your father?"

I thank the captain. *I'm certain to find legacy hardware and software to read it. Father never throws anything away.*

Uncle Justin oversees the transfer of crates from the *Twysog* to my shuttle and watches as they are strapped down to his satisfaction. His message is brusque. "I am ready to depart. Where are you?"

Hours later, I fight the storm to make a safe entry into the hanger at Fortress without any damage to my cargo. Father is there to greet his relatives. "You and your shipmates are creating history. Please show and tell the Privy Council what you have found and help us decide what we will tell the other Houses."

~~~~~

Uncle Justin and Aunt Carson have had years to prepare. Most of the Council of the Res Publica listens politely to their presentation. When they invite questions, Gens Tarren is first to speak. He doesn't question; he challenges. "These samples are nothing more than fakery, tissues created in Gens Bleddyn's secret genetics laboratories. We have wasted the day."

At a signal from Gens Bleddyn, the doors of the Council Chamber open, and medicos wheel in a gurney with the body of a Primate. "I thank His Grace, Gens Tarren, for the confidence he expresses in my genetics laboratory; however, I assure him and the Council we are incapable of creating what you see here, and invite

270

each house, Greater and Lesser, to send scientists to Fortress Bleddyn to take their own samples. Meanwhile, we will preserve the body of this creature."

Gens Tarren tries to show disinterest, but his face and voice show anger. "Even if these tests prove your claim, all you have shown us is that we are not alone. This does not prove the existence of the Adversary you invented to justify war."

~~~~~

Father makes Delwyn and Daffyd responsible for greeting scientists who arrive to examine the specimens. In his den, he scrolls through reports while I summarize them. Spring Stormtime damage to farms and orchards; acreage planted in silage, wheat, sorghum, and vegetables; number of calves and colts weaned; estimates of fish populations – the essential details of an agrarian civilization. When the reports end, Father says. "You have more."

"Yes, Father. Daffyd created a situation."

Father almost smiles. "Did he dump a month's supply of garlic into tonight's soup?" he asks.

"No, Father."

"Then Garreth is ahead on points." His smile disappears. "Something troubles you."

"Daffyd agreed to an endurance and navigation race with Marchant of Caerwyn and Aurin of Ellis. Cynwrig of Tarren – heir apparent until a child of the new Gens is born – learned of the race and added his challenge. Daffyd asks your decision on whether to allow Cynwrig into the race."

"Gens Tarren plots against us," Father says. "Cynwrig's shuttle will be equipped not only for speed and endurance but also for intelligence collection. The decision belongs to Daffyd, Aurin, and Marchant. There is risk, but by knowing Tarren's goals, we may better understand his tactics – and his weaknesses."

It is still early morning when Daffyd sits at his father's console in the house War Room and sets up an encrypted televisor conference with Aurin and Marchant.

Aurin's hair is disheveled and the collar of his tunic is open. "Do you have any idea how early it is in this time zone?"

"Two hours earlier than here," Marchant says. He yawns. "The message was marked *important* but did not have the code group for danger."

"I apologize to you both," Daffyd says, "but we need to answer Cynwrig lest he think we fear him. You asked me to make the decision, but I want you to know what I considered. Gens Tarren would like nothing better than an accident to destroy one of our shuttles – and one of us. He would not hesitate to order Cynwrig to create an accident. We installed new radar at the spaceport on Namhae. The racecourse is supposed to skirt Namhae, but Cynwrig might fly close enough to get electronic intelligence data on the radar."

"He would be penalized for missing a waypoint 'cause that's cheating," Marchant says.

"So would creating an accident – be cheating, I mean. Neither is beyond Tarren's capabilities or ambition."

"Your father enforces a no-fly zone around Sehwa and Namhae. He will shoot down anyone who gets too close," Aurin adds. " But, Cynwrig and Gens Tarren knows your father wouldn't order Cynwrig shot down during a race. It's a win-win for Tarren, even if Cynwrig loses the race."

"Two wins?" Marchant asks.

"One for getting electronic intelligence on the radar, one for tweaking Gens Bleddyn's nose and getting away with it," Aurin responds.

Daffyd fills in the silence with a proposal. "Aurin and my shuttles are evenly matched. Victory between the two of us will go to the better pilot."

"I know I have little chance against you two," Marchant says. "But I don't understand what you are saying."

"First, do not denigrate yourself. You may defeat both of us. Second – and this is the secret – I want to switch shuttles with Aurin," Daffyd says. Aurin and Marchant stare, blankly. More than the early hour causes their confusion.

"Our flight suits bear the colors of our houses. Our helmets cover our faces. Aurin and I are of the same height. No one will know if we exchange flight suits and then walk to the other's shuttle. Aurin is the better pilot, but I am the better combat pilot, and Cynwrig knows that. Gens Tarren hasn't forgiven House Ellis for allying with Caerwyn. If Cynwrig attacks anyone, it will be Aurin. It will be Aurin's shuttle he attacks, but I will be the pilot. I cannot lose."

"You will risk yourself for me," Aurin says. "You could die. Even if you didn't die, if anyone discovered this, I would be shamed."

"If I defeat Cynwrig, you and I will switch flight suits after the race before anyone sees us. If I lose, I will be dead and Bleddyn and Tarren will be in open war. You won't have time to feel shame. Besides, Marchant and our fathers will know of this."

Aurin and Marchant agree to the plan. Daffyd ends the call and sends a copy of the route to Cynwrig and an invitation to participate.

Four hours later, Daffyd calls Aurin. The conversation is brief. They agree to do whatever is necessary to protect Marchant, the youngest and most inexperienced pilot. "It is unlikely Cynwrig would attack Marchant," Daffyd says. "He is scarcely more than a child, and beneath Cynwrig's notice."

Spectators crowd the southern battlements of Fortress Bleddyn. Most are members of House Bleddyn; some, of Houses Caerwyn and Ellis. House Tarren did not send anyone. No one is surprised – or disappointed. Inspectors from neutral house Hywel confirm the shuttles' weapons are disabled and signal the race may begin.

The four pilots, helmeted and in flight suits, walk from a postern gate onto the greensward south of Fortress. Their shuttles, resplendent with house colors and imaginative creatures, stand ready. The crew chiefs salute the pilots and seal the doors behind them. After the pilots check in by radio with shuttle control, a signal is given. Nearly as one, they lift from the ground and dart southward. In an instant, they disappear. People leave the battlements, seeking breakfast.

Father and I monitor the race from the house War Room. Radar will follow the shuttles for most of the course; satellites will supplement where radar does not cover. Transponders on each shuttle will send identification codes and current position.

The race combines navigation skill and speed, which have to be balanced with power and engine performance. The shuttles can fly more than three times the speed of sound, but cannot keep that speed during the navigation part of the race. The route runs over the ocean, clockwise around the equatorial continent. Navigation legs weave among the islands of House Dolffin, the Free Islands, and the eastern islands of Houses Reese and Bleddyn, before a final leg from near Soando to Mesa. The race will take most of the day.

Little happens until nearly high sun when the racers pass the Free Islands and leave the radar coverage of allied House Hynafol. Without radar transponders, the shuttles' identification disappears.

"We will lose even the satellite view when they reach Rock Island," a controller says. His comment is unnecessary. The pass between the two thousand meter, shear cliffs of the island and the even steeper cliffs of the mainland is treacherous. Formed when a piece of the continent broke off, Rock Island Pass is nowhere more than twenty meters wide. The sea rushes from west to east, jumping and scattering spray, making visibility near zero for the first fifty meters or so. Above that, a constant westerly wind blusters through the pass, bouncing off the walls, creating eddies and vortexes. It is a point of pride for a shuttle pilot to navigate the pass. No sailing ship has ever done so.

"They're in the pass," I announce. My voice goes to every televisor in Fortress and is broadcast over the continent. "They'll have to slow, and will lose time. It will be about a quarter hour until we see them leave the pass."

My hands are clenched. Fingernails cut into my palms. I try to keep one eye on the clock and one on the screen. It doesn't work. A shuttle pops out of the pass. Without radar, it's impossible to know—

"Where are the others?" A controller gasps. A moment later, a second shuttle appears. It's a minute behind the first. A third leaves the pass, half a minute behind the second. Finally, the fourth shuttle appears, more than five minutes behind the leader.

"Something happened in the pass," Father says. He scans the display. "Get me radar. Penetrate Cythrual's War Room if necessary. I want to know more."

In moments, a controller replies. "Radar is available, sir. We have transponder codes from all four shuttles."

The images on the main screen ease Father's concern. Daffyd leads, Marchant is next, then Aurin. Cynwrig of Tarren is last.

"What happened to make such a great change?" I ask. It is a rhetorical question. We will not know until the pilots return.

Cynwrig cannot make up the time, especially when he is penalized for flying too close to the Reese island where the House Tarren spaceport lies. Just before sunset, three shuttles fly over Fortress Bleddyn. Daffyd's shuttle is in the lead. He makes a victory roll – a dangerous maneuver in any AG craft. Aurin made up time after the pass and his shuttle is second. Marchant is nearly tied for third. Only those with sharp eyes and the controllers with radar see Cynwrig – far behind the others – leave the race. His course turns westward to Tarren territory.

~~~~~

The pilots land on the greensward, leave their shuttles to be serviced by crew chiefs, and go directly to quarters. After showers and a change of clothes, Aurin, Marchant, and Daffyd report to Father. Garreth and I are waiting for them. Garreth runs to Daffyd, stopping short of hugging him. There is something in Daffyd's face that bothers my brother. "You don't act like you won," Garreth says.

"I didn't win, and you must never tell anyone," Daffyd says.

Garreth's eyes and mind are full of questions as Father invites us to sit in front of the fire and pours *dŵr y bywyd* – including a thimbleful for Garreth. He offers the salute. "To Aurin, the victory; to Daffyd the defeat of Cynwrig, and to Marchant, a battle well fought."

I see Garreth's confusion. He saw Daffyd's shuttle cross the finish line, first. I look at Daffyd, encouraging him to respond. "Aurin and I flew one another's shuttles. It was part of the challenge between us – to fly the race in an unfamiliar craft. There are people who might think this cheating, dishonorable, but the challenge was between Aurin, Marchant, and me, and we agreed to it."

276

Father breaks up the explanation. "What happened in the pass?"

"Cynwrig thought I was Aurin and tried to ram my shuttle, push me into the rocks," Daffyd says. "I rolled on my side and pointed my portside AG pod at his starboard pod. That pushed him away and tumbled his shuttle. He lost altitude and ended up in the sea mist. I pointed my starboard pod at the cliff to keep me from crashing into it. I tumbled, too, since my pods were asymmetric, but I planned for that and recovered quickly."

"You said you were the better combat pilot," Aurin said. "I could never have done that."

The next night, Father holds a traditional celebration, a barchedig, to honor the pilots. Aurin and Marchant's families have been at Fortress for three days. No one mentions Cynwrig and Gens Tarren. The head table on the dais holds three Gens. Marchant's eldest brother, Heir of Caerwyn and his wife, my sister, Bethan, also sit in places of honor. I smile at Garreth. I've made him responsible for his brother, Macca, who sits at the head table for the first time. Alaw, another youngster, sits at Garreth's left.

Father avoids mentioning winners and losers in his words. Gens Caerwyn and Ellis follow his example. I understand Father had shared the pilots' plan and plot with their Gens, and they are all pleased with the outcome.

~~~~~

Less than a month after the race and celebration, Father summons his Privy Council. I reach his den to find Garreth sitting at Father's desk. I give Father a memory stick and watch as he scrolls through the information. He shows Garreth how to follow the agenda during the meeting. *Father is grooming Garreth for something, a greater role. Is it because he knows Garreth has hidden talents? Will Garreth be his heir?*

Father told me this will be an important meeting, so I open it with the ancient words. "At the command and invitation of the Gens, the Privy Council is assembled to advise House Bleddyn."

Those words wake them up and everyone is alert when Aunt Carson begins her report. "My relatives and compères," she begins. "*Twysog* was the first of the *Vishnu Nerada* to bring home irrefutable proof an Adversary seeded not only our planet but others. We are not the only species created by this Adversary. We offered the proof to all houses. Some accepted it; some accepted it conditionally; others rejected it.

"I am a scientist and deal in facts. The facts point in only one direction. Another species is close enough in space to have seeded this planet. Does it wish us ill? Will it return to inspect its work? Should we fear it? These are not questions for science, but for this Council." She sits.

I signal Uncle Maddox. He stands and uses his communicator to control images presented on a viewscreen. "Two years ago, our Gens tasked us to create a special colony ship. It is known only to this council and our allies as *The Last Starship*. Should the Adversary attack World and is winning the battle, the leadership of House Bleddyn and its allies will escape on this ship. What you see is the design for the ship. It is the largest ship ever constructed on World."

Father stands. Our eyes turn to him. "House Bleddyn plans for millennia. Our plans assume World will continue the way we know it. The discovery of the Adversary requires we plan differently.

"We have made contact with species who lag us in technology. We have encountered an Adversary with advanced technology. It is reasonable to believe we will encounter other species whose technology is as advanced – or more advanced – than ours. These things have created a new paradigm.

"One hundred and forty thousand millennia ago, the Res Publica created a last-resort signaling system using tachyons to

278

report the death of a ship and its crew. Despite the limitations of the system, we received seven such messages. Three were from ships of the *Vishnu Nerada*. Even when we revealed our FTL comm system, no one thought to ask if we received signals from those ships before their destruction. The answer, for two of our ships, is *yes*. They reported being under attack by unknown forces. The tachyon signal of their destruction was the last thing we heard from them.

"Whether it is the Adversary I postulate, or another species, it is clear, enemies await us in the vast expanse of the galaxy."

Father sits and gestures. I know what he wants and why he wants it. I am to speak the most difficult part of his presentation. "There is another subject too sensitive to be held on any computer or tablet. To protect *The Last Starship* during its escape, we will build and install on World ground-to-space missiles with nuclear fission warheads. These will include single-use x-ray masers powered by a fission explosion. Our shipyard will arm selected corvettes and fighters of the Home Fleet with torpedoes with fission warheads. Clan Bleddyn will violate the Compact. We will place some weapons in space. We will place others on missiles hidden in silos throughout Clan territory. For these weapons to have sufficient coverage, we will recruit allies to place them in their territories."

I sit to allow the Councilors to think about what I said. In only a few minutes, Uncle Dewi stands and raises his arm in the house salute. The others follow. I catch Garreth's eye and nod to show him I expect him to be a part of this. I am proud of my brother when he stands and salutes.

After the Privy Council adjourns, Father and I sit with Garreth. A small fire burns in the hearth.

"Even though the haemocyanin in our blood thrives in the cold, we have a deep need for the warmth of a fire," Father muses. Then he speaks more forcefully.

"Telor, you will be in charge of the planning and preparation for the defense of Fortress, Namhae, and World, and for the escape of *The Last Starship*. You will have access to all weapons, both conventional and nuclear. I will recruit allies to join us and position weapons in their territories."

He looks at Garreth. "You know a great secret, Garreth. You know you must never speak nor hint of it."

"I swear, Father." Again, I find myself very proud of my brother.

~~~~~

Father's announced visit to House Dolffin's Songbaek Island surprises no one. House Bleddyn's long-time alliance with House Dolffin is not a secret, nor is Bleddyn's relationship with Gens Dolffin.

Father does surprise Gens Dolffin when he reveals the plan. "As far as we know, our species – the Res Publica and the thralls – is unique in this galaxy. We are the only sentient species known with haemocyanin as a carrier of oxygen. Our Adversary seeded countless planets with life, some of which holds the DNA capsules that will become their children – beings that should evolve to become like them."

"Should evolve?" Gens Dolffin asks.

"The Adversary's understanding of random mutation – an important part of evolution – seems lacking," Bleddyn says. "More important, it appears this Adversary doesn't want only to seed the galaxy. They also want to exterminate us." Gens Bleddyn shows Dolffin the evidence of battles between ships of the Res Publica and the Adversary.

"I fear for my house, but I also fear for our species. I call upon the ancient bonds between our houses to protect not only our houses, but the Res Publica – and the thralls."

Gens Dolffin is surprised, but she does not show it. "What can Dolffin do?"

Bleddyn relaxes. Dolffin feels the release of his tension.

"You know every colony ship we launch will carry the blood of House Bleddyn and our allies, and of thralls.

"The next colony ship will launch from Namhae in six months. You and other allies must each provide at least four hundred fifty of your houses and thralls to be part of its crew. Here is a list of skills needed by those people, prepared by the joint working group."

Bleddyn pauses. Dolffin fills in the silence. "It happens quickly. I understand. I will ensure my people understand. That may be the most difficult of my tasks."

"No, my friend. The most difficult of your tasks may be what I next propose. I am certain the Adversary will discover World and attack us. If it looks like we will lose the battle, *The Last Starship* will launch. Banned weapons will protect its escape. Nuclear fission weapons. Warheads on missiles capable of attacking the Adversary in space, but not in atmosphere or on the surface of World. We will not poison World. We will position these weapons in silos on Mesa, on Namhae and Kosong and, if you agree, on Songbaek and other of your islands."

Bleddyn pauses. "You know the history of House Kaetween and its destruction. Are you willing to accept the risk?"

Dolffin does not hesitate. "You have convinced me. Yes. My house will accept the risk."

When Gens Bleddyn nods, she adds, "If you plan to defend the entire continent, including all your allies, you will need launch sites all the way from Chindo Island to Namhae."

"No. Although we defeated Tarren in battle, he has been quick to rebuild his power and his allies. Powerful houses still give him their allegiance – and their support. We must make sure Tarren is unaware of our plans. I will approach our allies with this same request. I will tell you when I have additional sites. I may not be able to tell you where, just—"

Gens Dolffin puts her finger to Gens Bleddyn's lips. "Shhh. I know."

Chapter 23: A Murder, An Execution, and a Duel

An announcement, hidden among routine messages intercepted by our counter-intelligence squad, seizes my attention. Cynwrig Tarren, the challenger in the shuttle race, is dead. The details are sketchy, but enough for me to fill in the blanks. He failed his mission. He was executed, certainly on the orders of the Gens. This leaves Bräu as heir apparent until a child of the Gens is born. A little bit of arithmetic shows me Bräu will be in Garreth's class at Academy. And, if Academy is to be judged by the past, Gareth will need protection.

~~~~~

Father returns to Fortress in time for Harvest Festival. He arrives at night, and when I present his briefing the next morning, he says nothing of his visit with Gens Dolffin except, "… we will discuss it later. Now, we must continue the business and activities of the house as if everything were normal. Harvest Festival starts this morning. Are preparations complete?"

Harvest Festival is a time of celebration. Millennia ago, it marked the end of a successful year of farming and herding. It promised a house would have enough food to survive the winter and enough left to plant the next year. Today, sustainable farming and fishing, careful breeding of our herds, and tight human population control ensure we will not out-spend our resources but will have enough to feed everyone and to plant, next year and for many years to come.

Fortress Bleddyn is open to family, friends, allies, and thralls. In fact, the thralls are the main attraction. They are dressed in colorful clothing and offer for sale food, trinkets, and games.

283

Garreth's companion-guards know enough to anticipate his antics, and mostly keep him under control. Until something froward interrupts the fair.

Glint, Garreth's cousin from Namhae, accuses a thrall of having a concealed weapon. It quickly becomes clear the only way Glint could have known about the weapon is that Glint is a demon, someone who can see into the minds of others.

Garreth's companion-guards have no choice but to hold Glint and turn him over to Father for execution. The Compact says in certain terms, *Thou shalt not allow a demon to live.*

Garreth takes the death of his cousin and friend very hard. I try to visit him, but he closes and locks his door. I know his anger. Glint is dead. There is no appeal.

~~~~~

Half a year passes since Glint's execution. Garreth will never forget his friend, but he has strength to continue his training. Father and I provide lessons. However, not all is well and nothing is normal. Father asks me to take his seat at the first meeting of the Council after Spring Stormtime. I will be one of the thirteen people who decide the course of the Res Publica. Although the request is routine, the instructions from Father are neither routine nor simple. Our discussion is long.

The Council chamber is full. Tight lips part only to whisper, and a susurrus of sound echoes from the ancient walls until Gens Hywel, who holds the chair of First Speaker, opens the meeting with the customary polity. He welcomes the Gens present, and then recognizes Gens Cythrual.

Cythrual stands and looks along the High Dais. His eyes stop at me. "I have requested this convocation to set the price of House Bleddyn's imports of iridium, palladium, and certain other precious metals. House Bleddyn discovered several planets which have these metals, and—"

"Article Ten of the Compact negates Gens Cythrual's objection to House Bleddyn profiting from this trade," I interrupt. "This Council lacks the authority to set the cost of our metals. I ask the First Speaker to rule House Cythrual's request void and to adjourn this meeting."

"You will not interrupt me, boy, nor make demands." Gens Cythrual's voice and flared nostrils show his scorn. "You may sit in Gens Bleddyn's seat, but you are not he. Know your place and keep silent."

"I sit for my father. You offend him when you offend me, Cythrual," I reply. My voice is soft and even, like the sea during the Halcyon days of autumn. "You offend me."

"Young pup! You dare..." Gens Cythrual sputters. "I demand your apology."

"And I claim right to your apology, Cythrual," I say. Everyone notices my second failure to use an honorific. The whispers begin, again.

"Enough words!" Gens Cythrual says, and slams his fist on the dais. "I call you to the field."

If Gens Cythrual expects me to be afraid, or to retract my words, I disappoint him. I turn to the First Speaker. "Gens Hywel, I accept Cythrual's challenge. Please adjourn the Council to the field."

~~~~~~

Delwyn stands as my second. She carries only her grace knife. It will be her responsibility to kill me should I be wounded too badly to continue the fight. One of Gens Cythrual's soldiers stands beside him as second.

The Council of Greater Houses lines one side of the field in front of Council House; the Lesser Houses, the other side. Cythrual and I step away from our seconds and stop, one meter apart, in the center of the field.

I lift my sword in salute. Gens Cythrual sneers. He lifts his sword not in salute but in attack. I parry a barrage of quick, short strikes. I block Cythrual's blows, twisting my body to bring my blade into position. My feet never shift or leave the ground. Cythrual is power; I am grace. I step toward my opponent, who takes a step forward to meet me. Blades meet, again, and are deflected. We both step back. Gens Cythrual attempts a fleché, which proves his undoing. I parry. Before Cythrual regains his footing, my blade sweeps through Cythrual's neck, nearly severing the man's head. Cythrual's second does not need his grace knife.

~~~~~

The next day, I face my father.

"Given the time you spend with your books," Father says, "I often overlook that you are also a warrior. You understand why it had to be you and not I who challenged Gens Cythrual?"

"Yes, Father. Neither Cythrual nor the Council would believe you could be rash and impetuous. This 'young pup,' as Cythrual styled me, acts childishly and without restraint. Gens Cythrual was easy for me to bait. He could never have been confident or brave enough to call you to the field."

"We have eliminated a foolish enemy. Gens Cythrual pitted his heirs against one another and did not name a successor. I expect we will see some of them dead before the struggle for succession is over."

"This will change the balance of power," I say.

"Not enough," Father says. "We need an open alliance with one of the three unaligned Greater Houses, or to steal a Greater House from Tarren. Houses Lagon and Emrys have remained firmly neutral for millennia. They have weathered, unscathed, the wars and vendettas among other houses. Hywel is aligned with me, although only my closest allies know that. Emrys would not likely align with me. His territory abuts House Tarren, and would be vulnerable to attack. Helygen may be our best option."

Father does not always confide in me, although he always has confidence in me. I have trouble separating the two.

~~~~~

Not for the first time, Garreth has run away. Privately, I celebrate the determination and courage he shows to cut the locator from his thigh. Still, I can track him by other means. On my recommendation, Father sends agents to Cytgord, the city of mercenary auctions – Garreth's destination.

"Would he enroll as a mercenary?" I ask Father. "Would Garreth sell himself and his services?"

"I think not. If he does enter the auction he will be discovered – and I will ensure one of our agents buys his contract."

"He is under greater than normal stress. His vambrace will run out of drugs in seven or eight days – or fewer," I caution. Father only nods. He knows this, but has no instructions for me.

~~~~~

Twelve days later, Father returns to Fortress. Garreth and Brân, a young woman of unknown provenance, accompany him. Before I am allowed to see him, Garreth's vambrace is fully charged and I do not know what passes between Father, Garreth, and Brân, but Father treats her as an honored guest – and refuses to acknowledge the questions and raised eyebrows of his relatives.

Chapter 24: *Vishnu Nerada* Ship *Eofn*

Before Spring Stormtime, Father notifies all houses the Corvette *Eofn* is inbound and will land at Namhae in autumn. "The *Eofn* brings further proof of a Primate species with haemoglobin blood. They are sentient. They reached a bronze-age civilization 1,500 years ago." The announcement includes an invitation for all Gens to be present when the ship lands. "Let us hope," Father says to me, "at least some of them will bring scientists with microscopes."

"And open minds," I add.

On the day *Eofn* will arrive, Gens of twenty-four houses gather in a hanger where Uncle Maddox provides refreshments. He has set up chairs and tables to resemble a café. I know Father ordered *Eofn* to land in the early afternoon, to allow time for people to assemble, to relax, and to be greeted by members of House Bleddyn. *Always politics.*

If it were not for the announcement on the loud speakers, no one would have known *Eofn* was landing. Its antigravity engines are silent, and the tarmac was swept to make sure no debris would be thrown up. The watching crowd is silent as the ship until the landing skids extend and scrape the tarmac. It is the only sound. Then, someone applauds. Others follow. Gens Tarren joins the applause, although only languidly and briefly.

"Come, we will greet the captain," Father says.

The captain – Great Uncle Archwill – sees we are in uniform and salutes Father rather than bowing. Father returns the salute. "Welcome home, Uncle. This is your nephew, Telor who is

my son and House Chancellor. This nephew is Garreth, who is …
the most curious of my family, and Selwyn, my grandson."

The visiting Gens are anxious to enter the ship, to see for
themselves what was brought. The crew of the *Eofn,* except the
scientists, debarks. The Gens and other visitors climb aboard to see
the bodies of three Primates in cold-sleep canisters.

My Great Uncle understands my unspoken question. "No,
Nephew we did not kill them. They are sentient. These three died
of wounds in battle with others of their species. We retrieved the
bodies from the battlefield without being seen. We thawed this one
so our visitors may remove tissue samples for themselves."

I look at the bodies. They are male, and have the same male
parts as I. Their ears are not smooth and motile like mine, but
convoluted and firmly fixed to their heads. Their eyes are round
and not protected by the fold of skin that protects mine. Their skin
is deep brown, almost black. It is darker than the bronze skin of the
Res Publica. Their hair is not straight but tightly curled. Yet they
are human. They are not us, but they are our cousins.

Uncle Archwill's people provide scalpels, containers, and
preservative liquid. Father offers the first samples to House Tarren.
Gens Tarren watches his man remove one eyeball and one testicle.
At his request, one of our scientists makes an incision and spreads
the ribs, opening the torso. I see the internal organs of this man –
for I must call him that. They are the same as ours. The Tarren
scientist takes samples of the heart, liver, and lungs.

"I have seen enough, Uncle Archwill." I turn to leave, but
Garreth tugs my arm. He asks if he may stay. I signal one of
Father's guards, and then agree.

It is easy to match the tissues of the Primates with those of
our bodies. Aunt Carson sequences the DNA. It is a 97% match.
"We find greater DNA differences among our own species than
between these Primates and the Res Publica." Her words echo
through the chamber when the Council meets, ten days later. Even

290

Gens Tarren is convinced, but he will not say if his ships have encountered sentient life or if he believes Father's claim an Adversary is seeding planets.

~~~~~

Father is not surprised when the current Gens Tarren, once a member of the Praetorian Guard, is himself assassinated by another member of the Praetorian Guard who names himself Gens-Regent for Bräu – the last surviving son of the earlier Gens.

"He is unsure of himself," I say, "and hopes that by linking himself to Bräu, he will gain support from those whose loyalties lie in the past. A foolish notion, especially in that house. Their loyalties ebb and flow more deeply than does the tide among our islands. If he lives, Bräu will enter Academy next year – with Garreth." My question hovers in the air between us, but Father does not hesitate.

"I will ensure they are in the same element. It is a challenge that will strengthen Garreth." Father's plan is not quite what I had in mind.

~~~~~

When Winter Stormtime ends. Garreth's surrogate and I take him to Academy. We do not leave the shuttle, but watch the twelve-year-old Garreth approach the waiting faculty members and the training cadre of older cadets. I am proud to see he does not flinch or hesitate. *Brave and modest*, I think and hope Garreth remembers both words.

~~~~~

The New Year brings Father to the office of First Speaker. Father charges Aunt Aveta, his Privy Secretary, and me to prepare the agenda for the first meeting. Aunt Aveta assembles petitions that have arrived and I prepare the notice in the Ancient Language, and send it to all houses.

I've scarcely sent the message when my communicator chimes. It's the Senior Controller of the War Room. "Sir, Gens-Regent Tarren replied to your message. He refuses to attend a meeting called by Gens Bleddyn."

"What do you think, Aunt?" I say. "You've been Privy Secretary to the Gens long enough to have been through several cycles of the speakership. Is this the first time it has happened?"

"No, and it won't happen this time, either." She smiles at my puzzled look – head cocked to the left, and right eyebrow raised over my eye like a caterpillar.

"On the agenda is a petition to return to House Emrys a thousand hectares of ancestral lands Tarren occupied. Without Tarren present to argue against the petition, it will surely pass by an eight-to-four vote. Speak of this to your father. If he agrees, send that message to Tarren."

I deliver the message to Father. He rewards me with one of his rare smiles. "Send the message, and thank Aunt Aveta for that lesson. You know, of course, even an eight-to-five vote will not be enough to pass the measure."

"Yes, Father. The petition is reasonable, but it will fail."

Father compresses his lips. I sense his anger, and something else. "Perhaps not."

≈≈≈≈≈

Gens-Regent Tarren is both angry and sullen. He fills the Council Meeting with spiteful repartee that descends to mockery. No one hears what Gens Lagon says to Tarren during an early break, but afterwards the meeting is both quieter and more productive.

292

Gens Emrys introduces his petition on the second day. Tarren objects, and shows a deed to the disputed land.

"The deed is a forgery," Gens Emrys says.

Aunt Aveta and Father exchange glances. She nods. I cannot see what passes between them.

"Whether the deed is a forgery is not moot – not debatable," Father says. "The deed was not recorded in the Council archives. It is invalid."

"That is an ancient law," Tarren spits to show his distain.

"*Lex dura, sed lex*," Father says. "The law may be hard, but it is the law." Before Tarren can reply, Father calls for a vote.

The tokens are passed. Gens Caerwyn receives the first numbered token and stands. "Caerwyn supports the petition to return the land to Emrys."

The vote continues with Pugh denying the petition; Marredudd and Lagon supporting it; Maelon, Cythrual, and Tarren denying it. The last token is held by Helygen. The vote is eight-to-four to support the petition. Tarren smiles. Helygen's vote will tip the balance in Tarren's favor.

Helygen stands. "Helygen supports the petition." The vote is nine-to-four. The petition passes.

Tarren's face turns white. "You can't do that," he shouts.

Helygen is still standing. "I have the dais," he says. "When I received the agenda, I read most carefully the treaty between Helygen and Tarren. It calls for amity and mutual defense in time of war. It establishes terms for trade between us and for passage of our people through one another's territory. It provides for fostering children in one another's homes. The treaty does not require Helygen to support every position Tarren takes in Council. I may do this; I have done so."

Father hides his satisfaction when he orders Tarren to "remove all persons and property which belongs to House Tarren" from the land in twenty days, and appoints Gens Mynydd Judge of the Change.

As Spring Stormtime approaches, Garreth sends me the names of schoolmates he wants to bring home. I quickly approve Barri and Deryn. I wonder if Garreth susses they are his protectors, assigned by Father. Betsan is more difficult to vet. She is a member of an unaligned house, Griffin, which has a smallholding in the western mountains. I know no one from that house, and little about it. I will watch her closely during the visit, and I will repair this gap in my intelligence network. After I send Garreth approval, I pull up the roster of Academy cadets in my class, and look for members of House Griffin.

I watch Garreth and his friends join in games and play with his siblings and with my son Selwyn. I am pleased Garreth includes the boy. I also see how easily Betsan takes the role of elder sister to Alaw. I sense her loyalty and pride in her adopted role. She will make an excellent classmate for Garreth. On my recommendation, Father ensures she will remain in Garreth's element for at least another year.

~~~~~

On a fine spring day a month after Stormtime, Uncle Maddox reports *The Last Starship* ready for its test flight. I fly to Namhae to observe. The ship nearly crashes. At least, that's what seems to happen. The pilot is Uncle Maddox, who has more experience as a starship test pilot than any other person on World. He safely lands the wobbling ship. Tugs pull it into a hanger. The hanger was built to hold the ship and to conceal activities from observation.

"Perfect flight," Uncle Maddox tells me. "Two of Tarren's satellites made passes during the flight and should have picked up the wobble and seen the abrupt landing. Now, all we have to do is ensure Tarren knows of the design flaw that makes the ship useless."

"Father will do so at the next Council meeting."

~~~~~

Gens-Regent Tarren requests a meeting of the Council to present *important information*. His important information is an announcement.

"I understand your latest colony ship is flawed." He looks at Father and then sits. An obvious smile and a slight shake of his head show his smugness. Since he is blocking our telepathy with drugs, Father and I have to rely on body language, but Tarren is easy to read.

Father is prepared, and is quite composed when he responds. "Yes. We seem to have reached the limit of what we can do with antigravity engines. They lift ships from World by interacting with the world's mass, and then interact with the dark energy of the universe to propel the ships through space. Unless we come up with a new technology, we cannot build a successful ship any larger than our earlier colony ships."

"A costly lesson, I suspect," Gens-Regent Tarren says with the same smile and shake of his head.

"More than you realize, I'm afraid." Father looks down and shakes his own head. "The ship was not only larger, but the entire design was new. Engines, power, structure, and electronic systems – all are integrated. We cannot salvage anything except perhaps light fixtures, and not many of those. We are considering turning it into a training facility, but even that will be costly."

"Perhaps it could become a museum to hubris," Tarren says.

Rather than take offense, Father smiles. "Or a museum to hubris."

Tarren realizes he will not bait Father and that most of the attendees are not interested in his petty words. He sits, sullen, for the rest of the meeting.

Telor was right, Gens Bleddyn thinks. *Treating your enemies with kindness throws them off balance.*

I am in the library when my communicator chimes with a message from the War Room.

<<Distress call fishing vessel under attack by unknown ship northeast of Sehwa>>

I know Father has received the message; I hurry to the War Room where Father is being briefed by the Senior Controller. "We will have a satellite in range in a few minutes. The nearest ship – the *Caerodor* is 10 kilometers away, and will have to sail into the wind to reach the fishing ship. Perhaps half an hour."

"The attacker?"

"Unknown—" Our satellite comes in range. Two ships appear on the screen.

I am fastest to interpret what is on the screen. "Turtle ship ... Tarren design ... covered deck, cannons fore and aft ... square sail plus oarsmen. Probably crewed by Reese but on orders of Tarren."

"Our people are in life jackets, in the water. Our ship is foundering. The *Caerodor* is moving in. They know we have people in the water."

"The Reese ship is turning away." This is dishonorable. Even though Reese is the attacker, they have a duty to rescue survivors.

The satellite continues its southward orbit and the ships disappear from the display screen.

"Telor, put a satellite in synchronous orbit above the Reese islands," Father commands. "Close that gap in coverage."

An hour later, *Caerodor* reports rescue of the fishing boat's crew, who are en route to the hospital on Sehwa for checkups. Uncle Maddox promises to have another satellite constructed and put in orbit within a month. I report to Father.

"Tarren will learn about the new satellite and will protest, through Reese. Uncle Maddox said the satellite will have active defenses, but he wouldn't say what they are. I think he enjoys having secrets from me, but he will tell you. Tarren is already angry our radar at Namhae can monitor all of his launches from the Reese spaceport, and that we can track them through cislunar space. If Tarren attacks the satellite, we will know of it."

Father abruptly changes the subject. "Aunt Aveta sent my formal protest to Reese, moments before Reese's protest of our fishing vessel infringing on Reese waters. The argument will drag out for two or three years before Reese pays us restitution. Meanwhile, how shall we return this strike?"

"On Reese or Tarren?"

Father ducks his head slightly and looks at me from the top of his eyes. He says nothing.

"Tarren," I say.

I arrange the destruction of one of Tarren's robotic harvesters in a field of winter wheat exactly ten days after the attack on our fishing boat. The boat and the harvester are of equivalent value. There are no deaths in either attack. We have more fishing boats; Tarren has more harvesters. No one will go hungry. We both flexed our muscles. Vendetta should be satisfied, at least for a little while.

~~~~~

Bleddyn is not the only house with a receiver tuned to the tachyon system. Tarren has one, and there is one at Council House that relays information to every house, even those who cannot afford to build spaceships. At the House Bleddyn War Room, the tachyon signal comes in after an FTL message that one of our ships is under attack. There is no question in anyone's mind: we have lost a ship, but, to whom?

A controller clears the main display.

"Play it back, please," I say. "Play all the information and stop after each event. From the first FTL message to the tachyon signal."

The controller assembles a display that shows our ship near a standard star and its first message.

<<Unknown drive signature approaching inner planet.>> Technical details from their sensors are attached.

"Nothing more for two hours," the controller says. I order her to advance the timeline.

<<Confirmed Adversary ship headed for inner planet. We determined it was seeded.>>

"It looks like the Adversary didn't forget this one."

Again, details of the Adversary's drive signature and, perhaps more useful, our ship's report of its exploration of the inner planet are attached to the message.

"The next event is the tachyon signal," the controller reports. "Our ship was destroyed, but launched seven life pods."

"Will we be able to recover them?" A controller asks.

"The life pods will seek a libration point at the nearest habitable planet," I reply. "Unfortunately, that is the newly-seeded planet. We will try to rescue the life pods, but that may not be possible. If the Adversary detects them, they will destroy them or try to capture our people. Should the Adversary attempt to open a life pod, the pod will self-destruct, killing the occupant."

298

Gens-Regent Tarren objects again to being summoned to Council by Gens Bleddyn. However, after his defeat at the first meeting of the year he does not refuse to attend. Father's report of this fourth encounter with the Adversary on a line pointing toward World electrifies the Council. We have a new urgency to our efforts to protect World.

"Four could still be coincidence," Tarren says. Neither Father nor I can find more in his mind. He's blocking with the same drug Llywelyn used. Gens Merrick's disgust with Tarren is scarcely hidden when he adjourns the meeting.

~~~~~

Garreth and his element have completed their first year at Academy. Betsan, Cledwyn, and Nudd accept Garreth's invitation to visit Fortress during Winter Stormtime. Barri and Deryn accept, too. I expected that. Garreth's friends may hope for a fun time, but Father commands I fly to Namhae. I decide to give these young cadets a thrill and insist Garreth and his friends accompany me, no matter how unusual it is to fly shuttles during stormtime.

I take my racing shuttle. To save weight, it has no permanent passenger seats. The youngsters sit in canvas seats with five-point harnesses. Most seem unaffected by the bumps, dips, and dives, although Barri looks a little green, which is quite a trick given his bronze skin and clear blood.

Uncle Maddox takes us into a cavern under Namhae. The cavern's walls are smooth obsidian, and a perfect, fifty meter-diameter sphere except for the flat base. A bubble of gas in lava created the chamber millennia ago. Racks of computer equipment tended by a score of technicians cover the floor. The cadets' awe at their surroundings nearly keeps them from hearing Uncle Maddox describe the ship they will visit.

None of the cadets have any idea how big the ship is. In fact, they knew little except from video of the disastrous test flight

– video that Gens Tarren widely distributed. The ship's public name is *Dothineb Geraint* – in the old language, "Wisdom of Geraint." A suitable name for a training ship, I thought when I named it.

Once the cadets get over their initial awe, members of the trainee crew, close in age, greet them, show them around, and set up simulated launches, battles, and landings. After that, even Barri forgives me for the rough ride.

〰〰〰

I return Garreth and his element-mates to Fortress. They spend most of their time on the firing range after complaining they don't get enough practice at Academy. I am in the War Room when a message arrives from House Tarren. The Comm-O sends it to Father's terminal where I am monitoring calls for assistance. This stormtime is mild, and there are few calls. Expecting this message to be such a call, I am jolted.

<<Gens Tarren sends. Bräu is dead.>>

I notify Father immediately, but wait until after lunchtime to give the news to Garreth and his companions. Bräu was a member of their element, although I suspect none were close to him. Nevertheless, the news sobers the group until blood sugar elevated by a sweet dessert improves their mood.

Bräu would have graduated from Academy with Garreth's element in a few years. By custom, he would become Gens Tarren. It seems the man who declared himself Regent didn't want that to happen.

300

The next day, Father announces he will assign the twins, Daffyd and Delwyn, to separate starships and Guffudd will become heir presumptive. Father uses even his own children to further the goals of the house. For the children, it is not only their duty but also brings them honor. It will be two months before the twins' ships breach the cometary cloud and are far enough from the sun's gravity well to enter stardrive. By then, all but a few of the crew will be in cold-sleep.

The twins' mission profiles call for visits to planets we think were seeded by the Adversary and then forgotten. Some may be suitable for colonization. Some may have sentient life. Some of that life may be telepathic.

—Telor Bleddyn, Journal

Chapter 25: *Vishnu Nerada* Ship *Draig Aur*

Garreth brings Barri, Deryn, and Alwen to Fortress for Spring Stormtime. There is something troubling Garreth, but I cannot suss what it is. Only after he takes Barri and Deryn to meet Father do I understand. In Barri and Deryn, Garreth found the first persons to swear loyalty and fealty to him. I watch as Garreth shows he understands his obligation from their oaths.

Little of importance happens during the next nine months, but I am glad when Garreth joins me in the War Room for duty during Winter Stormtime. House Bleddyn is the focal point for emergency messages and requests for help from not only our allies but also those of Tarren's allies he ignores. Garreth is using the FTL system relayed through ships light years away to communicate with houses whose comms were destroyed by the storms. I am about to re-position a weather satellite when the Communication Officer sends me a message. I read it and forward it to Garreth.

The message is from the *Draig Aur*, an exploration ship launched a hundred millennia ago. We thought it was lost, but now it is returning. The ship is old and slow, and will not land until mid-year. Still, the news is exciting.

~~~~~

Before the *Draig Aur* lands, Gens Tarren asks Caerwyn, who is First Speaker, to call an "emergency meeting of the Council to address a grave situation." Father instructs me to accompany him and to be watchful. I understand he means for me to monitor the reactions of the other Gens, especially those not allied with him.

Father describes the message from the *Draig Aur* to all who will listen. Tarren's response to Father's announcement is one the Council and we have heard often.

"The only proofs of this Adversary are assertions of House Bleddyn – scientists who are on a ship thousands of light-years away. In the few years since we declared war, the fortunes of House Bleddyn have increased a hundred-fold through payments to their shipyards and for the FTL communication system.

"House Tarren herewith enters a motion before Council that House Bleddyn pay its fair share of the costs of this so-called war. Not the *even share* as in the past, but based on the house's wealth and income." Everyone expects Gens Maelon's second of the motion. Maelon is a known sycophant and ally of Gens Tarren. After the Free City of Ocsiwn was destroyed, Tarren is the only ally of Maelon.

Father signals and is recognized. "I can show you the genetic, evolutionary history of the Res Publica. I can compare that with the climatic history of our planet. I can show where haemocyanin offered an evolutionary advantage during an extended ice age. I can show when the species of the Res Publica and the thralls diverged from the beasts and cattle of the forest and fields and became human. The truth will convince no one whose mind is closed.

"There is only one proof you will accept. That proof is getting closer every day. You know of the message from the *Draig Aur* – a ship of the *Vishnu Nerada*. It will arrive in fewer than three hundred days. They have defeated a ship of the Adversary and bring with them both technology and bodies."

"Living bodies?" Gens Tarren pounces on Father's statement.

"Perhaps. What passes for blood in their bodies cannot tolerate our cold-sleep. My crew put two in their own long-sleep chambers. They may survive."

Father refuses to answer further questions, saying he has no more information but will bring everything before Council when the ship lands.

Despite Father's promise, Tarren demands a vote on his motion, but fails to receive a supermajority.

~~~~~

We return to Fortress late at night. Ignoring the hour, Father summons me to his den. It is not yet first light.

"Telor, your mind holds questions. What are they?"

He asks a question for which I am not prepared. My thoughts stumble, but he gives me time to think.

"Father, you have always trusted me and I have always trusted you. Even when I know you have not told me all you knew, I have trusted you. My trust comes from knowing your thoughts and knowing you hold me in the same hand you hold my siblings."

"I hold you thus," Father says, although his voice is mild and lacks the usual aura of command, "because you are the future of the house. While Guffudd is now my heir, you are already his chief counselor. Guffudd is very comfortable with that. And, like Guffudd, you do not kneel before me. Guffudd is also comfortable with that. He understands the balance of power and the need for it better than Llywelyn ever did.

"You want to know why I did not tell you about the *Draig Aur*'s cargo. I have known since I was a cadet. The ship carries not only bodies of the Adversary but also samples of their technology. Many millennia have passed since *Draig Aur* captured the ship. We should expect their technology to have advanced since then. However, these are the best and only samples we have.

"You wonder why I did not share this information with you."

Father stops speaking. He looks at the wall where portraits of his ancestors hang – Gens of generations past. "It was because of the oath I made to my father, and he to his. Does this disturb you?"

I answer easily. "No, Father."

There is something Father is not telling me, but I put it aside to deal with what is important and what is immediate.

~~~~~

Namhae Island was formed long ago by volcanoes whose tops we flattened to make a landing place. Bunkers surround the tarmac. Once the bunkers were control rooms for the launch of chemical-engine rockets carrying satellites and later, ships carrying explorers into space. A few kilometers away and reached by a monorail are the hangers and shops of the shipyard. Our radar stands sentinel to the protections we mount against enemies. Only Namhae is more secure than Fortress.

Summer Stormtime is several days away, but Father arranges an early release from Academy for Garreth and his friends. I travel to Namhae with Father, Garreth, Alaw, Selwyn, and Garreth's friends. Other shuttles hold what may be half the house's Home Guard. Armed shuttles fill the sky and warships ply the waters. All this is to deter House Tarren and their allies from attempting any mischief when the *Draig Aur* lands.

We watch from one of the bunkers and look through thick, tempered glass when the ancient rocket engines lower the ship. The infrasonic rumble of the engines penetrates even the massive concrete and shakes our bodies. Alaw screams in fright. Betsan sees and hugs the girl until the noise abruptly stops.

As soon as the tarmac cools, Father walks to the ship and greets the captain, our great-great uncle Derwin.

The rest of the morning is carefully orchestrated chaos. Medicos take charge of Uncle Derwin and the crew. Scientists and engineers swarm the ship, testing its systems and removing the equipment and parts of the Adversary ship that fill the holds. A

306

special medical-engineering team removes the long-sleep coffins containing the Adversaries.

Stormtime is felt across the continent, yet messages from the other Great Houses are becoming more insistent. Allies are requesting – and enemies are demanding – access to the Adversary's technology. Father orders everything – including the chambers holding the Adversaries – transported to Fortress. We arrive before the first major storm of the season strikes.

I return to Fortress in time for the Senior Controller to show me a message from Gens Maelon. It is an open secret that Gens Maelon's mouth speaks the words of Gens Tarren. "Your faster-than-light communication system would have brought news of this to you long before the ship landed, long before the announcement you made sixteen years ago and brought the Res Publica into a war. Gens Maelon calls for Gens Bleddyn to be open about what you know of the Adversary."

I thank the controller and take the message to Father. "How will you answer this?"

"Tell Maelon the blame lies with a faulty transmitter. When the *Draig Aur* was launched, the FTL system was in its infancy. Maelon may not believe us, but he cannot challenge us," Father replies.

Then, he tells me what Uncle Derwin spoke only to Father. "The FTL system did fail. When *Draig Aur* reached the orbit of Lau, she reported by medium wave because her FTL system no longer worked. They tested everything except the cube."

Father hands me a box. "The cube is here. Please take it to the laboratory."

~~~~~

It is the deepest hour of night when Uncle Grigor summons me to the laboratory where cubes for the FTL system are created.

Uncle Tahoma is with him. Their faces convey bad news, but their minds are too chaotic for me to understand. I think Uncle Grigor may be a telepath. He sees my confusion.

"The cube from the ship and the one in the console in the War Room are no longer entangled. Something we have suspected but had no proof until now. There's a rule in quantum theory, 'if anything is possible, given enough time it will happen.'"

"What happened," Uncle Tahoma picks up the narrative, "is what we call *quantum fluctuations* – small and inexplicable changes in random ways. They always occur in an otherwise homogeneous substance. The cubes can survive some of this, but eventually become untangled enough to destroy their interconnectedness."

There is silence while my uncles try to suss if I understand their explanation.

"I do understand," I say. "There is a natural force about which we know little and over which we have no control. This force may render useless the scores of communication links between World and ships – ours and those of other houses. The good news is this is not likely to happen immediately or all at once. The bad news is it will happen. This is a problem. I will ensure that Father understands, but I want a solution. Meanwhile, I will order all ships to return to World if they lose FTL comms."

My uncles exchange glances, and I see understanding.

≈≈≈≈≈

Soon after we return to Fortress, Father sends a call for the houses to assemble at Council House. The late Summer Stormtime weather continues to make travel hazardous, but Father insists. Thunder rumbles and penetrates even the Council chambers. Uncle Derwin and I accompany Father. The rest of our family and their stormtime guests must watch by televisor.

308

A captive walks, naked, into the Council Chamber. The First Speaker waits while conversations buzz.

"He looks like us…"

"No, look at his ears. They are crumpled …"

"His eyes …" another says. "…are round."

"Who are you? What is your name?" The voice of Gens Tarren cuts through the murmurs.

"He cannot answer," Gens Bleddyn says. "Not only does he not understand our speech, his mind did not survive the passage. He has no more brain than … than an earthworm."

Knowing the creature has no sentience, no mind, no intelligence, no feeling, I draw my grace knife and with one quick movement slice open the insensate captive's palm. I raise the man's hand and step away from the spreading pool of blood.

"Look!" I challenge. "His blood is red, like our cattle. He is not-of-the-blood. His people are anathema. This is the Adversary."

I signal a medico to bind the wound.

Father's voice cuts through the babble. "We will keep the two specimens alive and study them. I invite all houses to send doctors and scientists to our hospital on Sehwa to join those studies."

Father scores points with that. What he says next has potential to split the Res Publica.

"The Adversary ship was armed with torpedoes. We retrieved several of those. The crew destroyed the ship's power source and stardrive; however, the torpedoes have a near-light-speed drive, which may offer us clues. There was no information about the ship's power source or drive. Our crew broke into a vault containing a computer, but found it melted, utterly destroyed. They found no operating or repair manuals.

"We will continue to study the torpedoes. When we understand them, we will replicate and test them. Once that happens, we will share them with the rest of the Res Publica."

Father's voice cuts through Gens Tarren's shouted objection. "I remind you of what I said when we first became aware of the Adversary – the Galaxy has room for all the Res Publica, but not for these beasts. They attacked us more than once without warning; they seeded our planet and deserted us; they are not-of-the-blood. I call for the People of the Blood to remember this, and to join in opposition to them – and not to one another."

Gens Tarren is not happy. He sends messages to Father demanding he allow Tarren's engineers to study the Adversary's torpedoes. He knows House Bleddyn will be the first to understand the new technology. Father demurs but renews his promise to share the technology once it is understood.

~~~~~

A few days later, Gens Bleddyn enters Aunt Carson's laboratory. She greets him with the bow of family.

Bleddyn returns the bow, but a little deeper. "I understand you have examined samples of the Adversary bodies."

Aunt Carson's answer surprises him. "Do you know you have samples of flora and fauna returned by exploration ships beginning a hundred and twenty millennia ago? They sat in cryogenic vaults. No one was interested in them. They are being removed to my laboratory a few at a time. I am trying to sequence their DNA. Some samples are still viable, and I'm getting results."

"And the DNA of the Adversary?"

"It is sequenced. You believe the Adversary is seeding planets in our spiral arm of the galaxy. We have determined life encountered by our ships is too similar among itself and ours to have been formed simply by the coincidences of chemical determinism. This is the first DNA of the Adversary we have possessed. The best evidence to support your hypothesis will come from comparing the Adversary's DNA to DNA from many planets, including ours."

310

Two ten-days later, Aunt Carson reports her findings to the Privy Council. "We have confirmed this. All life encountered so far is genetically related. From the most microscopic of bacteria to the greatest of the animals, and to our species – the Res Publica and the thralls. It is conclusive. The Adversary's DNA is the genesis of this relationship and is older than any other DNA encountered. We are descended from Adversary DNA, although we have evolved along a different path, most notably in our blood, eyesight, and hearing.

"The Adversary's DNA – from these starship crewmembers – has many of the anti-aging genetic modifications we incorporate in the DNA of our starship crews. Telomeres tied off, editing genes strengthened. We and the Adversary developed this independently."

"We found no nanobots, however. We are more advanced, or rather more advanced than where they were nine millennia ago."

Father thanks Aunt Carson. "The Adversary modified the DNA of their starship crews for long life; they did not include this in the DNA with which they seeded planets."

Aunt Carson corrects her nephew. "Our natural life-span of more than three millennia without enhancements resulted from a mutation incorporated when we adapted to the cold with haemocyanin blood."

~~~~~

It is twelve years since Gens Tarren was assassinated, and Cadfael became Gens. Cadfael's brother, Aaron, killed Cadfael. A member of the Praetorian Guard killed Aaron. Another member of the Guard killed the first one, and set himself up as Gens-Regent for Bräu, the last of the old Gens Tarren's line. He killed Bräu and became Gens. House Tarren and its Gens hate my house. Gens Tarren seems more bored than angry when Aunt Carson reports to

Council. He doodles on a pad of paper, then surprises everyone when he announces his understanding.

"Years ago, House Tarren disputed House Bleddyn's claims. Bleddyn was correct. Millennia ago, our ancestors thought World was flat. That notion was preserved and reinforced by teachings of the Abrahamic sect. We know it is not true. It never was true.

"House Tarren scientists accept the judgment of House Bleddyn – in this matter."

He is careful his statement applies only to this particular matter, and to his scientists and not to himself. That leaves him wiggle room. He does not fool either Father or me.

~~~~~

Garreth is fifteen years old and has completed four years at Academy. I monitor the drugs in his vambrace and reduce them gradually. He is coping with not only his anger and the tendency for his mind to wander but also his telepathy. Father judges it time to remove Garreth's medical vambrace.

During Winter Stormtime, I take Garreth to his cousin, a medico. When the medico completes his task, I hand Garreth a soldier's vambrace, a symbol of his adulthood. It is leather and metal, and embossed with studs.

"I like this one much better, Brother," Garreth says as he straps on the new vambrace.

312

Chapter 26: *Vishnu Nerada* Ship *Titan*

Tarren's agreement at Council did not reduce the tension between our houses. Vendetta attacks continue. Tarren infiltration elements make spotty raids on our outlying territories and tie up our ground defenses. Ships flying the flag of the Pirates of the Free Islands attack two of our merchant ships south of Port Caerwyn. I suspect the pirates are Tarren forces sailing under false colors. Father and I are planning responses when the Senior Controller calls.

"Sir, message from the *Titan*." *Titan* was an early and very large explorer. The message is by ancient high-frequency radio in a binary code. It was received in the War Room – neither Father nor his predecessors ever discarded anything. The War Room decodes the message and displays it on the main screen.

"We thought *Titan* was lost millennia ago," I said.

"Apparently not," Father says. I feel his excitement, but his face does not show it. "They will land at Namhae in 25 days."

"The message was on an open channel, and it will be hard to hide preparations to land so large a ship," I say. "Tarren may take advantage of the situation; we should prepare."

Father issues orders. "Notify Uncle Maddox. Assemble forces to accompany me to Namhae for the landing. "Depending on winds, there may be time to assemble naval forces. Ensure they make sail for Namhae."

Then, Father turns. "I will meet this ship with Garreth. You and Guffudd will remain here to deal with Tarren and defend Fortress as necessary."

"Yes, Father."

The *Titan* lands on tongues of fire from ancient reaction engines that cushion its fall from space. Fighters and armed shuttles surround it. They prove unnecessary. There is no sign of Tarren forces. When the tarmac cools, a man walks down the boarding ramp.

"I am Gens Bleddyn," Father says. He looks at the insignia on the other man's uniform. "Captain, I am also your great-great-great grandnephew. I greet you as family."

Hours later, Father – Gens Bleddyn – and his many-greats granduncle – Captain Heddwyn Bleddyn – sit in Fathers' den. I pour tea and *dŵr y bywyd*.

The two men are linked by blood through only five generations, but the time compression of FTL starflight and millennia in cold-sleep separate them by at least a hundred millennia. They sit before a fireplace where spring winds pulse down the chimney and push the flames back and forth.

"I see the weather has not changed since we left," Captain Bleddyn says.

"The spring storms are still fierce," Gens Bleddyn replies.

Captain Bleddyn does not wait for Father to ask for his report. "We discovered a ship of the Adversary. Its power source and drive were intact. It had grounded on a planet. We do not know what happened afterwards, but suspect an attack by either disease or indigenous life forms.

"We were careful to maintain tight quarantine and found no pathogens." He chuckles. "Although we are a primitive ship by your standards, our medical skills are quite good."

"The Adversary ship?" Father prompts.

"The power source is a matter-energy converter. More efficient than our fission reactors, but it relies on being able to scoop up enough matter to make it work. It is effective where

314

hydrogen density is high – in young star clusters, for example. I do not know how effective it will be after most of the hydrogen created after the initial singularity is swept up to make stars.

"Their FTL drive is more advanced than ours … rather, it is more advanced than the one *Titan* had. My nephews, your Uncles Maddox and Grigor and nieces, your Aunt Calenda and Chooli, are excited about it."

"How does it operate?"

"Somehow, it punches a hole between realities and passes the ship in some kind of null-space before punching a hole back into our reality at its destination. I'm sorry, but I'm a geologist, and not a physicist."

"That's why the scientists are so interested," Gens Bleddyn says. "It is like our third generation drive. We may not have the edge in technology we thought."

~~~~~

Uncle Grigor and Aunt Calenda install new equipment in a laboratory deep below Fortress. They string cables to the top of the Keep, where oddly shaped antennas sit. Uncle Grigor oversees the secrets of the house's FTL communication system. Aunt Calenda's work with nuclear fission is even more secret. *What can possibly link those two sciences?*

I learn the answer when they summon me to the laboratory.

"Have you created a new communication system, Uncle?" I ask when I see the computers and displays.

"This is a new detection system, Nephew." My normally sedate uncle is excited. Words rush from his mouth, his hands wave and point to the equipment, he draws diagrams on a display screen. I struggle to absorb what he is showing me.

"When a ship – ours or the Adversary's – slips out of this universe into inter-plane space and when it returns, mirror-spin particles are created. The mirror-spin particles last only a femto-instant before reverting to normal particles—"

"Normal, as in quarks," I interrupt.

"Exactly."

"You know, don't you, there's nothing *normal* about a particle called a *strange quark* with a charge of two-thirds and a spin of one-half." This, however, gives me the clue I need to understand how Uncle Grigor and Aunt Calenda's work intersect.

Aunt Calenda chuckles while Uncle Grigor continues. "The particles interact with hydrogen atoms. They create a wave front that travels faster than light, like the blue light in one of Calenda's water-moderated reactors. That wave front cannot carry information. But, these interactions create a secondary signal."

Uncle Grigor waves his arms and seems to draw diagrams in the air. "The signal's wavelength is 21 centimeters, what we call the hydrogen line. Antennas on the roof detect it; computers interpret it. We need to build two more detectors and install them on ships at the Sun-World libration points to triangulate a location."

I think about the logistics of stationing two ships thousands of kilometers from World. "Could you automate the system, use solar power, include an FTL comm system, and put it in a satellite without crew?"

Uncle Grigor looks abashed. "I didn't think of that." His ebullience returns. "You always were a smart boy!"

Uncle Grigor promises a design for the satellites, and Father listens to my shorter description of the system and agrees Uncle Grigor and Aunt Calenda should proceed.

Chapter 27: Evolution Gone Wild

Captain Heddwyn Bleddyn clearly has more to say about his mission. Father gives him and his crew time to rest and then summons them and me to his den.

Heddwyn Bleddyn's abrupt announcement sets the agenda for the meeting. "I believe the science of the ship's drive and power source is less important than what we learned of the Adversary's seeding missions."

Father nods for him to continue.

"We explored thirty-seven planets in the comfort zone of their stars – close enough to the star for liquid water to exist, far enough away it hadn't boiled away. Five were barren of life. Seven held simple life, sometimes little more than viruses which might have come together from chemical determinism or floated through space until captured by the planets' gravity – an example of *panspermia*. On twenty-five, we found life too complex and too much like our own to be the result of panspermia or chemical determinism – or coincidence."

"You reached the same conclusion we did. Someone seeded those planets," Gens Bleddyn says, knowing Heddwyn and his crew had already discussed this with Aunt Carson. "But you have new information."

"The seeding took place aeons ago based on our analysis of the DNA, yet the sower of the seed allowed evolution to take its course. Sometimes, with disastrous results."

Heddwyn puts a video on the main screen. "Here is one planet seeded only with cyanobacteria to create an oxygen atmosphere, and with primitive sea creatures."

I looked at the video. A plant rises from the depths of the sea and spreads on the land. A writhing mass of vegetation fights for sunlight and covers the planet from pole to pole.

"The weed dies and rots, giving up carbon dioxide and methane, and taking up oxygen in a way that balances its growth."

"Here," Heddwyn shows another video, "a similar weed took over the land masses, but incorporates animal DNA." He zooms into a patch of weed, well inland from the sea. A pulsing mass of pink vegetation draws our attention.

"We sampled the mass. The pink is blood – haemoglobin-based blood. The mass is animal tissue living in symbiosis with the vegetation."

"I almost understand Gens Tarren's desire to destroy planets on which evolution has gone wild," Father says. "That will not be the policy of House Bleddyn. The galaxy is large enough for more than one kind of life."

The next day, we send data from the *Titan* to the rest of the Res Publica. Gens Tarren misconstrues the data and demands a Council meeting. There, he takes the Council dais without being recognized by the First Speaker. "Again, we depend on propaganda created and edited by Gens Bleddyn who speaks of planets on which evolution has *gone wild*. But, evolution is only a theory—"

"Gens Tarren does not know what *theory* means," Gens Merrick interrupts. "A theory is an explanation that fits all known facts and which explains those facts. No idea is declared to be a theory if any fact, truth, or proof shows it to be wrong. Gravity is *only a theory*, but I do not see Gens Tarren jumping from the tower of his Keep."

Gen Merrick sits, but not before he says, "I do not know why I say these things, for no truth can sway the mind of someone who has made up his mind and shut it to any contradicting evidence."

318

Gens Pugh speaks calmly at first. "Gens Merrick and I may disagree on theory, but we cannot disagree the ships of House Bleddyn have discovered planets on which live creatures very far removed from the Res Publica." His voice becomes shrill. "These creatures are not-of-the-blood, they are anathema. Their blood is Gens Bleddyn's justification for war with the Adversary. He cannot discard this, now."

After considerable discussion, Gens Caerwyn, the First Speaker, stands and raps his gavel. "Gens Bleddyn presents evidence that life on many planets is tied to one original seed. It is the same seed from which we sprang. On some planets, this seed evolved in ways different from us, creating things not-of-the-blood.

"We are agreed," he says. "Planets on which we find primate life, even if not-of-the-blood, will be watched. Planets on which simpler life exists will be opened for colonization."

"The planets with life that is not-of-the-blood must be sterilized!" Gens Tarren cries.

"Gens Tarren, we have not agreed to that. We are adjourned." Gens Caerwyn says and slams his gavel on the banque, ending the meeting.

~~~~~

I receive a request from Corporal Cos of Father's Mountain Company to remove Garreth from Academy for a mission. I take the message to Father and object. "Garreth trained with the Mountain Company, and is qualified for whatever mission they have in mind. I do not, however, think it appropriate to take him from Academy. That would increase the distance between him and his classmates."

Father overrules me. Something is more important than Garreth's schoolwork. I could draw the answer from Father's mind, but he would know. And, he decreed long ago that we would never dig into the other's mind. "If you knew my thoughts, and I yours,

319

we might think we had the solution to a problem and would stop questioning. *Doubt everything, for doubt leads to questioning and only by questioning can you find the truth,*" he said quoting Geraint.

Only two days later, I greet Garreth when he lands on the battlements in a shuttle. He brings someone he should not know. I take them through back halls and secret passages to Father's den.

Garreth gives Father a memory stick. "This holds evidence of a plot by Maelon and Helygen," he says.

Father takes the memory stick, and hands it to me before dismissing us.

After studying the information on the memory stick, I return to Father's den.

"You know now why I assigned Garreth to this mission?" he asks.

"Yes, Father. Has this information been been authenticated?"

"It has been corroborated by other sources. Garreth's contact was not our only agent in Sangtae. It is a bold plan, but we have enough information to identify the plotters – both among the Res Publica and among the southern thralls. The Mountain Company will deploy to Sangtae and deal with it."

Before I can speak he says, "No, Garreth will not participate."

~~~~~

Father orders the house to be free with information from our ships returning to World. It is too much to expect Gens Tarren will be as open. When our spies learn Tarren captured an Adversary's starchart, Father orders me to learn more and to take possession of the chart – or at least, make a copy.

320

Our agents copy the chart; however, we are disappointed. What Tarren calls a chart is a huge block of crystal into which a craftsperson inserted gems, presumably to mark stars with colonized planets. The chart covers only a small part of what we believe to be the Adversary's territory. We extrapolate coordinates from the positions of the gems. A computer finds the best fit with known stars in our spiral arm. Both the accuracy and the validity of the information are suspect. We have found many seeded planets not in the chart. However, the chart may help us avoid encounters.

~~~~~

The Council meets after Fall Stormtime to assess damage and review mutual support for recovery. By more recent practice, House Tarren limits its support to their closest allies. Father always offers aid to allies of Tarren, except Maelon and Tarren, himself. While not changing any alliances, this reduces tensions between House Bleddyn and some of Tarren's allies. This year, Father has a surprise for Council.

"House Bleddyn wishes to share new information about the Adversary." The room darkens, and I put the first image on the screens. It is a three-dimensional starchart, which rotates slowly. In the darkness, no one sees Tarren blanch.

"The information on this chart is at this moment being sent from my War Room to yours. It shows only a small part of our spiral arm of the galaxy. We copied it from a chart belonging to the Adversary. The chart has no galactic coordinates. The coordinates we offer were created by overlaying the chart on our starcharts until we found the best fit with the most standard stars. We believe they represent seeded and colonized planets the Adversary has not abandoned. Despite the uncertainty, I present this to be true and factual, and assure you House Bleddyn will make use of it."

~~~~

It has been seventeen years since the Res Publica declared war with the Adversary. For House Bleddyn, preparation for war and for the survival of the Res Publica and the thralls has been an overriding mission. House Tarren's hatred is strong, and they continue to conduct vendetta against us, even after acknowledging the existence of the Adversary.

Academy remains an island of stability. Every house, even the smallest, sends their best and brightest to Academy where – officially, at least – vendetta and house rivalry are set aside or sublimated by competition between elements, groups, and squadrons in games and academics.

Today, Garreth will graduate as commander of his element. The element ranks in the top ten percent of the graduating class. Father wants the rank to be higher and Garreth to be a Group or Squadron commander, but I convince him Garreth's experience has been of more value than points or positions at Academy.

I think Garreth's assignment as a crewmember of *Cardis*, a corvette in the *Vishnu Nerada*, will consume his attention. I am wrong. He still has questions for me.

"Garreth, you know one source of our house's power comes from the telepathy of the Gens and his highest counselors."

"Yes, Brother. You made that clear."

"The most important part of your mission is not to find planets suitable for colonization, but planets where life evolved into sentient beings. Father hopes you will find telepaths – and allies – on those planets."

Three months later, *Cardis* and the colony ship *Waldfa* drop from our reality. It will be years before we hear from them.

~~~~~

After House Bleddyn reveals our FTL communication system, we move the consoles linked to our ships and allies into the War Room. We keep the consoles that allow us to intercept the messages of others in a separate, secure location.

"Report from *Hedd Gwyn*, sir." The Senior Controller's voice betrays her excitement. "*Kobaya* crew rescued. All wakened from cold-sleep."

Father maintains his usual stoic demeanor. "Order the *Hedd Gwyn* to survey the system and then to return home at best speed. *Kobaya's* crew are heroes. And, they may have more information and insight into the Adversary than they are aware."

The *Hedd Gwyn* is a third generation corvette, and should arrive in fewer than ten years. That will give me time to plan the welcome and questioning.

~~~~~

One of our exploration ships finds a planet that meets the requirements for colonization: within the comfort zone, possessing a large moon, and about the same size as World. More important, it is marked "lost by the Adversary" on our starcharts.

The ship approaches silently – drifting with engines off and all systems except passive monitors and life support powered down. "Watch and learn," as Father would have said.

Hiding and listening allow our ship to capture and interpret the drive signatures of three ships that reach the system after them. They are ships of House Tarren. They all orbit the single planet in the comfort zone, dropping nuclear fission explosives at strategic points. Tarren does not target cities or infrastructure. The beings that inhabit this planet haven't advanced far enough to build such things. The targets are bays and estuaries upwind of the continents. Bombs vaporize and irradiate both water and mud and throw the results into the atmosphere to drift over the continents. The

323

radiation will be too strong for the DNA of the inchoate species on the planet to survive. Beta particles, gamma rays, and fast neutrons penetrate the cells of the animals and plants. The ionizing radiation burns, corrupts, and destroys the delicate strands of life. When Tarren's ships depart, the planet is sterile. Enough radiation is left to ensure it will remain so for millennia.

Father commands me to assemble a report for Council; however Tarren denies using fission weapons on a habitable planet, and Father's motion of censure fails.

~~~~~

In the past thirty years, House Bleddyn launched thirty colony ships, the most recent twenty-five with colonists of mixed houses and thralls. Even with the third generation stardrive, only five ships have reached their target planets. The ships land and colonists waken. In a room next to the War Room, a team representing all allied houses monitors progress, sends questions, and wrestles with problems faced by the colonists. Their job is to ensure future colonists learn from mistakes of the early ones. I am in the War Room, watching the team's deliberations on a vid screen, when a red symbol signals a message from Delwyn's ship, the corvette, *Baedd Du*.

<<Adversary ship encountered. Our fighters attacking. We are standing off.>>

The Comm-O sees I have read the message, and asks, "Sir, why does the *Baedd Du* stand off?"

"Their mission is exploration – and intelligence gathering." I then quote what Father says often, "Watch and learn."

What I don't say is the *Baedd Du* has an FTL system with bandwidth high enough to send reports from the ship's sensors to a

324

room closed to all but a few. The ship also has torpedoes with fission warheads.

I'm getting more and more nervous waiting for another message from *Baedd Du* when Aunt Chooli summons me to the room where she monitors the FTL system. She points to a screen. "Message from your sister."

<<Adversary ship has telepath on board in contact with telepath called "control" I can hear only ship's side of conversation.>>

I sit at a terminal and respond.

<<Language?>>

<<Not ours; telepathy doesn't need language>>

This is the first known contact with a telepath not of House Bleddyn. Telepathy not needing language is an important bit of information.

<<What saying?>>

<<Reports they encountered swarm of fighters and are responding but captain not optimistic and cannot flee>>

There is a pause, then another message from Delwyn.

<<Enemy ship exploded last message from telepath "captain ordered autodestruct.">>

I understand. Their warrior ethos is like ours in at least one way – do not allow yourself to become a hostage.

<<Thank you, Sister. Are you all right?>>

<<Yes, Brother, although I felt his death>>

I stand from the console and stretch my arms and legs. I have been sitting for ten hours. It is the middle of the night, but I call my father. He summons me to his den.

"How much of this should we share, and with whom?"

Father turns my question back. "What do we know, and what do we assume?"

"We know the enemy has telepaths. We assume all enemy ships have at least one telepath since this one spoke to a command element called 'control.' Their telepathy is long-range, since Delwyn heard only one side of the conversation. The captain destroyed the ship to avoid capture and disgrace, to protect technology and starcharts, and to keep us from capturing a telepath."

"You learned a great deal from Delwyn's messages. We cannot say Delwyn overheard a telepathic conversation. How might we explain our knowledge?"

The windows in Father's den are bright with dawn before we craft a satisfactory answer and a plan to present it to Council.

~~~~~

Without details, I display to Council images of a multi-ship battle with the Adversary in which the post-battle analysis shows enemy ships' movements synchronized over light-hours, suggesting an FTL comm system.

Most of the Council accepts our conclusions. Tarren scoffs and is eager for the meeting to adjourn.

The day after Father and I return from Council, Uncle Grigor shows us an intercepted FTL message. It is from Tarren to all his ships and allies.

<<Bleddyn claims Adversary has FTL comm system. Proof is believable. The Adversary's FTL system may use telepaths – demons. All ships are to seek and capture a telepath. If capture is impossible, kill it to break the link in the Adversary comm net.>>

"Several previous Gens Tarren believed you are a telepath," I say to Father after Uncle Grigor leaves. "This one believes the Adversary has telepaths which are the basis of their FTL comm system. He orders attacks on the Adversary to kill telepaths, but does not reveal his suspicions about you."

"Tarren waits until he can create a super-majority in Council," Father replies. "He will accuse me of being a demon only when he is sure he can win a vote to execute me. That would lead to a major war he knows he cannot win. I do not believe he will make this move."

It takes only two years before Tarren's assumption of a galaxy-wide telepathic network supporting the Adversary becomes common knowledge. Some houses suggest the Res Publica should try to breed telepaths, but the ancient prejudices are too strong. *Thou shalt not allow a demon to live.*

~~~~~

Months later, we receive a message from an exploration vessel. They watched a single House Tarren ship sterilizing a planet with fission bombs. Our ship then watched an Adversary ship pursue the Tarren ship and destroy it.

I put this information in the file of messages I save for our ships when they return to our universe.

~~~~~

"Telor, we have something you should see." Uncle Grigor's call summons me to the room in which we secretly intercept FTL messages sent by both allies and adversaries. Father is adamant we not take advantage of this capability, we never reveal it, and the aunt and uncles who operate the equipment do not say what they learn unless it presents a clear and present danger to the House of Wolf or the Res Publica. Knowing this, I hurry my steps despite the tumult in my mind.

Aunt Chooli explains what was discovered. "You know Tarren believes the Adversary has telepaths – which Tarren calls demons. He believes their telepathy has intra-galactic range and is instantaneous. It is much more powerful and useful than yours, for example. He bases his belief on intercepted Adversary radio communication."

I am surprised Aunt Chooli knows I am a telepath. *She is Father's sister. There's no reason she shouldn't be a telepath. If she is, there is no reason—*

"Tarren translated the Adversary's language," I say, interrupting my own thoughts.

"Indeed, he did." Aunt Chooli doesn't give me a chance to think. "And he unwittingly gave us enough information to allow us to do it, too. Further, Tarren discovered a planet seeded by the Adversary. Sentience and a civilization of sorts have developed, something like ours in the latter age of coal and petroleum before we exhausted those fuels and nearly destroyed our climate. They have penetrated space, but no farther than their own moon, and have abandoned crewed missions to send robotic explorers. They do not constitute a threat to the Res Publica, despite having discovered nuclear fission and fusion weapons. Tarren intercepted Adversary radio communication saying there is a telepath on the planet and the Adversary wants it. Gens Tarren ordered his forces

328

to kill the telepath and not allow it to be captured by the Adversary."

A console chimes and a message appears on the screen. Uncle Tahoma scans the message. "Nothing important."

Aunt Chooli continues her briefing. "Apparently, they have done so – killed the telepath. They released two weapons on the planet and then pursued and destroyed an Adversary ship. They report two ships escaped and one of their own ships was destroyed. A tachyon message confirms the destruction of a Tarren ship. The coordinates do not match any of the stars in the stolen starchart."

"The Adversary has secrets even from his own people," I say.

Father ponders this information while I stand, trying not to fidget. Despite the importance of the information, Father's words are unemotional. "Please continue monitoring and send similar messages to me. Send messages to our ships to record and send any enemy electromagnetic communication they intercept. Ask Uncle Maddox to install wide-band radio receivers in future ships. Send the nearest of our ships to that planet to investigate. And call the Privy Council into session. You may wait until after lunch to do that."

I think Father almost made a joke and try hard to keep from smiling.

After lunch the Privy Council meets. Before taking his seat, Father speaks. He reminds the council of Tarren's bombing a life-bearing planet years ago. He relates Aunt Chooli's information about Tarren bombing another planet – one with sentient life – to kill a telepath. After the whispers die down, he says, "Telepathy with galactic range is at the heart of the Adversary's faster-than-light communication system. I understand Tarren's motivation, but do not believe it justifies his methods."

Then, he presents the problem to the Privy Council. "How should House Bleddyn react toward the Adversary and toward House Tarren, given this new information?"

After the death of Aunt Belisiama, Great Uncle Grigor is the eldest member of the Privy Council. By custom, he begins the discussion. "We are at war with the Adversary and he is at war with us. This is a legitimate war, in which the Adversary struck the first blow. We are not at war with every planet seeded by the Adversary on which sentient life has developed. We are not at war with the Cats or any of the Primate species we have encountered. The Res Publica is not at war with the planet on which Tarren discovered a telepath, nor with the planets his forces have bombed."

An aunt summarizes what Uncle Grigor said. "Tarren committed violations of the Compact: an unjustified attack and use of fission weapons."

A cousin objects. "The Compact was written before we knew about life on other planets. It doesn't address that situation."

That is my cue to speak. "The Compact states, 'No attack on any person, house, or other entity shall be made before declaration of war or vendetta.' It does not define 'entity,' nor does it extend to other planets or species. However, the record of the Council's deliberations makes it clear this injunction was meant to be as broad as possible. Tarren violated the Compact."

"Bravo," Uncle Grigor says, putting his imprimatur on my words.

The Privy Council debates until time for evening meal, and agrees to continue the next day after breakfast. We have become accustomed to working in the long years of space travel, and even Father's questions do not seem to have great urgency. By high sun the next day, the Privy Council creates a strategy, which Father agrees to present at the next Council meeting.

Father's announcement we have translated the Adversary's language from intercepted radio messages angers Tarren. Tarren cannot admit having done this earlier and not sharing it, any more than he can admit having the stolen starchart and not sharing it. Father plays recordings of Adversary messages while translations flash on the screen. The messages discuss the sentient beings on the planet, their civilization, and the presence of a telepath. They describe what is clearly a Tarren ship dropping fission weapons on a hospital.

"Propaganda," Tarren declares. He stops short of calling Father a liar.

"The Council may decide the truth of what I present," Father replies. "House Bleddyn proposes House Tarren be censured for its attacks on several planets and the more recent attack on a sentient but non-threatening civilization. We propose no entity of the Res Publica shall attack any planet, even if the planet might have been seeded by the Adversary, until we determine the inhabitants of the planet pose a clear and present danger to the Res Publica and the Council has declared war on the planet. House Bleddyn proposes the Council permit the creation and use of fission weapons against the Adversary and his ships."

The Council deliberates briefly. Father planted the seeds of his proposals and nurtured them before the meeting. The vote on all proposals is nine-to-four to support the proposals except the censure of House Tarren.

My son, Selwyn is waiting when we return from Council. He is now a man, but with life-extension treatment he appears barely younger than me. He inherited my telepathy. He would not take information from my mind, any more than I would take information from his or Father's. But, without trying, Selwyn sees moods and emotions – something that saved him a great deal of punishment when he was growing up.

"Something is wrong," he says when we sit together in the library.

"You must not speak of this even though it will guide our thinking and our planning," I say. "Father created a conundrum and a new reality. In the past, despite vendetta, all houses respected the Compact and accepted the judgment of a super-majority of the Council. You know Father broke the Compact secretly when he first armed our ships with fission weapons and when he first built defenses for World. He feels uncomfortable, especially when he charges Tarren with a similar violation. He knows Tarren also broke the Compact, and with impunity. Even if the Council had voted to censure Tarren, it would have been an empty effort since censure would not bring any punishment."

~~~~~

The corvette *Caliban* reports arriving at a planet seeded and forgotten by the Adversary. Garreth's message is short but electrifying.

<<*Caliban* reports. Planet has sentient life. Primates with iron tools, agriculture, pastoralism, and writing.>>

Father's commands are unnecessary. His standing orders are clear. "Monitor; report; do not harm; do not interfere." It's the official version of "watch and learn."

While *Caliban* is on station, they detect another ship of the Res Publica. It is a battleship from House Tarren. The *Caliban* and the ship of House Tarren exchange radio messages. *Caliban* relays them to the War Room on the FTL system.

<<The planet harbors life of the Adversary. We will sterilize it>> the Tarren ship sends.

<<Negative until approved by Council we will notify our Gens you must notify yours>> *Caliban* responds.

The FTL systems from both ships go silent.

We hear nothing more the ships say to one another by radio until a tachyon burst marks the death of the Tarren ship. The FTL message from our ship follows the tachyon message by only a few seconds.

<<*Caliban* reports. Tarren battleship fired first; was destroyed. No survivors. Planet intact. Instructions?>>

I check with Aunt Chooli. She confirms we intercepted no other FTL message – the Tarren ship never contacted House Tarren.

"Send this message," Father commands. "*Caliban* crew will be honored upon your return. Do not speak of this until then."

~~~~~

I am on duty in the War Room. Even though the Senior Controller is in command, he or she always defers to Father or me if we are present.

"Message from Gens Tylluan, sir." The Senior Controller puts it on the main screen. "*Breuddwydio Tylluan* popped out near their target planet and launched a caravel and fighters to explore. The ship remains outside the system's cometary cloud."

I thank the Comm-O and report to Father. Aunt Chooli would have received the initial FTL message, but we keep secret our ability to overhear the messages of other houses. The ship reached its destination in record time. It is the first ship to have the third-generation stardrive.

A month later, the ship reports the planet is suitable for colonization.

<<Planet seeded through Wave 4 but DNA dating shows no Wave 5 seeding. Planet confirmed abandoned by Adversary. Colonists will land in 15 days.>>

Father is in the War Room when this message is relayed from House Tylluan. He orders the next colony ship, set to launch in less than two months, join the colonists on this new planet. We send that information to allied houses. The new ship will have 5,000 colonists, selected from all allied houses and thralls. Two more corvettes and their fighters – the nucleus of a planetary defense force in case the Adversary returns – will accompany it. The message is sent through Council channels so that Tarren will intercept the message and understand what it means.

~~~~~

I once spent most of my time in the library; now, I am usually in the War Room. Father expects me to coordinate space missions and ship construction. He wants daily updates on the status of colony ships, crew training, life-extension, and selection of future colonists with the skills they will need. I think he is worried.

I have returned from giving Father his daily briefing when a console chimes and a message appears on the screen. It is from one of our ships. The communication officer will tell me—

"Sir! It's the *Cardis* … the message, Lieutenant Garreth Bleddyn signed it."

I press the keys to display the message on my console, and type a reply. Then, I press the button on my communicator to notify Father.

Garreth and I have many opportunities to exchange personal messages. I report on births and deaths among family and important allies. When Garreth asks, I trace his offspring and those of Betsan, Barri, and Deryn and bring them to Fortress to communicate with the parents and grandparents they have never known.

I also tell Garreth about the loss of several of our ships, and their last known locations. We received a tachyon message from only one; the others had failed to report.

<<We do not know if they were destroyed or their FTL comms system failed.>> I send.

<<If their comm system failed, they should report to a rendezvous point for repairs.>>

<<Yes, and perhaps in a few centuries or a few millennia we will know more.>>

I almost hear the chuckle in Garreth's reply. <<House Bleddyn plans for millennia.>>

Garreth's ship, *Cardis,* guards the colony planet for half a local year, until the colony installs its own defenses. After a last exchange of messages with the house War Room, *Cardis* accelerates from the star's gravity well then pops into inter-plane space, moving toward its next assignment while the crew sleeps.

~~~~~

A few years after *Cardis* arrives at the second mission planet we receive a brief message.

<<Adversary ship encountered captain orders attack>>

I am summoned to the War Room, where I wait. *Battles in space are short*, I think, remembering something Geraint wrote. For days, I attempt contact. No reply. After the first message, there is nothing more from *Cardis*.

Something Father said when I was a child comes to mind. *Space is vast and unforgiving.* Those words play over and over while I walk from the War Room to Father's den.

"Father, *Cardis* is not responding to comm checks. They reported encountering an Adversary ship and firing on it. There has been no tachyon signal. We may hope the ship is safe and the FTL system no longer operates."

"The cubes should not have failed so quickly."

"Quantum uncertainty is uncertain. That is why I say *hope* and not *assume*."

Chapter 28: War Reaches World

Uncle Grigor installs a new display in the War Room. It links by cable to his laboratory deep in Fortress and by FTL to satellites in Sun-Lau libration points λ3, 4 and 5. It provides a three dimensional display of the entire solar system from the sun to a radius of 150,000 astronomical units – well past the cometary cloud. We watch our departing colony and exploration ships pass the cometary cloud and drop into the inter-sheet space on their way to new worlds. We can also see ships returning. Tarren still does not know we have the third-generation drive, but we monitor his ships' departures and returns using other systems.

On an early morning, twenty years after Garreth's ship fails to report, an alarm sounds. A bright yellow symbol appears. "Unknown ship materialized outside the cometary cloud," the Senior Controller announces. "Signature matches Adversary."

I have the command chair. "Speed? Direction?"

The Comm-O replies. "Message coming in now, sir. Picket ship reports velocity just below lightspeed but slowing and moving toward the sun."

Father is on Songbaek Island, certainly asleep at this hour. "Alert Military Command and send the information to them. Tell them we will launch corvettes and await their orders."

The Military Command controls armed ships and planetary defenses. Father tried to get cooperation from Gens Tarren by building Military Command at Fortress Lagon rather than on Mesa. No one was surprised when that didn't work. We duplicated the Military Command War Room at both Fortress Bleddyn and one other, even more secret, location.

"Launch three corvettes from Namhae, and set up a feed to them, to the House Dolffin War Room, and to Military Command," I order. Controllers respond. I press a single button on my communicator and wake Father.

He sounds alert; his words are quick. "I am here."

"An Adversary ship popped into our neighborhood, about 150 thousand AU from the Sun, now moving inward. I've launched corvettes. House Dolffin and Military Command have the details by now."

Father's decision is quick. "My mission to Songbaek is not complete. I will remain here. You are in command of house resources. Annihilate him."

I understand. Delwyn, aboard the corvette, *Baedd Du*, learned the Adversary has telepaths on their ships and their telepathy can instantly reach across the galaxy. When the crew of this ship realizes they are in our system – if they don't know already – they will report to their masters. We must destroy the ship first. When Father gives me command of house resources, he includes the fission warheads on the missiles carried by the corvettes and fighters.

"Orders to corvettes," I say. "Plot an intercept course at best speed. Launch fighters when in range. All weapons are released. Repeat, all weapons are released."

Now, the captains of the corvettes and the pilots of the fighters can launch fission weapons. Years ago, Father convinced Council we must use fission warheads against the Adversary. This is the first time we will do so in our own system.

~~~~~

Our defenses succeed; had they not, I might not be writing this. Two fighters intercepted the Adversary ship 0.25 light days from World and fired missiles with fission warheads at nearly the same time. The intruder ship was obliterated. Less than half-a-day

338

—Telor Bleddyn, Private Journal

~~~~~

The whine in Gens Tarren's voice and the frown on his face show his disdain. "Gens Bleddyn took independent action against a ship which entered our system. This is a direct assault on the understanding and agreement reached when this Council established the Military Command. Bleddyn launched two corvettes. The corvettes and their fighters were the only ships in the region. We detected two fission explosions. It is clear House Bleddyn employed fission weapons without approval from Gens Lagon at Military Command."

He wanders from his prepared remarks. "House Tarren has long suspected Bleddyn's motive for creating the planetary defenses is to conquer or annihilate those houses who are not subservient to him. We demand all components of the so-called defense system be disbanded. House Bleddyn must be declared anathema and its members scattered throughout World, house-less bastards."

Father and I sit quietly, keeping our faces immobile, allowing no one to see our reaction. When Tarren sits, Gens Hywel rises. "A member of my Home Guard, a daughter, piloted one of the corvettes. She is here. May she speak?"

Gens Lagon, the First Speaker, gives permission. A young woman stands in the benches. "Thank you, Your Grace. I was pilot of a fighter launched from the Corvette *Maxen*. It was my wingman and I who fired torpedoes with fission warheads at an Adversary ship. We operated under the authority specified in

339

Council resolution of the Tenth Month of Year 200,420 C.E., not under the command of Gens Bleddyn."

At Gens Lagon's nod, a son of his house describes the actions of the Military Command. "The signals we received were unmistakable. After Bleddyn's War Room ordered forces to launch, we assumed control, confirmed the order, and we ordered weapons release, including fission warheads." The young man looks at Gens Tarren without fear. "Our actions and those of House Bleddyn were in accord with the Compact and Council resolutions. Gens Tarren must have been drinking something other than *dŵr y bywyd* to have dreamed up his charges."

Gens Tarren's lips curl into a snarl, but he says nothing. The young man is too confident for him to challenge.

Tarren does, however, demand a vote on the charge Bleddyn violated the compact. The Gens of the Greater Houses vote ten-to-three to defeat Gens Tarren's charges. The three unaligned Great Houses vote in our favor. They have soldiers in training with our house. All three know *The Last Starship* has places for their blood. Helygen's vote to support House Bleddyn is no longer unexpected, but Cythrual's is a surprise.

That evening at family supper, Father breaks one of his rules, and describes the encounter and the outcome. Younger children sit, enraptured, while their food grows cold. Older children and adults pretend they are not equally fascinated, but their eating slows. Father is a good storyteller.

"The unanswered question," Father concludes, "is whether the telepath on the Adversary ship reported before he or she died. We must assume the worst.

"We have launched a colony ship every year for one hundred years. It seems the old estimate of the Adversary's discovery of World was wrong. Telor, ask your Uncle Maddox to speed construction of colony ships. He is to have first call on all resources of the house. We must get as many people as possible

340

away from World. He already knows to ensure *The Last Starship* is ready to launch. Tell him to bring the crew, including the corvette and fighter crews, to full strength."

Father's words are not only a command but also a dismissal. I look at the uneaten food on my plate, then leave for the War Room to carry out Father's orders.

~~~~~

War reaches World fifty years after that first incursion. Early warning comes from a picket ship snuggled up to a ball of methane ice at the outer edge of the cometary cloud, 100,000 AU from the sun.

<<P23 unknown multiple power signatures approaching +05/160/100k>>

The translation goes on the main screen of the War Room and a dot appears on a three-dimensional display.

Picket 23 reports unknown ships approaching from 5 degrees above the ecliptic, 160 degrees from baseline, at 100,000 AU from the sun.

A second message provides the velocity: a thousand AU per day toward the sun.

"The sun isn't their target. They will reach our orbit in 99 days," a junior controller says.

I catch his eye and tilt my head. He realizes he's overlooked something. "If their speed does not change," he says.

"Why did Uncle Grigor's system not alert us?" a cousin asks.

"Because they dropped from their FTL drive outside the range of his detectors," I answer. "That is not important, now. They are here."

Father arrives and takes only a moment to absorb the information. "Notify all houses of an inbound enemy force and summon them to Council. Ensure Military Command has this information. Set up a link between Gens Lagon and me."

The Senior Controller is my Granddaughter by Selwyn, and the Great-granddaughter of Gens Bleddyn. It is she who sends the notification to all houses: *The Res Publica is in danger. Come immediately.* The message is identical to one sent by Father more than one hundred fifty years ago. The irony is not lost on her or me. Or, when he sees it, on Father, who grants the young woman one of his rare smiles.

Two more messages, separated by an hour, come in.

<<P23 46 drive signatures 00/160/100k/1k>>

"Still moving at the same speed," someone observes.
"They've dropped into the ecliptic. They will hide behind planets and among asteroids," another suggests.

<<P23/00/160/100k/1k 18 battleships 28 corvettes their radar painted us will soon realize we're not a snowball>>

"Eighteen battleships and 28 corvettes is quite an armada. The question is, are more coming from another direction or will these disperse into a battle pattern or will the Adversary do something else? What is the likelihood they have detected Picket 23?"

"Low, Father," I reply. "We know their torpedoes can reach near-light speed in less than a minute. If they had detected a picket ship earlier, they likely would have destroyed it."

342

"Is there a second force approaching from a different direction?" Father asks. We have discussed the Adversary's likely strategy long into the night, but are not close to an answer.

"As you said, Father, this is quite an armada. It represents more ships than the total we have encountered since the Corvette *Gorlassar* was destroyed. For the moment, I would focus half our forces on this incursion."

"For the moment?" Father says.

He sees my certainty. After more than a century as chancellor, I am no longer embarrassed when he questions me. "Yes, Father. Until we know more, we should not commit all our forces in one direction."

Another message appears on the screen.

<<P23 torps fired/returning—>>

The picket ship is too small to have a tachyon signaling system, but we know he is gone.

"The attack has begun. Notify allied houses to execute Operation Assemble," Father orders. This will position passengers on *The Last Starship*, in cold-sleep, waiting a command to launch.

After sending the message and logging acknowledgements, I move to stand beside Father. "Lau stands between the Adversary fleet and us. If they plan to use it for cover, detectors on Lau's moons will spot them."

Father nods. "At their present speed, we have enough time to implement Assemble. Notify me if the fleet changes speed or formation. Telor, it is time for you to leave for Namhae."

I do not hesitate. "Selwyn, my daughter, and my grandson are already aboard *The Last Starship*. They are my escape and my immortality. There is much to be done, here. I will stay with you." I hold my breath after saying this. It is the first time I have refused an order from my father. I've disagreed with him – often in private and rarely in public – but never refused an order.

Father turns and I feel a flash of anger, quickly replaced by something I cannot interpret. He stares at me for a moment, nods his head, and turns back to the screen. "Selwyn will be a fine captain."

I watch the displays in the War Room as allied houses report shuttle launches. Our satellites are already jamming the radar of our enemies. It is something we do randomly and frequently. We hope Tarren will not discover we are assembling on Namhae lest he suss we are fleeing World.

Then, I receive a signal from a source that should not exist.

"Father? I have a message on a medium wave circuit. It's from one of the Free Islands."

"Put it on the screen."

The message is terse, but strange. "We cede control of our forces to House Lagon. We are not entirely isolated and, although we are house-less bastards, this is our world, too. A shuttle with my son and two daughters will reach Namhae in a very few minutes. Do you have a place for them?"

"Send this reply, copy to Selwyn and Lagon." Father commands. "The Res Publica thanks you for your support of the war, and will make best use of your forces. Our people on Namhae have a place for your blood, which will be received with honor."

After I've sent the messages and received replies, I look toward Father. He knows my question.

"Sometimes, it is necessary to create relationships that might be anathema to one's allies. Such a relationship with the leaders of the so-called pirates of the Free Islands would have been seen that way by the other Greater Houses. The message came from a man who has led the Free Islands for millennia."

"Of what use are his forces?" I ask.

Father allows one of his rare smiles. "None, unless the Adversary were to land wooden sailing ships on our oceans. However, this man's ships, flying the flag of House Dolffin, have protected her fleet for the past century."

344

Another screen shows the readiness of *The Last Starship*. The ship has been kept prepared, with a crew aboard, for more than 100 years. Now, it will receive the last colony to leave World – the heirs of House Bleddyn and our allies, plus crafts-persons from among the Res Publica and thralls. The ship will carry the hope of their houses. Tools, medicines, books, clothing, musical instruments, cryogenic containers of eggs and seed of the Res Publica and thralls and of the beasts of the field and denizens of the sea, seeds of trees, food-plants, and flowers, and hundreds of other things have long ago been loaded.

Selwyn arrives on Namhae and establishes a secure link between the ship's bridge and the War Room. We have the same readiness displays, but it is easier to talk about progress than read numbers and charts on a screen. Besides, I know this will be the last time I talk to my son.

"The crews of corvettes and fighters who were in barracks have boarded their ships," Selwyn says as that number goes from yellow to blue. Corvette and fighter crews understand their role. They will screen the fleeing colony ship from enemy attack. If they are successful in obliterating the enemy and then are fast enough, they will reach the ship where cold-sleep canisters wait for them. It is a long shot, but the fighter crews know their eggs or seed are safely aboard, and their blood will live – if *The Last Starship* lives.

"It's a good thing the Adversary comes now," Father muses.

"Why?"

"In the past century and a half, we have dispatched one hundred sixty two colony ships, each with 5,000 of the best of our people   members of House Bleddyn, allied houses, and thralls. We have barely enough people left to maintain the farms and fisheries, the mines and merchant fleets, to keep up the pretense we are too strong for Tarren to attack. If the Adversary had not arrived soon, we might have abandoned World to Tarren, and I would not want to do that."

345

Tarren and his allies reluctantly attend Council. We have stopped jamming his radar, but Tarren is angry and snaps at Father.

"Gens Tarren, the jamming comes from space," Father replies. "You and I both launch satellites for other houses. Who can say which satellites are responsible for the jamming?"

Father's words incite Tarren rather than calm him. However, even Tarren cannot believe Father would send word of an invasion unless it were true.

The Council Meeting is strained. Our allies and we are adamant we will defend World with all our resources. Gens Lagon invites Tarren to attach his forces to the Military Command, but – as in the past – Tarren refuses.

"No one doubts Lagon follows Bleddyn's orders," Tarren spits. "He is in command, and Lagon is your puppet."

Lagon stands. Tarren insults him and he has cause to call Tarren to the field. Instead, he replies to the insult only with biting words. "I hope you speak from ignorance and not malice, for ignorance can be cured but malice is likely too deeply rooted to be overcome."

Gens Tarren stands. His fists are clenched in the boyhood sign for challenge. Before he can speak, the First Speaker raps his gavel. "We have no time for bickering. Tarren, your concerns are noted and will be considered, but your anger does not help. It is clear an Adversary force—"

He stops when a courier runs to Father with a message. Father stands and is recognized. "A sensor near Law reports half the Adversary fleet turned toward the sun. The other half is decelerating and continues toward World. We believe half the force will spin around the sun and attack from a second direction."

346

"Your Grace," Gens Lagon addresses the First Speaker. "I would be of more use at Military Command. I move the Council adjourn."

The motion to adjourn may be made at any time and without discussion. The vote is thirteen-to-zero; only the second time I remember a unanimous vote in the history of the Council. The first was the declaration of this war. Father and I return quickly to our War Room and link with Military Command.

"Half the Adversary will spin through the sun's gravity and come at us from a different direction. Should we launch *The Last Starship*?" a controller asks.

"No," I say. "They would see it, and likely give chase. We will not launch *The Last Starship* until it is clear we will lose World. Before the launch, we must destroy as many of the Adversary as possible."

"They're staying in the ecliptic," another controller observes. "They're not thinking in three dimensions."

Father nods. "Notify our defenses."

The situation seems to stabilize over the next few days. A controller, monitoring Adversary movement, reports. "The first force is now at 10^{-5} lightspeed. They are no longer decelerating, but have maneuvered into a long line of ships, nearly nose to tail. They will attack *en passant* in perhaps four days. After that, I don't know."

"*Jang sa jin*, the long snake formation," Dirgel replies, reminding us of an Academy formation for *Bo-taoshi*. "They will pass quickly and strike us one at a time, then spin around the sun and return."

"Let us hope," I say, "none will return. Where is the second wave?"

"They are at the same speed and formation – long snake – but they will arrive from sunward at least a day later than the first formation." Mindful of an earlier mistake, the controller adds, "If they don't change speed or formation."

"Dirgel, what defensive formation do you recommend?"

"*Hagik-jin*, crane wing formation, but in three dimensions using half of our forces for each Adversary force," Dirgel says. "It's the best defense against the long snake in our two dimensional naval battles."

"Make it so," Father says. Dirgel relays Father's order to Military Command.

≈≈≈≈≈

The Adversary is a day away. I take several hours to sleep and refresh myself. I don a clean and pressed uniform before returning to the War Room to watch the first contact between our forces and the Adversary. I fear it is the last time ever I will sleep.

"The first wave is only half-a-day away. We can expect them to launch torpedoes at any moment," Dirgel reports.

"They still have time and opportunity to change course," Father says. "Do not relax your guard."

"The second wave from sunward is now only half-a-day behind the first. They made up some time."

"Dirgel, how can we best take advantage of this, and do we have time to do so?" I ask.

"It depends on what the first force does," Dirgel replies. "We must keep the crane wing open until we know, and we must not draw our second crane wing from the second force."

At that moment, the Adversary's first wave unleashes torpedoes. Our ships have formed a cup – a three-dimensional crane wing. It allows them to focus masers on enemy ships when they arrive one-at-a-time. Many of our displays blank as radiation overwhelms sensors.

The first battle lasts less than an hour. The long snake of Adversary ships passes through our crane wing. They lost a tenth

348

of their forces. We lost nearly half our ships. The Adversary targeted first the battleships and corvettes, ignoring the fighters. The *Titan*, refurbished and made flagship of one half of our forces, is destroyed. "Their ships are spaceborne arsenals," Dirgel says. "Much more heavily armed than ours."

Once past the crane wing, the Adversary spins and decelerates. "They're still moving away, but at that rate of deceleration, they'll be back here in…" Dirgel pauses to calculate. "…in less than a day."

There is little time for damage assessment. The second wave of Adversary ships is due in a few hours.

~~~~~

Dirgel orders the survivors of the first battle to reinforce the second crane wing. The extra ships help. We destroy nearly a third of the Adversary's ships but suffer eighty percent losses. The Adversary's second wing spins and decelerates, then accelerates toward World. Caught between two Adversary armadas, our remaining ships are annihilated. No space defenses are left. World is open to the Adversary.

Father and Gens Lagon confer and agree to release the weapons of last resort. These are the missiles based on World, hidden until now, weapons which hold the x-ray masers and powerful fission warheads.

"Why were these not used, earlier?" A controller asks. Father gestures me to answer.

"Our goal was to keep the battle in space as long as possible, to spare World from attack and protect *The Last Starship*. This is no longer an option."

The missiles rise from silos across the continent, from Dolffin's islands, Ellis's volcanoes, the mountains of Griffin and Itan, from Mesa and Merrick, ripping into Adversary ships.

The Adversary responds as predicted and bombards World. Most of their fission bombs land on the Equatorial Continent; some, on the Southern Continent; a few, in the ocean.

Radar shows three corvettes lifting from Tarren's spaceport. "Tarren has committed forces," the Senior Controller announces.

"No," he says a few moments later. "Their trajectories take them away from World. They are fleeing."

"The Adversary pursues," another controller says. We watch five of the smaller Adversary ships – which we call corvettes – turn toward the Tarren ships.

"If Tarren will not help defend World, at least he draws Adversary forces away," another controller says.

I turn to the War Plans Controller, who has little to do except watch his orders being carried out by others. "Dirgel, considering Tarren's flight, the Adversary's pursuit, and our remaining weapons, plot the best, safest escape route for *The Last Starship*. Keep it current in this fluid situation. Your computers are more powerful than those on the ship – and you are a better tactician. Send them updates as needed."

Dirgel acknowledges and sends orders to his team in their own War Room a few dozen meters away. I smile when I think of Dirgel's history. In the past hundred years or so, he rose from senior floater mechanic to leader of the Operations Plans Division. I also know Dirgel's son is a crewmember on *The Last Starship*.

Father scans the displays, then encodes a message. It will be received on *The Last Starship* and preserved for the time it lands on a suitable world. "Selwyn is Heir of Bleddyn." Since we have integrated the houses on all colonies for the past century or more, it is uncertain how important this message will be in a millennium or two. However, I find myself oddly happy.

"Fortress has fallen. We in the War Room are the only ones still alive. More than half our systems are inoperable." My report is correct, but still disheartening. Father uses an FTL link through a starship a thousand light-years away to contact Gens Lagon. Lagon's reply is no more optimistic than my report. Father and Lagon agree to a plan known only to them, me, and one other.

At Father's command, I use an FTL link to speak to Martyn Tylluan. "Martyn, there will be no more shuttle races. Fortress Bleddyn has fallen. Military Command is destroyed. The defense of World rests with you and your house's War Room. Father and Gens Lagon pass the flag to you. Are you able—"

"We are able, Brother," Martyn replies. "What is the strategy?"

"Protect Namhae and *The Last Starship*. If we lose contact with you, then order its launch when you think best. That is all."

"And World?" Martyn asks.

"World is lost," I reply. "What is not reduced to rubble will emit ionizing radiation for millennia. Even the Southern Continent is devastated."

"I hear and understand, Brother. I know your son and others of your blood are aboard, and that my blood, also, rests in cold-sleep, awaiting escape. You may be sure of me. Goodbye, Brother."

"Goodbye, Brother."

~~~~~

Control of the battle is now in the hands of Tylluan. Our role is reduced to monitoring comm systems and occasionally establishing a link between someone and Tylluan.

Father and I stand together in the War Room. Father holds a book. The book was found on the planet attacked by Tarren to kill a telepath. Father recites to our surviving forces the words of an ancient Admiral honored by his people. "Do not weep, do not announce my death. Beat the drums, blow the trumpets, wave the flag for advance. We are still fighting. Finish the enemy to the last one."

Martyn Tylluan fires the last of World's defenses and sends a signal ordering the launch of *The Last Starship*. The ship lifts from Namhae and flies through a cloud of radioactive dust as it pushes high above the ecliptic toward its destiny.

Selwyn reports pursuit by fighters, the only remaining ships of the Adversary. "Our fighters outnumber theirs. Our masers are defending against the few torpedoes launched at us. We will be able to slip away in thirty hours."

The Adversary's radiation weapons, what we call masers, have turned the upper levels of Fortress into molten rock. Radiation penetrates even the War Room. The controllers, Father, and I are already dead, although our bodies and minds continue to function.

The battle is over. Our surviving systems do not sense any Adversary ships. It is a pyrrhic victory. World is effectively destroyed. All life on World will end. We can only hope a hundred and fifty years of colonization will ensure the survival of our species – the bronze Res Publica and the white thralls.

My thoughts are interrupted when Uncle Grigor's system signals. *The Last Starship* passes the cometary cloud and slips from our universe into the space between universes. They are safe from the Adversary, at least for the moment, but their adventure has just begun.

"Telor, son-of-the-blood and son of my heart ..." I hear faintly, before darkness falls.

Finis

Characters and Glossary

Words in quotation marks at the end of entries are the meaning of the entry in one of several ancient languages. EA III refers to Earth Analogue III, in which you are reading this.

Aaron: Third son of Gens Tarren. "heir."

Aberwith: Port north of the border between the territories of Greater House Bleddyn and Lesser House Eryr. An "open city" which, in theory, is available to all Houses without dispute or rancor. "mouth of the river"

Abrahamic Sect: A pseudo-religious sect among the thralls around the time of the wars of conquest, which taught its followers that a death-sacrifice (e.g., as a suicide bomber) would be rewarded in an afterlife. The sect faded once their leaders were shown to be charlatans, and their so-called theology was exposed to the light of reason.

Academy: Military school. Entry is at age 12; survivors of the training graduate after six years or "Forms." Cadets are assigned to elements of 18 cadets of their age. Four elements of the same Form are aggregated into a group (72 cadets). One group of each form (total of six groups) is aggregated into a squadron of 360 cadets. The squadrons constitute the Cadet Wing.

ADD/ADHD: See "vambrace."

Aderyn: Female of the Third Rank of House Bleddyn; a spy. "a bird."

Adrenaline: A natural hormone and neurotransmitter produced when a person is faced with danger or surprise. The current name on Earth Analogue III is Epinephrine. One of the drugs in a vambrace. It triggers the fight-or-flight reaction, which

355

includes drawing blood to the major muscle groups and away from the face.

Adversary: Res Publica name for the Founders. See "The Stuff of Life: Book I."

Aelwen: Garreth's Sister-plus-six. "fair browed"

Afon: Scion of House Mynydd. Member of Llywelyn's companions until recalled. "grey"

AG: Antigravity. Primary propulsion of floaters, shuttles, and starships.

Ahnwyn: From ancient lore. "a place of torture or destruction"

Alaw: Garreth's Sister-minus-three. "water lily"

Alun: Corvette of the *Vishnu Nerada* involved in a battle against an Adversary ship. "harmony."

Anatol's Equivalent Retaliation Strategy: A *quid pro quo*, or "tit-for-tat" strategy, highly effective in an iterated exchange. Named for the equivalent retaliation strategy introduced into the Prisoner's Dilemma by Anatol Rapoport in Earth Analogue III.

Ancient Language: Language spoken until shortly after the War of Conquest. The source of the Res Publica language which evolved over the next two hundred or so millennia. The ancient language is still used in formal occasions and oaths, and for names.

Anja: Captain in the Home Guard of House Itan; wife of Captain Joyhan; mother of Niniwed.

Anrhydeus [an rye day us]: Name given to scion and later Gens of House Mynydd. "honorable." (The young man's original name was Medrus "skillful").

ap-: Patronymic prefix to house names; honorific which signifies someone adopted into the house.

Apothegm: An aphorism; a concise and often clever saying which might contain some truth.

Archwill: Aptly named Great Uncle, by several generations, of Garreth Bleddyn. Captain of the Corvette, *Eofn*. "explorer"

Ardeth: Nephew of Gens Bleddyn, a spy.

Arth: Mercenary, one of three whom Soosong meets. "bear"

Asant: Private in the House Bleddyn Second Company of the Home Guard; sergeant in the house's intelligent corps.

Astin: Lesser House. Nonaligned.

Astrogator/astrogation: Stellar navigator/stellar navigation.

Astronomical Unit (AU): The distance from a planet to its star, equivalent to one mean orbital radius. On Earth Analogue III, one AU equals about 150 million km or 93 million miles, The AU for the World of the Res Publica is somewhat larger. Their sun is hotter than Sol, and World's yearly orbit requires 595 days of approximately 25 hours each.

Aurin: Scion of Lesser House Ellis. In Academy Element with Daffyd and Delwyn Bleddyn. Swears to Daffyd.

Aveta: Aunt of Garreth Bleddyn, sister of Gens Bleddyn. She serves as Gens Bleddyn's Privy Secretary.

Baedd Du: *Vishnu Nerada* corvette to which Delwyn Bleddyn was assigned. "Black Boar"

Banque: (1) The "bench" at which representatives of the 13 Greater Houses sit in Council. Same as Dais. (2) The "banque d' Bleddyn" is the seat in the courtroom of House Bleddyn where the Gens sits in judgment.

Barchedlg [bach a dig]: Act or ceremony honoring a person of power. May be as simple as a bow or as elaborate as a banquet. "revered"

Barri: Blood of House Hynafol. Member of Garreth's Element at Academy. Element Commander, First Form. "summit."

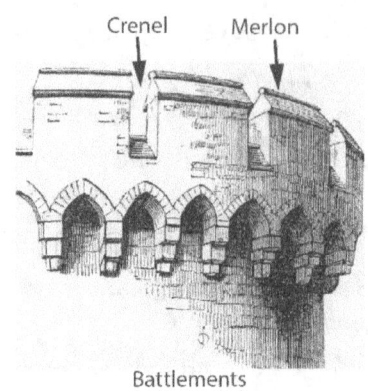

Crenel   Merlon

Battlements

Bastard: (1) A person not acknowledged by his or her father or mother. (2) Any person of the Res Publica of low status, often a person without house.

Battlements: (1) The parapet at the top of a wall, usually of a fortress or castle with spaced openings ("crenels" or "embrasures") between merlons. (2) The portion of roof enclosed by this parapet.

Belisiama [bell EES ah ma]: Garreth's great-great-aunt; member of Gens Bleddyn's Privy Council. An honored teacher.

Beta particle: High-energy and fast-moving electrons created by radioactive decay of an atomic nucleus. They are a type of ionizing radiation.

Bethan: A daughter of Gens Bleddyn, Garreth's Sister-plus-fifteen. "daughter of the Gens"

Betsan of House Griffin (unaligned): Female member of Garreth's Academy element; Garreth's second. "shortened form of Elizabeth"

Big Bang: See "Initial Singularity."

Bleddyn: Greater House. Telor and Garreth's house and patronymic. "wolf." House colors: orange, black, and gold. House crest: *an escutcheon or, a wolf, proper, couped* (on a golden shield, the head of a wolf as if severed cleanly from the body, in profile and in natural colors). Also, *a full moon tenné, a wolf couped sable* (on an orange moon, the head of a wolf, black). On banners, ancients, and flags, the wolf rampant or couchant may be used.

Blevins: Uncle of Gens Bleddyn. One of Garreth's tutors. "son of the wolf"

Bloody: Usually used in a curse (e.g., "bloody fool"); considered extremely vulgar.

Boleadoras (Bola or Bolas): A weapon consisting of three balls of steel or stone tied together with wire, leather thongs, or fiber which are spun once around a hunter's head and released to wrap around the legs of prey.

Bo-taoshi: Battle game played at the Japanese Self Defense Force School, Earth Analogue III. See Pole Pull-down, below, and the bibliography for links to YouTube.

Book of Proverbs: A document, compiled by a legendary historian and poet, Taliesin. The book contains the wisdom of both Geraint and Karmet, q.v.

Brân: Bastard whom Garreth meets when he runs away. "crow" or "raven"

Bräu: Male, scion of Gens Tarren. Assigned to Garreth's element in the last Form.

Brawin: Female of House Pugh; element mate of Llywelyn Bleddyn.

Breuddwydio Tylluan: "Dream of Tylluan." Starship, corvette class, first ship launched by House Bleddyn for a Lesser House.

Brotherhood: The closest oath that can be made other than fealty. Brotherhood may be between two boys, two girls, or a boy and a girl.

Bugail: Member of Llywelyn Bleddyn's coterie. "shepherd boy"

C: The speed of light.

Cadfael: First son of Gens Tarren. At one time, heir apparent and later Gens Tarren. "battle prince"

Cadre: Select members of a military unit or cadet corps charged with training new soldiers or cadets.

Caerodor: Fishing vessel in *Vishnu Nerada* surface fleet. Involved in a rescue operation.

Caerwyn: House located on the south coast of the Equatorial Continent. Blood-kin to House Bleddyn. "white fort"

Caitlan: Girl of House Dolffin, member of Delwyn and Daffyd Bleddyn's Element at Academy.

Calenda: An aunt of Gens Bleddyn. Physicist.

Calendar: The year on world is 595 days long, and is divided into four quarters by the solstices and equinoxes. On Earth Analogue III these are December 21 and June 21, and March 21 and September 21. The New Year begins at the winter solstice, a custom established when the Res Publica were ignorant of science and believed that weather and the "return of the sun" after the winter solstice was the province of an imaginary, magical being. Academy years ("Forms") start just after Winter Stormtime. Twelve months of approximately 50 days each are marked by the phases of World's largest moon. Years are numbered C.E. for "Conquest Era," after the conquest of the Southern Continent by the Res Publica and B.C.E. for Before the Conquest Era.

Caliban: *Vishnu Nerada* corvette involved in a battle with a House Tarren battleship.

Call to the Field: Phrase meaning to challenge to a duel.

Cammies: Nickname for camouflage uniforms.

Caravel: (1) Fast starship used for scouting and exploration. One or more caravels may be carried on a corvette or other larger starship. (2) A wooden boat usually with three masts, two with square sales and the aft mast being lateen-rigged.

Cardis: *Vishnu Nerada* corvette (starship). Garreth's assignment after graduation from Academy.

Carson: Aunt (many generations removed) of Gens Bleddyn; biologist on exploration ship *Twysog* of the *Vishnu Nerada* fleet.

Caitlan: Female member of Delwyn's element. Member of House Dolffin.

C.E.: Year of the Conquest Era (see Calendar).

Chancellor: The most senior official on the staff of a house's leader (Gens). Among other duties, presides at meetings of the Privy Council not attended by the Gens and serves as emissary to other houses.

Chandler: Person or company that supplies ships.

360

Chang Sa Jin: Long snake formation. A line of soldiers or ships pointing to the enemy to minimize exposure to enemy fire, attacking one at a time then turning to allow the next soldier/ship in the line to attack. A tactic used by Admiral Yi Sun-sin (Earth Analogue III); see the references.

Chemical determinism: The tendency for certain chemical compounds to form in ways that minimize the energy of their bonds.

Chemist: A pharmacist, a dealer in herbs and drugs both legal and illegal.

Chido: Uninhabited western island claimed by House Dolffin. Site of element training, part of House Dolffin's school.

Chojeom: "Focal point." Similar to the German, Schwerpunkt (Earth Analogue III). The literal translation is "main focus, main emphasis, or focal point." In military parlance, a Schwerpunkt or *chojeom* attack means "striking the enemy at a point that is both vital and weakly defended." Chojeom is one of the most common initial attack strategies of *Bo-taoshi* (pole pull-down).

Chooli: Sister of Gens Bleddyn, scientist, one of three people charged with creation of the house's FTL comm system. "mountain" (signifying strength)

Cislunar Space: The space between a planet and the orbit of its primary moon.

Cledwyn: Scion of House Caerwyn and male member of Garreth's Element. "a river"

Cold-sleep: A form of suspended animation entered by starship crews of the Res Publica that allows them to exist in stasis for millennia during long star flights.

Colonizer: A class of starships carrying c. 5,000 colonists in cold-sleep. Will also carry shuttles, fighters, and caravels.

Cometary Cloud: Like the Oort cloud believed to surround the solar system of Earth Analogue III, World's cometary cloud is a bubble of icy debris (comets, planetoids, dust) that surrounds the sun at a distance of between 5,000 and 100,000 of World's orbital radii. [See "astronomical unit."]

Comfort Zone: A band around a star in which a planet is close enough for liquid water to exist but far enough away the water doesn't boil off. On Earth Analogue III, call the "Goldilocks zone" (not too hot, not too cold, just right).

Commander: The military title of a Gens within his Home Guard.

Comm-O: Communication officer in a War Room, aboard a ship, or attached to an infantry unit.

Compact, First: The agreement among the houses created after a despotic king, Gens Triumph Tarren, was overthrown and the Council established. Originally, the Compact set up the Council of Gens of the Greater Houses as the government of the Res Publica and the first mission of the Council – the conquest of the Southern Continent. Additional provisions were made over the millennia, including rules for vendetta, enforcement of an agreement banning nuclear fission, abolishment of primogeniture (more honored by some in the breach than in the observance), the abolishment of slavery, creation and maintenance of the tachyon signaling system, and rules for the operation of Academy.

Companion: A friend, or someone in a more formal relationship.

Companion-Guard: A formal relationship that exists between a scion of a Greater House and older relatives and members of sworn houses who are charged with the scion's safety. Sometimes shortened to "guard."

Companion-Playmate: A formal relationship that exists between a scion of a Greater House and close kin or members of sworn houses of the scion's age who may be fostered to the Greater House. Sometimes shortened to "playmate" or "companion."

Companion-Student: A formal relationship that exists among cadets assigned to the same Academy Element and Group.

362

It requires a degree of amity, respect, and courtesy, and (in theory) excludes vendetta.

Conquest, War of: The war in which the Res Publica conquered the people of the Southern Continent. Occurred approximately two hundred millennia before this narrative begins.

Constable: This word derives from Earth Analogue III Latin, *comes stabuli*, "official of the stable," and originally meant a commander of cavalry.

Contre Quarte: A move in which an épée makes a circular or oval shape.

Corps-à-corps: [noun or adverb] Body-to-body. The situation that exists when two swordsmen's bodies come into physical contact.

Corvette: A class of starship. Corvettes normally carry twenty fighter and two caravels. Newer corvettes may also carry as many as a hundred colonists in freeze-sleep.

Cos: Male corporal in the Mountain Company of House Bleddyn's Home Guard.

Coterie: A noun of venery; a collective noun often associated with lesser creatures, such as vultures.

Council: Ruling body of the Res Publica comprising the patriarchs/matriarchs ("Gens") of the thirteen Greater Houses.

Council House: Complex of buildings on Mesa where Council meets and the Res Publica conducts business.

Crenel: See "Battlements."

Crest: Most often used to mean the symbol of a House. May be a stylized letter from the alphabet, an animal, or other figure. It may appear in two or three dimensions (on a document or badge, or at the top of the haft of a dagger, for example).

Crëyr: Female mercenary. "heron"

Cynwrig [SIN rig]: Fourth son of Gens Tarren. "having the quality of a chief or hero"

Cytgord [SIT gord]: Town within the territory of Gens Bleddyn, location of a mercenary auction. Inhabitants are both thralls and members of the Res Publica. Anyone entering the town must agree to a truce. "harmony, concord"

Cythrual [KITH rowel]: Greater House sworn to House Tarren.

Daffyd: A son of Gens Bleddyn, Telor's Brother-minus-eight-years.

Dagger: A knife, usually thin, with a blade length of about 45 cm.

Dark Energy: The universe comprises ordinary matter, dark matter, and dark energy at approximately 4%, 23%, and 73%, respectively. While dark matter seems to exist (mostly) in a "halo" around the edges of galaxies, dark energy pervades the entire universe.

Dark Matter: An unknown substance which does not interact with electromagnetic energy (which includes light) in any known way, but which does create gravity. It makes up approximately 23% of the universe. Its existence is inferred from the gravitational interactions with ordinary matter in galaxies.

Data Key, Data Stick: Similar to a thumb drive, flash drive, or a flash memory drive.

de facto: In fact, but perhaps not officially or in law. Telor was for several years Gens Bleddyn's *de facto* aide-de-camp because he performs the duties although he has not been appointed to the position. Later, he became chancellor, *de jure*.

Delwyn: Telor's Sister-minus-eight. A twin of Daffyd. "pretty and white"

Deri: Male member of Garreth's Element. "oak"

Derwin: Many-generations "great uncle" of Telor. Captain of the starship *Draig Aur*. "oak"

Deryn: Of House Hynafol. Member of Garreth's Academy Element. "falcon"

Dewi: Uncle of Telor, brother of Gens Bleddyn. Senior Member of the House after the Gens, although not in line of succession.

Dirgel [DIRGE ell]: Scion of House Reese (aligned with House Tarren). Academy-mate of Llywelyn Bleddyn and a member of Llywelyn's coterie following graduation. "clever."

Dobok: [Dough bock]: Uniform worn when practicing martial arts.

Doethineb Geraint: Public name of *The Last Starship*. "Wisdom of Geraint."

Dojo: A gymnasium dedicated to the martial arts.

Dolffin: Lesser house subject of a history story by Gens Bleddyn. Ally with blood ties to House Bleddyn. Gens Dolffin has been for millennia a woman.

Draig Aur: Ship of the *Vishnu Nerada*, the House Bleddyn Fleet. "Golden Dragon."

Dŵr y bywyd: Five-times distilled and 1000-year-aged liquor drunk only for ceremonial purposes. "water of life."

Ecliptic: The plane created by the path of a planet around its sun.

Element: (1) A squad of eighteen soldiers usually commanded by a Sergeant with a Corporal as second. (2) Eighteen Academy cadets of the same age who train together. Supervision is provided by Tactical Officers ("Tacs"). Leadership is provided by age-group peers. (3): A flight of two or three starships that operate under a single commander.

Element 92: Uranium.

Elevation: The ceremony at which a child is presented to family or to the Council of the Res Publica and declared legitimate.

Elint: Electronic Intelligence. Information gathered about an enemy's radar and similar detection systems.

Ellis: Lesser house once aligned with House Tarren. House crest: Phoenix rising from a red and yellow fire.

Emlyn: Thrall child whom Soosong meets in Cytgord. "industrious"

Empath: An individual who can sense emotions but not read thoughts. See also "telepath."

Emrys: Greater House, unaligned.

En passant: "In passing." An attack as one force element passes another, often at a high speed. From a move in chess, Earth Analogue III.

Energy weapons (pistol, rifle): Weapon based on laser technology. In Telor's time, the weapons can accept a replaceable magazine.

Entente cordial: A truce or suspension of hostilities.

Entrée: The right to enter or join a group, house, sept, element, etc.

Eofn [E O fin]: Corvette of the *Vishnu Nerada*. Ship which discovered the species labeled Primate III. "dauntless"

Épée: A dueling sword, light and with a sharp point. Blade is stiff and triangular in cross-section and has a v-shaped groove called a fuller or (incorrectly) a blood-gutter.

Epididymis: A convoluted duct between the testis and the vas deferens through which sperm, created in the testis, travel and mature.

Equatorial Continent: The main body of land inhabited by the Res Publica. Approximately 4,500 miles wide, 2,500 miles from north to south.

Eryr [EYE are]: Lesser House allied with House Tarren until 200,372 C.E., when the house aligns with House Bleddyn. "eagle" Nickname of house: "Mountain Eagles."

Ethanol: Ethyl alcohol – C_2H_5OH – consumable alcohol.

Eukaryotic: Said of a cell that has a nucleus holding DNA and other organelles, which perform various functions for the cell. "true nut"

Eurion: Telor's Brother-minus-thirty. "golden"

Evan: Member of Daffyd and Delwyn's element at Academy. "strong"

Fast neutrons: High-energy neutrons produced by nuclear fission reactions. Their high energy means they can more easily penetrate the nuclei of atoms they encounter. "Fallout" from the detonation of a nuclear fission weapon is a mix of fission products from the weapon, itself, plus atoms of water and dirt that are made radioactive by fast neutrons from the explosion.

Field Marshall: The highest rank (other than the Gens) is a house's Home Guard. The Gens' rank is Commander.

Fighter: One of several types of shuttlecraft. Until c. 200,365 C.E., fighters were merely armed shuttlecraft with engines capable of operation in a planet's atmosphere or in space. Around that time, House Bleddyn designed and built fighters more streamlined, with less room for crew but more powerful offensive arms, stronger armor, more powerful, and capable of longer range operation.

Fire Wolf (Fire Wolves): Andirons, sometimes called "fire dogs," that hold wood above the floor of a fireplace ensuring a draft to encourage burning. They are usually of wrought iron, and may be decorated with fanciful images.

First Speaker: Chairperson of the Council of Res Publica. Position rotates among the thirteen Greater Houses, annually. Inspired by Isaac Asimov's "Foundation and Empire" series of Earth Analogue III.

Flame weapon: An improvised explosive device (IED) that can throw fire against an enemy. See https://en.wikipedia.org/wiki/Fougasse_(weapon).

Fleché: A move in fencing or sword fight intended to land the point of an épée or sword on the opponent's chest or to skewer him. "arrow"

Floater: Any of several models of anti-gravity sleds, shaped something like a toboggan, usually less than three meters long and a meter or so wide. Most are designed for one person, lying prone and with legs and torso clamped into a cradle, facing down into a display from a forward-looking camera. A transparent wind-screen protects the pilot's face. Two-person models are used for training.

The military floater is capable of an altitude of perhaps 500 meters and a speed of more than 100 kilometers per hour. Its display includes visual and radar sensors, a satellite location system, and targeting systems for its armament. Floaters used in mock combat may have paintball guns and may be equipped with laser tag lasers and sensors. Floaters used for military operations are usually equipped with rocket grenades. Floaters used by exploratory vessels may be larger and have a greater cargo capacity. The basic civilian model is limited to an altitude of 100 meters above ground level and a speed of 50 kilometers per hour.

Folant: Male member of Daffyd and Delwyn's element at Academy. "young warrior"

Footie: A game resembling soccer with four goals rather than two and teams that change composition as players are forced into time-out after scoring, and as new players enter the game.

Force-blade: A knife or sword, the blade of which is reinforced by an energy field making it capable of penetrating most personal armor. Inspired by Isaac Asimov's "Lucky Star, Space Ranger" Earth Analogue III.

Forensic, Forensic Team: As used herein, forensics is the application of science to crime investigation.

Form: A year at Academy. Enrollment usually lasts for six forms (years), rarely five or seven. Forms begin immediately after Winter Stormtime (q.v.) and end just before the next Winter Stormtime. Membership in an element may change during the first two Forms, but usually stabilizes at the beginning of Third Form.

Froward (FRO ward): An Earth Analogue III English word, although archaic, meaning "difficult to deal with." It is related to "toward," pronounced "TWO ward," as in "to and fro." A toward child is tractable and obedient; a froward child is contrary. Something that is toward is appropriate; something froward, inappropriate.

Fychan: Lesser house, aligned with House Maelon. Ambitious, desires to become a Greater House. "small"

368

Gamma-ray: Electromagnetic radiation of wavelength usually less than 10^{-11} meters and the highest known photon energy (about 100,000 electron Volts). Gamma rays are ionizing radiation and can be extremely hazardous to biological material.

Garreth: Tenth child (ninth in line of succession) of Gens Bleddyn. "brave and modest"

Gawain: Son of Gens Dolffin, about Telor Bleddyn's age. "courteous"

Gens: Title of the leader of a House of the Res Publica. Plural: Gens. Singular and plural possessive: Gens'.

Geraint: A historical figure and philosopher known for his wisdom. A great teacher whose name is invoked in rituals binding protégés and mentors. A pacifist, he lacks respect from the more militant members of the Res Publica. "old" [On Earth Analogue III, Geraint is a character in Welsh folk tales and the Arthurian legend.]

Geraint's Cannon: A log, painted black to resemble a real weapon, which is positioned to fool an enemy into believing it faced greater arms than exist. Named for the followers of Geraint, who were largely pacifists. After the "Quaker cannon" or "Quaker gun" of Earth Analogue III.

Glint: Cousin of Telor and Garreth, from Namhae.

Glöwr: Thrall. Chief shift supervisor at House Bleddyn's mines on the island of Soando. "miner"

Goldilocks Zone: The outdated notion among scientists of EA III that life can begin and develop only on a planet located close enough to its star for liquid water to exist but far enough away that solar heat and radiation haven't boiled away all water. (Not too hot; not too cold; just right.) This notion has been challenged by the discovery of *extremophiles*, creatures that thrive in the incredible heat and pressure of hydrothermal vents at the ocean bottom of Earth Analogue III. A more recent definition requires only that a suitable solvent in liquid form be able to exist.

Gorlassar: Corvette of the *Vishnu Nerada*, mother ship of the Caravel *Kobaya*. The *Gorlassar* was destroyed in the first known encounter of the *Vishnu Nerada* with the Adversary of the Res Publica. "above the sky"

Grace knife: A long, thin blade used to administer the final blow to a wounded enemy or a comrade wounded too badly to survive. "coup de grâce"

Grach: Scion of House Dolffin. Female member of Delwyn and Daffyd's element at Academy.

Griffin: Lesser house, unaligned. "king's hand"

Grigor: Uncle of Gens Bleddyn; one of three relatives who are responsible for the secrets of the faster-than-light communication system.

Group: Four Academy Elements (i.e., 72 cadets) of the same age (Form) who attend class and engage in pole pull-down (*Bo-Taoshi*) and other activities as a unit.

Guffudd: Telor's Brother-minus-nine. "the king's strong grip"

Gwenallt: Name given to Soosong by Llywelyn Bleddyn.

Gwydion [gwid ee on]: Niece of Gens Bleddyn, a spy not known to the rest of the family. "magician"

Gymnosperm: "Naked seed." A tree, such as a pine whose seeds are usually carried on the wind.

Hagik-jin: Crane-wing formation. A semi-circular formation of soldiers or ships that creates a killing zone in the middle. May involve luring the enemy into the killing zone. After that used by Admiral Yi Sun-sin in the Battle of Hansan (Hansando), 8th Day of 7th Moon, 1592 C.E., Earth Analogue III.

Halcyon Days (of Autumn): From Earth Analogue III Greek.

Hectare (HEK ter): 10,000 square meters (about 2.5 acres in Imperial measurement).

Hedd Gwyn: Ship of the *Vishnu Nerada*; "white hart."

370

Heddwyn: Captain of *Vishnu Nerada* battle ship, *Titan*; blood of House Bleddyn. "peace"

Heir Apparent and **Heir Presumptive**: The heir apparent is someone whose claim to the throne or a title cannot be set aside by the birth of another heir. He or she is the person most likely to succeed to the throne or title. The heir presumptive is a person whose claim to a throne or title could be severed by the birth of another heir. These titles apply to both males and females.

Helygen: Greater House allied with House Tarren. "willow"

Hominid: A primate of the family *Hominidae* that includes (on Earth Analogue III) modern humans and extinct relatives (e.g., Neanderthals) and ancestors (e.g., *Homo erectus*). From Garreth's perspective, where evolution was "skipped" by virtue of the Founders' seeding, it is used to designate many species of human-like creatures discovered on other worlds.

Home Guard: A house's private army. Subject to being ordered into action by the Council, for example, to put down a rebellion among the thralls or, in extreme circumstances, to stop a war between rival houses.

House: An extended family related by blood and fealty, ruled by a senior patriarch or matriarch who is addressed as "Gens." The thirteen original houses (the Greater Houses) trace their origin to antiquity. Some of the Lesser Houses were formed following a dynastic war within a Greater House.

Hubris: Overwhelming pride, considered by the Greeks of Earth Analogue III to be a grave sin, marking a person for destruction by the gods.

Huw: Second son of Gens Tarren. Member of Daffyd and Delwyn's element at Academy.

Hynafol: Greater House. Allied with House Bleddyn. "ancient"

Hywel: Greater House. Gens Hywel is always a woman. "founder of laws."

Ilja-jin: One line formation. A tactical formation consisting of lines of soldiers or ships facing one another. It allows volley fire but sacrifices maneuverability. Used effectively by Admiral Yi Sun-sin, Earth Analogue III.

Ilk: From the archaic Scottish of Earth Analogue III, meaning those of the same name. Anyone of "that ilk" or "his ilk" in the case of a Gens (house leader) shares membership or relationship with a house of the Res Publica.

Infiltration Element: Strike teams of about eighteen soldiers trained to operate independently, live off the land, strike from concealment, and conduct guerilla warfare. Created by House Bleddyn c. 100,000 C.E. in response to House Tarren's creation of large land armies.

Infrared: Light shorter than 380 nanometers (nm), and beyond the eyesight of humans of Earth Analogue III. The eyesight of the Res Publica and thralls can detect light waves as short as about 200 nm, something that began as a survival characteristic during the coldest time of the Res Publica's evolution.

Infrasonic: Vibration below the audible level.

Initial Singularity: Res Publica term for what is known on Earth Analogue III as "the big bang."

Iona: One of Bethan's bodyguards while at Academy. "January" or "beginning"

Isoquant: House Bleddyn-developed faster-than-light communication system. See "Spooky Action at a Distance."

Isotope: A variety of an element with the same atomic number (number of protons) but a different number of neutrons, giving it a different atomic weight.

Itan: Lesser House.

Itol Lagon: Archivist and Recorder. After the diarist and polymath of Bronson Beta, from "After Worlds Collide" by Philip Wylie and Edwin Balmer, Earth Analogue III.

***Jang sa jin* (long snake formation)**: A line of soldiers or ships pointing toward the enemy to minimize exposure. The force elements will move forward and attack one at a time before turning, retreating to rearm, and allowing the next force element to attack. After a strategy employed by Admiral Yi Sun Sin, Earth Analogue III.

Jaryeondo: Literally, "self-training-way," meaning a method of training or discipline. It is the name of the martial art that many children of the Res Publica study.

Joyhan [JOY han]: Captain in the Home Guard of House Itan; husband of Captain Anja; father of Niniwed.

Judge of the Change: An official with complete authority to resolve disputes during a specified action or event.

Justin: Uncle, many generations removed, of Gens Bleddyn. Biologist on the exploration ship *Twysog* of the *Vishnu Nerada* fleet.

Kaetween [kate WEEN]: Ancient house destroyed c. 20,000 B.C.E. by all other houses, united, after employing a nuclear fission weapon in combat.

Karmet: An ancient philosopher whose art of war resembles that of Sun Tzu of Earth Analogue III.

Kata: A system or series of choreographed training exercises for practitioners of martial arts including *Jaryeondo*, q.v.

Kilogram: A measure of mass equivalent to 2.2 pounds.

Knot: Nautical mile, nautical miles per hour. A nautical mile is about 1.85 km or about 1.15 statute miles.

Kobaya: A caravel, which survived the first known encounter of the Res Publica with their Adversary. Its crew of scientists unraveled the DNA on a seeded world, leading to the war between the Res Publica and their Adversary.

Kosong: House Bleddyn island located off the eastern edge of the Equatorial Continent.

Lagon: Greater House which historically has maintained neutrality and which keeps the history of the Res Publica.

Last Starship Out: A colony ship designed to allow the leadership of Houses Bleddyn and allies to escape World should the Adversary attack the home planet.

Lau: Gas giant planet in the Res Publica solar system. About the size and distance of Jupiter in Earth's solar system. "Jupiter"

Lawri: Bastard. Member of Garreth's element during several Forms.

Leiaf [LEE aff]: Scion of House Astin; companion of Llywelyn Bleddyn. "least, smallest."

Lesser House(s): See House.

Libration point: A point in space where the combined gravitational forces of two large bodies, such as World and its largest moon. are equal to the centrifugal force experienced by a much smaller body. This interaction creates points of equilibrium where a spacecraft may be secured. Only two of the points are completely stable without the expenditure of energy. On Earth Analogue III, these are more often called the Lagrangian points.

Life span, life-extension treatment: Normal life span is about one-to-three millennia. Early life-extension involved modification of the DNA, especially the HOX genes, the telomeres at the end of DNA strands, and editing genes and RNA. This gives the already long-lived people of World life spans of tens of millennia (assuming they're not assassinated of killed in vendetta). More recent treatment includes injecting nanobots to repair damaged cells and tissues.

Lighter pine: Also "lightered pine." Sap-laden heartwood from a pine tree often used as kindling to more easily start a fire.

Lloyd: Field Marshall, commander of House Bleddyn's Home Guard. "gray haired"

Llywelyn: Telor's Brother-plus-two. Heir Apparent of House Bleddyn. "lion"

Lowri: Female member of Garreth's element.

Macca: Telor's Brother-minus-twenty-six. "hammer"

Maddox: Glint's father; Telor's uncle. "champion"

Maelon: Gens allied with Gens Tarren. "a follower"

Maldwyn: Uncle of Telor and his siblings. Assassin. "brave friend"

Mammal: A class of vertebrates usually distinguished by hair, three middle ear bones, a neocortex, and females with mammary glands. On Earth Analogue III, mammals include whales, dogs, and humans. On Garreth's world, where evolution was modified by the Adversary, other mammals include the saber-toothed cats and their smaller relatives, and mastodons, *inter alia*.

Marchant [MAR shant]: Eldest son of Gens Caerwyn, six years younger than Daffyd Bleddyn and Aurin of Ellis.

Marches: Borderlands between two countries. Originally, the border areas between England and Wales/Scotland of Earth Analogue III, both areas subject to continuous feuding and battles.

Marredudd: Greater house, aligned with House Bleddyn. "great lord"

Markham: Woman; member of Gens Bleddyn's Praetorian Guard.

Martyn: Son of Gens Tylluan; in Telor's element at Academy.

Marwin: Son of Gens Dolffin. "sea hill"

Maser: "Microwave amplification by stimulated emission of radiation." A device to excite atoms to generate a coherent and beam of electromagnetic radiation of a single frequency. A "laser" is an example of a maser operating in the band of visible radiation.

Master-genes: The genes that appear to turn on and off other genes especially during gestation of an embryo.

Maxen: Corvette of the *Vishnu Nerada* involved in a battle with an Adversary ship. "great warrior"

Medico: A doctor of medicine or a combat medic.

Melatonin: A natural hormone produced by the pineal gland. It regulates sleep and wakefulness.

Merlon: See "Battlements."

Merrick: Greater House aligned with Gens Bleddyn.

Mesa: The elevated land upon which stand Academy, Fortress, Bleddyn, and Council House.

Methane: Main component of natural gas, CH_4OH. Created by the decomposition of organic matter. A greenhouse gas. When methane burns in air, it produces two other greenhouse gasses: carbon dioxide and water vapor. ($4CH_4OH + 7\ O_2 \rightarrow 4CO_2 + 10H_2O$)

Millennium: A thousand years.

Mob shower: A shower room in which there are multiple showerheads frequently located on a circular fixture in the center of the room.

Moiety: Either of two parts into which a family, social group, or ritual group can be divided.

Moot: Something subject to debate or dispute. (The expression, "a mute point," used colloquially to describe something subject to debate or not subject to debate is incorrect in either sense.)

Mount Elgon: An extinct shield volcano north of Mesa, rising 4,321 meters above sea level. Part of the Arista Mountains.

Mufti: Non-uniform, "civilian" clothes.

Mynydd [MUN you'd]: Lesser house aligned with House Bleddyn. "mountain"

Myrmidon: (MUHR mi duhn) Name of chairman of a board of inquiry at Academy. From Greek mythology, Earth Analogue III: one who unquestioningly follows orders.

Namhae: Island off the southeast coast of the Equatorial Continent of World. Site of House Bleddyn's spaceport.

Nana: Nickname from infant's speech of Garreth's surrogate.

Nanobot: Microscopic robot.

Naphtha: More accurately, benzene. C_6H_6. Flammable liquid distilled from methane.

Natural-born: Said of a member of the Res Publica who was born of intercourse rather than implantation in a surrogate. Some natural-born children are bastards; others are not, depending on the nature of their birth and whether or not the parent who is member of the higher house acknowledges the child.

Niniwed [NINNY wed]: Name of kidnapped scion of Gens Itan. "innocent"

Nudd: Member of Garreth's Element at Academy. "fog."

Obaith: A town, not too far from the lands of Gens Bleddyn, which Garreth visits, briefly, and where he meets Brân. "hope."

OCD: Obsessive-Compulsive Disorder. See also "vambrace."

Ocsiwn [OXI win]: City in the mountains between the territories of Houses Maelon and Mynydd. A "free city" owing allegiance to no house, but under the control of Maelon.

Open City: Specified locations such as the cities of Aberwith and Cytgord in which a truce of non-violence holds.

Orbit: (1) the path taken by one body around another usually dictated by mass and gravitational attraction. (2) The distance from the sun to World, used as a measure of other distances in World's solar system. For example, the cometary cloud is between 5,000 and 100,000 "orbital radii" from the sun. See also "Astronomical Unit (AU)."

Organelle: Any one of several semi-independent components in a eukaryotic cell.

Ötsi: Nephew of Gens Ellis and Academy rival of Llywelyn Bleddyn.

Panspermia: Hypothesis that life (which had to originate somewhere, perhaps through chemical determinism, q.v.) was spread through the galaxy on comets, meteorites, dust particles driven by solar winds, etc.

Peace Bond: Agreement or oath to not use weapons, engage in vendetta, etc. which may be applied to persons entering a town, for example. May be symbolized by colored yarn wrapped around hafts of swords, through trigger guards, etc.

Pitch: Any sports field.

Pole Pull-down: Game and competition, based on *Bo-taoshi*, a competition conducted at the National Defense Academy of Japan, Earth Analogue III. See episodes by Googling "YouTube Bo-taoshi".

Postern Gate: A small gate or door in a fortification, often in a hidden location, that allows coming and going without opening a main gate.

Praetorian Guard: Soldiers selected for ability and loyalty to guard important people including a Gens. In some cases, they may also act as secret police. From the history of Rome, Earth Analogue III.

Pride: Noun of venery; collective noun for a group of lions or similar animals, including homotheria.

Primate: A mammal of the order that includes monkeys, apes, and humans.

Primogeniture: Succession to a title or property going to the first-born child.

Progenitor: The biological parent of a House. In pre-history, it was common for the male house leader to be the only male to have children. When one house defeated another in battle, it was common for all males of the losing house to be killed and the females impregnated by the winning house's progenitor. When birth by surrogate became possible, a female house leader might be the only one whose eggs were fertilized. These practices largely fell out of practice c. 50,000 C.E. [Conquest Era, or "after the conquest].

Provost: A senior administrative officer of a school. From Earth Analogue III Latin, *praepositus*, "head, chief."

Pugh [PEW]: Greater House aligned with House Tarren. "son of Hugh"

Pyrrhic victory: (peer ick) A victory won at great cost, making it more like a defeat than a victory.

Quantum-fluctuation Death: The deviation of quantum cubes in the Res Publica FTL system that renders them no longer entangled and therefore useless for communication. Does not occur until a "significant" fraction of the buckyball molecules degrade.

Reaches: The borderlands of a territory. Those parts of a house's territory that might be challenged by another, bordering, house.

Recce: Short for "reconnaissance."

Reese: Lesser House, aligned with House Tarren. Territory consists of several large islands to the southeast of the Equatorial Continent. One island holds the spaceport used by House Tarren and its allies. "enthusiasm"

Remembrance: A ceremony conducted after someone's death during which friends and family express their grief at the person's death, share stories of his or her life, and experience catharsis. The person's body may be cremated at this time.

Res Publica: World's dominant civilization; from the Earth Analogue III Latin: *common good, commonwealth, body politic.*

Rhiannon: Garreth's horse, a creature equivalent to a large Pliohippus from Earth's evolutionary history.

Rhingyll [RING ill]: Master Sergeant and Company Commander of House Bleddyn's Mountain Company. He is the only non-commissioned officer to command a company, and has repeatedly refused promotion to an officer grade.

Rodric: Telor's Brother-minus-seventeen-years.

Rocket grenade: Short for "rocket-propelled grenade." A weapon consisting of a warhead and a solid-fuel rocket propulsion system. Used to attack a crowd of people, an armored vehicle, a floater, a shuttle, or a fixed structure. Different versions and sizes may be fired from a corvette, shuttle, floater, an over-and-under slug rifle, or a bazooka-like hand-held launcher.

Sally Port: An opening in the wall of a fortress through which troops can "sally forth" to battle.

SAM: Surface-to-air missile.

Sangtae: Coastal city on the Southern Continent.

Sani: Member of Southern people, thrall to Gens Bleddyn, second mentor to Garreth. "old one"

Sarcopterygian: The Sarcopterygii are a class of bony fishes of which, on Earth Analogue III, the coelacanth is the only living related fish, the others having become extinct during the Late Cretaceous period. By the strictest definition, their clade includes the terrestrial vertebrates, including humans.

Sawel: Scion and heir of Gens Eryr.

Scion: A descendant of a noble family, usually a son or daughter, sometimes a niece or nephew.

Scullery: (1) A place where pots, pans, and dishes are washed. (2) A servant whose duties are in the scullery.

Scuttlebutt: (1) A cask containing fresh water, from which sailors drink. Like the water fountain in offices on Earth Analogue III, it is also a place where gossip often occurs. (2) Such gossip.

Second: (1) Short for "second in command." (2) The person who stands with a participant in a duel until the duel begins. Seconds are armed with only grace knives. Since all adult duels are to the death, the seconds of adult combatants have the responsibility to kill the combatant to whom they are seconded should the combatant be wounded too badly to continue to fight.

Secund: To lend an employee or soldier by one employer (or house) to another. From the Earth Analogue III Latin, *secundus*, "following."

Sehwa: House Bleddyn island. Nearest the equator. Location of a hospital.

Selwyn: Son of Llywelyn Bleddyn and Gwenallt. "friend"

Sept: A lesser family not of house status, or a division of a House. May be derived from Latin of Earth Analogue III, *septum*, meaning "partition."

Shuttle: An AG-powered vehicle. Larger versions are used to carry freight. Racing shuttles are capable of speeds of about 3.2 times the speed of sound (Mach 3.2 or about 4,000 kph).

Slade: Scion of Maelon, member of Llywelyn's companions.

Soando: Volcanic island off southeast coast of equatorial continent. Location of House Bleddyn's mines, a military garrison, a population of thralls, and little else.

Solar storms: See "Stormtime."

Soldiers' Oath: "I swear always to live by honor, to be valorous in battle and loyal to my Gens, house, and the Res Publica." This is often abbreviated as "Honor, valor, loyalty."

Songbaek: Island slightly southwest of the Equatorial Continent in House Dolffin territory. Home of House Dolffin's school and Fortress Dolffin.

Soosong: Academy cadet, assassin. "a humble person of low status or class"

Southern People, Southerners: The thralls. The same species as the Res Publica, but whose genotype diverged slightly when the southern and northern continents were separated by tectonic plate movement. At one time enemies, the Southerners were defeated millennia before this story begins and are servants or employees of the Res Publica

Spooky Action at a Distance: Also "quantum entanglement." Basis for the Res Publica faster-than-light "isoquant" communication system. [Iso = same; quant = quantum.]

Squadron Raptor: The Academy squadron into which Daffyd and Delwyn's element is inducted.

Stardrive: Same as faster-than-light drive.

Status quo: "that which is" or "that which was." For example, *status quo ante bellum* means "the way it was before the war."

Stormtime: The period before and after extreme weather that occurs at the winter and summer solstices and the spring and fall equinoxes. The storms may be called "solar storms." Much of the planet is shut down and people seek shelters for five-to-seven days before and after the times of peak weather.

Surrogate: A child's foster mother and frequently birth mother who may also serve as a companion of a man whose wife is away on duty.

Suss: *verb, transitive.* To figure out, to puzzle out, to grasp as an idea or concept.

Tac: Short for Tactical Officer. Adult military officer or non-commissioned officer who supervises an Element at Academy. The Tac is not the Element Commander although his or her orders are to be obeyed.

Tachyon: A hypothetical particle that can travel (and carry information) faster than the speed of light.

Tahoma: Brother of Gens Bleddyn. One of three relatives, scientists, charged with creating the house's FTL comm system. "waters edge"

Taliesin: Recorder of past history, compiler of the *Book of Proverbs*. Poet and Chief of Poets. "shining brow"

Tarren: Greater House. Historical enemy of House Bleddyn. House colors: black and gray. "burnt lands"

Telor: Son of Gens Bleddyn by a mistress. Eldest of the children of Gens Bleddyn. Member-by-blood of the Gens. In line of succession after siblings born of Gens Bleddyn and his wife's egg. "singer."

Telepath: An individual who is able to communicate mentally with others of his or her kind. Someone able to read the thoughts of others. In the vernacular of the Res Publica, a demon.

Temperature: The Res Publica temperature scale is identical to the Centigrade/Celsius scale on Earth Analogue III: 0 is the freezing point of water; 100 is the boiling point. On EA III, this presumes a sea-level atmospheric pressure, which is lower than the sea-level pressure on World.

Terrwyn: Lieutenant and commander of the Prime Element of Gens Bleddyn's Praetorian Guard (the First Company of the house's Home Guard). Male. Often acts as Gens Bleddyn's conduit to the Field Marshall commander of that guard. "brave"

Thrall: A member of the species of the Res Publica whose ancestors occupied the Southern Continent, and who subsequently lost nearly all the melanin in their skin in order to absorb sufficient sunlight to create what on Earth Analogue III is called "Vitamin D." They were conquered about two hundred millennia ago by the Res Publica. (Dates are given as "C.E." meaning "Conquest Era.") By the time of this narrative, thralls are free and independent people, but are still subject to some institutionalized racism. Many are servants; some occupy positions of great importance and trust.

Time (Clock): Day and night are broken into hours. There are twenty hours in one solar day. The first hour is that which begins at dawn on the Spring Equinox (6:00 AM Earth Analogue III equivalent). At one time, day and night were divided into ten hours, each, which meant that winter day hours were much shorter than winter night hours, and summer day hours were much longer than summer night hours. As the Res Publica civilization developed, this custom was abandoned for the timing of atomic clocks.

Tirion [TIER ee on]: One of two guards in Bethan's element during Academy. "gentle and happy"

Titan: Warship of the *Vishnu Nerada*, Gens Bleddyn's fleet.

To the field: A "call to the field" is a challenge to a duel. Duels between adults are always to the death.

Tom: (1) A male cat of any feline species. (2) Boy; member of House Ellis, caught in Tarren lands with his family when House Ellis changed alignment. Later, a member of House Bleddyn's Home Guard.

Triumph: Name of an ancient, despotic, and psychotic leader of House Tarren.

Turtle ship 거북선 (Kŏbuk-ok-sŏn): From the navy of Admiral Yi Sun-sin, Earth Analogue III, first used in the Sach'ŏn Battle 29th of the 5th Moon, 1592 C.E. An iron-clad ship with cannon, gun ports, sails, and oars.

Twysog [TRY sog]: Corvette of the *Vishnu Nerada* which discovered the planet with the species designated Primate II. "prince"

Tylluan: Lesser house initially non-aligned; later aligned with House Bleddyn. Colors: red and yellow or red and gold. Logo, a dragon.

Tywyll: Commander of House Bleddyn garrison on the island of Soando. Later assigned to House Dolffin's school. "dark"

Vambrace: Traditionally, a piece of armor that protects the lower arm. It may be made of metal or leather. It may cover part of the arm, and be held on with leather straps or completely encircle the arm. The vambraces worn by younger members of the Res Publica are metal. They completely encircle the arm. They contain sensors that monitor blood chemistry and contain drugs that are injected to maintain specified blood chemistry. The vambraces monitor for the hormones and electrochemicals associated with Attention Deficit Disorder/Attention Deficit Hyperactivity Disorder (ADD/ADHD), Obsessive Compulsive Disorder (OCD), Bipolar syndrome, and Mood Disorders that affect all people on World (Res Publica and thralls) from about the onset of puberty until about age eighteen. Thrall children are subject to these same syndromes (disorders). Those whose families are wealthy enough may have a vambrace. Lesser children must rely on pills or herbal medicines.

Vaward: The forefront of an attack formation.

Vet: *verb transitive* To investigate someone's academic credentials, experience, personal history, etc. and positively assert the truth of their claims or loyalty.

384

Vishnu Nerada: The Fleet of Gens Bleddyn. From Earth Analogue III, a four-armed Hindu god and an Australian tea.

Vision (eyesight): The vision of the Res Publica evolved during major fluctuations in the temperature of World, during ice ages. They can see from the near infrared to the far ultraviolet. Like birds of Earth Analogue III, they have four types of cones in their eyes.

Volemic shock: More correctly, hypovolemic shock. A situation that exist when a body looses more than about 20% of its blood, making it impossible for the heart to pump the remaining blood.

Waldfa [WALD fa]: Colony ship of the *Vishnu Nerada*, accompanies Garreth Bleddyn on his first space mission.

World: The common name for the planet of Garreth's people, the Res Publica.

Year: World circles a young, hot, blue star at an average distance of 218.5 million km. Its year is 590 days.

Yosok Maru: Corvette, starship belonging to Gens Bleddyn and on which Gwenallt is stationed.

Your Grace: Formal term of address for a Gens, especially Gens of the Greater Houses.

Acknowledgements

I am especially indebted to beta readers Mary L. "Lani" Clancy, Charlotte Elizabeth Robinson, and Michael Weinstock. Their advice and expertise over the years have been invaluable.

Many of the early chapters were reviewed by The Peachtree City, Georgia, Library Writers' Circle, including David Allman, Alexandria Bolden, Pat Butler, Patricia and Chuck Cruzan, Petra Engish, Sharon Marchisello, Mark Myers, Delayne Ryms, Susan Samson, Robin Strickland, and Rebecca Watts (Writers' Circle Leader and Facilitator). They have been very generous with their time and talents.

The expression, "Never invest in anything that eats," is most often attributed to Billy Rose, a figure from EA III. He was speaking of horses.

A number of the battles, especially those at sea, were drawn from accounts of the life and career of Korean Admiral and Tongjesa Yi Sun-sin (1545-1589 CE), posthumously honored as Chung Mu Gong Yi (Duke of Loyalty and Warfare) and other titles. The message read by Gens Tarren and Telor near the end of "House of Wolf" was spoken by Admiral Yi after being mortally wounded in battle.

A young friend and linguist, Shi Ho Kim, was very helpful in showing me how to modernize the spelling of historical locations in Korea which allowed me to track Admiral Yi's battles. Shi Ho also created the name of Garreth's martial art (Jaryeondo), using his knowledge of Korean, Chinese, and English.

I am especially grateful to the Korean Spirit and Cultural Promotion Project for their generous donation of the books on Korean culture and history listed in the bibliography.

The story of the boy and the wolf cub was transmogrified from Plutarch's *Life of Lycurgus*. The stories of the wolf and the pterodactyl, the boy and the bully, the boy who carried the flag of House Hynafol, the mouse and the wolf, the swallow and the hemp, and likely others were transmogrified from various editions of *Aesop's Fables*, all in the public domain. The moral of the wolf and pterodactyl story as Sani presented it, "Live and work for the benefit of all," is an expression of *Hongik Ingan*, the unofficial motto of South Korea. See the bibliography.

"May his days be few; and let another take his place," is a curse from Psalm 109:8 (King James Version of the Bible).

The form of warfare practiced by House Bleddyn's Infiltration Elements was perhaps first practiced on Earth Analogue III by Fabius Maximus (280-203 B. C. E.) who earned the title "Cunctator" (from the Latin: *cunctari*, to hesitate or delay) for his tactics in not engaging the enemy directly when he was outnumbered.

The aphorism, "Wars are fought with weapons, but they are won by men," is attributed to General George Patton, US Army, Earth Analogue III.

The aphorism, "A fool can think only foolish thoughts" is from the movie, "Roshamon," directed by Akira Kurosawa.

Quotations from the Res Publica's *Book of Proverbs – The Wisdom of Geraint and Karmet*, were taken largely from Machiavelli (*The Prince*), Plato, Sun Tzu (*The Art of War*), Von Clausewitz (*On War*), Yi Sun-sin (*War Diary* and *Memorials [Memoranda] to the Court)*, William Shakespeare, Peter Abelard, and Benjamin Franklin (*Poor Richard's Almanac*).

The notion that the society of the Res Publica is a fluid hierarchy, dependent upon not only strength but also coalitions, was inspired by Ian Tattersall's "Masters of the Planet: The Search for our Human Origins." (Kindle Edition)

"In quantum physics if something is not forbidden it necessarily happens with some non-zero probability."
—Alexander Vilenkin, Tufts University 2013 Earth Analogue III

388

Bibliography and References

_____, *Admiral Yi Sun-sin: A brief overview of his life and achievements*. Diamond Sutra Recitation Group. Undated.

_____, *The Practice of Hongik Ingan: Lives of Queen Seondeok, Shin Saimdang and Yi Yulgok."* Korean Spirit and Cultural Project, published by the Diamond Sutra Recitation Group, March 2011. (The book, "To Live, to Work, to Benefit All," which Gens Bleddyn gives Telor is an analogue of this book.)

Briegel, Hans J. "Versatile cluster entangled light," *Science Magazine*, 28 October 2016.

Hawking, Stephen, and Mlodinow, Leonard. *The Grand Design*. Random House Publishing Group, 2010. Kindle edition.

Jeong Byeong-Jo. "Master Wonhyo: An Overview of His Life and Teachings," Korean Spirit & Cultural Promotion Project, 2010.

Machiavelli, *The Prince*.

Musser, George, "Spooky Action at a Distance," Scientific American Press, Kindle Edition.

Plato, *The Republic*.

Sun Tzu, *The Art of War*.

Yi Sun-sin, *War Dairy (Nangjung Ilgi)* 1598 and *Memorials to the Court* (English editions).

≈

390

The Science of
"The Stuff of Life" Tetrology

Telepathy is a genetic trait. The Founders ("The Stuff of Life: Book I") were convinced it was created by environmental factors acting on somatic cells. The Res Publica ("Enemy Planet" books) understood that it was genetic. Telepathy is instantaneous (thus breaking the speed of light) but it is subject to the inverse-square law. (The power of the message is reduced by the square of the distance from the sender.)

Res Publica FTL Communication System: Based on what Einstein (Earth Analogue III) called "spooky action at a distance," and "entanglement," a term coined by Erwin Schrödinger (1877-1961 C.E.). More recently called "quantum entanglement."

Both telepathy and the FTL communication system become nearly impossible to use when a ship approaches about 0.7 the speed of light (C), and are useless when a ship is between branes or universes.

~~~~~

Might faster-than-light travel and communication be possible? Please consider the following:

"Any sufficiently advanced technology is indistinguishable from magic." Arthur C. Clark, Third Law. On the other hand, "When a distinguished but elderly scientist states that something is possible, he is almost certainly right. When he states that something is impossible, he is very probably wrong." Clark's First Law.

"Both branches of magic, the homoeopathic and the contagious, may conveniently be comprehended under the general name of Sympathetic Magic, since both assume that things act on each other at a distance through a secret sympathy, the impulse being transmitted from one to the other by means of what we may conceive as a kind of invisible ether, not unlike that which is postulated by modern science for a precisely similar purpose, namely, to explain how things can physically affect each other through a space which appears to be empty." Frazer, Sir James George. "The Golden Bough" (Kindle Locations 366-367). Kindle Edition

Other Books by the Author

"The Stuff of Life"

Years ago, the people of a planet near the center of the Milky Way Galaxy sent out ships whose mission was to seed planets with the stuff of life: single-cell animals and plants; eggs of reptiles, amphibians, birds, and fish; and infant mammals. The people's purpose: to prepare these planets for their children. Each ship's crew includes at least one telepath. In 2002, a telepath is born in the hospital at Fort Hood, Texas. In 2015, he contacts one of these seeding ships. This is their story.

"The Cry of the Innocents"

The bodies of young people – Navajo, Hopi, Apache – are found in the high desert, desecrated. A serial killer? Gang wars? Animals? Organ harvesters? A kiva society of young men recruit a forensic anthropologist and an investigative reporter to seek the answer.

"On Ty Ty Creek: Sweet Potato Pie, Moonshine and Other Southern Traditions

A boy growing up on a farm in rural Georgia during the Great Depression of the early 20th Century faces a crisis of faith when his little brother dies. For the rest of his life, he struggles to reconcile what he learns from the church he attends with what he sees around him, including the racial divide, Klan murders, hypocrisy, abject poverty, law-breaking, and the different

393

message he hears from his grandfather, preacher at the biggest church in Athens and who has his own radio program.

"Holy Fire"

"Holy Fire" describes a dystopian future in which plutocrats, politicians, and preachers – whose only motivation is money and power – gain control of the USA. Their goals are, at first, similar enough to make them allies, but what happens when greed and lust overtake them? What happens when a few people, guided by the principles of The Enlightenment, rebel? Can they make a difference? Can they stop the forces of war, pestilence, disease, and famine – the Four Horsemen of the Apocalypse, and the Fifth Horseman, Climate Change – before it is too late?

All books are available in hardcover and Kindle at
www.amazon.com/author/paullentz
or link from
www.PaulLentzAuthor.com

www.ingramcontent.com/pod-product-compliance
Lightning Source LLC
Chambersburg PA
CBHW060144260626
47160CB00001B/117